BOOKS BY KAREN ROBARDS

Loving Julia
Night Magic
To Love a Man
Wild Orchids

Published by
WARNER BOOKS

WILD ORCHIDS

KAREN ROBARDS

WARNER BOOKS

A Time Warner Company

WARNER BOOKS EDITION

Copyright © 1986 by Karen Robards
All rights reserved.

Cover design by Diane Luger
Cover illustration by Michael Racz
Hand lettering by Carl Dellacroce

Warner Books, Inc.
1271 Avenue of the Americas
New York, NY 10020

Ⓦ A Time Warner Company

Printed in the United States of America

First Printing: January, 1986

Reissued: September, 1994

10 9 8 7 6 5 4 3

I
___

One moment he was a faceless stranger standing on a Mexican street corner; the next, he was opening the passenger side door and sliding into the rented orange Volkswagen Rabbit beside her.

Lora Harding's hands clenched on the steering wheel. Her throat went dry. Her heart began knocking like a jackhammer in her chest. This could not be happening, not to her, she thought, and the thought took on the fervency of a prayer. Horrified, she stared dumbly at the menacing looking man folded into the brown vinyl bucket seat beside her. The glint of something shiny in the vicinity of his blue jeaned thighs caught her eye. She looked down at his lap to see the blue metallic barrel of a gun poking out at her from beneath the folds of a grimy sarape that had been carried over his arm as he stood on the street corner, and now rested in an untidy heap on his legs. Her eyes widened with fright, and flew back up to his face. The wide straw brim of a battered sombrero

obsured all but a square chin covered by several days' growth
of bristly black beard and a grim mouth that was nearly
hidden by an evil looking black mustache. But one thing she
could see: the man was big. Overwhelmingly so, as he sat so
close that she could feel his hard muscled arm crowding hers,
so close that she could smell the tangy aroma of male sweat.
The gaudy Hawaiian print shirt he wore stretched tautly over
shoulders that could have graced a linebacker for the Kansas
City Chiefs. Corded muscles covered in sleek, bronzed flesh
bulged beneath the shirt's short sleeves. A wide chest tapered
down to a narrow waist and flat belly. Muscles bulged again
in his thighs, straining against the faded denim covering the
long legs jackknifed under the dash. Dusty maroon and silver
running shoes in what must have been a size eleven encased
his feet. As her eyes ran back up over him with lightning
speed, Lora swallowed. Although she was no dwarf herself,
she saw at once that in any straight physical fight for her life
against this man she stood not a chance. Fight for her
life . . . She shuddered. This could not be happening. It simply could not be happening. Inoffensive schoolteachers from
small towns in Kansas were not routinely shanghaied while
on vacation in Mexico. Mexico was safe, for goodness sake!
Her travel agent had assured her of that! Certainly this
ferocious looking man could not be meaning to kidnap *her*. It
was impossible. . . .

"Sir—uh, *señor,*" she began faintly, knowing there must
be some mistake. She would laugh when she discovered what
it was. . . .

"Drive," he said in American-accented English, and to
remove any possibility of error pulled back the folds of the
sarape so that the gun was clearly visible.

Lora tried. She really did. But she had never driven a
clutch-type vehicle before nine o'clock that morning when

she had rented the tiny VW from the desk of her hotel. Now terror mixed with her natural mechanical incompetence, and in her agitation she let up on the clutch too fast. The car lurched into the intersection, which was fortunately (unfortunately? she was in too much of a quake to decide) empty, then died. She cast a quick, scared glance at the hulking figure beside her to gauge his reaction. The shabby sombrero hid his expression from her—but there was no mistaking the import of the gun that was suddenly jammed hard into her side. Lora flinched, gasping with pain and fright.

"No! Please. . . ."

"I said drive!"

Her hands and knees trembled in unison as Lora went through the motions of restarting the car. Feverishly she prayed that this time the balky vehicle would obey her without argument. Would he shoot her if he thought she was deliberately malingering? What would it feel like to be shot? Would she die instantly, or slowly, or . . . ? Lora shuddered. At her involuntary movement the gun jabbed into her side again in a wordless threat. Her palms went icy cold, and she felt sweat start to bead on her upper lip. When the engine turned over, then the car slid through the intersection and on across the bridge over the lagoon without mishap, he grunted and withdrew the gun to his lap again. Lora's terror subsided only marginally. What happened now?

Establish communication with your attacker. Make him think of you as a person, an individual like himself. Be friendly and polite, but above all be calm . . . The words of the instructor at the rape prevention course she had taken along with many of the other teachers and nearly all the girl students at Augusta High School began to filter into her shocked brain. So did one important rule for never finding oneself in a situation where acting on such advice would be necessary: Always keep your car doors locked, even when you're inside. Well, it was too late now. Lora took a deep breath, praying it would steady her.

"Where do you want to go?" she asked in what she hoped was a reasonably level voice.

"Shut up and drive." The snarl was accompanied by a threatening gesture with the gun.

So much for communication, she thought, shivering. Though the car's air conditioner worked only sporadically, she suddenly felt very cold. Wetting her lips, she shut up and drove past the Convention Center into the town of Cancun itself.

Cancun was the newest and swankiest of the "in" Mexican resort towns—the travel agent who had sold her the package tour had assured her that it had supplanted even Acapulco—and even in the middle of July, which was about as off-season as one could get, it was crowded with tourists. Every hotel on the luxurious strip along the beach was filled to capacity, and the town itself had only the very worst accommodations still to let. Usually the single road leading from the hotel area into the town was packed with traffic. Speeding local taxis vied with lumbering buses, private cars, bicycles and pedestrians for space. The streets of the town itself were normally jammed with free-spending *turistas* and locals trying their wily best to persuade the visitors to buy everything from papier-mâché marionettes to "real" Mayan silver. But not now, Lora realized with a sinking sensation. It was two o'clock, the siesta hour, and the streets and sidewalks were almost deserted. The only individuals in sight were two shopkeepers who had settled down to nap in rickety wooden chairs just outside their establishment doors. Like the man beside her, they had huge sombreros tilted over their faces to keep out the blazing afternoon sun. Unlike the man beside her, whose electric blue nylon shirt embellished with bright parrots and palm trees screamed that he was a tourist, the native shopkeepers wore loose, short-sleeved shirts of pastel embroidered cotton in deference to the ferocious heat, which topped one hundred degrees as it had every day of the five Lora had already spent in Cancun. During the day, she had discovered, this fabulous, fun-filled resort was griddle hot; at night it was infested with insects.

Glancing nervously sideways, Lora saw that her captor's overbright shirt was damp with sweat, causing it to cling faithfully to the hard muscles of his chest. He was very muscular... Lora jerked her eyes back to the road, feeling cold all over again. This man with the body builder's physique might well be the death of her....

Clearly there was no help to be had from the somnolent shopkeepers. Even if they had been awake and aware, how could she convey to them that she needed help—and would they help her if they understood her plight? Since arriving for this once-in-a-lifetime vacation, she had discovered that Mexico's was a distinctly male-dominated society. Women got many smiling glances, but little respect. Tourists were treated much the same way. Apparently the natives had long since made up their minds that all *turistas* were crazy at best and that the most satisfactory way to deal with this infusion of wealthy foreigners was to smile and agree to everything the *gringos* said while proceeding to do just as they liked.

"Turn left at the next corner." The low growl brought her attention effectively back to her present straits. Lora chanced a quick glance at her captor to find that he appeared to be looking straight ahead, his eyes on the road. The gun rested lightly on his thighs with the little hole at the end pointed straight at her hipbone. He did not seem to be holding it very tightly. Lora risked another darting glance up at what she could see of his face. He really did not seem to be paying much attention to her at all. He appeared lost in thought . . . Was there any way she could grab the gun? Lora considered the possibility for a moment. She could stealthily lift one hand from the wheel, reach over, and snatch the thing away from him before he was even aware of what she intended. It was what the heroine in her favorite detective show on TV would do, she was sure. But she wasn't Laura Holt, and this wasn't TV. It was real life—*her* life. If she grabbed for the gun, it would very likely fire. Of course, there was always a chance that it was unloaded, that the man beside her was bluffing, but she didn't think so. He seemed frighteningly sure of himself—and of her. If the gun went off, the chances were good that she would be shot, and that was exactly the circumstance she was trying to avoid. Besides, if she did somehow manage to get her hands on the gun, what would she do with it? She had never shot a gun in her life. And her captor would certainly not just be placidly sitting there beside her, watching as she tried to figure out how to work the dratted thing. . . .

"Damn it, I said turn left!"

The menacing snarl just beside her right ear made her jump at least a foot in the air. Dear Lord, she had been so lost in thought that she had almost missed the turn. In fact, she had missed it. The gun gouged her ribs again. Lora cringed, trembling. Her hands swung the wheel around violently. The VW practically stood on its two left tires as it spun, bumping over the curb to finally end up heading in the direction he had wanted it to take. As she righted the car, Lora had a faint, sneaking hope that perhaps her wild driving might attract the attention of the local *policía*. . . .

"Listen, bitch, you pull something like that again and

I'll blow you all the way to Alaska. You drive right, within the speed limit, and no more fancy stuff. I need you for cover, but I don't need you that bad. And I got no aversion to hurting women. You better keep that in mind.'' The gun was jabbed into her rib cage as her captor released the dashboard, which he had grabbed for balance during her little maneuver, and leaned over to grab her by the throat. Lora started as she felt his hand, large and calloused and hot, tightening around her soft neck. Her eyes were huge with fear as they flew to his face. What she saw there terrified her. He looked cruel, all harsh planes and jutting angles and bronzed, weathered skin. His eyes beneath thick scowling black brows were black, too, and narrowed with a deadly obsidian gleam.

"I'm sorry—please. . . ." She stuttered in her haste to convince him.

"You drive right, bitch," he growled, and released her throat, moving back to his seat. Lora was trembling as she shifted her eyes back to the road just in time to avoid running up on the sidewalk. Dear God, he would probably kill her if she did. She righted the car, practically deafened by the pounding of blood in her ears as the true horror of her situation began to sink in. If she wanted to get out of this nightmare with a whole skin, it would behoove her to do exactly as he told her—at least until she could figure out any kind of sensible alternative.

There had to *be* an alternative. She could not just meekly drive until he told her to stop, at which point he would quite likely order her out of the car, put a bullet in her brain and drive merrily on his way. She had to do something, and the need grew more urgent as the car headed implacably toward the outskirts of town. If she was going to act, her best chance would be now, while there were still people within shouting distance—how did one scream help in Spanish, for God's sake? Would a simple, generic scream of terror suffice? One was bubbling in her throat at that very moment. But she obviously couldn't scream while still inside the car. That would be worse than useless—it would probably provoke him into killing her instantly. No, she had to get out of the car, and persuading him to stop pointing that gun at her was the obvious first step. If he would only put the gun away, she could slam the car into park—could one do that with a manual transmission? She prayed one could—throw open the door, and run for her life. Or would it be better to jump from the moving vehicle? Lora pondered for an instant. If she jumped while the car was moving, she would have more time to escape, but she might seriously injure herself in the process. On the other hand, if she threw the car into park— could she do that? Why hadn't she paid the small additional amount an automatic would have cost?—he would be thrown off balance by the sudden and unexpected stop, which he would not be expecting. All things considered, she decided it would be best to throw the car into park before jumping. (Should she depress the clutch first? Who knew?) But when? Now?

"Could you please put that gun away? It makes me very nervous. I—I promise I'll do whatever you say." The quaver in her words made them very convincing, Lora felt. She threw a pleading glance at her captor, hoping that for once her face, which had been described as wholesome and honest looking so often that the terms nauseated her, would aid her cause. He didn't even look at her, didn't even grunt. And the gun didn't shift by so much as a millimeter.

They were passing through the slums of the city now, well away from the places where tourists usually went. The streets were narrow and filled with trash, the buildings on either side of them tumbledown and squalid. Perhaps seven half-naked children darted, screaming and laughing, from behind what appeared to be a ramshackle residential hotel to run across the street in front of the car and disappear behind a one-story cinderblock building on the opposite side of the road. Besides the children, whose laughter could still be heard although they were now out of sight, the only other denizen of the area appeared to be a large, half-starved dog. Should she try it now?

She would do it. She would throw the car into park and . . . In preparation for what she feared would be the last act of her life, Lora looked down at the gear box to locate park. There was no park. There was first gear, second gear, third gear, reverse, and neutral . . . There had to be a park—but if there was she couldn't find it.

"Keep your eyes on the road!"

Lora jerked her eyes back up to the road, terrified that he might guess her intention—and discovered that it was too late to carry out her plan in any case. They were just driving through the outskirts of town, past a sign that announced that it was one hundred fifty kilometers to Chichén Itzá. Stunted palm trees laced together with dense vegetation crowded forward at the edge of the cleared area surrounding the town, while the blacktop highway itself stretched before them, gleaming and deserted under the blazing afternoon sun. Lora stared blankly at the sun-baked road as the tires seemed to swish out a rhythm of, Too late, too late.

They drove without speaking for maybe twenty minutes, Lora's mind whirling with fear and various plans to save herself—none of which seemed particularly workable—while her captor radiated silent menace. With every sneaking glance she cast him, her terror grew proportionally larger. Quite apart from his size, which was intimidating in itself, there was an aura of violence about him that terrified her. What little she could see of his face looked brutal, and his hand held the gun with an easy familiarity that told its own story. He had no aversion to hurting women . . . She felt her palms grow damp, and clutched the steering wheel harder to prevent her hands from sliding. The man was clearly a criminal—a violent criminal—and maybe deranged as well. Perhaps he had robbed a bank or something. Why had he abducted her? That was the key. He'd said he needed her for cover. Of course, whoever was after him would be searching for a man alone. They would not be on the lookout for a couple. So maybe that made her chances of survival a little better. At least for a while . . . Lora took another look at the cruel set of his mouth and shivered. He looked more than capable of rape—and murder.

Lora frantically put her mind to work again. She was only twenty-seven, her whole life was still ahead of her. She hadn't even begun to live—crazily, the words from that song by the Carpenters ran through her mind: "We've only just begun . . ." She banished the melody, but the words were essentially true. For so many years she had lived her life for others, had done what was best for her family instead of what she had wanted to do. Her older sister, Janice, had married right out of high school as girls frequently did in their small hometown, and Lora might well have followed in her footsteps if fate had not chosen to intervene.

She had been seventeen, a senior in high school when her dearly loved father had been killed in the crash of the car he was driving. Her mother was severely injured in the same crash, and never fully recovered. Emily Harding spent the rest of her life as an invalid, first in a wheelchair and then in bed, growing increasingly bitter as her health deteriorated. As the only daughter left at home, Lora had become nurse, companion, and chief scapegoat rolled into one. Not that anyone had ever asked her to give up her plans for a life of her own to stay home and care for her mother. Everyone, including Janice and even herself, had simply assumed that she would do so. And she had; for ten long years, until this past March when Emily died at last from pnuemonia, which Dr. Ramsey had told her frequently claimed the bedridden.

Lora had grieved when Emily died—she had loved her mother dearly despite the querulousness and vitriolic tongue which had gradually overwhelmed the warm smiles and kind words that had guided Lora's younger days—but secretly, shamefully, she had been glad as well. It meant blessed freedom at last. Freedom for her mother, of course, but Lora was honest enough to admit that the tremendous sense of release she felt was just as much on her own behalf. For the first time in ten years, she was free to live life as she wanted, to do as she pleased without having to consider anyone but herself. It was such a relief to go to bed knowing that she would be able to sleep through the night without her mother calling her two or three times to get her a glass of water, or help her to the bathroom, or perform any of the innumerable mundane tasks that Emily was no longer able to do for herself. It was such a relief to get up in the morning and know that she had only herself to do for; she no longer had to bathe and dress and feed her mother as well; she no longer had to wait for the neighbor who stayed with her mother during the day, or miss work if that neighbor was sick or otherwise unable to come. At last she was free to stay late at the school if some student should need to talk with her without feeling a horrible sense of guilt because her mother was home waiting for her. At last she was able to go away for the weekend, to take a vacation. . . . Since the accident, she had never been able to leave her mother as long as overnight. Emily did not like to be cared for by other than "family," and Janice was "too busy" with her own husband and two daughters to take care of their mother long enough to give Lora even a brief respite. After one abortive weekend which Lora had attempted to spend at a teacher's meeting in Topeka—her mother had fallen out of bed, broken her hip, and been rushed to the hospital, all because, Emily quavered, of Lora's selfishness— Lora had never again been gone for more than a few hours at a time. But now she was free—free.

Three days after her mother's funeral, feeling guilty but wonderfully lighthearted for all that, she walked into Augusta's largest travel agency and gathered up all the brochures on all the exotic places she could find. Emily had left her small estate to be divided equally between her daughters, so Lora had some money. She had used part of the life insurance proceeds plus a dauntingly large bank loan to buy the half-interest in the house from her sister, but there was still nearly ten thousand dollars left. Most of it she would sensibly bank, but some of it—fifteen hundred of it as it turned out—she would spend on a fabulous vacation. Somewhere exotic, with a beach and sun and ocean, and sights to see and . . .

That somewhere had turned out to be Cancun, Mexico. Even from the beginning, when she had stepped off the airplane to be enveloped by the smell of rotting vegetation and a swarming cloud of ravenous mosquitoes, she had suspected that her dream vacation might not turn out to be quite what she had expected. Between broken air conditioners that might, or might not, be repaired *mañana* (how she had grown to dread that ubiquitous tomorrow, which could just as easily mean next week, or next month, or next year!), inedible food, the mosquitoes that feasted on her fair skin every time she set foot outdoors after dark and the sun that broiled her alive during the day, a tour bus that had been broken for four days while its driver waited unconcernedly for a part that would surely arrive *mañana*, she had had to work hard to keep her wonderful vacation from turning into nothing but an expensive exercise in aggravation. Still, Lora had determinedly overlooked the myriad irritations, meaning to enjoy herself no matter what. She had even decided that she would no longer be a hostage to a broken tour bus. She wanted to see the Mayan ruins at Chichén Itzá—the small ruin off the beach near her hotel had merely whetted her appetite for more—and see the ruins she would, whether the rest of the tour group did or not. So she had rented a car and headed out—and here she was, abducted at gunpoint by a criminal. Some dream vacation.

"What's your name?"

Lora started at the question, which was growled near her ear. She flicked a quick look sideways to find that the obsidian eyes were once again visible beneath the brim of the hat. They were regarding her without any sign of emotion at all. She thought, Those are the eyes of a cold-blooded killer, and had to take a deep breath to calm her pounding heart before she replied.

"You got papers with you—driver's license and so on?" Lora nodded.

"If we get stopped by the police, you show them what they ask for and stay inside the car. Don't try anything fancy or you're dead. You got that?"

Lora nodded again, swallowing as she gave him another quick, scared look.

"You here on your own?"

Lora's eyes widened at that. He must be beginning to wonder how long it would be before she would be missed. If she admitted that she was traveling alone, that no one would miss her until the tour group got together to board the chartered plane for home the day after tomorrow, her chances for surviving this would be even less than they were already, she calculated.

"No. I'm with my family. My husband and two children." Her voice was perfectly even. She had never been a good liar, but looking death in the face fortunately seemed to bring out all her latent deceitful instincts.

"You are, huh?" Listening to him speak, Lora grew more and more certain that he was an American. Not only the accent, which she thought sounded vaguely Texan with its slow drawl, but the slang he used, the way he put his words together, was typical of the careless English of the United States. The knowledge that he was a fellow citizen (if he had not been stripped of his citizenship for some nefarious deed) should have made her feel better. After another quick glance at that hard, mustachioed face, it did not.

"Where's your wedding ring?" he shot at her. Lora was taken by surprise by the question, and could not resist shooting a quick glance down at the bare ring finger of her left hand. Good point, she thought, and also registered that he did not entirely believe her story. Why not? Was there something about her that made it seem implausible that she could be married and the mother of two? Surely she did not look old-maidish at twenty-seven! She was reasonably slim and attractive, and her not-quite-blond hair and guileless blue eyes had always led people to assume she was younger than her years. But she certainly looked old enough to be a wife and mother. And probably would have been by now, if not for that car crash. . . .

"I left it at home. I was told that I would be safer in Mexico without expensive jewelry. Because of the criminal element." She could not quite prevent a sardonic inflection from creeping into those last words. He ignored it as his eyes rested briefly on the finger in question.

"Your skin is very smooth. Not a mark on it—as there would be if you wore a ring habitually."

"My ring is very loose." That was the best she could come up with. Lora had to give him points for intelligence. He might be a thug, but he was not a stupid thug. Possibly a sociopath. She had read that they were usually highly intelligent. . . . She refused to remember the other things she had read about sociopaths. Panic could not help her.

He grunted, then suddenly bent forward to fish for something beneath his feet. Her purse, she saw as he straightened to open it without so much as a by-your-leave. She thought about protesting, but instinct warned her against it. Compared to kidnapping, and possibly murder and God knew what other acts of mayhem, opening her purse without her permission was a mere bagatelle.

"What are your kids' names?" He had extracted her billfold from the purse and was opening the clasp as he spoke. Suddenly she realized that he was looking for some way of ascertaining whether or not she was telling the truth. Lora smiled with inward triumph. She had pictures of her two little nieces in that billfold.

"Heather and Becky." He had found the pictures of the two blonde girls and was staring at them. The pictures were over a year old, taken when Heather was six and Becky was four. The girls looked adorable—who could murder the mother of such sweet looking children?—and enough like herself to be convincing.

"And this is your husband?" He was looking at the picture of the man she had been engaged to for the last four years. A math teacher at Augusta High, Brian was thirty-five, good looking in a scholarly way, but perhaps a little set in his ways. But he was kind and thoughtful, and would make a good husband and father some day. And she cared for him a lot.

They could have a good life together. If their relationship sometimes seemed to lack a certain something, well, that was life. Certainly having tastes and attitudes in common were more important. And in most of the areas in which they disagreed, Brian turned out to be right; certainly it did make more sense to save all they could of their combined salaries in tax-sheltered investments for retirement rather than squandering a thousand or so on a diamond engagement ring. She didn't *need* a ring. . . .

"What's his name?"

"Brian."

"Brian Harding?"

"Yes." He was looking at her credit cards and driver's license now. Lora thought quickly, but she couldn't remember anything on any of them that might betray her.

"So why weren't he and the kiddies with you in the car?" She breathed a little easier. Apparently there was nothing.

"I wanted to see the ruins at Chichén Itzá. Brian didn't, and we both felt that, since the girls get carsick, it would be best if they stayed with him since I would only be gone for a few hours." Lora was pardonably proud of the calm certainty of her tone. If she hadn't known better, she would have believed what she was saying. Why then was her captor fixing her with those narrow, suspicious eyes?

"What will he do when you don't turn up? Hubby, I mean?"

"I imagine he will call the local police. And possibly the American Embassy. He will be out of his mind with worry. I have very regular habits."

"I can believe that." The words were dry. He sent a quick assessing glance over her that left her with the impression that he did not find her particularly attractive.

Ridiculously, Lora felt a little stab of feminine pique. She was no raving beauty, she knew, but she was generally considered reasonably pretty. Her sky blue sundress and flat white sandals were inexpensive but immaculate. Perhaps she was a little too generously endowed with breasts and hips, but the men of her acquaintance had never seemed to mind, and anyway her waist and legs were slender. The chin-length pageboy style of her fair hair was possibly a little staid (Janice thought so), but it was neat and shining, even in this heat. Her face would never launch a thousand ships, but it was well enough: oval in shape, with a softly rounded chin and forehead, and cheeks to match—she had often despaired of finding her cheekbones, although she knew they had to be in there somewhere—and a small, pert nose and well-shaped lips that were neither too full nor too thin. Nothing objectionable there at all. Her eyes were her best feature, large and guilelessly blue, innocent eyes her friends often said. They were greatly helped by a generous coating of black mascara on both top and bottom lashes; like her hair, her lashes were fair, although they were reasonably long and thick. They just needed a little enhancement. But because of the blazing heat and dense humidity, she wasn't wearing any mascara at the moment, or any other makeup, for that matter. She had found that it disappeared after a scant half hour in this climate. She had put on a pink lip gloss before she had left the hotel, but from the dry feel of her lips, that too had vanished. She had good skin—next to her eyes, she considered her smooth, almost poreless-looking ivory skin her best feature—and so she never worried about not wearing cosmetics.

Now she realized that she must be looking distinctly washed out. Like a pale, uninteresting nonentity, in fact. Which maybe she was—and in any case she would certainly be glad if her abductor thought so! Perhaps she would not then have to fear rape . . . Or maybe he would attack her regardless of whether or not he found her physically attractive. Her self-defense instructor had said that rape was not a crime of passion at all, but aggression and hostility against women. And he certainly was hostile, she thought, feeling her palms start to sweat again as she cast that jutting chin and thin, black-mustachioed mouth—the rest of his face was once again hidden by the sombrero—an assessing look. He had no aversion to hurting women . . . Yes, she decided, shivering anew, he was definitely capable of rape. What on earth was she going to do?

"What are you doing?" The protest sprang involuntarily from her lips as she watched him extract a sheaf of mingled pesos and dollars and her traveler's checks—several hundred dollars' worth—from the inner compartment of her billfold.

"What does it look like?" He was stuffing the money into the front pocket of his jeans, clearly unconcerned that she had seen him do so. He was robbing her, she thought indignantly, but in almost the same instant realized that there was nothing she could do about it. He was likely to do far worse than rob her if she could not think of a way to prevent him.

She said nothing more, just stared out at the road and continued to drive. Tepid air blew in spurts from the air conditioning vents. Her body was beginning to stick to the vinyl seat even through her dress. Rolling down a window would be worse than useless with the ennervating heat outside— if he would even permit her to do so. She risked another quick sideways look. He was sweating, too. . . .

Once they were within the city limits, which would only be another few minutes, she would make her move, she decided. If necessary, she would run the car into the side of a building.

But she would escape, or die in the attempt. Better to go down fighting than to wait for him to do his worst. . . .

"Pull over."

The command was so unexpected that Lora gaped at him.

"I said pull over." The menace was definitely back in his voice. Lora looked around in alarm. They were still some distance outside Chichén Itzá, and had just come around a bend in the road. There was not a car, a person, or even so much as a dog in sight. The tropical rain forest, with its profusion of trees and other vegetation, grew close to the road. On the left there was a little layby which, she supposed, was designed to allow cars to turn around. The setup was altogether too desolate for Lora's peace of mind. With inescapable dread she imagined his intent: he meant to kill her, and whatever else he intended to do with her, here, before she had a chance to reach another town and perhaps try to escape. Out here, all alone with him, she would be at his mercy. . . .

If she was going to act, it had to be now.

She slammed on the brakes as hard as she could, sending the car skidding sideways with a protesting squeal. Her captor was thrown violently forward—so was she, but she had expected the car's motion and so avoided striking her head on the windshield as he did, with considerable force, too, from the sound of the crack and his resultant cursing. Her left hand found the door latch and released it. While the motion of the car sent the door careening open, her right hand pushed against the wheel and she was suddenly flying through space to land with considerable force on the roadway. Her knees and hands, which bore the brunt of the impact, hurt horribly. But there was no time to reflect on that. With a single scared glance over her shoulder at the car—which was now travel-ing fractionally more slowly toward the dense line of trees at the opposite side of the road—Lora scrambled to her feet and started to run as if her life depended on it. Which, she realized as she heard the crash as the car made contact with the trees, it probably did.

II
—

He was chasing her. Lora knew it before she saw him, before she heard the pounding of his feet on the pavement or the rough pant of his breathing. She could sense him coming behind her like something out of a nightmare. She ran as she had never run before in her life, ran until her heart felt as though it would burst and her lungs threatened to explode from lack of air, knowing all the while that it would be useless. He was going to catch her. . . .

He did. She felt his hand close on her hair, yanking her painfully backward. She cried out, staggering as her head was wrenched almost off her neck, one hand clutching mindlessly at his where it made a tight fist in her hair. She was being dragged back against a hard, huge overheated body, enveloped by the smell of sweat and just plain man, crushed by a steel-muscled arm that locked around her neck . . . Her head was forced back against his massive shoulder. He was not wearing the sombrero; the brilliant sunlight blinded her as she

21

looked up into this face, trying to read his intentions toward
her in his expression. Her eyes readjusted to find his harsh
features twisted with savagery. Those obsidian eyes seared
down into hers, glittering with fury—and murder? Lora
screamed. The sound sliced through the thick hot air, hung
shrill and shivering—and then was abruptly silenced by his
hand clamping down hard over her mouth.

"Shut your damned mouth!" he rasped into her ear.

His hand was crushing her nose and mouth, cutting off her
breath. She couldn't breathe! Was he trying to suffocate her?
Terror filled her eyes as she fought to get away from him. He
held her in a viselike grip, crushing her ribs, hurting her. Her
frantic struggles increased; he controlled them easily. His face
was ugly with anger, his eyes filled with it. She could see a
line of surprisingly white, even teeth beneath the evil looking
mustache as his mouth contorted into a feral grin. He enjoyed
hurting her . . . She clawed at the hand that was smothering
her, her nails scraping savagely across its back. He swore,
and the arm around her neck tightened in reprisal until she
thought she might faint. Dear God, she couldn't breathe,
couldn't breathe . . . ! Her nails dug deep into his hard-muscled
forearm as her hands flew to claw at this new threat. He
swore again, viciously. The hand holding her mouth dropped
to pull her nails from his arm. He pinioned her arms with one
of his while the other tightened mercilessly around her neck. . . .

Facing death, her brain became acutely aware of physical
sensations: the harsh pounding of blood in her ears, the salty
taste of his skin as his calloused hand crushed into her mouth,
the salad that had comprised her lunch heaving in her stomach, the air that was all about her but could not reach her
starving lungs . . . She could feel her eyes bulging as she
stared up into the merciless face of her murderer. Her last
sight on earth would be of heavy black eyebrows meeting in a

vicious scowl over thick-lashed eyes so dark they resembled bits of shiny black jet, a long, high-bridged nose with a hump in the middle and a faint quirk to the left, that desperado's mustache and cruel, grinning mouth . . . Dear God, his nose! His nose!

Out of the deep recesses of her memory sprang the motions she had learned in the self-defense class to take control of her body. Without even knowing that she meant to do so, she kicked savagely backward. Her heel made jarring contact with his right kneecap. He shouted in pained surprise, and his hold loosened enough to allow her to turn in his arms. She punched him, openhanded as she had been taught, the edge of her palm coming up hard under his nose and driving upward with all the force she could throw behind it. Her hand made contact with a satisfying thunk! He howled, releasing her as his hands flew to his injured nose. Lora staggered backward, wanting nothing so much as to sink to the ground and gasp for air. But she could not. She had to run. . . .

She looked up to find that his hands were already falling away from his face. Twin streams of bright crimson flowed from his nostrils, running down into his mustache and mouth. He swiped at the blood with a brown forearm and stood staring at the red smears on his skin. Then his eyes lifted to hers. If she had thought the expression on his face was savage before, she had not words to describe the way he was looking at her now. His fists clenched at his sides; profanities fell from his mouth in a steady, filthy stream. Lora almost wished that he didn't speak English; she would rather not have heard the things he was calling her.

The blazing sun, beating down on them as they stood facing each other with perhaps six feet between them, could not warm the chill that sent shivers shooting up and down her spine. He was terrifying as he stood there glaring at her, murder plain in his eyes, big and muscular and savagely angry—at her. The Incredible Hulk in bronzed skin and a Hawaiian shirt. Lora felt a hysterical giggle bubble up in her throat. She had always secretly liked the Incredible Hulk... She couldn't run, she realized sickly, he would catch her in seconds.... And the idea of beating him in a fight was laughable. She had only managed to break away from him before because she had caught him by surprise. Even that small advantage was denied to her now. He would not give her the chance to do that to him again....

He lunged toward her. Lora shrieked and whirled to run, regardless of the sense of it. It was too late to even try. His hand closed over her shoulder, and he jerked her back against him. Once again she was smothered by the sheer enormous size and strength of him. Terrified, she reacted instinctively, screaming and struggling furiously in an effort to save herself. In this moment of crisis, her self-defense lessons rose to the fore again, and she stomped hard on his instep. Her flat sandal made no perceptable impression on his sneaker-clad foot. She squirmed in his hold, screaming and trying futilely to kick his shins. One of his steel-muscled arms encircled her waist, imprisoning her arms. Then he was lifting her clear off her feet, holding her helplessly crushed against his broad chest.

"Unless you want me to hurt you—and I mean really hurt you, you vicious little bitch—you'd better shut up and hold still!" His arms squeezed her so hard that she feared for her ribs.

Tears of fright rose in her eyes, and Lora realized the fight was over. To struggle more would only provoke him further.... She subsided with a whimper, going limp in his arms, waiting for another move from him. If he thought to terrify her into meek obedience, he was doing a good job of it. He stared down at her inimically for a few seconds while she lay against him, quivering with terror.

"That's better." He held her a moment longer, brutally tight, then slowly, slowly, set her back on her feet. Lora barely had time to enjoy the feel of solid ground beneath her before he was wrenching one arm behind her back, holding it at a painful angle. She cried out, but his grip didn't loosen by so much as a fraction. Grasping her by the nape of her neck, he turned her around and pushed her stumbling back in the direction from which they had come.

"Walk!" he ordered tersely. With him so close behind her, ready to exert punishing persuasion on her already aching arm, she had little choice. She walked.

"Damn it, woman, I ought to strangle you on the spot! I'm bleeding like a stuck pig, and just look at the goddamned car!" He still sounded murderously angry as they approached the VW, which had come to rest against the trunk of a now crazily leaning palm tree. The front end of the vehicle was crushed in the middle like a Pepsi can that had been squeezed by a huge hand. The hood was still latched in the center, but either side of it lifted skyward like wings poised for takeoff. A faint plume of steam rose lazily from the nether parts of the engine; its upward progress was accompanied by a sibilant hissing sound.

"God in heaven!" She could almost hear him gnashing his teeth as he surveyed the carnage.

"Ohhh!" She uttered the small sound involuntarily as he walked up to the car, dragging her with him. The pressure on her arm was excruciatingly painful. . . .

"Please. . . ." She could not help herself. She would beg if she had to.

"Please what?" To her surprise, he had actually stopped

and turned to look at her. So what if there was a taunt to his voice? If only he would ease the pressure on her arm!

"Please," she said again, hating herself for sounding so humble but unable to do anything about it. "Please let go of my arm. I won't try to escape again, I swear it."

He laughed, the sound brutal. Lora felt a chill race down her spine. He liked hearing her beg, she thought. And the thought frightened her almost more than anything else that had happened so far on this dreadful day.

"Damn right you won't. Because you know that next time—if there is a next time—you won't walk away from it with only a bad fright and a sore arm. Next time I'll be playing for keeps. Understand?"

"Y—yes." She would agree to anything if only he would let go of her arm—and not hurt her further. . . .

"Remember what I said."

She groaned as he gave one final upward tug on her imprisoned arm before releasing it. Bringing it forward slowly, she rubbed her aching muscles as she turned to face him. Those obsidian eyes, narrowed and dangerous, fixed hers. Her own eyes dropped nervously away from the blood-smeared face.

"Remember," he said again, menacingly, and she nodded.

Without taking his eyes off her, he opened the driver's door and got into the car, leaving the door open behind him. Lora stood watching him while trying not to meet his eyes. She had read that looking a vicious dog directly in the eyes could provoke an attack, and it was possible that vicious men might react in the same way. As she watched without appearing to, he looked at himself in the rearview mirror, grimaced, picked up his sarape, and used it to mop the blood from his face. Then he wadded the sarape up and threw it into the backseat, glaring at her through the windshield before turning his attention to the car.

The keys were still in the ignition, and Lora watched nervously as he turned them. There was a dry heave from the engine, then a series of grinding groans. Lora paled. If the car would not start, what would happen to her? As far as she could see, his alternatives were these: kill her and try the kidnapping bit again, or let her go and do the same. But he wouldn't let her go; he would be certain that she would immediately go to the police.

A gutteral curse made her look fearfully at him. He was getting out of the car, casting her a killing glare as he did so. He walked around to the trunk, opened it, and rooted around for a moment. As the trunk hid him from her view, it occurred to Lora that now would be a perfect time to run. He thought he had her thoroughly cowed . . . She remembered his threat of what he would do to her if she tried to escape again. He had meant it . . . She shivered. Then she thought of what he would probably do to her anyway. She could not wait meekly for her own execution. . . . The sun glinted blindingly off the shiny orange paint on the raised trunk; of her captor, Lora could see only the top of his rough black head. Taking a deep breath, she ran for her life, her gait made unexpectedly awkward by her skinned knees. She ran on regardless. But not along the road, where her recapture would certainly be only a matter of a couple of minutes. This time she ran for the jungle, where she might be able to hide. She would by far rather take her chances with the wild rain forest than with the man who held her prisoner. . . .

The plant life at the edge of the jungle was so dense that it was like running headlong into a wall. Lora threw herself at the intertwined branches and bushes and vines, praying that she would break through. She did, to more of the same.

"Goddamn it!"

The infuriated roar from behind her spurred her on. She clawed and pushed and leaped in an effort to make some headway, but her gains could be measured in inches rather than yards. The undergrowth was so thick . . . The soft, spongy jungle floor sucked at her feet like quicksand. Lora sank ankle deep every time her foot touched the ground. The leaves brushing her bare arms and legs felt cool and almost slimy. Others had sharp, thorny edges . . . Birds squawked and took wing as she blundered through the tangled vegetation. She refused to speculate on what besides birds the jungle might house. . . . She could hear him crashing through the forest behind her, and panic gave her added impetus; he would kill her if he caught her, she knew. Bending almost double, she put her arms over her head to protect her face and pushed onward. Even as she did so, she realized that she had done the most foolish thing imaginable in trying to escape again. He would certainly catch her . . . But she hadn't known the jungle would be so inpenetrable. She had had to try. . . .

Something closed on her hair, jerking her head backward. He had caught her . . . She screamed, fire engine loud, trying frantically to pull away. Then she saw that her hair was caught on the low-hanging branches of a tree. . . .

"You lying little bitch." The words were gritted right behind her. Lora jerked around, eyes wide with fear, as he pushed through the wall of foliage. She was caught fast, unable to get away because of the snarl of branches in her hair. Clearly he was aware of her predicament, because he moved forward unhurriedly. His face was dark with anger, his black eyes alive with it. A long scratch, from a branch as he chased after her through the jungle no doubt, bisected the bronzed skin of his left cheek from the edge of that fearsome mustache to his earlobe. His mouth was twisted into a nasty smile. As he loomed beside her, Lora cringed.

His hands went beneath the hem of that awful shirt. Horrified, Lora remembered the gun. Would he shoot her now? She whimpered, cringing as far away from him as she could, her hands tearing at her trapped hair futilely while she kept her eyes fixed on his every move. The branch in her hair held firm as she pulled frantically against it. She could feel strands of her hair tearing out of her head. . . .

His hands were moving beneath the edge of the shirt. Then they were in view again, pulling free of the beltloops of his jeans an overlong leather thong that, wrapped twice around his waist, had served him as a belt. Lora sagged with relief. At least it wasn't the gun . . . Holding the thong in one hand, he reached for her with the other. She shrank away, but he caught her. His fingers bit into the soft bare flesh of her upper arm as he turned her so that her back was to him. Dragging her hands roughly behind her, he used the thong to tie her wrists tightly together behind her back. The leather was soft and supple, but that did not keep it from biting into her skin. . . .

"Please don't hurt me." The soft whimper was hers. She was terrified, shaking with fear as she tried to look over her shoulder to see what he was doing. His hands were in her hair now, untangling it from the branches with little care for the tender scalp to which it was attached. Lora winced at the short, sharp stings of pain. She was very much afraid there was worse to come. . . .

He didn't say a word as he dragged her after him out of the jungle, his fingers biting into her soft upper arm. She stumbled several times, nearly falling, but he pulled her roughly on.

At the edge of the jungle, he turned to look at her. The sun striking those black eyes made them glitter with an unholy light. His mouth was tight beneath the fierce mustache.

"I warned you, lady," he gritted, lifting a hand toward her. Lora cowered, and big tears slowly filled her eyes to run down her cheeks.

"Please," she whispered, hating her own cowardice. "Please don't hurt me. I—I—please. . . ."

"Goddamn." His hand dropped as he surveyed her pleading face. The white-hot anger that had so terrified her faded from his eyes, to be replaced by something that very much resembled self-disgust. "Don't cry, lady. I'm not going to hurt you, okay? If you'll just give me a little cooperation. But you've got to understand that I'm on the run for my life. If you put me in a position where it's you or me, well . . . But if you're smart, you'll be fine. Only no more stunts like this one. I don't need the hassle."

Lora stared at him, still quivering. He was not going to hurt her—if she did as he told her. He said she would be fine . . . Slowly, the shaking ceased and the flow of tears stopped. He still frightened her, but as she looked up at him some of the sick terror he had engendered in her faded. His voice had been reasonable, his expression irritable rather than murderous. He seemed almost human, in fact. . . .

"Do we have a deal?"

Lora nodded, not trusting herself to speak. He was not going to hurt her. Relief made her lightheaded. She offered no resistance as he led her back to where the car waited.

"Sit," he said, pushing her down next to a stunted palm tree only a few feet from the car. Lora sat, not caring that the sharp, prickly grass jabbed at her through the thin cotton blend of her dress.

Crouching behind her, he untied her wrists, dragged them

behind the tree trunk and tied them again, a little looser this time. Then he stood up, looking down at her.

"That's for insurance while I try to fix the mess you made of the car."

He turned to walk back to the still-open car trunk. Lora watched him go, sagging back against the tree in relief. He limped slightly, she noticed, favoring his right knee. She had kicked him in that knee—she hadn't realized that she packed that much of a wallop. Her knees and palms stung a little, a legacy from her leap from the car, but she hardly noticed. She felt lucky just to be alive. She had been so certain he would kill her—but he hadn't. He said he wouldn't hurt her if she did as he said. Could she believe him?

Apparently, there were some tools in the trunk, because he had a small metal box open at his feet and a wrench in his hand as he bent over the hood, which he had managed to raise after some effort. In deference to the blistering heat, he discarded the sleazy shirt, affording her an excellent view of his bare torso. Watching streams of perspiration run down the rippling muscles of his back, Lora thanked heaven that she was tethered in the shade.

He was working with concentrated effort, scowling down at the engine and cursing under his breath as he discarded first one tool and then another, finally returning to the wrench. A sound from back down the highway brought his head swinging around. A car! Lora stiffened with excitement, ready to scream for help as soon as the vehicle's occupants were within hearing distance. Then she looked warily back at her captor. He had sprinted to the passenger's door, opened it, leaned in and straightened again, shutting the door, all before the approaching vehicle—which turned out to be a dusty, battered pickup truck loaded down with skinny Mexican children and squawking chickens—had done much more than come into view.

Turning, he snatched up his shirt from the ground and strode toward her, the limp more pronounced as his movements quickened. Lora froze with renewed fear as she saw that he carried the gun. Scowling at her with an expression that would have silenced a far braver soul than she, he hunkered down beside her. Lora shivered as one long, bare, hard-muscled arm encircled her waist in what must have appeared, to anyone who didn't know better, to be a loving embrace. She could feel the heat and strength of that arm and the dampness of his skin through her dress. He had dropped his shirt in her lap; the hand belonging to the arm around her waist burrowed beneath it. Lora flinched as she felt the hard barrel of the gun press against her stomach.

"Behave yourself," he muttered warningly. Lora nodded.

The approaching truck was almost even with the layby by this time; its driver must have seen them, because it was slowing. The dark-skinned children in back leaned over the rickety wooden slats that fenced in the sides of the truck bed, craning their necks and chattering among themselves as they stared at first the wrecked car resting against the crazily leaning palm tree and then at the couple cuddling so affectionately just a few yards away. The passenger side window was open; a plump, harassed looking Mexican woman whom Lora assumed was the children's mother stuck her head out to call to them.

"*Señor! Que pasa?*" The woman sounded as if she didn't much care if they were having trouble.

With a swift glance at the man beside her, Lora frantically weighed her odds if she decided to risk the gun and call for help. Should she? Her captor must have sensed what was in her mind, because he tightened his grip; she felt his body hot and close against her side as the hard nose of the gun prodded deeper into her stomach.

"Smile!" he hissed, his voice deadly. Lora smiled. His closeness was overwhelming. She was aware of him with every nerve of her body; the strength of the muscles that enfolded her against him; the heat that emanated from him like a stove; the smell of sweat; the hardness of his arms and chest; the dampness of his bare skin where it touched her and the prickling of the hairs on his chest against her arm. . . .

"*Nada, señora, gracias! No problema!*" he called back, lifting the hand that was not holding the gun in a careless wave.

Lora tried frantically to signal with her eyes that something was wrong—she didn't dare do anything else with the gun and the man pressing ever closer—but the woman apparently saw nothing out of the ordinary.

"*Adios!*" She waved once, the children grabbed hold, and the truck was underway again. Lora watched forlornly as it rattled down the road and out of sight.

"Smart girl," he approved then, removing his arm and the gun simultaneously.

Lora shivered as he stood. She cast a quick, resentful glare up at her captor as he stood over her, his shirt in one hand and the gun in the other.

He left her, returning to the car and to work. Lora watched as his head and shoulders disappeared under the hood with a piece of hose. She was struck suddenly by how well-proportioned his body was. When he had first crowded into the VW beside her, she had thought that he was almost as stocky as he was tall. Now she saw that that was not true at all. His shoulders were wide and heavily muscled, but his torso was lean and sculpted. Sweat gleamed on the bronzed skin of his shoulder-blades, then trickled down his spine to disappear into a spreading patch of wetness at the waistband of his jeans. Her arm still tingled from contact with the wedge of curling black hair that covered the muscular planes of his chest. He was leaning into the engine, so most of his chest was out of her sight. But his backside was not . . . His hips were narrow, his legs long and straight. As her eyes ran back up over them she could not help but notice that his rear was small and tight in the faded jeans that fit him like the advertisements promised they could. All at once he straightened, turning to look directly at her. Lora realized with a stab of acute discomfort that she had been staring—and where. Dear God, had he seen? Would he take it for encouragement?

"I think I managed to fix it." He was coming toward her, still moving with that slight limp, wiping his hands on a rag as he spoke. She was relieved to see him put on his shirt, carelessly doing up the buttons with one hand. He would not put on his shirt if he was intent on rape. . . .

"Goody." Her response was distinctly unenthusiastic.

He grinned then, a real, human, honest-to-God grin, and Lora stared. Amazing what a swathe of white teeth and a crinkling of black eyes could do for a face! He looked almost—handsome. No, not handsome, with that too aggressive face and villainous mustache, to say nothing of the remaining smears of blood from the wounds she and the jungle between them had inflicted. But attractive, which was not the right word, either. Lora was a stickler for the right word; as an English teacher, she demanded it of her students in their compositions and she would not now accept less of herself. And that word was, she reluctantly realized, sexy. The man was sexy as hell. She shuddered away from the thought. Under the circumstances, how could she possibly find him sexy? Was she crazy? Masochistic, maybe? If so, she had never recognized signs of it in herself before now.

He was behind her, his hands on her wrists as he untied the thong. She flinched from even that impersonal touch. His fingers seemed unbearably hot against her soft skin. . . .

"Come on, let's go." He caught her upper arm to help her to her feet. Lora jerked away from him reflexively, and he let her go. She could feel his eyes boring into her back as she walked ahead of him to the car. She was suddenly, frighteningly aware of his blatant masculinity, and in self-defense tried to suppress the natural feminine sway of her hips, with what success she couldn't guess. He stood watching until she was installed in the driver's seat, then got in himself before handing her the keys. Taking them, she was careful not to touch his fingers. His glittering black eyes on her face gave her the shivers. . . .

"Don't try any more tricks," he warned softly as she started the car. The gun lay across his lap, gleaming starkly in the bright sunlight pouring in through the windshield. Lora flicked a quick, nervous glance down at it. His hand on the grip seemed idle, but the nose was pointed directly at her. "I've been very patient with you so far, but don't push your luck. Remember, you'll be okay as long as you do exactly what I tell you. If you don't—I'll do what I have to."

Lora swallowed, and nodded without speaking. Carefully, she depressed the clutch, put the car into first, and pulled out onto the highway. That unprecedented stab of sexual awareness she had just experienced toward him had unnerved her completely. Never in her life had she been so aware of a man as a man . . . She shifted into second; there was an ear-shattering grinding sound as the gears crashed. Lora winced, and he grimaced. The car jerked off down the road as Lora awkwardly manipulated the stick shift and tried to remember when to step on the clutch and when to release it.

"You can't drive worth a damn, can you?" he said when at last she had managed to wrestle the transmission into fourth gear and the car was moving more or less smoothly down the highway.

"Would you like to drive?" she demanded irritably before she thought.

"Then I wouldn't need you, would I?" he answered, his voice very soft. "But you never know, I may decide that the off-chance that the police will pull us over isn't worth putting up with your god-awful driving. Then where will you be?"

Lora cast him a quick, nervous look. He was staring out at the road, and his face was as unreadable as stone. She quickly looked away again, but the image of that grim profile was etched indelibly into her memory. Sexy or not, he would kill her if he had to. She had best not make the mistake of forgetting that again.

III

They drove without stopping until long past dark. Lora grew increasingly anxious as he made no attempt at conversation, merely shifting in his seat with growing restlessness as the sun sank beneath the horizon and mile after mile of blacktop highway passed beneath the wheels. He was uneasy, she could sense it. His shoulders and legs filled his side of the small car; she was acutely aware of every movement he made. When he leaned forward to scan the road ahead of them, or turned to survey cars approaching them from behind, she could feel the tautness of his body, as if he was waiting for something, expecting something to happen. Watching for the police, perhaps? She had no doubts that he was a criminal; clearly he was on the run from the law, or maybe from his fellow criminals—or both. The questions was, what would happen if he was caught while she was with him? With the police, it would just be a matter of making them understand that she was his victim, not his confederate—if they could be made to listen before bullets started flying—but with criminals as desperate as her abductor she might be dispatched along with him whether she was an innocent victim of circumstances or not. She hoped against hope that it was the police he seemed so desperately wary of—they would realize that she was a victim; after all, they were the police, they didn't make mistakes like that—and that they would catch up with him soon. If not, what would he do to her? Despite his promise, would he kill her? Maybe he had just said what he had to assure her cooperation until he no longer needed her.

If he didn't kill her, would he rape her? That, she decided, was a very real possibility. Sooner or later, they would have to stop and rest, and then, she was very much afraid, she would learn the worst. She kept remembering how he had said that he didn't mind hurting women. The memory made her shudder. Would he rape her? Dear God, she prayed he would not. It was impossible to imagine herself being subjected to such horror . . . But then, this morning it would have been equally impossible to imagine herself being kidnapped by a terrifyingly real, terrifyingly serious version of the Frito Bandido. And it had happened. If he were to initiate a sexual overture, what should she do? Would he hurt her if she resisted him? Just because she thought he was sexy—detestable word, she had been around sixteen-year-old girls too long—did not mean that she would willingly have sex with him. Far from it! First of all, he scared her senseless. And second, where she came from, there were only two types of females: ladies and all others. And ladies did not, definitely did not, have sex with men they had known for less than a day, regardless of how physically attractive said men might be. And a lady would certainly never voluntarily have sex with a violent and possibly crazed criminal who had abducted her at gunpoint. And Lora had always been, indisputably, a lady.

The sticking point was what he would do when she rejected him. He might take her rejection philosophically or, as seemed far more likely from what she already knew of him, he might not. And that's where the spectre of forcible rape came in. Because he could force her, she knew. No matter how hard she might fight, he could easily overpower her. Her self-defense course had not turned her into a female Bruce Lee, after all. She had gotten lucky, before, but she could not count on it happening again. Against a six-foot-four or thereabouts hunk of honed muscle and bone that looked like it should be playing fullback for the Dallas Cowboys, she didn't stand a chance.

While she was sitting there ruminating, casting the man beside her the occasional worried glance, Lora gradually became aware of an ever-more-pressing concern: she had to go to the bathroom. At first she ignored her bladder's signals, but as the minutes and miles passed she became increasingly uncomfortable. Hunger and sleepiness she could, and would, hold at bay for some hours longer. But she had to go to the bathroom! The problem was, she was afraid to tell him so, afraid that mention of such an unmentionable subject might give him ideas, in case he didn't have them already. Besides, she was afraid to stop, period. While she was driving the car, she felt relatively safe. Once she was not, who knew what he might take it into his head to do to her?

She squirmed as discreetly as possible on the uncomfortable vinyl seat, tightening her muscles and trying to think of something else. He was staring out at the road ahead of them, which was deserted now. Except for the faint light of their own headlights, they were surrounded by darkness. Uneven expanses of fields rolled away from the highway on both sides, products of the slash and burn method of reclaiming farmland from the jungle. Even the blacktop highway itself stretching away into an infinity of unseen miles contributed to the overall impression of inpenetrable night. Except for the occasional lowing of a cow or cry of a night animal, they could have been alone in the world.

'What the hell are you wiggling about?'' After about fifteen minutes of what she had thought were her imperceptible movements, his voice barked at her over the faint hum of the engine.

''Nothing,'' she answered defensively, refusing to look at him although she knew he was glaring at her. Quite apart from fearing what he might do to her if he started thinking along those lines, she found that she simply could not tell a strange man of the problem that afflicted her. It would be too embarrassing.

''Then for God's sake, sit still.'' He sounded more irritable than threatening, but Lora didn't want to push her luck. She concentrated on ignoring her difficulty, and almost succeeded. Until the first fat drop of rain plopped down on the windshield, to be followed by another and another in a rapidly quickening assault.

''Oh, no.'' The mere sound of water flowing threatened to be her undoing. She clamped her thighs even tighter.

''What are you moaning about?'' He turned to face her as he spoke, his eyes glittering points of light in the darkness. She could feel them moving down over her body and then back up to her face again. Her hands tightened on the wheel; she did not like the speculative way he was looking at her body. Of course, he could merely be trying to decipher the cause of her obvious discomfort, but along the way he was making no bones about eyeing her curves. Lora slowed the car to a crawl as the quickening droplets turned without warning into sheets of pouring rain; modesty and fear battled with urgent need. Need won.

"I have to stop."

He snorted. "We'll stop when I say stop. It's not raining that hard."

Lora stared out into the raging downpour. He probably would call a hurricane a little rainstorm, she grumbled inwardly. But in any case that was not her problem at the moment.

"I need to stop," she said tightly, without looking at him.

"You heard what I said."

"I have to go to the bathroom!" The words burst out of her mouth. Furious that he had made her admit something so intimate, she shot a glare at him. His eyes moved swiftly over her once again, and then he settled back into his seat. To her angry embarrassment, she caught the glimmer of a faint grin as it came and went on his mouth.

"Oh."

When, after a few minutes, it became obvious that that was all the response he meant to give to what was rapidly becoming the driving force of her life, she shot him another furious look.

"Is that all you can say?"

"What do you want me to say? In case you haven't noticed, it's raining cats and dogs out there. I would say that you are welcome to stop the car and go behind a bush if you like, but I'd have to get out with you and I'm damned if I'm going to get soaked to the skin. You'll just have to exercise some self-control."

"Self-control!" Lora spluttered, thinking of the miles that she had been doing just that. He looked over at her, and once again she caught that faint, glimmering grin before it disappeared and his mouth became as hard and uncompromising as ever.

"Unless you have a jar in the backseat."

"A jar!" Words failed her. She seethed silently, steering

the car through the driving rain with gritted teeth, not really caring whether or not they stayed on the roadway. More by good luck than by good management they did, but she was at the point where it made not the slightest difference to her. She had to go to the bathroom!

The gun was lying in his lap, its nose pointed toward the dashboard, his hand resting negligently on the handle. Even if it had been pointed directly at her, she wouldn't have cared. There were no restrooms or even any buildings in sight, nor had there been for miles, there was no jar in the backseat, and there was no way she was going to wet her pants.

"I'm stopping," she said through her teeth, suiting the action to the words. "You can shoot me if you want to, but I have to go to the bathroom!"

He turned to stare at her as she threw the car into neutral, set the brake, and opened the door, stepping out into the downpour. She heard him curse, and saw his brown hand tighten on the gun as she shut the door behind her with a bang. He got out onto the roadway, clapping the sombrero on his head as he emerged, and stood scowling at her over the roof of the VW. The gun, pointed directly at her, was in one hand while with the other he tried to hold the folded sarape over it to protect it from the cascading torrents.

Lora ignored both him and the gun, walking away from the car into the quagmire at the side of the road. She was already soaked to the skin. Water streamed over her face and hair, and her dress was plastered to her body. Mud oozed slimily over the sides of her sandals, sucking at her feet with every step. A most unaromatic smell assaulted her nostrils. She sniffed, barely avoided getting a nose full of water, and identified the odor's source. Mexican farmers fertilized their fields with human excrement. Shuddering, she stopped in her tracks. There was no way she was venturing into one of those fields.

She narrowed her eyes against the rain and peered back toward the car. He had walked around it and now stood with feet braced apart and the gun pointed in her direction. With only the car's headlights behind him for illumination, she could not see his face but the rest of him looked very big and dark and dangerous. She caught the mutter of his voice over the pouring of the rain, and guessed that he was cursing her with expert fluency.

"Turn your back!"

He didn't hear her the first time, so she cupped her hands around her mouth and shouted. For a moment he stood irresolute, staring at her, but then he must have decided that she had no intention of doing what needed to be done while he stood and watched her. He turned his back. Lora had a brief moment of thankfulness that she wasn't wearing pantyhose, and then the whole business was concluded with satisfying speed. Feeling much better despite the fact that she was soaked to the skin, she stood, adjusted her clothing, walked around him back to the car, and got in. The thought of running did briefly occur to her, only to be quickly dismissed. When he caught her—and he would—he would be in a filthy temper, and she had already learned a healthy respect for his temper. Besides, the idea of slogging through acres of mud teeming with the source of that smell was off-putting in the extreme.

"I ought to shoot you. I'm wet as a drowned duck." Those were his first words as he got back in beside her. The gun was raised threateningly, but even its shiny blue-black barrel was not as ominous as the scowl on his face. The straw sombrero had been no match for the rain; he threw it and the soaked sarape into the backseat with a gesture of disgust. He

was as wet as she. Water still ran from his soaking hair down
his face and dripped from the end of his thick eyebrows and
mustache. His shirt clung wetly to his broad chest and his
drenched jeans hugged his thighs, emphasizing taut muscles
and sinews. Through the wet closeness of his shirt, she saw
the dark shadow of body hair. Hairy chested men had always
secretly appealed to her . . . Lora's eyes flickered at the thought.
Averting her face with a belligerent lift of her chin, she
reached to yank the car into first. It bucked forward, then, as
she shifted with a loud grinding of gears, lurched on down the
wet road.

"Goddamn it!" He clutched the dashboard for support,
and let the gun drop into his lap. Running his hand over his
wet face, he sluiced away what water he could. Lora didn't
even look at him as some of the droplets struck her arms and
neck. She was so wet already, she couldn't get any wetter.

They drove that way for perhaps fifteen minutes, while
Lora grew clammier and clammier. He shut off the air
conditioner, but that wasn't much help. He must have been as
cold and uncomfortable as she was, because finally, with a
muffled growl, he reached over and flicked on the heater. A
musty smell was the only tangible result. Lora waited vainly
for some evidence that the car was getting warmer, but if it
was she couldn't tell.

"Pull over," he ordered moments later, sounding fed up to
his back teeth. Lora cast him a quick look. For some reason
the black scowl that greeted her was almost reassuring. He
nearly always looked like that; she imagined that, if he was
planning to kill her for her temerity in making him get wet,
he would wear quite a different expression.

When she had done as he ordered, he reached out to grab
her roughly by the arm and leaned forward so that his face
was only inches away. Lora was very conscious of the rough

masculinity of him as he loomed so near. She stared at him wide-eyed, and tried not to wonder how the bristle on his chin would feel against her skin. . . .

'If I'm not mistaken, there's an *ejido*—a cooperative farm— down that track,'' he said with a jerk of his head in the direction he meant. ''We're going to drive down there, and if they'll have us we're going to spend what's left of the night. You're my wife, and I'm Brian Harding. Have you got that?''

Lora stared at him, then nodded jerkily. She wasn't sure, but she thought that this new arrangement might be something that could be turned to her advantage. If they were to be in the company of other people, surely she would have the opportunity to acquaint them with her plight. . . .

''If you try anything,'' his voice lowered, became the menacing growl he had used when he had first abducted her, ''if you try anything, so help me God, I'll kill you and them too. Understand me?''

He meant it. Lora's eyes widened as she registered that, and she shrank as far away from him as she could in the close confines of the car. She was no longer even remotely curious about how his unshaven chin would feel. He was an animal, a murderous brute, and she had temporarily allowed herself to forget that fact. How could she have felt even briefly attracted to him?

''Good.'' Her shrinking must have told him all he wanted to know, because he nodded as if satisfied. With a gesture he ordered her to start the car again. She did, and at his direction turned left onto a gravel track, only the track seemed to be more mud than gravel.

They had gone only a little way before the car plowed to a halt. Lora hit the accelerator, but the only response was the sound of spinning wheels. They were stuck in the mud. Lora licked her lips, and looked nervously over at her captor, who was scowling.

"Hell, what next?" The hand on the gun tightened, and Lora shrank back toward the door.

"I couldn't help it!" she protested hurriedly, and his scowl intensified.

"Did I say you could?" He reached toward her, and she shrank even further, but he only turned off the ignition and removed the keys, putting them in his pocket.

"So we walk," he said, leaning over again to open her door and push her out into the rain. Lora tumbled out, instinctively grabbing for her purse, nearly falling in the mud surrounding the car as he pulled the door closed again. She heard the faint click as he locked it after her. Then, before she even had time to think of trying to run, he was out of the car and closing the door behind him. The soaked and useless sombrero was plopped on his head, and the sarape was once again folded over his arm and hand to protect the gun.

"Come on." He was beside her now, catching her arm in that same rough grasp and propelling her through the down-pour. She struggled through ankle-deep mud as they waded down the track toward a cluster of low, dark buildings that were just visible through the pouring rain. Would the people here help her? she wondered as they slogged ever closer to the quiet houses. Did she dare even ask for help? She cast a scared glance up at the man who was dragging her along beside him like a recalcitrant dog on a leash. The answer was: she just didn't know.

IV
—

After their initial surprise and wariness at being disturbed in the middle of the night by *gringo* strangers was soothed by her captor's glib explanation—he spoke functional Spanish, of which Lora understood no more than two words in a hundred—and some of her own cash, which she was slightly affronted to watch him fish out of his pocket and hand out so liberally, their impromptu hosts were hospitality itself. Her captor's sombrero was taken from him—he smilingly rejected all attempts to remove the sarape, too—and both he and Lora were exclaimed over as they were ushered inside the small, cinderblock dwelling.

The middle-aged farmer whose house it apparently was introduced himself as Carlos Rodriguez as he put down the ancient rifle with which he had greeted them and tugged self-consciously on the obviously hastily donned trousers which were his only garment. A slender, black-plaited young girl with a woven blanket draped over his shoulders to cover

47

her nightgown regarded them with unblinking black eyes from behind Carlos's beefy shoulder. If Lora correctly understood one of the few words that had meaning for her in the reciprocal torrent of Spanish, this was Carlos's wife, Juana. A tiny, wizened old woman addressed by both Rodriguez and his wife as Mamacita peered at them from the depths of a large iron bedstead in one corner of the single room that made up the lower level of the house. Three big-eyed children snuggled on either side of Mamacita, goggling at the newcomers from beneath the protection of bedcoverings. The single electric bulb dangling from a cord in the center of the ceiling cast a dim light over what, as far as Lora could tell, was an immaculate, if shabby, dwelling. Her abductor, whose supposedly loving arm hugged her shoulders while the gun nuzzled her rib cage beneath the sheltering sarape, soon seemed to be on the easiest of terms with the entire family.

"*Veni, señor y señora* Harding." With a beckoning gesture, Juana at last led the way to a ladder set into the wall at the back of the room. Lora's psuedo-husband followed, bringing Lora with him.

After one swift, despairing look around as he stood aside for her to precede him, Lora climbed the ladder, a trifle awkwardly because of the encumbrance of her purse, which she clutched in one hand. There was clearly no help for her here. To begin with, none of these people seemed to speak a word of English. And even if they had, she could not bring herself to put them in danger. If anything went wrong, her captor might very well kill them all, children included, to save himself from whoever or whatever he was running from. He could not take them all captive, not if he meant to travel. And she certainly didn't think that he would leave witnesses behind to contact the police. She doubted that they could help her anyway. Rodriguez was a farmer, not a fighter, and even with his ancient rifle he was no match for the hard brutality of the man who was even now climbing the ladder below her.

Lora clambered off the ladder through an open trapdoor to find herself on her hands and knees in what seemed to be a loft. She could not be sure because the only light came from the room below. Except for the area just around the opening, the room was pitch dark. Cautiously, Lora stayed within the perimeter of light as her captor's head and shoulders appeared through the opening. Bracing his hands on the floor, he hoisted himself up beside her. Juana called out something, and he dropped the sarape and thrust the gun into his waistband before reaching down through the opening to emerge holding a smoking kerosene lantern. Like Lora, he was on his hands and knees; he sank back on his haunches and held up the lantern to survey the space in which they found themselves.

The floor was made of rough wood planks. The thatched roof angled down on both sides so that only in the very center could a person stand upright. A painted iron bedstead like the one below stood in the middle of the room. Near its foot was a battered tin pail into which a steady series of drips fell with rhythmic plops. The windowless room had a close, musty odor that was not helped by the smell of burning kerosene. Lora felt a sudden surge of nausea and grimaced. Of course she felt sick, and it wasn't just the smell. She hadn't eaten a thing in nearly twelve hours.

He scooped up the pistol and dripping sarape as he stood, stooping in the space that had never been intended to accommodate someone of his height. Walking over to the bed, he set the lantern and pistol down on a small table beside it, and draped the sarape over the back of the single straight-backed chair. "You did very well, wife," he said with a flickering smile as he turned up the wick so that every corner of the small room was illuminated. "Keep that up and we'll get along fine." Then he turned to look at her. Lora, still on her hands and knees beside the opening, regarded him warily. She was at his mercy—and she didn't like the looks of that bed.

"Hungry?"

Lora nodded, her eyes never leaving him as she contemplated her situation. Would he dare try to rape her with the entire Rodriguez family right below? With another long look at him, Lora thought, Yes, he'd dare.

"The price of a night's stay also included a meal. Señora Rodriguez is probably preparing it now. In the meantime, I suggest you get out of those wet clothes and into bed. We've turned the Rodriguez couple out of what is obviously their love nest, so we may as well enjoy it."

"I—I'm fine," Lora stuttered, her eyes widening. Did he mean what she feared he did by that last? Determinedly, she ignored the chills that were running up and down her spine. She was soaked to the skin, her hair sending icy streamers of water down her neck, her dress clinging clammily to her goose-bump-riddled body. Even her sandals were miserably awash with mud and water, and slid uncomfortably around on her feet. Every cell in her body longed to be out of the wet, filthy clothes—except those in her brain. They shrieked at her to remain fully dressed at all cost. Love nest, indeed!

"What do you mean, you're fine? Thanks to your idiocy, we're both as wet as a pair of fish. I'm going to strip off, and if you have any sense you will, too." He looked very big and intimidating as he stood eyeing her from beneath scowling brows. The effect was in no way mitigated by the forced bowing of his head in deference to the low roof. Lora sidled back toward the trapdoor, which was still open. If it actually came down to attempted rape, she would scream like a banshee and let the chips fall were they would.

He still stood near the foot of the bed, looking big and dark and frightening as he waited for her reply. The lantern cast weird shadows over his face making him look like some evil demon risen from the netherworld to terrorize her. His black brows were drawn together over glittering eyes that were no less dark. His mouth was compressed grimly beneath the mustache that was just what was needed to make him look the part of a desperate criminal. The square, unshaven jaw and gleaming wet black hair, the height of him and breadth of his shoulders, the length and strength of his limbs all combined with the knowledge that she was his helpless prisoner to scare her through to the very marrow of her bones.

"Are you going to get undressed or not?" He was regarding her in a way that made Lora feel sick. His hands hung loose and flexed at his sides. Any minute now he would come across the room and grab her, she thought, and she would scream because she would not be able to help it and the innocent Mexican family downstairs would come tumbling up the ladder to see what ailed their guests and they would all, herself included, likely end up dead. . . .

"No." Her voice was hoarse with dread. This is where he came storming across the room to rip the clothes from her shrinking body. . . .

"Suit yourself, then," he said, turning his back on her. "If you want to sit around freezing in wet clothes, it's no skin off my back." And with that he started to unbutton his shirt.

Lora didn't know whether to feel relieved or freshly alarmed. She watched, both frightened and fascinated, as he stripped off his shirt to reveal those massive shoulders and that lean, muscular back. His skin gleamed in the lamplight like bronze silk. The muscles underneath rippled as he moved . . . His hands were on the narrow leather thong that served him as a belt, pulling it free, and Lora understood that he meant to take off his clothes with as little regard for her presence as if she had not been there at all. She stared, unable to look away as he kicked the silver and maroon running shoes from his feet and then pushed his jeans down over thighs and calves that were dark with hair and ridged with muscle. Clad only in a pair of white jockey shorts that seemed to be as wet as the rest of his clothes from the way they molded every hard curve and shadowed indention in his rump, he sat down on the bed to remove his white athletic socks. Lora watched, mesmerized by the play of muscles in his arms and chest as he bared long, narrow brown feet. That done, he stood up again, holding his socks in one hand as he gathered the rest of his clothes from the floor and spread them carefully over the iron footboard to dry. As he moved, Lora saw the spiderweb design of silvery white scars that marred the front of his right knee. So that was the reason for his limp. She didn't think she had kicked him that hard... If Lora thought the underpants revealed his backside, it was nothing to what they did to his front. She looked at the soft bulge beneath the doubled material of his fly, then kept on looking because she couldn't help herself.

"*Señor! Señora!*" The voice from below brought Lora back to reality with a jerk. She blinked, and felt her face color hotly. Thank the Lord that Señora Rodriguez had interrupted when she had, before he had seen the fascination that must have been written all too plainly on her face. What was the matter with her, that she could find such a man sexually exciting? That was the question that plagued her as she wet her embarrassingly dry lips and, in response to his gesture, leaned down through the trapdoor to answer Señora Rodriguez's call.

The Mexican woman handed up two chipped crockery plates filled with a steamy concoction of beans and tortillas, the scent of which made Lora's mouth water, a bottle and glasses, and two rough towels.

As Lora took the provisions and set them on the floor next to her purse, she realized that this might be her only chance to alert her hosts to her predicament. Perhaps Señor Rodriguez could summon the police while her captor slept, and he would be captured and she freed by morning. Throwing a quick, nervous look over her shoulder, she saw that he was occupied with dragging a blanket from the bed, his back to her. She leaned down through the opening again, her eyes fixed pleadingly on the other woman's face as she tried to remember enough Spanish to ask for help.

"*Aidez-moi.*" Drat, that was French. Why hadn't she studied Spanish in school instead? French had never done her a lick of good, and now her lack of Spanish might very well end up costing her her life. Señora Rodriguez was staring up at her with a slight frown wrinkling her brow. She obviously had not the slightest inkling of what Lora was trying to say.

"*Como dice?*" The question sounded puzzled. Lora abandoned her attempt to find the right Spanish phrase. She leaned further out of the opening, her voice hoarse with urgency as she whispered.

"I need help. Please. You must fetch—" She had been going to say *la policía*, one of the few Spanish words she knew, but was stopped in midsentence by a rough hand closing around the nape of her neck.

Lora cast a single, terrified look back at her captor as his steel-like fingers threatened to crush the vertebrae in the back of her neck. She couldn't move, couldn't utter a sound, and didn't know if it was from fear or from some kung fu hold that he was using on her. He drew her inexorably backward, then leaned forward, a smile on his face, to speak to Señora Rodriguez.

"Perdóname, Señor Harding, no entiendo la señora..." Señora Rodriguez began, an apologetic smile on her smooth young face.

"No es importa," he answered, smiling. Lora was amazed at the charm he could put into his voice and face as he continued soothingly. The only other phrase Lora caught was something about *mi esposa,* which she knew meant wife and guessed referred to herself. She could have sworn that he had not a trouble in the world as he concluded with, *"Buenas noches, señora, y muchas gracias."*

"De nada, señor. Buenas noches, señor y señora Harding." He had apparently managed to allay any slight puzzlement she might have aroused in Señora Rodriguez, because the woman walked away from the ladder without a backward look. He bent, never letting go of Lora's neck, and closed the trapdoor very gently. Then he straightened and turned to look at her. Despite her chilled state, Lora felt sweat break out all over her at the look in his eyes.

V
—

"You don't learn very fast, do you?"

She was still on her knees with his hand on her neck forcing her head back so that she had to look up at him. He loomed over her, the striped blanket he had wrapped around himself to speak with Señora Rodriquez dropping from his shoulders so that he was once again clad only in his underpants. His body was huge and dark-furred and menacing, and his eyes glittered fiercely in the harshly carved face. Combined with the strength of the steely fingers that threatened to snap her neck, the homicidal look in his eyes terrified the wits out of her. The soft voice which had put the question to her only intensified her fear. She sat dumbly, quivering from head to toe as she stared up at him. At her lack of reply, his fingers tightened cruelly on her neck. Lora's hands half rose to grasp his arm in an instinctive effort to free herself of the excruciating grip, but something warned her that any resistance on her part now would be a grave mistake.

"You just exhausted my patience, lady. Stand up." The fingers on her neck dragged her upright without giving her a chance to obey under her own steam. Lora stood with her back to him, her eyes huge, her mouth shaking. He pushed her in the direction of the bed, and she went. His hand never left her neck.

He let her go near the foot of the bed. The relief of being suddenly free of those cruel fingers was such that her knees sagged. Her hand came up automatically to massage the tingling ache as she turned to face him. Her eyes sought him fearfully. What would he do to her now?

"I was just—just trying to ask her about—about a bathroom." Her newfound deceitful instincts rushed to her aid.

He snorted. "Yeah, and I'm Bugs Bunny," he retorted, his face hard. "Get undressed."

Lora stared at him, blanching. He was close, perhaps three feet away. She could feel the anger in him, feel the heat and sheer power of that barely clad body as if he stood mere inches from her. Those glittering black eyes impaled her. The grim mouth barely moved as he spoke. Lora's mouth quivered piteously as the hot sting of tears burned her eyes. It was going to happen now, the rape she had feared; by her own actions she had brought about just the crisis she had most dreaded. Dear God, what should she do?

He was regarding her falling tears without pity this time. Those obsidian eyes were dark and hard as twin coals. "I said get undressed."

The harsh bite of his voice told her that he would tolerate no further delay. Lora quivered, biting her lower lip, looking at him piteously as her hand moved, slowly, slowly, to the top of the zipper at the back of her dress. He watched her without the slightest softening. She started to pull the zipper down, her eyes never leaving him. Soon she would be naked and vulnerable . . . Suddenly, Lora knew that she could not do it. She could not submit to this degradation without a fight.

Her hand dropped back to her side, her chin came up, and she met his eyes defiantly while the tears dried on her cheeks.

"No," she said. He stared at her for a moment as if unable to believe his ears. Then his mouth tightened and his face darkened ominously. He moved, and she stepped back nervously.

"If you touch me I'll scream," she warned in a high-pitched whisper. Her knees were quivering with fear, but he couldn't know that.

He stood stock still, staring at her for a long moment without speaking. Then he turned away. Lora sagged with relief. She had called his bluff, and she had won. . . .

"So you'll scream, will you?" He turned back toward her, speaking with a fierce satisfaction. Lora's eyes widened with horror as she saw that he now held the pistol, which was pointed right at her heart. "I don't think so. Not if you want to live to be a day older. Now take off your clothes!"

The last sentence was savage, but not as savage as the light in his eyes. Lora stared at that pistol, and felt the sick horror return. She did not doubt that he would use it if she did not obey. The choice was between submitting to the unspeakable degradation of a sexual assault or dying. Her mouth quivered. She did not want to die. Her hand moved back to the zipper while he watched with narrowed, glinting eyes.

Her hands shook as she pulled the zipper down past her waist as slowly as she dared. When the dress was loose she shrugged out of the narrow straps and let it fall down her body. Staring fixedly at a point on the opposite wall so that she would not have to look at him, she stepped out of the soggy, crumpled circle of blue, and bent to pick it up. Carefully, she shook it out and hung it with his discarded clothes on the footboard. She felt his eyes on her all the while. Unable to resist the compulsion, she darted a quick, frightened glance at him, then just as hastily looked away. His face was predatory as he took in the sight of her clad only in her white strapless bra with the innocent little pink rosebud between the cups that she filled almost to overflowing and the matching panties that circled her slender waist with a narrow band of elastic decorated with yet another rosebud before flaring out to hug her curving hips with silky white nylon. The underwear was newly bought for the trip, and while it was pretty and feminine it was also modest. Or at least, it had been in the department store. Now, dampened, it clung to her skin so that she might as well have been naked. Looking down at herself, Lora was mortified to discover that her nipples, reacting to the chill, stood erect, pressing wantonly against the whisper-thin nylon that seemed to gleam in the flickering lamplight. Their rosy pink color was clearly discernable, as was the darker hue of the circle surrounding them. And, further down her body, could be seen the triangular shadow between her thighs.

"Take that off, too. Everything."

Lora clasped her hands before her, her fingers twining in an unconscious nervous gesture. To strip naked before this monster, this animal who was deliberately forcing her to humiliate herself as a prelude to heaping even worse brutalities on her, was absolutely beyond her. She could not do it . . . She looked up, directly at him for the first time since she had started taking off her clothes. The cold blue metal of the gun gleamed at her. His eyes were just as hard and cold as they met hers. Would he shoot her? With the Rodriquez family downstairs? If he shot her, he would have to kill them as well. Would he think of that? Would he care?

"Did you hear me?" The quiet rasp was ominous in its softness.

Lora's hands twisted again. She looked up at him helplessly. The gun in his hand terrified her, the man himself terrified her—but the thought of standing naked before him terrified her too.

"You won't shoot me."

"What?" He sounded dumbfounded.

Lora swallowed. She had barely managed to get the words out the first time. It wasn't surprising that he thought he might have misunderstood the hoarse croak.

"You won't shoot me." Her voice was a little stronger this time. He stood staring at her as if she had suddenly sprouted horns before his eyes.

"You have a death wish, or what?" he asked, eyes glittering as his mouth compressed. Lora quivered as the gun came up, pointed while his hand tightened. "I'm giving you one more chance, and one only. Take off those clothes!"

"If you shoot me, you'll have to shoot all of them, too. Downstairs. The police will come, and then they'll really be after you. The whole country will be after you. . . ."

"Goddamn it!" The words were no less ferocious for being muttered. Before Lora realized what was happening, he grabbed her, shoved her against the wall, and pinioned her there with one hand around her throat. He squeezed just hard enough so that she had to gasp for air. Her eyes were wide and terrified as they met his. He was smiling savagely.

"You're right, lady: I'm not going to shoot you, not here. But there's not one thing in hell to keep me from strangling you!" His hand tightened while her eyes bulged, as much from panic as lack of air. His hand loosened just enough so that she could draw breath.

"Give me any more trouble, make one more sound, and that's just what I'll do. Understand?"

Without waiting for her response, he pressed a tiny red

button on the side of the pistol, tossed it on the bed, then reached behind her with his free hand to unhook her bra. She quivered as he yanked it from her, her arms coming up to hug her breasts in a gesture of frantic protectiveness. He tossed the bra on the bed beside the gun, then hooked his hand in the waistband of her panties, dragging them down her legs, yanking at them as they entwined her ankles so that she was forced to step out of them.

She was naked. Lora absorbed the shame of it, her face crimsoning as she felt the cool texture of whitewashed cinderblock against her back and the body heat of the man who, nearly as naked as she, leaned so close. Lora shrank against the wall, her arms trying to protect her body from him, but he was having none of that. His hand moved around to the nape of her neck again, squeezing painfully as he dragged her away from the wall and shoved her onto the bed. She fell forward, hitting her knee on the pistol. It hurt, and she winced. Then she was rolling over to find him leaning close . . . She scrambled up the bed in an effort to escape, scooting with her elbows and her feet as she came up hard against the cold iron bars of the headboard. He picked up the gun, hefting it once as he looked at her.

Lora cringed, her eyes running fearfully over the grim face, over the hard muscles and hair-roughened skin of his shoulders and chest to focus with horrified attention on the front of his briefs. Sweat broke out all over her body as she saw that the once soft bulge was growing before her eyes. Bigger and bigger . . . He set the gun down on the small table, then turned to look at her again. His eyes ran over her shrinking body with deliberate slowness.

"Scream and I swear I'll strangle you," he hissed through clenched teeth, and then he was on the bed beside her, catching her in his arms so that she was pressed close against his chest. Lora was terrifyingly aware of the immense heat of him, the roughness of his body hair against her own smooth skin, the hard, rippling muscles crushing her softness, the smell of rain-wet man. Then he was on top of her, his big body completely covering her smaller one, the weight of him forcing the air from her lungs so that she couldn't have made a sound louder than a grunt even if the thick pelt of hair on his chest had not been crushing her nose and mouth. She could feel the hot satiny texture and dampness of his skin with her every pore . . . The hard muscles of his arms and legs had her pinned helplessly beneath him. Against her soft thighs, she could feel the cloth of his briefs. And beneath the cloth was the rock hardness that told her what was to come.

Her brain shut down, leaving only instinct to respond. Her body bucked frantically, trying to throw him off her. Caught by surprise, he shifted so that she was partially free. Twisting, she clawed for the side of the bed, her nails sinking deep into the pile of blankets and her feet kicking desperately at the unyielding strength of his legs that still imprisoned hers. He grabbed her, grappling to hold her, one hand clamping over her mouth that had opened to scream regardless of the consequences as he crushed her to him with his other arm around her waist. His hand spread out over the curve of her round bottom, his fingers digging painfully into the soft flesh.

The intimacy of his grip galvanized her. Frenziedly she kicked and writhed, but it was like trying to kick free of an octopus; his hold on her was unbreakable. Unable to escape, she swiveled toward him, her nails going for his eyes as her knee came up hard, aiming for his groin. He grunted, ducking just in time. Her nails missed his face, raking harmlessly across the blanket instead. Her knee made jarring contact with solid hard flesh—too solid and hard; she had managed to knee him in the thigh. He grunted again and his grip shifted so that she was once again pinned helplessly beneath him. He raised himself slightly so that he could look down at her. The expression on his face was diabolical. Lora quivered with reaction. He must have felt her tremors and taken them as a signal of surrender because he slowly lifted his hand from her mouth. Staring straight into his eyes, Lora waited until his hand had moved down before opening her mouth with terrified abandon. Threats or no, she would scream loud enough to knock the house down... She managed only to draw a lungful of air before he crammed something, a soft roll of cloth, down her throat, gagging her.

"You goddamn stupid little bitch, I ought to beat hell out of you. I ought to take my belt and wrap it around your windpipe and pull till your neck snaps. I ought to..."

He was straddling her now, his face crimson with rage, his eyes alive with it, his mouth tight with it. Those massive shoulders loomed over her, casting an enormous shadow across her quivering form. His hands were painfully tight around her wrists. She kicked and twisted beneath him, trying frantically to spit out the cloth that was threatening to suffocate her. He tightened his grip on her wrists until she whimpered into the muffling gag, and lay still. Then he transferred both her wrists to one of his big hands, crushing them ruthlessly as he reached behind him. His hand came back holding the leather thong. Lora's eyes widened with horror as she realized what he meant to do. She twisted again, kicking and squirming, but he was ready for her now and her struggles did not appear to bother him in the least. In just a matter of minutes he had her hands tied together above her head to the iron bars of the headboard, and her ankles wound up in her panties and secured by his shirt to the footboard. Her naked body, quivering with a combination of fear, outrage and shame, was stretched helplessly between.

The roll of cloth in her mouth—one of the towels that Señora Rodriguez had given them—had been supplemented by her bra, which he had passed between her open jaws and tied securely behind her head. She was trussed as securely as a hog for the slaughter—or a virgin sacrifice.

He gave a final tug to the knots holding her ankles and got off the bed to stand looking down at her with grim satisfaction. He was sweating; perspiration stood out in beads on his temples and the mat of dark hair on his chest was damp with it. The broad bronzed shoulders and corded arms gleamed in the flickering lamplight as if they had been oiled. Muscles formed a ridged wall across the breadth of his chest all the way down to his flat abdomen, where his navel peeped over the waistband of his briefs. If Lora hadn't been so frightened, she might have appreciated him for the magnificent male animal he was. Under the circumstances, however, all she could think of was that she was naked and helpless to do anything to prevent his raping her. . . .

She was also helpless to do anything to prevent his eyes from roving where they chose. He looked her up and down, thoroughly, slowly, his eyes lingering on the puckered pink tips of her breasts, the soft belly and thighs and the nest of curling hair at their apex. Lora wanted to squirm beneath the searing regard, but she was afraid that any movement on her part might incite him to attack her. She lay motionless, only her eyes moving as they watched his face, hoping for some change of expression to give her a clue as to what he was thinking. There was none. His face was completely expressionless except for the gleaming of his eyes as they crawled over her body.

Fatalistically, Lora accepted the fact that she could only await the inevitable. Any minute now he would lay his hands and his mouth and his body on her, forcing her . . . And there was absolutely nothing she could do to prevent him. He could do anything he wanted—rape her, even kill her. Oh, God, why had she not swallowed her impatience and waited for that damned bus to go to Chichén Itzá?

He leaned forward, placing his hands on either side of her head and lowering his upper body until his face was just inches from hers and his chest hair brushed maddeningly against the sensitive tips of her breasts. Lora's eyes widened, and her heart speeded up so that its pounding nearly deafened her. It was starting. . . .

"Am I scaring you?" The harsh whisper that he had been using ever since he had closed the trapdoor sent shivers up and down her spine. Once again it occurred to her that this man might get his kicks from tormenting his victims. Sadism— that was the word for it. The man showed a strong tendency toward it. . . .

"I can do anything I want to you," he continued as if he were savoring the possibilities. "Anything at all."

Lora quivered, and he lifted himself a little away from her while his eyes wandered from her face down her body. Her pale skin was dappled with goosebumps, both from the night chill and from fright. With her arms stretched tautly over her head, her full breasts thrust prominently upward, their soft firmness crested with puckered pink-brown circles. In the center of those circles her nipples stood painfully erect. From the cold, of course . . . His eyes rested on those embarrassingly hardened peaks for a long moment, the lids lowered so that she could not read his expression. Then they crawled further down her body, lingering over her small waist and curving hips and sliding the length of her legs before returning with an equal lack of haste to appraise the curling triangle of reddish hair between her thighs. Lora could not stop an involuntary shifting of her legs as she sought to cover herself.

It was useless, of course, tied as she was. She had to let him look as long as he liked. Do anything he liked. . . .

Suddenly one brown, callous-tipped finger was on her skin, tracing a rough line from the hollow of her throat down the silky skin between her breasts over her diaphragm and stomach to her navel.

Lora froze again, quivering helplessly. There was nothing she could do, nothing she could say that would stop him . . . Her eyes squeezed shut as she awaited what he would do next. She could only hope that he would not be brutal. . . .

His finger moved back up her body, traced a tiny circle in the valley between her breasts, lifted . . . Then his hand gripped her chin hard.

"Look at me."

The growling voice brooked no disobedience. Lora opened her eyes and looked at him fearfully. He was eyeing her grimly, his mouth set hard beneath that coal black mustache, his eyes dark and narrow on hers. He looked very large and very tough as he bent over her. His hand hurt her chin.

"You ever been raped?"

Sobs crowded in Lora's throat as she stared up at him wild-eyed. Oh, God. . . .

"Answer me. You ever been raped?" The hand tightened on her chin.

Chest heaving with frightened sobs that could find no outlet past the gag, eyes huge as they fixed on his harsh face, Lora shook her head.

"Want to try it?"

Oh, God, why was he torturing her this way? If he had to do it, why didn't he just go ahead and get it over with? She was going to die of fright. . . .

"Answer me!"

Despairingly, Lora shook her head again. If the gag in her

mouth had not muffled all utterance, she would have been bawling with terror. Maybe then he would show her some mercy. . . .

He leaned closer so that his hairy chest once again brushed her breasts. The dark mustachioed face with its unshaven jaw was so close she could see the tiny lines radiating out from the corners of his eyes and feel his warm breath on her face.

"Next time you pull a stunt like this one tonight, I'll take it for an invitation." His lips curved in a twisted parody of a smile. "You're lucky I don't go ahead now. I'd kind of like to make it with you. I go for broads with big tits."

And with that he straightened suddenly to stand looking down at her again, his arms folded over that hairy chest and some indecipherable gleam in his eyes. Before Lora could even begin to assimilate the fact that he apparently wasn't going to rape her after all, he stepped away from the bed for an instant and returned with the blanket that he had discarded earlier by the trapdoor. Lora's head whirled as he dropped it over her, covering her nakedness. She thought she might faint with relief . . . He was not going to rape her. . . .

Lora knew her eyes must have betrayed her feelings. She felt limp all over at the unexpected reprieve. He stood looking down at her a moment longer, his eyes on her face now that the rest of her was decently covered, then grinned maliciously. Moving away, he rescued the plates of food from where Lora had left them by the door. He set one on the bedside table near her head, so that the appetizing aroma wafted across her dilating nostrils. He held the other in his hand, scooping up a mouthful of beans and forking it into his mouth while he chewed with obvious enjoyment.

"Mmmmm, this is great." He looked down at her again as he forked in another heaping mouthful. "Hungry?"

Eagerly, Lora nodded. He wasn't so bad after all. He

hadn't raped her, despite scaring her half out of her wits, and he was going to feed her. . . .

"Isn't it too bad that I had to tie you up? You won't be able to eat," he said with apparent regret, wolfing another forkful. Lora's eyes widened with outrage as she realized what he was doing: teaching her a lesson. First, he had frightened her worse than she'd ever been frightened in her life, and now he was eating his meal—and hers, too!—right in front of her starving eyes as a lesson in obedience. The filthy swine! He had not raped her, no, but he had terrorized and humiliated her and now he was starving her while he stuffed himself.

Lora glared at him furiously. He grinned at her, finishing the food with a loud, aggravating and probably purposeful burp. He then patted his stomach and set the empty plates aside and took a healthy swig of whatever drink was contained in the bottle. Lora's mouth was already painfully dry from the gag, and she longed for the liquid in the bottle almost more than she longed for food. Glaring at him ferociously as he drank again, Lora mentally called him every filthy name she had ever heard.

Finally, he set the bottle down, yawned widely, and leaned over to blow out the light. Then the blankets beneath her were dragged free, not without some effort, leaving her lying on a cool, rough woven sheet. He spread another blanket on top of the one that already covered her. Then Lora heard him move to the other side of the bed, felt the mattress sink beneath his weight, rolling her slightly toward him.

The blankets moved. Lora felt the hard, hot length of a hairy leg brush her, then a shoulder settled just millimeters from her upstretched arm. She could feel him next to her, smell him, hear him breathing. He shifted, and the bed shifted with him. If she had not been tied, she would have rolled against him. His weight made a considerable valley on his side of the bed. As it was, her hands and ankles pulled painfully as they held her body in place. He moved again, and she could hear the faint thump of a pillow being shoved into place.

"Pleasant dreams," he murmured just inches from her ear.

Lora jerked, and she could have sworn she heard him chuckle. She lay there, seething with anger and something else she refused to acknowledge as his body heat wafted all around her. Tied as she was, she could not escape the occasional brush of shoulder or arm or leg as he shifted position. His skin was so hot . . . With every pore of her skin she was maddeningly conscious of his body next to hers—and her own nakedness. She hated him, feared him—but she could not for the life of her get the image of him as he had looked earlier, clad only in his underpants, out of her head.

He shifted again and his hair-roughened thigh brushed her hip. Lora gritted her teeth, feeling as though hundreds of centipedes with fiery hot feet were swarming out all over her body from that central spot. It was no use, she might as well admit it to herself. He was getting to her. She could not forget the way the lamplight has emphasized the muscles that rippled and played beneath tanned satiny skin; the dark hair that formed a wedge on his chest to trail past his navel and then disappear into the snug white briefs; the linebacker's shoulders tapering to a narrow waist and hips; the hard, strong arms and thighs that had crushed her beneath him, the calloused hands. . . .

Lora swallowed. She must be going out of her mind. He was a sadistic animal who had enjoyed scaring her to tears earlier, who had reveled in denying her food and was probably even now delighting in the knowledge that she was suffering miserable discomfort from the way he had her tied. He was a criminal guilty of God knew how many vicious acts, he had threatened her with rape and he was quite likely to murder her before this nightmare was over. How could she let herself be excited by his body? It was insane. Nothing like it had ever happened to her before. Not even for Brian had she felt this aching physical awareness—and Brian had always been a perfectly satisfactory lover. It was not as if she was sexually frustrated or anything. She enjoyed making love with Brian. This man had scared the hell out of her, humiliated her, caused her physical discomfort, as her stretched taut arms and legs that were already falling asleep reminded her. How could he possibly excite her? Sheer physical chemistry, perhaps? She had read about the irresistable pull of one particular set of glands for another in romance novels, but she had never really believed it could happen. At least, not to her. Not to sensible, level-headed Lora Harding. But *something* was happening. Was she the only one to feel it? Was he experiencing this unwelcome attraction as well?

A faint but unmistakable snore put an end to Lora's speculations. She stiffened. The no good son of a gun was asleep! So much for mutual chemistry, she fumed, squirming angrily in an effort to find a comfortable enough position so that she could imitate his nonchalance and fall asleep herself. Temporary insanity was more like it. And she meant to fight it for everything she was worth!

VI

Stockholm Syndrome. That was the answer. Lora awoke from a miserably uncomfortable sleep with the words flashing like a neon sign in her brain. She had read about it, of course. A psychologist had documented cases where hostages had begun to identify and even fall in love with their captors. It was some sort of defense mechanism designed to reduce the stress of an otherwise unbearable situation. Anyway, it perfectly explained her otherwise incomprehensible reaction to the brute who still snored blithely beside her. She was not attracted to him at all; her mind was merely playing tricks on her in an effort to keep her from fully experiencing the horror of being kidnapped by a violent stranger.

Despite the dryness of her mouth—she was sure her tongue must be swollen to three times its normal size—and the lack of feeling in her arms and legs, which had gone numb hours ago, she felt much better. It boosted her morale considerably to know that what ailed her body was a recognized psychological condition that even had a name. Now, if she had only paid more attention to the article, perhaps she could remember the cure . . . But probably just knowing what was happening to her would be enough. Certainly she was no longer in any danger of succumbing to his dubious charms. . . .

"Sleep well?"

Her nemesis was awake. She turned her head to glare at him. By the faint glow of sunlight filtering in through the roof, she saw that he was very close. . . . He looked very male, very sexy with his black hair ruffled all around his head and what must have been a week's growth of bristly black beard roughening that tough jaw. He also looked very well rested. She eyed him resentfully, her resentment increased by the inescapable fact that the bandido's mustache became him very well. It made him look rakish and wicked, like a modern-day buccaneer. She wondered if it was soft or prickly to the touch, then caught herself up sharply. Stockholm Syndrome, she reminded herself, and to drive the point home shifted her toes and fingers so that red-hot needles seemed to sear through her limbs. After that, she managed a truly ferocious glare.

"Cat got your tongue?" He was grinning as he reached around behind her head to fumble at the knot he had tied in her bra. Lora shrank from his touch—but not very far. She couldn't. Then he was lifting the bra away from her mouth and the towel, too, and suddenly Lora was no longer thinking of him. Her mouth hurt! Her jaw ached and her tongue was dry and swollen, and her lips were probably swollen too. Just closing her mouth was agonizingly painful. She passed her tongue over her lips instinctively, wincing at the feel of the two dry tissues coming together. She would never be able to talk again. . . .

"Drink this." He had rooted around the floor by the bed

and come up with the bottle he had been drinking from the night before. Sitting up, the blankets falling to his waist so that his bronzed, hairy chest was bared, he slid one hand behind her head to lift it and held the bottle to her lips. With a single glare at him Lora complied. The way she was feeling, she would have accepted water from the devil himself, which he was not far from being. Only it wasn't water. She choked as the unidentifiable liquor burned across her lips and tongue and down her raw throat. He kept pouring, and she spluttered, turning her head so that the liquid ran down the side of her face and onto the bed. His hand tightened on the back of her head.

"Drink some more. You need it." He put the bottle to her lips again, and she had to drink. When he judged that she had had enough, he took the bottle away and turned to set it on the floor.

Lora experimentally tried running her tongue over her lips again. Her whole mouth tingled from the nasty tasting liquor, but she had to admit that it felt somewhat better, no longer so painfully dry.

He got out of bed. Lora was further annoyed to find that, Stockholm Syndrome or not, she still thought he looked good in his underpants. His limp was more noticeable this morning, as he walked around to the foot of the bed to pick up his jeans, feeling them to see if they were dry. Lora wondered if his knee had stiffened during the night—she hoped it had, and she especially hoped that something she did was the reason. Apparently, the jeans were dry, because he stepped into them, pulling up the zipper and fastening the button at the top of the fly without regard for her interested if resentful stare. Then he reached down to pull at the blankets so that her feet were exposed to the air. It took him more than a few minutes to untie them; apparently, her twisting movements during the night had tightened the knots in the cheap nylon material of his shirt. When at last they were free, he moved up to the head of the bed while Lora gingerly bent her knees, drawing them up toward her chest, and flexed her ankles. Pain shot along her nerve endings; she moaned. When at last her hands, too, were free, Lora lowered them slowly, wincing as she rubbed her chafed wrists.

"You bastard," she said venomously as she sat up, her tortured arms and legs screaming for vengeance as blood began to circulate through them. She rarely swore, but on this occasion, for this man, she was willing to make an exception. Under the circumstances, the epithet so exactly expressed her feelings that she could not regret it. Unless, of course, he chose to take some violent reprisal.

"My, my, you're going to hurt my feelings if you're not careful."

He shrugged into his badly wrinkled shirt as he spoke, buttoning the front of it and stuffing the ends into the worn jeans. Lora glared at him, hating him so much that it was all she could do not to throw the nearest object at him. As that object happened to be a flat pillow, it would have done little but possibly relieve her feelings, so she allowed good judgment to win out over spleen and refrained. Her arms and legs ached miserably, her tongue still felt about twice its normal size, and her head hurt, either from hunger or from the position she had been forced to lie in all night, or possibly a combination of both. While he—he looked positively blooming—and had the nerve to mock her. If looks could kill, the one she threw at him would have felled him on the spot.

To her surprise, he sat down on the end of the bed and reached for one of her slim bare feet. Lora tried to jerk her foot away, but she was hampered by the necessity of maintaining her grip on the pile of covers that were clamped under her armpits and held across her bosom. He held onto the prize easily, crossing one muscular thigh over the other and positioning her bare calf across his lap as he began to rub the traumatized muscles of her foot and leg. Lora scowled at him, but those hard warm fingers on her skin felt so good that she quit tugging at her foot and surrendered to his ministrations. When at last he put one foot aside and reached for the other, she eyed him warily but made no resistance. His brows knit in concentrated effort as he kneaded and probed the tendons and ligaments he had abused, finally flexing her foot several times before looking up at her.

"Better?" he asked with a slight, quizzing grin.

Lora, all too conscious of that large, brown hand wrapped around her own pale foot—a foot that was by no means dainty, although the blatant masculinity of that large hand made it appear so—recovered herself enough to jerk her foot out of his lap.

"No." This was said with a bite. He grinned, a real grin this time, as if he were genuinely amused.

"Bitch," he said without heat. "You're lucky you're still in one piece after what you tried to pull last night. I told you before, I'm on the run for my life. It it comes to a choice between you and me—well, there's no choice, so I'd keep that in mind, if I were you. I won't hurt you unless you make me, but I'll do whatever I have to do to get out of this damned country in one piece. Now, get your ass out of bed and get dressed. We've got a long way to go today."

Lora glowered at him from the depths of the bed, still clutching the blankets under her arms. He was a brute, and a bully, and . . .

He reached down, grabbed the covers, and yanked them off her. Lora gasped, covering herself with her arms as she scrambled to put something, a pillow, anything, between her body and his eyes.

"I said get up. I've already seen everything you've got, so there's no point in worrying about modesty. On the other hand, if you're not into your clothes and ready to go in three minutes flat, I will give you something to worry about. So move!"

He grabbed her arm, hauling her out of the bed and then, when her feet were on the floor, throwing her clothes at her. Lora caught the dress but missed the bra and panties. Turning her back after a single furious glare at the man who stood watching her with gleaming attention, she dressed. When she had trouble getting the zipper all the way up, having to stretch her arms into pretzel-like contortions as she fought with the tiny metal tab, he came over to help her. Lora felt his hands on her spine and shivered. Jerking away, she glared at him over her shoulder and finished the job herself. He shrugged, and sat down on the edge of the bed to pull on his mud-caked sneakers. Lora's sandals were in no better shape, and she regarded them with revulsion before forcing the warped leather straps on her feet.

"Here." He was standing now, and as she looked at him he tossed her purse to her. She caught it instinctively with both hands as it thudded against her stomach. "You look like something the cat dragged home on a bad night. Brush your hair, put on some lipstick, do whatever it is women do to make themselves look human. But do it fast. There's some water in the washstand over there." He pointed to the far side of the room.

Nestled underneath the eaves was a small wooden table with a pitcher and bowl on top. Last night, with only the lantern for light, it must have been hidden in the deep shadows which had shrouded the corners of the room. Now

Lora was glad to see it, primitive as it was. Crossing to it with a single scathing glance at her captor, she opened her purse and extracted her small makeup case. Besides her few cosmetics, it contained a travel-sized toothbrush, toothpaste, soap, and a bottle of sunscreen. There was a small mirror on the washstand too; Lora took one look at herself in it and had to repress a shudder.

At the best of times she was no beauty, but at least she was reasonably attractive and certainly neat. Today, with her lips chapped and swollen from that repulsive gag, red marks creasing her cheeks from where her bra had cut into them during the night, her eyelids heavy and dark circles under the eyes themselves from lack of sleep, she looked dreadful. Added to that, her face was sunburned from exposure during the hottest part of the day yesterday—the sunscreen had to be diligently reapplied to be effective—and her hair, usually a smooth, shining cap that curved gently under just at her jaw, was a tumble of riotous curls. The rain, of course. Her hair was naturally wavy, and to achieve her usual dignified style she needed a blow dryer and a round brush. To add insult to injury, the blue dress was stiff with dirt and terribly wrinkled. Lora grimaced, then almost had to smile as she remembered having suspected her captor of lusting after her the night before. No man in his right mind would lust after her looking like this! She tore her eyes away from the awful sight in the mirror and went to work with a will, washing her face and as much of her body as she decently could with him watching her. That done, she applied sunscreen in place of the moisturizer she usually used, and looked at herself in the mirror critically. The sun had tinted her forehead and chin and particularly her nose a rosy pink, while somehow missing her cheeks. The result was that the center of her face was bright with color, while the sides looked unnaturally white in comparison. Pride compelled her to do something about it. She could not go about the world looking like this!

Digging through her small cosmetics case, she unearthed a sample-sized pot of blush in a brilliant shade of strawberry pink. Lora remembered that Janice had gotten it as part of a bonus makeup kit offered by a department store in Wichita, along with a matching lipstick and a tiny powder compact. Lora had never worn the blush or lipstick before, and had never expected to. She had only brought them with her because they were travel-sized and fit well in her cosmetics case. But now the neon pink seemed just what she needed to balance out the already glowing center of her face. She dabbed a little blush on her cheeks, rubbed it in, and, emboldened by the results—it was not nearly as garish on her skin as it had appeared in the pot—added a little more. That done, she smoothed the matching creamy lipstick over her sore lips—surprising how soothing lipstick could feel—and stood back to survey the results. Not half bad, she thought, surprised. She was now rosy pink from her forehead to her chin and from ear to ear, but the color was surprisingly becoming. Her denim blue eyes seemed much livelier, brighter, and her tousled, mousy colored hair looked almost a true blond. Lora blinked at herself, mildly amazed. She would never have believed how much a little added color could do for her face. Interesting. . . .

"For God's sake, hurry up! I didn't mean for you to primp for hours. Let's go."

The impatient voice snapped Lora back to the unpleasant present. She threw a loathing look over her shoulder at her captor, ran the comb she had extracted from her purse through her hair, and moved stiffly toward where he waited by the trapdoor, the still-damp sarape tossed carelessly over his shoulder. As she approached he put a hand on her arm. When she looked at him inquiringly, he patted the faint bulge at his waist that she knew was the gun. Then, without waiting for a response from her, he lifted the door and swung himself through the opening and down the ladder. Left alone, Lora toyed with the idea of slamming the trapdoor after him and sitting on it, but reluctantly dismissed the idea. It just wasn't worth it. He would get her back one way or another—she had seen enough of the way he operated to be sure of that—and the consequences would be distinctly unpleasant. To say nothing of what might happen to the innocent Rodriguez family.

The hour was early, but the sun was dazzling and the Rodriguezes, along with their older children, were already out in the fields. Mamacita was left with the three youngest, two toddlers who looked to be less than a year apart and an infant. Her suspicious looks at the two *norteamericanos* and the childrens' wide-eyed fascination did not encourage them to linger. Her captor said something in Spanish, to which Mamacita responded by thrusting the ruined sombrero, which he had removed out of politeness and left downstairs the night before, and a package wrapped in a clean cloth into his hands.

"*Gracias,*" he replied with a curt nod, and catching Lora by the upper arm, propelled her with him through the door.

Lora was given only a brief moment to look around as he hustled her along the track that was still thick with mud. As she had thought, the Rodriguez house was situated at the very edge of a small village of shabby cinderblock dwellings. Muddy fields burned out of the jungle stretched away on all sides, and the older residents of the village could be seen laboring on their hands and knees among the growing crops. Dogs and chickens and very small children seemed to wander about at will. All seemed fascinated with the *gringos,* and soon there was quite a little procession following them back toward where they had abandoned the VW. Lora, looking over her shoulder at four solemn-faced toddlers with huge dark eyes, three mangy dogs almost bristling with fleas, a round dozen pecking hens and a single strutting bantam rooster, had to smile despite herself. Her captor, seeing her smile and glancing over his own shoulder to discover the reason for it, scowled fiercely and wheeled to face the ill-assorted gang of camp followers.

"*Vamos!*" he roared with a shooing motion, and the group scattered to the accompaniment of wailing children, barking dogs, and clucking hens. Only the little rooster stood his ground, the rusty feathers around his neck rising like a dog's hackles.

As Lora watched, he uttered a ferocious squawk and launched himself with a fanatic's intensity at the legs of the man beside her. Her captor let out a squawk that rivaled the rooster's in volume as he found himself under attack, and kicked and jumped as the valiant fowl assaulted his shins with beak and claws. Lora was helpless with laughter by the time the rooster, obviously considering himself the victor, flapped off to crow in a nearby clump of palmettos. Her captor had to drag her along after him as he retreated with ignominious haste to the safety of the car, casting wary looks behind him all the way. Lora was gasping for breath by the time he thrust her into the driver's seat and shut the door on her.

"Start the car," he growled, and while she did he went around behind to push. It took no more than a single heave from that powerful body to wrest the small car free of the ruts. Before Lora could even consider driving away and leaving him standing, he was in the car beside her, scowling.

"Very funny," he said sourly at her continued giggles.

Lora went into fresh gales of laughter as he pulled up first one and then the other pants leg to check for injuries to his ankles and calves. There were none that she could see—apparently the sturdy material of his jeans had saved him. Putting his feet back on the floor, he cast her a disgruntled look and held up the package that Mamacita had given him.

"If you don't shut up, I won't feed you." He unwrapped the cloth to reveal a stack of tortillas.

Lora hastily smothered her mirth as well as she could—isolated chortles struggled at intervals to burst forth, but in the face of starvation she did what she could to suppress them—and eagerly held out her hand. Ordinarily, a plain corn tortilla would have been less than appetizing, but this morning it tasted like ambrosia. She ate two and could have managed more, except that he had wolfed the other two himself. She looked longingly after the last bite as it disappeared into his mouth.

"Drive," he said as he had the day before, and winced as Lora thrust the car into gear and they jolted off down the road.

At his direction, they had turned off on Route 180 onto Highway 295 just before reaching Chichén Itzá the day before. The *ejido* where they had spent the night was located just off the two-lane road, perhaps some forty or fifty miles farther along, Lora calculated, appalled to discover that yesterday they had covered just a little over two hundred miles. At home, even zealously obeying the speed limit, that would have taken perhaps four hours. Yesterday they had driven for almost ten—but then, there had been a few interruptions, like the rain, and her own escape attempt that had left the Volkswagen's front end looking distinctly the worse for wear. Today, she hoped that they would make better time. The sooner they reached wherever he was going, the sooner she would be free of him. She hoped.

"What does your husband do?"

"What?" The question, out of the blue after more than an hour of driving in silence, surprised Lora.

"I said, what does your husband do?"

Momentarily at a loss, Lora took a few seconds to remember the family she had invented for him the day before.

"He's a math teacher." It was probably safer to stick with the truth as much as possible. That way, she wouldn't forget anything.

"Another teacher, huh? Wow, wherever you're from, they must really be behind their education system one hundred percent. I never would have guessed that even two teachers' salaries would have stretched to cover a jet-set vacation for the whole family."

"It wasn't as expensive as you'd think," Lora mumbled. To tell the truth, there was no way she could have managed this trip to Cancun on her salary in a million years, and no way that she and a husband both earning approximately the same thing could have afforded to bring themselves and their two children to Mexico's newest playground for the international rich. "Besides, it was paid for with an inheritance."

This last was inspired, she thought, and had the advantage of being the absolute truth as well, at least as far as it went.

He snorted. "Cut the crap, Lora."

Her hands tightened on the steering wheel and she flicked a quick glance sideways at him. He was looking at her with a narrow-eyed gleam that made her nervous. He could not know she lied—could he? How could she have possibly given herself away?

"Who do the kids belong to?"

"Are you talking about my children?" She tried to inject a note of amazement into her voice.

"Don't give me that. You don't have any kids. And you're not married."

"What on earth makes you say that?" This time, she thought, the amazement was rather better done. She *did* wonder what made him think it. Personally, she thought her tale had been pretty convincing.

"Two things. First, the way you react to a man."

"What do you mean by that?" She sounded both defensive and startled.

He snorted again. "When I started taking off my clothes, you looked as if you'd swallowed a jalapeño pepper. It was obvious that you weren't used to seeing a man in his shorts—to say nothing of in the buff. Therefore, it stands to reason you're not married."

"Maybe I'm just not used to seeing a man other than my husband undressing," Lora said stiffly, feeling heat creep up her neck to her cheeks and ears and beyond.

He merely raised his eyebrows at her skeptically. "Want to hear what else makes me think you're not a loving wife and mother?"

"No!"

"No stretch marks," he said succinctly.

Lora's eyes widened, and she felt another wave of embarrassed heat wash up her neck as she remembered that he was certainly in a position to know. He had seen every inch of her skin.

"Not all women get them, you know."

"Most do. Almost all when they're as fair as you. But there's not a mark on your skin. It's smooth as a baby's."

"So maybe I'm one of the lucky ones."

"And maybe you're not. Come on, come clean. Who do the cute little girls belong to?"

"They're my nieces," Lora said, giving up. For some strange reason, she was not altogether sorry that her make-believe family was being laid to rest. She didn't like telling

lies, and she wasn't particularly good at it, as this denoue-
ment proved. And there was another reason, one that occurred to her to be immediately vanquished: she didn't like
the idea of this man, whose body wildly excited her despite
every grain of sense she possessed, believing that she was
married and a mother. Just why that was, she refused to
speculate.

"And the math teacher? *Is* there a math teacher?"

"My fiancé."

"Do you sleep with him?" The question was so deceptively
casual that it took a moment to sink in.

"That's none of your business," Lora yelped.

"Suppose I make it my business?" he asked with an
exaggerated leer that made Lora want to grind her teeth.
When he wasn't scaring her to death, he was totally outrageous, totally infuriating. . . .

She was on the verge of losing her temper, Lora realized
with surprise. And she never lost her temper. Not anymore.
Not since Janice had grown up and left home and stopped
stealing her clothes, her cosmetics, and her boyfriends. Janice
said that those few occasions in their childhood were the only
times she had ever heard her inhibited little sister really
yelling, and Lora supposed Janice was right. She was a rather
low-key person, now that she thought about it. Maybe she
should have her blood pressure tested or something. Maybe it
wasn't high enough. She had read about people with that kind
of problem. . . .

"Christ, hit the brakes! Stop!"

She had been looking at him ruminatively. When he shouted,
his eyes widening with alarm, she jumped. Instinctively, her
eyes shot back to the road before her foot even began moving
for the brake. What she saw sent her leg stomping frantically
downward. A large brown cow stood placidly in the middle of

the road not fifteen feet away, chewing her cud as she watched with disinterest as the orange Volkswagen rattled toward her. Lora gasped, her foot came down hard on the brake—and the car gasped too before hesitating briefly, belching, and bucking forward. The cow didn't budge.

"Christ, that was the clutch!" He was yelling in her ear. "Hit the goddamn brakes, woman!"

Lora tried again, and this time she got it right. The car squealed to a halt not more than two feet from the animal's sleek, brown hide. Lora sat with her hands curled tightly around the wheel, staring disbelievingly at the still chewing cow who was regarding them with mild interest through the windshield. Her captor let out his breath and reached over to slide the transmission into neutral.

"You have to be the worst damned driver I have ever seen in my entire life."

"I'd only driven automatics before yesterday."

"Good God in heaven." He shut his eyes, leaning his head back against the seat briefly before sitting up again. "Well, no harm done. Honk the horn, and let's get moving."

Lora obediently honked the horn, then when the cow didn't budge honked it again. The cow flicked her ears forward, an expression of interest briefly lighting her eyes. When nothing else happened, she apparently dismissed the sound as unimportant. Her attention shifted to her fellow cows, who had been lunching by the roadside and were now wandering over to see what was going on. All the while, she remained planted solidly in the middle of the road, calmly digesting her lunch.

"Now what?" Lora asked.

"Now you get out there and shoo her away."

"You must be joking." Lora turned to look at him, aghast. He was grinning—strange how that grin altered his whole face, changing him instantaneously from a ferocious looking criminal to someone who looked like he could, with no effort at all, charm the birds off the trees, or in this case the cow out of the road.

"Nope." The laconic reply made Lora shake her head vigorously.

"You do it. I'm afraid of cows."

"A Kansas farm girl, and you're afraid of cows? Come on."

"I am. One chased me once when I was a little girl and I had to climb a tree to get away from it. It stood underneath mooing and shaking its head until my grandfather came looking for me and chased it away. I hate cows."

"Too bad."

Before Lora knew what was happening, he had leaned over, opening her door and thrusting her out of the car before slamming the door shut again and locking it. She scratched frantically for the handle, pleading for admittance. The sadistic swine heaved his big body over into the driver's seat and rolled the window down about an inch.

"This pays you back for the rooster."

"That wasn't my fault—I only laughed—oh, please, oh, no, oh, please open the door!"

This last was a near shriek, uttered because the cow, finally seeing something of interest to investigate, started to move— right toward Lora. Lora gave up trying to get into the car, moving frantically around the back as the cow, both ears pricked forward, followed. The other cows, interested by this new game, came swarming up the bank to join in. Lora ran to the passenger door, moaning with fear, and tugged desperately at its handle as the whole herd of cows trotted after her. To her relief, the handle gave. She jerked the door open and dove inside, slamming the door almost on the intrigued cow's nose as she sank into the seat to the accompaniment of uproarious laughter.

"Bastard," she said feelingly as the car moved forward—smoothly, of course, since he was driving. Casting him a venomous look, she again thought longingly of blunt objects. How she would like to bash in that unfeeling black head. . . .

"Ho, ho, for a girl who's afraid of cows you handled that pretty well. Sort of reminded me of the Pied Piper. . . ."

"Oh, shut up."

"Nasty, nasty . . ." He shook his head in mock reproof. "I bet you don't say that to Brian."

"You're not Brian," Lora retorted, glaring, and then had to grin herself. She was willing to bet that she had looked pretty funny, dancing around the back of the Volkswagen with a whole herd of curious cows trailing behind.

"You're pretty when you smile."

It was an offhand remark, sort of thrown at her, and it took Lora a moment to catch it. Then she looked at him, her expression a mixture of pleasure and wariness. He was concentrating on the smooth blacktop surface of the road, his hands competent on the wheel, his big body jacknifed into the little space like the folded insert in one of those cards with punchlines that pop out. His eyes were narrowed against the sun that beat down through the window, finding reddish glints in the bristles on his chin and in the silky mustache that matched the ones in the rough black curls at his nape that the sun just touched. He looked completely unaware of having paid her a compliment, and Lora had to replay the words carefully in her mind to be sure she had heard what she thought.

"Thank you." If his compliment—if he had even meant it to be a compliment—was offhand, her response was shy. He acknowledged it with a curt nod, his eyes never leaving the road. Able to think of nothing else to say, Lora too looked at the road. Only then did it occur to her that they had switched places.

"You're driving," she said, surprised.

He grunted, his expression wry as those black eyes flicked in her direction. "I don't think there's much possibility that we'll get pulled over out here. And I've had about all I can take of watching you abuse this poor car. We—the car and I—deserve a little peace."

Lora frowned at him for this slur on her driving, but only half-heartedly. Quite honestly, she was glad to have him take the wheel. It was good to have a rest—and besides, an escape, should she decide to try one again, would be much easier to orchestrate from the passenger seat... She lapsed into meditative silence, and they passed through the town of Felipe Carrillo Puerto without speaking.

Soon afterward, the view changed. Highway 295 became Highway 307, and cleared fields no longer fell away on either side. The road had been hacked out through the dense jungles of the state of Quintana Roo; dense walls of vegetation on either side seemed to constantly threaten encroachment on the cleared areas. Moisture from yesterday's rain rose steamily upward through the trees to hang over the low-ceilinged jungle like a thin cloud of white vapor. The smell of rotting vegetation was everywhere, seeping through the air conditioning vents to make Lora slightly sick at her stomach. Or maybe her stomach was acting up out of hunger. She didn't know, but the pungent smell certainly didn't help.

They passed through the village of Cafeta, and then drove for a while along the shores of a gorgeous blue lake, which could just be glimpsed through the trees. Lora was lost in its untamed beauty when a sudden, savage curse from the man beside her brought her head swinging around.

"Slide over here. Come on, hurry up."

"What?"

"There's a goddamned roadblock. I can't turn around, they'll wonder why. So slide your ass over here and be damned quick about it."

"But—"

"Do it!"

Lora didn't know quite how she managed it, but she did. The fierce tone in which he had flung the last order at her told her she'd better figure out a way. As she squirmed over the gearshift, he caught her and pulled her onto his lap, setting her hands on the wheel and letting her feet find the pedals before sliding out from under her. The car lurched as she took over the pedals, but she managed to keep it on the road and in gear as he slid over into the passenger seat. Once there, he reached in the back for the disreputable sarape, pulled the gun from where he had thrust it inside the waistband of his jeans, and placed it on his lap with one hand on it and the folded sarape neatly hiding it from view.

"I'm your husband, Brian Harding, math teacher. If they want to see my papers, I left them back at the hotel. We only thought we'd need yours, since you're doing the driving. Those two kids are ours. Got it?"

Lora nodded, darting an alarmed look at him. To think she had once again been on the verge of forgetting that he was an armed desperado who had abducted her at gunpoint. She had almost been liking him—and now the criminal was back, hard and tough and at bay, willing to do anything—including, she thought, murder her—to save his own skin. She switched her attention back to the road, swallowing.

"This pistol will be pointed straight at your guts the whole time. Say anything else and I'll blow you in half."

Lora nodded again, jerkily, feeling sweat starting to form

on the palms of her hands. Suppose the police should recognize him and start shooting—or she should slip up and say the wrong thing, or . . .

"Don't forget what I said." It was a harsh warning.

"I—I won't."

"Good. Now be careful."

Lora could feel her heart pounding against her breastbone as she pulled into the line of cars that were being let through the police checkpoint, one by one.

VII

By the time the car in front of them had passed through the checkpoint and driven away into the distance, Lora was afraid that she might have a heart attack, her heart was pounding so wildly. Just why she should be so afraid, she really couldn't pinpoint. After all, *she* hadn't done anything wrong, the police weren't after her. But her companion's grim face and taut mouth, the steely glint in his eyes, the tension that seemed to emanate from his body like heat from the sun, all had their effect on her. To say nothing of the gun that was pointed squarely at her midsection. Though she could not see it beneath the sheltering sarape, she felt it with every tiny hair on her skin. The question was, would he, in a pinch, pull the trigger? The answer was, she did not want to find out.

Then it was their turn, and Lora had no more time to worry. She pulled the car up to where the uniformed police-man waited beside one of the two police cars that partially blocked the road, and rolled down her window with what she hoped was an enquiring smile.

"*Buenos tardes, señora.*" He bent to look in the car, his brown eyes lighting on her companion and running over him. Lora could feel her captor's tension like electricity in the air, but when she risked a quick, apprehensive sideways glance at him she didn't know whether to be relieved or sorry. He looked completely relaxed, as if he didn't have a care in the world. Even the folded sarape on his lap looked totally innocuous.

"*Señor.*" The policeman nodded politely at him, then turned his attention back to Lora, who smiled nervously. "What is your business in this part of the country, *por favor?*"

Lora felt the truth rush wildly to her tongue, and swallowed it. She had almost blurted it out—but nothing else came to mind. Horrified, she realized that the policeman was waiting for her reply. And her mind was absolutely, totally blank.

"My wife and I are American tourists, *señor.* We wanted to see some of your beautiful country." He lied so smoothly that Lora almost believed him. She nodded her agreement, relieved and annoyed at the same time. Couldn't the dratted policeman see that the unkempt thug beside her could not possibly be her husband? Couldn't he sense her fear—and her captor's tension? Darn it, there was a huge loaded gun pointed at her midsection—or possibly at the policeman by now, she couldn't be sure—and the man didn't seem to have the slightest inkling that anything was wrong. Columbo would have sensed it, Lora knew.

"May I see your papers, *señora?*"

Lora swallowed and reached into the back seat for her purse. A large tanned masculine hand was before her. Calmly, he handed her purse to her and watched while Lora fished through the assorted paraphernalia for her billfold. She extracted her Kansas driver's license and her passport and handed them to the waiting policeman. He seemed to study both documents carefully, then lifted his head to fix suddenly severe eyes on Lora. Her breath seemed to stop as she met his gaze.

"And have you insurance for this vehicle, *señora?*"

Lora felt her breath expel like a deflating balloon. "Yes, I—the car is rented from my—our—hotel. Insurance was included in the price."

"You have proof of this?"

"I—I have the rental papers."

"May I see them, please?"

Silently, Lora extracted them from her purse and handed them over. The car was rented in her name—and her name alone—and the papers clearly showed this. Would he then deduce that her companion was not her husband, and demand an explanation? And when the explanation was unsatisfactory, as it surely would be to anyone with a modicum of intelligence, would he then ask them both to get out of the car and detain them while he determined the truth? To judge from her captor's tension, he had good reason to believe that the police were looking for him. Surely it would not take them long to determine that "Brian Harding" was in reality the man they sought. . . .

"These do not seem to be quite in order." Lora stared up at the policeman, her eyes widening. He was looking back at her severely.

"I don't understand."

"There is a little matter of an unpaid tax . . . for driving in the interior, you understand."

"But—" The people at the hotel hadn't said anything about a tax. Surely. . . .

"How much, *señor?*" Her captor broke in curtly. Lora

looked at him in surprise. She was sure there was some mistake.

"One hundred pesos."

"Just a moment." He fished in his jeans pocket, withdrew Lora's cash, and counted out the necessary bills. He held it out to the policeman, who accepted it with a smile.

"The problem is now solved. *Gracias, señor, señora.* Have a good trip."

To Lora's surprise, the policeman handed all her papers back to her with a nod and another smile, then stepped back from the car and waved for them to proceed as he deftly pocketed the money. Lora gaped from him to the documents in her hand. She couldn't believe that she was this close to rescue, and yet was not going to be freed. She couldn't believe . . .

"All he wanted was a bribe!" The realization rose with bubbling outrage to her lips. He had not been interested in her companion at all. He had not been interested in her. All—

"Drive on, woman!" The fierce hiss brought her eyes jerking around to him. He glared at her, motioning forward with one hand.

With a feeling of fatalism, Lora depressed the clutch and shifted into gear. The car didn't even lurch as it moved off down the highway. Lora didn't know whether to laugh or to cry as she watched through the rearview mirror as the policeman stopped car after car. Then the VW swung around a curve and the roadblock was lost from sight.

"You lie about as well as you drive. Was that on purpose?" He sounded disgruntled.

Lora shot him a quick look as she eased down the visor that shielded her eyes from the glaring sun. He was frowning heavily at the road in front of him. The scowl made him look extremely forbidding.

"No, I was—just nervous," Lora said, and it was the truth. She had not stumbled over her answers in a purposeful attempt to alert the policeman. Her stuttering had been a natural reaction to fear. The man beside her grunted, folding his arms over his chest and staring out through the windshield. Lora looked at him for an instant, then returned her attention to her driving. He did not speak again, and neither did she.

They drove for hours, stopping only once for gas at a delapidated Pemex station at the edge of a tiny village. Her captor bought Cokes and candy bars at an ancient vending machine—with her money, of course—and they both wolfed them down as they drove along. The candy tasted as old as the machine had looked, and the Coke had a peculiar tang to it, but Lora was too hungry to care. She had not eaten a meal, a real meal, for more than twenty-four hours, and she was ravenous. Talk about a crash diet . . .

"Look, would you please tell me where we're going? I'm tired of jolting through potholes that would make the Great Salt Lake look like a puddle and driving through miles of smelly jungle without having any idea of where we're going to end up. For goodness sake, I'm not going to tell anybody. There's nobody here to tell." Hunger was making her peevish, and a fierce glare at him accompanied her words.

He looked at her thoughtfully for a moment, then shook his head. "You don't need to know. I'll tell you when to stop."

His reply didn't surprise her, not really. She had not truly supposed he would tell her anything so concrete as where they were going. He was too secretive for that. What had he done anyway? She had no idea, couldn't even begin to guess, although she suspected that it must be something pretty awful. He looked the type to do something awful. . . . He, he, he! *He* had taken over her entire life, and she didn't even know his name! For some reason that infuriated her almost more than anything else, and she said as much, spitting the words at him.

"I don't suppose there's any harm in telling you that much," he finally said after some moments of silent deliberation. "You can call me Max."

"Just Max? Is that it? I've had dogs with longer names!" Her tone was as nasty as she could make it.

He frowned, slanting a look at her with those obsidian eyes, and Lora could see that she had managed to annoy him. The way she felt at the moment, annoying him was something to do for sport, like bear baiting, but she was afraid that the results might be similar as well. And she would be the one who would end up hurt. . . .

"All right, Max it is. At least it's an improvement on Hey, you!"

"Right," he answered curtly. "Now, could you please shut up and keep your eyes on the road? You're a bad enough driver under the best circumstances."

Lora cast him a fulminating glance. "And you're a—a—" Words failed her. At least, she thought of several that were appropriate, but at the last moment she decided that discretion was the better part of valor and refrained from using them.

Highway 307 had long since turned into Route 186, which cut due west through the states of Quintana Roo and Campeche. This was wild jungle country, and dense green walls of trees and vegetation crowded in on both sides of the narrow roadway. Craterous potholes abounded. Lora was forced to slow to a crawl, and when the obligatory afternoon downpour came she had to stop altogether. Her captor—it was hard to think of him as Max, although she thought the hard, cruel-sounding name with its shades of the Third Reich suited him to a tee—was not agreeable to merely waiting the deluge out.

In consequence, he took the wheel, and Lora got some little satisfaction from watching him negotiate at a snail's pace the road which soon more nearly resembled a roaring river. He didn't seem particularly concerned about her trying to escape, and looking out the windows at the pounding sheets of rain Lora could understand why: she would drown if she were foolish enough to leave the protection of the car. And even if she waited until the rain stopped—which it would, as abruptly as it had started—she shuddered at the thought of being alone and on foot in jungle country. The twisting trees and vines looked both forbidding and inpenetrable. She knew that the rain forest was almost completely uninhabited—by humans, at least. Just before the downpour had started, Lora had braked to avoid hitting a large, flat black furry creature that at first glance had seemed to be no more than a spot on the road. Then one thin leg moved, to be followed by another and another. . . . Steering around it, she had frowned at the creature curiously, trying to determine what it was, when Max casually identified it as a tarantula. They were quite common in these parts, he told her with a grin, obviously relishing her convulsive shudder. No, she thought, remembering, it wasn't surprising that he didn't seem to fear an escape attempt. She wouldn't set foot outside the car for a million dollars. Even he was preferable to a close encounter with a tarantula!

At the tiny village of Francisco Escárcega, which was scarcely more than a collection of huts, nature's call overpowered hunger as her primary discomfort, and she managed to prevail upon Max to stop. Again he didn't seem worried about her getting away from him, and as she climbed out of the car to be surrounded by a swarm of Indian women and children she began to understand why. None of the villagers spoke English— at least, none that she heard—and the village was so small that there was no way she could have hidden from him even if she had tried to run. There was a rusty looking pay telephone in front of a larger cinderblock building that she understood from the picture of an envelope out front to be a post office, but the thought of trying to place a call through a Mexican operator in the limited amount of time she was sure to have before he caught up with her boggled the mind. Besides, she didn't have so much as a penny to her name. That unspeakable man had robbed her of every cent she possessed.

Shrugging resignedly, she abandoned the idea of trying to outwit her captor for the moment and allowed herself to be pointed toward a public outhouse which she thankfully made use of while her captor, she presumed, relieved himself outside. As they were leaving a toothless old woman thrust another packet of the ubiquitous tortillas into Max's hand in return for a few pesos. He drove, for which Lora was grateful as it left her free to eat. When the last crumb of tortilla was consumed, she succumbed to the combined effects of nervous tension and her almost sleepless night and leaned her head back against the vinyl headrest to fall asleep within minutes.

When she woke again, they had just reached a village that rivaled Escárcega for lack of size. A faded road sign proclaimed it Catazaja. Here they turned south off the main highway and found themselves on a narrow, poorly paved road that rose and fell with the increasingly mountainous landscape while twisting in and out upon itself in a way that threatened to make Lora sick to her stomach. In the aftermath of the rain, droplets sparkled like diamonds on the dense jade green of the jungle foliage. Parrots and other exotic birds squawked noisily, and plumes of steam drifted from the roadway toward the sky. The scenery was wildly beautiful, as exotic as anything from *Lost Horizon*. The only ugly thing was the smell. Composed of rotting vegetation and, she feared, the decomposing corpses of animals, the stench was heavy and sweet, and did her already queasy stomach no good at all.

Finally, after more than an hour's drive, they rounded another hairpin bend—and despite her incipient nausea Lora caught her breath. Before them, shining white against the deep green of the rain forest, was a city of temples and pyramids that looked as though it belonged on the white sands of an Egyptian desert. Surrounded by the untamed savagery of the jungle, completely hidden from sight until they rounded that last bend, the ruins dazzled with the mystery and grandeur of a lost civilization.

"Palenque," he said. "I thought you'd like it."

"It's gorgeous," Lora replied as he drove along the narrow road that wound through the lower part of the town where the villagers lived in cheerful poverty. The thatch-roofed huts Max called *tiendas,* many bearing signs advertising Coca-Cola and Seven-Up, and colorfully dressed Indians hawking held no fascination for her at the moment. She had eyes only for the magnificence on the hill. "Can we stop?"

There was a short silence, and then he laughed caustically. "Forgotten where you are, baby? You're being kidnapped, remember? Hell, no, we can't stop. You'll have to come back another time—with your math teacher."

There was a distinct sneer in the last words, but Lora, jerked so rudely back to reality, did not hear it. Gazing at the ruins with disappointment as they rounded another bend and the whole town disappeared like a mirage behind a protective curtain of jungle, she realized that she had, indeed, forgotten her situation. For a moment there, he had been no more or less than any other companion, a friend who could enjoy the magnificence of the ancient city with her. The unpleasant truth came as a jolt.

After Palenque, the jungle grew even more inhospitable.

The roars of unseen beasts that he identified as jaguars or maybe wild boars could be heard from time to time over the fitful hum of the air conditioning. Lizards the size of small alligators lay sunning themselves on the warm pavement, moving sluggishly out of the way with a great deal of tail lashing and baring of teeth only after repeated honks of the horn. Monkeys—she hoped—shrieked ear splittingly from somewhere inside the tangle of trees, and winged insects, some several inches long, launched incessant kamikaze assaults on the windshield with stomach churning results. As night approached, Lora began to grow uneasy. Would they reach their destination soon? She did not relish the idea of remaining in this untamed wilderness after dark.

Finally, about an hour after nightfall, the jungle seemed to clear fractionally, and by the beam of the car's headlights Lora could see that they had reached another tiny village. Max drove to the far edge of the little gathering of huts and pulled to the side of the road, stopping the car. Lora, who had been about to doze off again, sat up, looking around at the dark village and the even darker jungle.

"Where are we?" she asked faintly.

He turned without answering and reached into the backseat for the battered sarape. "I'm going to have to blindfold you," he said, turning toward her with the now filthy garment dangling from one hand.

"What? Why?" Lora spluttered a protest even as he began to wrap the sarape loosely over her eyes and around the top of her head. She lifted her hands instinctively to pull the heavy, musty smelling cloth away. He caught both her hands in his, squeezing with just enough power so that she was forced to remember his strength, and how much in his power she truly was.

"Don't try to look where we're going. It'll be better for

you if you see as little as possible. Even this way, the friend we're visiting is not going to like me bringing you along, but I don't seem to have much choice. Unless you would rather I killed you, of course.''

''You wouldn't, would you?'' Lora asked in a small voice, no longer fighting the shrouding cloth that was giving her a headache to match her unwell stomach. Her hands lay quietly in her lap as he started the car again before he answered.

''Not unless you make me. But my friend isn't as nice as I am, so behave yourself.''

Lora behaved herself, for the moment at least, sitting quietly in the passenger seat as the car bumped its way along what she could only surmise to be a dirt track. It wound every which way, and after the third or fourth turn Lora had lost all sense of direction. The blindfold was making her claustrophobic, and despite the fact that her nose and mouth were free, she felt as if she were being smothered. Twice her hands twitched upwards in a reflexive need to tear the cloth from her eyes, but both times she managed to restrain herself. Something in his manner told her that the matter of the blindfold was deadly serious. Nervously, she wondered about this ''friend'' of his. Another criminal like himself obviously. . . .

A gunshot sounded, close at hand, followed immediately by the sound of running footsteps and the glare of lights that barely glimmered through the weave of the wool about her eyes. Lora started, instinctively reaching for the blindfold as the car rocked to a stop.

''Don't you dare touch that thing now, or you won't get out of here alive.'' Max growled at her as he caught her hand. Frightened, Lora turned her fingers so that they were clasping his, taking ridiculous comfort from the feel of that warm, strong hand in hers as something metallic—a rifle butt? —rapped sharply at Max's window. He squeezed her fingers once, then released her hand. She heard him rolling down the window, and a short, sharp exchange followed that left her all at sea because it was conducted in the most colloquial form of Mexican Spanish. Then the man who had been talking to Max stepped away from the car, shouting something presumably to others nearby. Lora heard the car window being rolled up, and then the car started. Wetting her lips, she reached blindly for Max's arm.

"Easy, now. My friend doesn't like being surprised, so he has a few guards keeping an eye out. By the way, you're my lady friend for the duration. You won't be asked any questions, but you'll be safer if he doesn't realize that you're liable to go running and screaming to the police the first chance you get."

"I won't—"

"You will. You're the type." There was a grim note in his voice, and Lora didn't like it. He was right, or course, she would go straight to the police when she was free of him, but she didn't like him thinking so. He might decide that the only way to stop her was to kill her. . . .

"I . . ." She tried again to disabuse him of his all too accurate notion.

"Shut up. We're here. Keep your mouth shut and keep close to me, and you'll be all right. And for God's sake, try not to look like I scare you down to your prim little panties. It'll make him wonder, and he doesn't like to wonder about people. Makes him itchy."

"Who is he?" Lora asked shakily as the car stopped. Max didn't answer. She heard his door open and slam shut, and then her door was opening and he gripped her arm, helping her out. When she was on her feet, he unwound the sarape so that she could see again.

The sudden glare of lights hurt her eyes. She squinted

against the brightness that seemed to be made up of dozens of spotlights. They were in some sort of walled compound, she saw. A huge, white painted adobe hacienda stood immediately in front of where Max had parked on the curved drive. A young Mexican was already climbing into the VW and driving it away. Other men, armed to the teeth with ammunition belts crossed over their chests like guerrillas in a bad movie, were everywhere, on top of the yard-thick cement block wall surrounding the complex, by the garage-door-sized solid metal gate through which they had driven, on the hacienda's red-tiled roof, and standing at attention one on either side of the door.

As Lora stared at these last two, the massive oak doors were flung open and a short, stocky man whose thick features told of Indian ancestry strode into view. He was dressed in a blue dress shirt that was open at the throat and what Lora guessed to be a very expensive tropical suit, white linen or silk from the slubs in the material, which nevertheless did not seem to fit him properly. The vest was unbuttoned from halfway down his chest so that his stomach, which was more solid than fat, but definitely there, was more obvious than it might have been. The slacks seemed just a tad too tight at the waist, and consequently rode beneath the stomach bulge to the detriment of both. The coattails flapped behind him like wings as, despite his bulk, he ran lightly down the circular stairs to meet them.

"Max, my friend!"

"Ortega!"

To Lora's surprise—Max seemed too much the embodiment of the Mexican concept of machismo to ever participate in a show of emotion, especially toward another man—the two exchanged a hearty embrace. Then Ortega stepped back, still holding Max by the arms as he shook him lightly.

"It has been a long time, *amigo*. Too long for this to be merely a social call. There is trouble?"

"There is trouble," Max confirmed with a wry twist to his mouth. "I'll fill you in later." He cast a significant glance at the men around them, who all immediately shifted their interested eyes elsewhere. Ortega nodded.

"Yes. Later." He turned to look at Lora. There was a faint hardness in his eyes that sent her shrinking imperceptibly closer to Max's side.

"You're married, *amigo?* Perhaps that is what has kept you away so long?"

Her captor laughed, and Lora felt a sudden strong urge to kick him.

"Would I do such a thing, *amigo?* This is but a lady friend. She has been very helpful to me in this time of trouble. She brings no problems with her, you have my word on it." He made another short comment in Spanish which Lora, to her mingled regret and relief, couldn't follow. Whatever he said, it had the effect of making the Mexican's eyes gleam with interest as they passed over her once again.

"*Es muy linda,*" he said to Max with what appeared to be a touch of regret.

"*Sí,*" replied her captor briefly, his hand tightening on her arm as he led her in the wake of his friend, who had turned away to usher them inside. Lora went with him up the carved stone steps in thoughtful silence. Her Spanish might be deficient, but she had understood that last exchange: the stranger had said that she was very pretty, and Max had agreed with him. Despite the nervousness that was gnawing at her stomach, this second affirmation that Max thought her pretty was oddly warming.

Inside, the hacienda was magnificent, very much in the grand Spanish style with large, airy, whitewashed rooms, cool tile floors, and lots of dark furniture and paintings. As Ortega yelled from the vast front hallway for someone named Lucia, Lora's eyes lit on a huge painting of an elongated, one-eyed woman that adorned one roughly textured wall. She was just thinking that it was strange that a man who showed so little signs of taste in his person would find a painting in the style of Pablo Picasso appealing, when her gaze fell on the signature. Good Lord! It *was* a Picasso, or at least an excellent forgery. To find one here, in the home of a Mexican *bandido* in the back of beyond was mind boggling. Just what did Ortega do for a living, anyway? Lora had a funny feeling that she was better off not knowing.

The entrance of a middle-aged, slightly plump Mexican woman in the traditional black uniform and white apron of a maid interrupted his musings. Ortega said something to her in Spanish, to which the woman responded with a bob of the head. Then Orgega turned those hard eyes on her.

"I regret, *señorita,* that I must steal your *novio* away for a while. We have things to discuss, you understand. I hope you will not think us rude."

"Not at all," Lora responded politely, looking into those little black eyes and thinking that the man reminded her of a toad, a malevolent toad. How could he be a friend of Max's? But of course, they were fellow criminals. Despite Max's hard good looks and the effect they had on her, it would never do to forget that he and Ortega were two of a kind: renegades who considered themselves above the laws that governed other people.

"Lucia will show you to your rooms. Max will join you before long, I promise you." This was accompanied by a sly smile that made Lora stiffen with distaste. She did not like this man. . . .

"Have a bath, Lora, and go on to bed. Ortega, do you

think you could organize something in the way of clothes for her? We came away in rather a hurry.''

Max's mention of a bath struck a cord in Lora's heart. There were few luxuries that appealed to her more at the moment.

"Certainly. Lucia will see to it.'' Ortega addressed a few short orders to the maid, who nodded again without speaking. *"Buenos noches, señorita Lora."*

"Good night, Mr. Ortega. Good night, Max. Don't rush your meeting on my account.'' This last was said with a sugary smile at Max as she prepared to follow the silent Lucia, who stood waiting impassively.

"I won't.'' He leaned over, catching her by the shoulders and, to Lora's astonishment, brushing her mouth with his.

The brief touch—it could scarcely be called a kiss—stunned her so that she was barely aware of him whispering, ''Remember!'' in warning tones against her lips. When he let her go, she stood staring at him until he gave her a little push in the direction of the maid. As she followed Lucia from the hall, she heard Ortega chuckle.

"Still a devil with the women, eh, *amigo?*''

It didn't take Max's laughing rejoinder to send blood rushing with searing intensity along her veins. She had responded to that whisper-soft touch of his lips like a starry-eyed schoolgirl after her first kiss! Conjuring up a picture of the way she must have looked standing there gaping up at him, Lora wanted to drop through the floor in shame.

The hacienda was shaped like a huge U, and Lora would have been greatly impressed with the size and sheer magnificence of it if she had been in a state to be impressed by anything. As it was, all she could think of was Max. He had to be aware of how that brief kiss had affected her. He was too much of a man not to be. Her response had been all too obvious. Now that he knew how vulnerable she was where he was concerned, would he find some way to take advantage of her weakness? Of course he would. It was the nature of the beast.

"*Su cuarto de dormir, señorita.*" Lucia had stopped and was opening a door of carved, dark wood. She then stood back so that Lora could precede her inside.

Lora entered a trifle hesitantly, not sure of what to expect. But the sumptuously furnished bedroom was empty. Lucia entered behind her, crossing the room to throw open a door to an equally luxurious bathroom. Lora stood in the middle of the floor, marveling at the amenities which would not have disgraced a deluxe hotel. From the king-sized bed with its quilted, mauve satin spread, to the voluptuous thickness of the beige carpet beneath her feet, to the huge magenta and mauve bath sheets that Lucia was even now laying out for her, the hacienda did itself proud. Added to that, the place apparently had electricity. Lucia was switching on a pair of tall brass lamps on either side of the bed, and now that Lora thought about it the rest of the hacienda and the grounds as well had been well lit too. How on earth, in the middle of one of the remotest jungles in the world, had Ortega managed that? Unless the fortress, for that was what it was, was equipped with its own generator. That was the only explanation.

Lucia disappeared into the bathroom, and Lora heard the sound of water running. It was unbelievable. In an area where water was still fetched in buckets from a single pump in the middle of a village, running water was an even greater miracle than electricity.

"*Su baño, señorita.*" Lucia emerged from the bathroom, gesturing in a way that made the words obvious even to Lora. Her bath was ready.

"*Gracias, Lucia.*" Lora made use of one of her few

Spanish phrases and Lucia, suddenly beaming, answered with a torrent of Spanish that stopped only when it became clear that Lora understood not one word of what had been said. With a philosophical shrug, Lucia waved Lora toward the bathroom and left the room herself.

After a moment's hesitation, Lora crossed the room and examined the door, hoping that it might have some sort of lock that she could secure from the inside. She did not relish the idea of Max—or anyone else, for that matter—walking in on her while she bathed. But there was no lock, and the bath was too tempting to forego. She would hop in and hop out. . . .

As it happened, she was in there for much longer than she had expected. First, she had to rinse out her underclothes and hang them to dry on a towel rod. Then the bath was made of rose marble with swirls of darker and lighter pink highlighting the creamy stone, and Lucia had added a perfumed bath oil to the blissfully hot water so that the resulting steam smelled deliciously of roses. Lora bathed with rose scented soap, lathering her body with abandon. At home, she never spent money on luxuries like perfumed bath oil and soap. There was even an expensive brand of shampoo, conditioner—and a blow dryer! Miracles would never cease! By the time Lora, wrapped in one of the huge bath sheets, had finished blow drying her hair into its customary smooth style and had given the shiny finish imparted by the conditioner one last admiring glance in the mirror she had constantly to wipe clear of steam, more than an hour had passed. She opened the bathroom door, shivering slightly as the colder air from the bedroom struck her still damp body, and padded back into the bedroom wondering what she could find to sleep in. Only direst necessity would make her put on her own filthy clothes . . . She stopped short. There, lounging in a velvet armchair by the bed, was Max. He was clad in a navy silk bathrobe that left his calves and most of his chest bare. A cigar was in his mouth, a glass of amber liquid in his hand—and his eyes were on her.

"You took your own sweet time in there." He spoke around the cigar.

Lora clutched the towel more closely to her, feeling trapped. She no longer feared rape, or even him, exactly. Or at least not much. But she was beginning to fear herself. Something about him attracted her madly. And after her reaction to that kiss, he had to know it. Remembering the hot touch of his mouth, a flicker of excitement ran over her skin. To be closely followed by intense embarrassment. Stockholm Syndrome, she reminded herself fiercely, much as a drowning man might grab at a passing branch. Think Stockholm Syndrome.

"Did you finish your chat with your friend?" To her surprise, her voice sounded composed. Taking courage from that, she moved a few steps nearer, her eyes leaving him—she refused to stare at a hairy male chest and muscular legs like some nymphomaniacal groupie—to wander around the room. They lit on the bed, and to her alarm the association embarrassed her anew. She felt herself blushing, and only hoped that he would attribute her rosy glow to the heat of her recent bath.

"Yes."

He was not exactly talkative, Lora thought grumpily, disgusted that such a man should appeal to her so strongly. She had always thought that she was attracted to intellectual types, not to—to brawny hunks of beefcake! It certainly didn't say much for her intelligence, to say the least.

He swallowed the rest of his liquor with a gulp, set the glass on the floor, and stood up. Lora's eyes flew to his face, and she automatically retreated a step. His mouth twisted sardonically.

"Your supper is over there on that table. Lucia brought it, and some clothes. I haven't looked at them, but I assume they're suitable. Whether they are or not, they'll have to do. That blue dress has had it."

"Whose fault is that?" She rounded on him, wanting to pick a quarrel so that she would not feel so ridiculously vulnerable. He merely shrugged, and bent to stub his cigar out in a crystal ashtray on the table next to the chair. Then his hand moved to the robe's belt, and he began to untie the knot. . . .

"What are you doing?" Her voice rose in a squeak. His hands paused for a moment, then resumed what they were doing. As the robe parted, Lora's eyes widened for a moment. Then, horrified at what she was doing, she dragged them away to focus blindly on the whitewashed wall. He was magnificent naked—and she was determined not to care.

"I'm getting ready to take a bath." A faint impatience tinged his tone. "While I'm bathing, I suggest you eat and get into bed. And don't try any funny tricks. The door doesn't lock, so short of tying you up again I have no way to keep you out of trouble other than to warn you: Ortega is not a pleasant man to run afoul of. We've been acquainted for a number of years; he trusts me, but he doesn't know you, and he's suspicious of strangers. Give him one reason to suspect you're anything other than what you seem and he won't have a second thought about killing you. I'm sure he'd consider kidnap victims to be high risk visitors given their affinity for the police, and Ortega doesn't deal in risks. Not if he doesn't have to."

Without waiting for her answer, he went into the bathroom. Lora heard a splash as he climbed into the water she had left. He would come out smelling like a rose . . . The thought tugged her lips upward in a small, reluctant smile.

VIII

A black silk and lace peignoir set lay across the foot of the turned down bed. Lora gaped at it for a moment, touching the nightgown with disbelief. It was beautiful, what there was of it. Long and slinky, with spaghetti straps and a bodice that was nothing more than flowery panels of lace to the waist. It was a sexy dream of a nightgown—and there was no way she was going to sleep in it. Not with Max sharing her bed. It was bound to give him ideas, if he didn't have them already. It gave *her* ideas, and that was quite bad enough.

Dropping the nightgown as if it had burned her, Lora looked with some desperation about the room. Her own clothes were gone, but there was a neat pile of things folded upon the rose plush overstuffed chair that was twin to the one Max had vacated. Examining them, Lora saw to her relief that there were jeans, a hot pink t-shirt with the words "Go for it!" scrawled across the front, and a rainproof jacket. There was also a pair of panties, tiny black satin and lace

111

panties which must have belonged to the owner of the peignoir set. Evidently, the lady did not believe in bras, or Lucia had forgotten to include that necessity. In any case, there was no bra to be found, though Lora searched through the pile twice in case it should have gotten caught up with the other clothes. Other than that, there was everything she needed, including a pair of sneakers. Ortega was well prepared for female visitors, it seemed. Perhaps there was even a woman staying here? The place was huge enough so that two dozen guests would never know of each other's presence if their host did not wish it.

Lora heard splashing from the bathroom and started. She wanted to be dressed by the time he returned. Hurriedly, she pulled on the french cut panties, which barely covered her most vital parts, and the jeans, which were designer variety and so tight that she had to hold the zipper closed with one hand and zip with the other. The knit t-shirt was snug, too; without a bra Lora felt positively indecent. The owner of the clothes was a size smaller than Lora about the hips and perhaps two sizes smaller through the bosom. Grimacing at what she could see of herself, Lora crossed to the mirror set into the wall opposite the bed, fearing the worst.

Looking at her reflection, she saw that her fears were confirmed, and then some. Dressed in the too-tight jeans and the hot pink t-shirt with no bra, she looked more like a sex-hungry adolescent than a conservative Republican high school English teacher. If Howard Birnbaum, the principal, ever saw her like this, he would probably fire her on the spot. The tight jeans molded her hips and legs, emphasizing the curves of one and the length of the other; Lora was afraid to turn around and observe the affect on her behind. The clingy material of the t-shirt did not conceal a thing. Instead, it emphasized the full curves of her breasts, hugging the soft round globes and the taut nipples. She would have to wear the jacket over the t-shirt at all times, or at least until her bra dried, but she couldn't very well wear a waterproof jacket to bed—could she?

Lora thought about it, then shook her head. No, she couldn't. Casting a wary glance at the open bathroom door— the immodest swine didn't seem particularly worried about the possibility that she might walk in on him—she was reassured to hear an off-key hum and the sound of more splashing. If she ate quickly, she could be in bed with the covers up to her chin by the time he got out of the tub.

The dinner was excellent. Lora fell upon it like a starving person, regretting only that she did not have time to really enjoy the chicken baked in some kind of dark, savory sauce and the accompanying side dishes. She wolfed every bite, barely chewing as she kept an ear and an eye trained on the bathroom. There was coffee, too, darker and more bitter than she was accustomed too, but surprisingly good and served in a delicate china cup with an intricately wrought silver teaspoon. Looking at her now empty plate, Lora saw that it too was china. Sevres china, to be exact, she discovered with surprise, looking at the mark on the bottom. Ortega certainly lived first class, she thought, and that raised the question for the dozenth time: What exactly was it that he did? She probably was better off not knowing. . . .

A louder splash warned her that her reprieve was at an end. Springing up while the last gulp of coffee burned her throat, she sprinted for the bed, diving under the covers and pulling them up to her chin. The bed had just stopped quivering when he walked into the room clad only in a bathsheet that he had wrapped around his waist and that hung nearly to his ankles, making it look as if her were wearing a long, native style skirt. His hair was damp and tousled from the steam, and the overlong ends curled around his neck and ears. He had shaved the stubble from his chin, revealing a light cleft in its center. Without the bristle, he looked younger, handsomer, not so much the thug. If he had only rid himself of the swooping mustache, Lora thought, he could have passed for a businessman or lawyer. Beads of water still clung to the broad bronzed shoulders and hair-roughened chest, emphasizing the clean lines of muscle and sinew. She was surprised once again by how lean his waist and hips were in comparison with those massive shoulders. . . .

"Look all you want, babe, but I feel I ought to warn you that I'm getting ready to drop the towel."

The dry voice brought Lora's eyes shooting back up to his face. She had been staring, she realized with squirming embarrassment as her eyes met his. There was a gleam in those obsidian depths that she didn't dare try to analyze. He knew that she liked what she saw when she looked at him, knew that she found him attractive. She knew that he did. It was humiliating in the extreme, but there it was. She could only hope that he would not take advantage of her weakness.

Lora had been so busy being embarrassed that she had quite forgotten what he had said. When he dropped the towel, his eyes steady on hers and his face quite unembarrassed, she gasped.

"I did warn you," he said as Lora shut her eyes. But it was too late. The image of that hard-muscled, hair-shaded, beautifully male body was seared into her brain. Without his clothes, he was gorgeous. . . .

She kept her eyes shut and her face turned away until she felt the bed sink with his weight as he got into it at the opposite side. The bed was enormous; they needn't touch at all, Lora thought with relief. She heard the click of the lamp on his side being switched off, and relaxed a little. They both needed sleep . . . Just because they were sharing a bed was no reason to be so uptight. He had not tried anything the night before, despite the humiliation he put her through. He would not try anything tonight. . . . All she had to do was control her imagination—and her wayward impulses—and go to sleep.

She felt the weight of his upper body across hers, and shrieked. The shriek was automatic, and she was swallowing it even before his hand clamped over her mouth. Her eyes had flown open along with her mouth. She stared up at him wide-eyed, alarmed, uncertain, and yes, if she had to admit it, even secretly a little excited. That sexy hairy naked chest was just inches from her barely covered breasts and electricity seemed to be coursing between them where they didn't quite touch. He was staring down at her, his eyes alive with some emotion she couldn't name. He wanted her just as she wanted him. Should she fight him, or . . .

"What in hell is the matter with you?" The growled question made her blink. Funny, it didn't sound at all loverlike. . . .

"You—I—"

Her stammerings, coupled with her expression, must have given him the picture, because the scowl lines puckering his forehead and bracketing that hard looking mouth eased. The mouth itself twisted slightly. Lora, staring up at him from her prone position just inches beneath him, was more confused that ever. No, she thought, he definitely didn't look loverlike. . . .

"My God, you do have rape on the brain, don't you? I was just reaching over to turn out the lamp. You left it on."

He sounded disgusted. Lora felt her face turn beet red, and didn't even attempt to deny that she had thought what he thought she had thought as he continued his aborted movement to turn off the lamp.

When the room clicked into darkness, he returned to his

side of the bed and turned his back to her. Lora was left staring, mortified, into nothingness. She had made a fool out of herself, again. The only thing that was saving her from suffering the most abject humiliation was that he seemed to think she feared rape. Lora made a face in the darkness. He was wrong; she didn't fear rape, but she did fear him. And the affect he had on her.

Lora supposed that she was a little old-fashioned about sex. She was not a virgin; she let Brian make love to her just about whenever he wanted to, which usually worked out to about once a month, logistics being what they were. And before Brian there had been a boy at the beginning of her senior year in high school, Mark Dyer, with whom she had "done it," in his vernacular, exactly twice. Both times in the backseat of his ancient Mustang; the first time she had been a virgin, so she could not have been expected to enjoy it. The second time, while not physically painful, could best be described as embarrassing. All that fumbling, and his hands hot and sweaty against her skin . . . They had been going steady, and she had thought they were in love. Certainly he had told her that he loved her while he wheedled her into letting him go a little further on every date. They might have gotten engaged and married right after high school as a lot of kids did but for the accident. After that, she had been needed at home, and Mark had just sort of faded out of her life. He went away to college, and later she heard that he graduated and took a job selling insurance. Anyway, he never came back to Augusta. She stayed home and, after a year, started taking classes at the local community college.

It had taken almost six years of juggling her mother's care, part-time jobs, and classes to get her degree, but it had been worth it. She had always wanted to teach. And if teaching hadn't turned out to be precisely what she had expected, well, she enjoyed it anyway. She liked the kids, she was good at it, it gave her self-respect and a livable if not large income. What more could one ask of one's job?

A slight snore told her that, unbelievably, in the few seconds she had been ruminating, he had fallen asleep. He went to sleep quicker than anyone she had ever known. Lora glared at the shape of his broad back through the darkness. Deliberately, she made herself concentrate on the husky rumbles that emerged from his throat. A snoring man was classically unsexy, she thought, concentrating on the soft but unmistakable sounds. He *snores,* she told herself over and over, snores, snores snores ... Contrary to all she had read about snoring and its effect on the snorer's bedmates, even his damned snore struck her as sexy. Punching her pillow as if it was his head, Lora turned her back and shut her eyes. She would go to sleep ... Finally, in desperation, she started counting the detestable man's rhythmic growls. . . .

She felt toasty warm, she thought, enfolded in warmth, enveloped in warmth ... Her eyes opened drowsily, seeking the source of that warmth. Abruptly her body stiffened. A bare masculine arm encircled her waist; a long-fingered male hand lay against her rib cage, just inches from her right breast; soft male breathing ruffled the hair just over her ear. Her back was pressed against a naked male chest, her bottom cuddled into the saddle of equally naked male hips. And even through the too-tight jeans, she could feel his male reaction to her closeness. He was hot for her, hot and hard and ready—and asleep.

This knowledge, which Lora confirmed with a sneaking glance backward at his face, eased her trepidation slightly. She liked lying against him this way, liked the tingles that radiated out along her nerves from every place where their bodies touched. She liked feeling the naked heat and strength of him—without any real risk. What harm could there be in lying here enjoying the delicious feelings he conjured up in her, as long as he knew nothing about it? She could close her eyes, and fantasize. . . .

She did, and her fantasies were of him. The image of him as he looked without his shirt, without any clothes at all, tantalized her. All those bronzed muscles and that thick mat of hair—he was so big, so strong, so male. And he was touching her, holding her . . . Lora felt her body quicken, and for just an instant her eyes fluttered open. She should end this fantasy, before it reached its logical conclusion and entangled her even more thoroughly in this mess. But he felt so good against her, and her body was aching, and he was asleep. . . .

He sighed, shifting slightly, and his hand moved to cover her breast. Lora froze, her eyes wide open now. She should push him away, push herself away, get up, do anything but just lie there burning beneath his touch. But he wasn't moving, and another lightning glance back at his face showed her that his lashes still lay dark and heavy against his lean cheeks, and his mouth was still parted slightly as he breathed in and out. He was asleep—and she could enjoy the fantasy a moment longer.

Slowly, she relaxed, her whole being concentrated on the heat of that strong hand as it gently held her breast. His hand was so light on her, and yet so heavy and warm. . . . Her nipple tightened against his hand, butting into the cupping heat in a silent demand for attention. Lora felt the tightness throughout her body. She squirmed a little in answer, and her breast inadvertently pushed against his palm. His hand tightened in response—and Lora sucked in her breath. But he still seemed to sleep. Other than that one small, seemingly involuntary reaction, he did not move.

Her body felt as if it had suddenly burst into flames. The fire radiated from the hand that held her throbbing breast, from the feel of his hardness burning through the jeans covering her round bottom, from the heat and strength of every inch of his flesh where it seared her through her clothes . . . Her insides were turning to liquid because of him, and he wasn't even awake. Thank goodness he wasn't awake. Her bottom shifted in involuntary reaction to her body's needs, pressing closer against the tantalizing shaft that didn't even know she was alive.

His hand tightened on her breast again. Lora's eyes fluttered up once more, but this time she was too caught up in the clamoring of her blood to care very much if he was awake. She wanted to be touched—she wanted him to touch her. She wanted to be stroked and caressed by that long-fingered hand that was driving her out of her mind just by holding her breast. . . .

His fingers were moving, slowly, to probe the hardened nipple. Lora felt his touch through the thin material of her t-shirt and had to bite her lip to keep from moaning. Her eyelids felt heavy; they closed despite her halfhearted battle to keep them open. She should pull away from him . . . Those fingers were gently squeezing, pinching her nipple, torturing her until her breast arched instinctively against his fingers. He rewarded it by sliding his hand down her rib cage under the hem of her shirt and up again. At the touch of his hand against her bare skin, all Lora's nerves went haywire. His hand felt so good! Her eyes shut tight, pretending that it wasn't she who was squirming with need, arching her back so that her breast pressed wantonly against his stroking palm, thrusting her bottom backwards so that it came into even closer contact with his hard flesh. Panting, she gave herself over to the fantasy that had been consuming her for days. She wanted this—she wanted this—she wanted . . .

His other arm snaked beneath her now, holding her back

against him while he rubbed her breast with one hand and the other slid down, down over her rib cage and around to the snap that closed her jeans. She held her breath as he unsnapped it, then slid the zipper down. The faint zipping noise acted like the most potent aphrodisiac on her already overheated nerves. She mewed as she felt his hand on the softness of her belly, one finger testing the hollow of her belly button before moving down. . . . The hand stopped for an instant at the edge of the tiny bikini pants, and Lora quivered with frustration. This was her fantasy, and he couldn't stop now. . . .

He didn't. The large, warm hand slid inside her panties, slid down until it covered the soft mound of hair, until his fingers were probing the moist secrets of her, gently touching the most exquisite pleasure points until she gasped, squirming, clamping her legs against that hand that felt marvelous between her thighs. . . . The fingers were bolder now, stroking her, exploring her, parting the quivering folds of flesh and sliding inside her. Lora gasped, feeling as if she might die as those fingers teased her, moving in and out and then lingering inside her before being withdrawn to stroke her weeping flesh again and then slide back inside. . . .

Gasping, panting, quaking against him, Lora was aware of nothing but the exquisite torture that was going on between her thighs. Desire was like a spring inside her, and with every movement of that hard, hot hand he was twisting it ever tighter until at last, at last she could stand it no longer. She cried out, her head thrown back, her eyes closed tight as her body quaked and quivered with pulsating release.

Her mind fell back to earth a little slower than her body, but when it did the result was infinitely more painful. She lay there, aware that she was still cradled in his arms with his hand still in her pants and his manhood still throbbing against her, afraid to open her eyes. Dear God, what had she done?

What had she let—no, be honest—egged him into doing? How could she have allowed him to . . . ? She couldn't even put it into words. She had never, ever engaged in such an act before, not to—to completion. With Brian, there was always only a little preliminary touching. Certainly he had never tried—and she had never wanted him to—to please her in that way. She had never even thought that she could be so devastatingly pleased by such an act. Was her reaction normal? And what about him?

Thinking that, Lora could no longer ignore the throbbing thrust of him against her backside. Though she was satiated to the point of numbness if one disregarded the burning shame that was threatening to rouse her, he was clearly unfulfilled. Lora chewed her lip, trying not to make the decision that had to be made. After what had just passed, he had every reason to assume that she would now make passionate love with him. Much as she hated to face the fact, she was largely to blame for that assumption. If he chose to go ahead now, she certainly could not cry rape. . . .

He removed his hand from her pants and sat up. Lora knew that she could postpone the confrontation no longer. Rolling onto her back and gritting her teeth, she fastened her jeans, pulled down her shirt—and opened her eyes.

Light was beginning to filter through the curtains that entirely covered one wall. Despite the lingering gloom, she could see him clearly. His black hair was wildly tousled, his naked torso formidable as he half turned to meet her gaze. Those obsidian eyes glinted down at her from beneath frowning brows. His mouth was straight, expressionless beneath that villainous mustache. He looked poised for action, yet he was looking at her as if waiting for her to say something. Perhaps he expected her to moan about how wonderful it had been for her as she invited him to continue? She snorted to herself.

Not hardly, to use her students' vernacular. She would let him make love to her—it seemed only fair, under the circumstances— but she didn't intend to enjoy it. And she meant to make that clear.

"Well, go ahead," she said, glaring at him. He lifted his eyebrows at her without saying anything. Lora's scowl darkened, losing nothing because of the bright red flush that suffused her skin. This man had just performed an extremely intimate act on her, and yet he was looking at her as if she were a bug on a pin.

"If you're going to do it, do it and get it over with. I won't stop you." She wasn't being quite fair, she knew, but she couldn't help it. Intellectually, she realized that he was hardly to blame for her humiliation—she had initiated the contact, however much it pained her to admit it—but that didn't lessen her hostility toward him. He probably felt she owed him . . . Well, she would pay in the coin he expected, but she wouldn't enjoy it and she would let him know it.

"Generous." The word was dry. His eyes, as they swept over her before returning to meet hers, were hooded. "But don't strain yourself to be nice, babe. I like my women hungry. Like you were earlier . . . " His mouth curved into a nasty smile.

She flinched at the reminder of how she had been, feeling humiliation burn into her flesh. He smiled grimly at her reaction, then got out of bed without regard for his nakedness or her eyes on him, and began to dress.

IX

It was barely past dawn, but sunlight was already filtering brightly into the compound when they left Ortega's fortress some half hour later. The procedure for leaving was the same as entering: armed men watched from different vantage points about the grounds as Lora was blindfolded and then Max drove away. Lora did not protest the blindfold; after what had happened between them, she was speaking to Max only when absolutely necessary. He was speaking to her even less than that. He had, perhaps, grunted twice at her since ordering her to get dressed as he did so himself. Shame was the uppermost of the emotions keeping her silent; from the grim set of his mouth, he was just plain mad.

Lora took the blindfold off herself, finally. After nearly forty minutes of driving, during which Max said not one word to indicate that they were safely away, Lora finally got the idea that he would leave her to swelter under the blasted sarape all day if she didn't do something about it. He gave her a single hard look as she emerged, blinking, from the swathing folds of cloth, and turned his attention back to the narrow road. Lora cast him a glance of loathing, and turned her attention to the view outside her window. If he was going to sulk, why, that was fine with her. Sulking was exactly what she felt like doing herself.

It was a beautiful morning. Water droplets glistened like diamonds on the deep green of the jungle foliage. The road twisted through the densest part of the rain forest, climbing steadily into the mountains all the while. Parrots and a multitude of smaller birds that Lora could not identify squawked overhead, their brilliant plummage gleaming in the sunlight as they fluttered from tree to tree. More tarantulas scuttled across the road. Lora counted three before they had driven more than ten miles. The encroaching undergrowth on either side of the road rustled intermittently, and Lora did not like to imagine what kind of animal might be causing the movements. Like nearly everything else associated with this man and the nightmare trip he had forced her on, it was probably better not to know.

The car was slowing. Lora saw that they were approaching a rickety wooden bridge. The thing was only wide enough to permit one car to pass at a time, and it looked as if it was as old as Mexico.

"You're not going to drive across that, are you?" The first civil words that she had spoken to him that morning squeaked from her lips as she stared, appalled, at the bridge that wasn't more than twenty feet from their front tires.

He said nothing, just shot her a narrow-eyed look from those glittering eyes. Lora glared at him, folded her arms, and determined not to say another word. Even if he was bent on killing them—which, from the looks of that bridge, he was—she would endure it in bitter silence.

The car crept onto the narrow planks. As the structure was forced to bear the combined weight of the orange Volkswagen and two adult humans it groaned loudly. Lora knew she must have whitened; her nails bit into her upper arms through the windbreaker and shirt as she fought to stifle a terrified protest. The car crept forward, the moan intensified, the bridge swayed . . . Lora shut her eyes.

"Oh, for God's sake!" The unexpected sound of Max's voice made Lora's eyes fly open again. She found that his expression was as unfriendly as his tone, but it was surprisingly comforting just to hear his voice, under the hair-raising circumstances. "The damned bridge is perfectly safe. I've crossed it before, in a lot heavier vehicles than this."

"But it's—moaning." Lora was too worried about falling into the swirling brown waters of the river far below to remember that she was not speaking to him. She was all in favor of letting bygones be bygones—at least until they reached solid ground again.

"It's something in the structure of the bridge. I tell you, it's perfectly safe."

"So you say." The words were muttered under her breath, but from the glinty-eyed look he shot her, he heard. Lora said nothing else, barely breathing until the Volkswagen reached the other side and crawled safely on into the jungle.

She drew in a deep breath, then frowned. Just around the first turn past the bridge two vehicles were parked at the side of the road, a nondescript brown sedan and a battered pickup truck. Except for the vehicles in Ortega's fortress, Lora had not seen another car along this road since they had left Palenque. Something about them, parked end to end and seemingly deserted in this impenetrable jungle, seemed odd to her. What . . .

Without warning, what appeared to be an entire platoon of armed men burst from the jungle, forming a line across the road and aiming their weapons at the Volkswagen. Lora uttered a little choked scream, ducking her head instinctively beneath the dash. Were they police or terrorists or maybe more *bandidos*? They would certainly start shooting at any second. . . . She gritted her teeth and prayed that she would not be struck by any stray bullets as she waited for the fusillade to start. The car was slowing. Max pulled off the road just behind the other vehicles and stopped the car. Lora sat up, eyes huge as the armed men—she saw now that there were only four, armed with large pistols like the one Max had stuck in his jeans—surrounded the car.

"Max, do you know them? What do we do?" Her voice was a hoarse whisper. She prayed that they were friends of his—until she remembered Ortega and had second thoughts. His friends were as scary as his enemies, to her at least. The men outside were looking in through the windows at them now. They stood, one on either side of the VW and two in front of it. Their weapons were ready. . . .

"You drive straight down this road for maybe another twenty miles and you'll run into 190. It's a major highway, and it'll take you anywhere you want to go. When you get to a town, you can ask directions back to Cancun. I wouldn't suggest going back the way we came. Especially not the way you drive."

"But—but—" Lora spluttered. The huge black man on the driver's side of the car tapped on the window with the barrel of his pistol and gestured for Max to get out. Max nodded once, curtly, then turned back to Lora. She was looking at him, horrified.

"You're not going to just leave, are you? We're in the middle of the jungle. What if something happens? The car breaks down, or . . ." Her voice rose as she considered the possibilities. Her eyes, as she looked from the huge black man glaring in through the window to Max, were enormous.

He shook his head impatiently. "You'll be all right. I've got to go. Lora . . ." he hesitated, then with a muttered, "Hell!" swooped over her. Before she knew what was happening, he had her pinned back against the seat and his mouth was on hers, hard and hot and almost brutal in its demand. His hand was rough and warm on her breast. Lora's senses exploded. She forgot the men outside the car, her anger with Max, everything as she wrapped her arms around his neck and kissed him back with a hunger that had been building inside her forever. . . .

It was over almost before it began. Max lifted himself away from her, his hands moving to open the door. Lora blinked at him. She was still in shock from that kiss.

"One more thing, Lora: Don't go to the police." Without another word he was out of the car, slamming the door behind him.

Lora sat stunned for an instant longer, then scooted into the driver's seat and feverishly rolled down the window.

"Max!"

He walked on as if he hadn't heard.

"Max!"

Lora stared after him in disbelief as he walked over to the brown sedan and got into the backseat. Two of the armed men got in beside him, and the two others slid into the front seat. None of them so much as glanced her way. Then the engine turned over, and a second after that the sedan was moving off down the road. . . .

"Bastard!" Lora glared after it until it disappeared around

a bend and a muted roar from somewhere close at hand reminded her of where she was. Hastily, she rolled up the window and locked both doors, shivering with dread. She was alone . . . She should be glad. She *was* glad. Her ordeal was over. She was free, free, free . . . And alive and unharmed. Her captor had vanished as suddenly as he had appeared. Except for the pickup truck abandoned beside the road, and the fact that she was alone in a tiny Volkswagen in the middle of the Mexican jungle, the whole thing might never have happened. She had never dreamed that he would vanish, just like that. In the beginning, when she had visualized getting rid of him, she had pictured something dramatic, like a police shoot-out. And after a while, she hadn't even pictured that. For the better part of a day, she was chagrined to realize, she hadn't even really wanted to be rid of him. She had almost liked him, more than liked him in fact. And she had wanted his body. . . .

That last thought brought memories of the morning with it. Lora felt embarrassed heat steal over her skin. What kind of woman was she, to be sitting here in the middle of nowhere mooning over a man who had terrorized and abused her? Well, maybe not abused, she temporized, then realized that she was trying to find excuses for him. He had kidnapped her, tried to strangle her, tied her up, and threatened her with death. If that was not abuse, what was? she demanded of herself. There was something wrong with her not to be utterly, devoutly thankful that he was gone. Something very wrong. So she would never see him again. So what? She should be celebrating instead of feeling as if someone had just kicked her in the stomach. What horrible twist of her personality had he tapped to make her feel this way about him, a brutal, lawless criminal? She shuddered at the idea of a dark side to herself that she had never before faced. Then the solution occurred to her, and she seized on it thankfully. Stockholm Syndrome, she repeated to herself. Stockholm Syndrome.

By the time she reached Route 190, the Pan-American Highway, without incident—no thanks to Max!—she was furious. She had been manipulated from the word go. Clearly Max was no murderer, at least not unless circumstances forced him to it. But he had wanted to make sure that she would not go to the police with what she knew. His last words to her proved it. After that searing kiss, all he could think of to say by way of farewell was, "Don't go to the police." That was why he had kissed her, probably why he had done what he had to her body that morning. Remembering her avid response both times, she squirmed, and her temper grew even hotter. He must be very sure of himself now, she thought, turning south without even thinking about where she was going. He was probably congratulating himself for his handling of a sex-hungry, old maid school teacher, who after being exposed to his brand of body heat would never even dream of betraying him by going to the police.

Like hell! she thought furiously, and glared at the road as if it were Max until she reached the town of Comitan. The small colonial community set into the side of a mountain was charmingly picturesque, but Lora probably would have driven straight through without even noticing if it had not come to her attention that the car was almost out of gas. Accordingly, she pulled off the highway and drove through the town, looking for a Pemex station. She finally found one after negotiating a maze of torturously steep streets. It was near the town square, and Lora looked at the peculiar six-sided building in the center of the square opposite without much interest as she waited for the attendant to come out and attend his customer. Probably some kind of church . . . *Mañana, mañana,* she thought, and vowed to go home as soon as she could get a plane. She was sick of this lunatic country. . . .

"*Sí, señorita?*" The attendant was a Mexican Indian not much taller than the roof of the VW. As he peered in at her, the inevitable sombrero on his head reminded her all too vividly of Max. At least she had the dratted hat to remember him by . . . It was still in the backseat, along with the crumpled sarape.

"Fill it up," she snapped, angered anew at the reminder. At his look of imcomprehension, she realized what she had said, and sighed.

"*Por favor*," she began laboriously, but he had already gotten the idea. With a questioning look at her, the attendant picked up the nozzle attached to the ancient gas pump and gestured at the cap over her gas tank. Lora nodded, relieved.

He began to unscrew the cap, and she was just settling back in the seat when a horrible thought occurred to her.

"Wait!" she cried, hanging out the door and gesturing wildly at him to stop.

He frowned, perplexed, staring at her with the nozzle in one hand and her gas cap in the other.

Lora climbed out of the car. "I don't have any money! That swine stole my money!"

She had been talking more to herself than the attendant, and seeing his bewilderment she shook her head, took the gas cap from his unresisting hand, and screwed it firmly back in place.

"No gas!" she said loudly, shaking her head.

He stared at her as if she was *loco* as she got back in the car and started the engine, a furious scowl darkening her face.

"That tears it!" she muttered as she put the car in gear, then leaned out to call to the attendant who stood staring bemusedly after her with the nozzle still in his hand. "*La policía!* Where?"

He frowned, took a step backward, and pointed down the street.

"*Gracias,*" Lora called, then pulled out into the dizzyingly steep street to look for the police station among the collection of colonial dwellings that dotted the hills.

X
―

"So you were kidnapped, *señorita*?" The boredom in the round-faced young policeman's voice was unmistakable.

Lora gritted her teeth and tried to hold on to her patience. Her temper was still flaring, and this Mexican bureaucrat's attitude was doing nothing to smother the flames.

"Yes, I was kidnapped."

"There has been no report of such a crime occurring."

"I am making the report. Now."

"Ahhh." He scratched his chin with the eraser of his pencil, stared at the pile of paperwork on the desk in front of him, and then looked up at her without much interest through the small window separating the reception area from the inside of the police station.

"You want to report your own kidnapping, *señorita*?"

Put that way it sounded ridiculous. Lora glowered. "Yes!" she gritted.

The policeman sighed, turning to call something over his

shoulder to an unseen confederate. There was an answering guffaw. Then the man in front of her got wearily to his feet and opened a small door at the side for her to enter.

"I will take a report, *señorita*." He gestured for her to take a rickety wooden chair placed at a right angle to his desk just beneath the reception window.

Lora sat down, trying not to look at the other two officers who were staring at her with undisguised curiosity. Was a blond *norteamericana* in too-tight jeans and a hot pink t-shirt really such an oddity? Lora thought about it, and decided that ones who wanted to report their own kidnapping must be. She tried to ignore the blatant stares, looking at everything except the two men as the officer taking the report laboriously located paper and pencil. The cinderblock walls, with their untidy bulletin boards and cheap framed prints, held little of interest. Her eyes returned to the two men again. They were still staring avidly. She tried a new tactic: staring boldly back. To her chagrin, this only seemed to increase their interest. The work in front of them was forgotten as they drank in every detail of her appearance. Flustered, wishing she had not surrendered to the baking heat and left her windbreaker in the car, Lora looked at the walls again.

"Now, *señorita*, suppose you tell me of this kidnap." The officer interviewing her sighed.

Looking into his disinterested brown eyes, Lora felt the first faltering of her resolve. Maybe she should just forget it. . . . Incredibly, she was beginning to feel guilty—as though she was somehow betraying Max, the no-good swine. . . .

"*Señorita?*" the officer prompted.

Second thoughts were hitting her like bricks in the head. Her eyes wandered desperately around the room again as she tried to untangle her snarled emotions. Despite her fury, which was not so much over the stolen money as it was over

being used by a master manipulator—and so easily, too!
—Lora found that she could no longer launch into the story
that would set the police—maybe a lot of police—on Max's
trail. She would just forget the whole thing ... Chalk it up as
an interesting experience and go home. Mind made up, she
swung her eyes back around to the patiently waiting officer—
and did a double take. There, on the bulletin board behind the
desk of the very man she was talking to, was a full face photo
of Max. It was a blurry, black and white picture and not very
good, but there was no mistaking the dark face with its square
chin—unshaven then, too—and narrowed eyes beneath thick
frowning brows. There was no mistaking the slightly crooked
nose, or the hard, straight mouth below the fierce black
mustache ... It was a wanted poster! The truth burst in Lora's
brain like a bomb.

"Señorita?" the policeman's voice was puzzled as he
turned to see what had riveted her attention. He followed her
eyes to the poster, and suddenly sat up straight.

"Is that the man, *señorita*? The man who kidnapped you?"
He sounded excited. Without waiting for her reply, he spoke
rapidly to the two other policemen, who jumped up with a
scraping of chairs and crossed to join them at the desk.

Lora, tearing her eyes away from the poster with an effort,
felt a sinking sensation in the pit of her stomach. They were
interested in what she had to say now. ... Whatever Max had
done, he was obviously in big trouble. She couldn't add to it.

"No, no, it was just—just an interesting face ..." Her
words trailed off as it became obvious no one was listening.
They were talking excitedly among themselves. One crossed
to knock on a door at the rear of the room. A middle-aged
man, obviously the others' superior, opened the door, barking
an irritable question. The torrent of Spanish that answered
him caused him to stare hard at Lora, vanish back inside the

door for an instant, then emerge pulling on his uniform coat. Lora swallowed nervously as she watched him approach.

"Uh, never mind, I made a mistake. Isn't that silly? I . . ." Lora babbled, getting to her feet.

"Please sit down, *señorita*." The senior officer fixed her with a stern look.

Lora looked back at him, despairing, then sank back into the chair. Oh, Lord, what had she done?

"Now, *señorita*, suppose you start at the beginning. What is your name?"

Lora told him. What else could she do?

"You have identification?"

Lora wordlessly produced her driver's license from her purse. He studied it, then handed it back with a nod.

"Do you have knowledge of this man? This John Roberts Maxwell?"

So that was Max's full name. Lora registered this information as she looked apprehensively up into the senior officer's lined face. The way his sun-thickened skin folded back in on itself in a myriad of deep wrinkles around mournful brown eyes reminded her irresistibly of a basset hound. She only hoped that he had a basset hound's amiable disposition. . . .

"No—I don't know anything about him."

"You claimed you were kidnapped, *señorita*. At least, according to Jorge, here." He indicated the policeman who had knocked on his door. "Is that not correct?"

"No, I—I was just—it was a mistake. A joke. Ha, ha!" Her explanation sounded unconvincing even to her own ears. The officer frowned.

"*Senorita*, lying to a police officer is a serious offense. Now, please, look at this picture and tell me if you have knowledge of this man."

At his gesture, the officer called Jorge took the poster from the bulletin board and handed it to Lora, who sat looking at it helplessly. The writing on it was in Spanish, so she was no wiser than before about the nature of Max's crimes, but the grainy photograph was, unmistakably, Max. She stared at it unhappily, wanting to kick herself for letting an unaccustomed surge of temper get her into this mess. Why had she ever come to the police in the first place? She did not want to get Max into any more trouble—or aid the police in finding him. But now that she had gone this far, she had to tell at least some of what had happened. Not to do so would mean getting herself in very big trouble, too. Lora took a quick glance up at the four men who formed a circle around her chair, staring down at her with identical frowns on their faces. These men meant business, she had no doubt.

"*Señorita,* I will ask you once more: is this John Roberts Maxwell the man who kidnapped you?" The senior officer's voice was stern.

Lora swallowed and nodded slowly. It was foolish, she knew, but she was going to fudge the truth a bit. If she could make them think that Max had left her the day before, maybe jumped out of the car in the middle of the jungle somewhere, then they would be no closer to the truth than they were now. Well, at least not much closer.

She nodded unhappily.

"Please tell me what happened." He gestured to one of the junior policemen, who, with a hastily muttered, "*Sí, capitán,*" dragged over his own chair and placed it in front of Lora with a flourish. The captain sat down, straddling the seat, folding his arms on the back of the chair and cradling his chin on his arms. His eyes never left Lora all the while.

Wetting her lips, Lora began a tangled account of her association with Max, most of which was at least partially true. She left out places and times, and most of the violence, and ended up describing how he had leaped out of the car in the middle of nowhere the day before and vanished into the jungle. When she had finished, the captain merely looked at her for a long moment. Then he lifted his head from his folded arms and sighed heavily.

"So you say this John Roberts Maxwell left you yesterday, and you are only now reporting the crime? Please tell me why that is, *señorita*?"

Those basset hound eyes were fixed on her face, and they were decidedly unamiable. Lora resisted the impulse to squirm guiltily beneath their unblinking regard.

"Because I was—afraid," she replied after the briefest of hesitations. "He—warned me not to go to the police." That much was the absolute truth. Lora didn't add that she fervently wished she had heeded his warning.

"Hmph." The captain, clearly dissatisfied with her story, stood up. He said something to his men. The third of the junior officers crossed to his desk and picked up the telephone, dialing. The others stood looking at her, faces identical in suspicion.

"Is—is that all? May I go now?" Lora didn't like the way they were looking at her. She rose nervously, lifting her purse from the desk where it had rested since she had showed the captain her identification, her eyes moving from one dark, unfriendly face to another.

"I regret, *Señorita* Harding, that we will have to keep you with us for a while. I hope it will not inconvenience you," the captain said.

"What do you mean, keep me with you? For how long?"

"Just until we check a few facts of your story." The policeman called Jorge spoke soothingly. "It should not take long."

"How long?" Lora felt panic rise in her throat. She had had experience with Mexicans' ideas of "not long."

"A day—two," he replied, while the captain said something to him in Spanish. "Until an officer of the Federal Judicial Police can arrive to talk with you. Then, I am sure, you will be free to go."

Lora was struck speechless at the idea of having to remain in the police station for the length of time that would probably take. At the rate things moved in Mexico, it could be several weeks, or a month! Or more . . . As she groped for the right words to persuade the captain of his error, Jorge took her arm and started to gently propel her from the room. Lora stared wildly around as she went with him. The captain had already vanished back into his office, and the other policemen were busy talking excitedly on the telephone. There was no help for her here. . . .

Her feet dragged with reluctance as Jorge steered her through a door into a tiny, cell-like room. There was another metal door, which he unlocked. Then Lora found herself in a long corridor. Steel bars were set at intervals into a double row of cinderblock walls. Before Lora had properly assimilated the fact that she was being taken to jail, he had unlocked one of the doors and was pushing her gently, but firmly, inside.

"No—I want to talk to someone from the American Embassy! I want a lawyer! Please . . ." She grabbed frantically, at the bars as he closed the door with a clang and turned the key in the lock. The steel bars were cold and unyielding beneath her grasping hands.

"You can't do this!" Lora cried as he turned away. "I am a United States citizen! You can't just lock me up for no reason! I demand to speak with an officer of the American Embassy!"

"Perhaps *mañana*," the response came floating back to her

as Jorge let himself out of the cell block area. Lora, staring at the closing door with her head resting dispiritedly against the steel bars, could have wept.

Lora's half disbelieving apprehension turned to real fear as hours passed and no one came to tell her that it had all been a mistake and they were setting her free. Alternating with the fear was anger. She hadn't done anything, damn it! These suspicious-minded policemen were treating her like a criminal! Max was the criminal, while she was the victim of his crime. They did not seem to be able to make that distinction.

The jail itself was not nearly as bad as she had been led to believe Mexican prisons were. Perhaps because it was merely in a small town and not a government run detention center. In any case, the cell in which she alternately paced and sat was reasonably clean. The furnishings were meager, consisting of a thin mattress covered with a blanket lying on the concrete floor and a pail of water with a dipper. There was a primitive toilet in the corner, open to the view of anyone who happened to be passing in the corridor. Although no one ever was, so far Lora had resisted the urge to make use of the facility. The way her luck was running today, just as surely as she did one of the young policemen would come by.

She could hear other prisoners talking, laughing, and occasionally fighting among themselves. From their voices she deduced that she was not the only woman prisoner. At least, she heard what sounded like female voices. She supposed that she could count herself lucky that she had not been put in with the others, who were, as far as she could tell, either in one large cell or a group of adjoining cells. Apparently, she had been given special accommodations. Because of her nationality or the fact that she had not been charged with a crime, she did not know.

A single bare bulb in the ceiling provided illumination. It

flickered on automatically when it got dark outside. No sooner had the light come on than Lora heard a rattling of keys, and the voices of the other prisoners picked up with interest and excitement. As hers was the first cell off the police station, she was afforded the first view of Jorge pushing a cart loaded with metal trays.

"Please—when are you going to let me out of here? I haven't done anything!" Lora rushed to hang onto the steel bars and look out at him with a mixture of pleading and anger. Jorge returned her look impassively as he picked up one tray and bent to shove it through a small opening at the bottom of the door.

"*El capitán* has sent to Mexico City for an officer of the Federal Judicial Police to talk with you. In the meantime, we no longer have the authority to do anything, even if we should want to. You will have to wait, as will we."

"For how long?" Lora was outraged, and her voice rose with it.

Jorge shrugged, already pushing the cart down the hall and out of her sight. "Who knows? It is in the hands of God."

"You can't do this! I haven't done anything! I demand that you contact the American Embassy! Or at least my hotel, so that they can call my sister. Are you listening to me?"

From the lack of reply, it became obvious that he was not. Lora felt like screaming, crying, picking up the metal tray with the unappetizing looking dinner and flinging it against the steel bars, but she did not. She had a feeling that she would do better not to antagonize these policemen too much. It was being borne in on her with an awful sense of helplessness that no one, no one in the whole entire world who might be interested, knew where she was. These men could keep her imprisoned for days, weeks, months, even years, and no one would do anything because no one would know of it. This wasn't the United States, where one had a right to a speedy trial and no one was just thrown into jail and kept there for nothing. This was Mexico. She seemed to remember reading that one could be held indefinitely in Mexico without any charges being filed. The thought made her shiver. She had to get out of here—what could she say or do to make them see reason? Maybe if she told the whole truth about Max . . . No, she couldn't change her story now. That would only make them even more suspicious. Oh, why hadn't she listened to Max in the first place and stayed away from the police? Damn him anyway! This was all, every little bit of it, his fault!

When Jorge came back by her door with the now empty cart, Lora tried once again to reason with him. He only shrugged in reply, and went out, closing the door behind him. Lora heard the click as the lock went home. Trying to talk to these men was useless, she was beginning to realize. She would have to offer them something, anything—but what? Remembering the policeman at the roadblock, Lora decided that a bribe would probably work best. But, thanks to Max, she had no money. And she doubted that they would take a check, or her Visa. . . . Disconsolately, Lora picked up the tray from the floor and carried it over to the mattress, where she sank down cross-legged and began to eat. As she halfheartedly chewed the stale tacos and cold beans that had been provided, she noted absently that she could already feel the concrete floor through the foam rubber cushion that could not have been more than two inches thick. Shifting in a futile effort to find a more comfortable position, she wondered what it would feel like to try to sleep on such a mattress.

Miserable was the answer, as Lora discovered fairly shortly. The lights went out immediately after Jorge came to collect the trays. (Lora didn't even try to talk to him this time, merely treated him to a sullen stare that didn't seem to bother him in the least.) Then there was nothing else to do but try to sleep. The other residents of the cell block apparently had reached the same conclusion, because soon only rattling snores punctured the darkness. Lora lay down on the mattress, wrapping herself in the threadbare blanket and trying not to despair. They couldn't—*couldn't*—hold her long. She was an American citizen! Tomorrow everything would look much better. Perhaps she could persuade the captain to let her go—or at least call the American Embassy, or even her sister. Janice would do something to help her, she knew, though she couldn't imagine precisely what. Contact their congressman? That could take years. . . .

A rattling of keys and the sound of the lock in the door to the cellblock clicking open caught Lora's attention. She sat up, desperate for any diversion to take her mind off her situation. What was happening? she wondered as a flashlight beamed past her door, accompanied by the rumble of male voices speaking Spanish and the shuffle of feet. A late arrival? A nighttime bed check?

The men—she thought there were two of them—stopped outside her cell. The flashlight swung around so that it shone directly on her. One man said something to the other in Spanish. The reply was, even to Lora, clearly an affirmative. A key slid into the lock on her door. Lora got shakily to her feet as the door swung open.

"What do you want?" Visions of rape and murder danced in her brain. Secretly, she had feared it all along. No one knew where she was—they could do as they liked with her—this was why they had kept her. She had been crazy to go to the police in a country like Mexico. It was very likely that she would never see the light of day again. . . . She had brought this on herself, idiot that she was. No, Max had brought it on her. . . .

"I am from the Federal Judicial Police, *Señorita* Harding. I would like to ask you a few questions, please."

He spoke excellent English. That alone was enough to make Lora feel a little better. But just a little. Why did he want to ask her a few questions in the middle of the night? Lora hung back. Visions of glaring lights and police brutality swam through her mind. Was she to be interrogated TV movie style?

"Come, *Señorita* Harding, I do not have all night."

Lora could see nothing of the two men except for dark outlines. The glare of the flashlight in her face prevented her from determining if the taller man was one of the policemen who had interviewed her earlier. He was not Jorge. . . . The man who was from the Federal Judicial Police was short even for a Mexican. Maybe two inches shorter than she, which would make him about five-feet-four. He was brusque, clearly in a hurry, and that made her uneasy. If she did not answer his questions to his satisfaction, she did not like to consider what his reaction might be. . . .

The policeman—the taller man was one of the policemen, the third one—reached in and grasped her arm, pulling her out of the cell and pushing her before him, through the door and into the lighted police station. Lora blinked at the brightness, turning to look apprehensively at the men who followed her through the door.

The shorter man, Mexican like the beefier policeman, was thin and wiry and dressed in a conservative blue business suit that would not have been out of place on an American businessman. He frowned as he looked around the room, then shook his head and asked a question in Spanish. The young policeman, who appeared to be the only one on duty at this time of the night, nodded and led the way to the door from which the captain had emerged earlier that day.

"I have asked him if there is a place we can go to be private," the other man said to Lora, and motioned for her to precede him through the door. She did, reluctantly, visions of cattle prods dancing in her brain. Turning to face the self-possessed man who followed her into what appeared to be the captain's office, she clutched her hands together nervously. The young policeman closed the door behind them, and she was alone with this officer from the Federal Judicial Police.

"Stay where you are." The order was crisp. Lora watched, bewildered, as the man pushed by her and crossed to the single small window set high in the wall. It was shuttered, and as the man dragged a chair beneath it and climbed up on it, opening the shutters to look out, Lora saw that the window was fortified with more steel bars set deep into the cinderblock walls. He pressed his face against the bars, then thrust a hand through them to wave at someone who was presumably outside. Lora stared, feeling more and more nervous. What was he doing? After a moment he stepped down from the chair, holding up a hand when she would have said something.

"One moment."

"Blammm!" the sound of an explosion nearby nearly deafened her. She whirled, jumping a foot in the air, to stare at the closed door, behind which she heard a yell and the sound of running feet. From somewhere near at hand came the sound of crashing walls, and then the scream of a siren.

"What . . . " She turned back nervously to glance at the officer, who was looking pleased.

"Good, it is on time," he said. Lora stared at him, then took a small step backwards. What on earth was going on? There was a rattling noise at the window, and Lora looked up to see a heavy iron chain being passed around the bars.

"What . . ." she started once more, but again he held up that silencing hand.

"In a moment."

Beyond the window, Lora heard the sound of a car engine. The chain tightened—and then the window, bars, frame and all, popped out of the wall, falling to the ground outside with a crash and the rattle of dislodged mortar. Lora was left gaping at the jagged hole.

"Out the window. Hurry!"

At once all of Lora's suspicions crystallized into rampant paranoia, and she started slowly backing away. An officer of the Federal Judicial Police should not be telling her to climb out the window. . . . Was it possible that she was being set up? But for what? So that she could be killed while supposedly trying to escape? But how would that benefit anyone?

"*Por Dios, Señorita* Harding, I have been sent by Max! To rescue you! He is waiting for us outside! We must go instantly, or we are discovered!"

"I don't believe you." She was right, it was a set-up. There was no way Max could know where she was. And the idea of him rescuing her—a wanted criminal rescuing her from the police—was laughable. This was an elaborate charade devised by someone, she felt sure, to get her to admit that she knew far more about Max than she had told. Perhaps they suspected she was his girfriend. . . .

"*Madre de Dios!*" From the sound of his voice, it was a curse, and the expression in his chocolate brown eyes as they met hers was distinctly unfriendly. He moved toward her, his hands reaching for her, the expression in his eyes determined—and Lora backed away just as determinedly.

"Don't make me use force, *Señorita* Harding! Max might not like it."

"I don't know anything about Max. And I don't want to know anything about Max. Just go away and leave me alone. Please."

"Cristos!" He stopped, glared at her, and swung on his heel, stepping up to the window in a single movement and leaning out, whistling softly. Lora watched, interested despite her wariness. What was he up to now?

The man said something, apparently to someone outside the window. Then he jumped down from the chair with the air of a conjurer and gave her a smug look. Outside the window there was a thump and a scraping sound—and then a rough black head and a pair of broad shoulders appeared, followed in short order by the rest of him. Max!

"What are you doing here?" Lora gasped the words, casting a scared glance over her shoulder at the closed door. Sirens wailed madly outside, accompanied by shouts and screams and the sound of squealing tires and running feet. The police would probably come bursting in here at any instant. . . .

"I just happened to be in the neighborhood," Max said with withering sarcasm, glaring at her from his perch in the ruined window. He was dressed in the same ordinary white t-shirt and blue jeans that he had worn since Ortega's—and nothing had ever looked so good to her in her life. The smaller man said something to him in Spanish, and Max grunted.

"Come on, Lora, we don't have all night. We have to get out of here."

"I can't go with you. I'm under arrest—sort of."

"And you'll stay under arrest—sort of—for the next twenty years if you don't come with me now. For God's sake, Lora, I told you not to go to the police! It'll take 'em a year just to make up their minds what to do with you, and then I'll bet a thousand dollars they'll decide you're an accomplice of mine and lock you up for the rest of your life."

"I can't just—escape!"

"Why not? People do it all the time. Believe me, I know." His eyes narrowed at her. He took a deep breath. "This is a hell of a time to be having this conversation. Clemente and I are leaving. You can come with us or not, it's up to you. But if I were you, I wouldn't want to still be here in the morning."

"Why not?"

"Look around you. Do you want to try to explain that you had nothing to do with any of this—or the explosion?"

"You did that!" she gasped, listening to the commotion that seemed to be coming from the far end of the jail. Max was no longer listening. He had jumped down into the room, jerking his thumb at Clemente to indicate that the man could leave. Clemente needed no second urging. He leaped to the chair and wriggled out of the window with the agility of a snake. Max turned to look at Lora.

"Well?"

She stared at him, thoughts tripping over each other as they rioted through her mind. She couldn't just escape—but, as he said, did she want to be here tomorrow to explain tonight's happenings to the sour-faced captain on top of everything else? She shuddered.

"All right, I'm coming!"

He already had a foot on the chair, but he turned back to offer her a hand. She let him pull her up beside him, and then she was scrambling headfirst through the jagged-edged window with his hand on her behind giving her a helpful boost. The feel of his hand against that part of her anatomy made her jerk away. She lost her balance and would have crashed to the ground on the other side if he had not grabbed her ankle, stopping her headlong descent. Dangling head down, she had just a second to notice that the opposite end of the jail seemed to have been reduced to rubble. People she assumed were fellow prisoners were fleeing every which way into the darkness while policemen armed with flashlights and pistols ran after them, weapons firing with sharp pops. The siren wailed from directly overhead, and Lora assumed that it must be set into the top of the building. Three police cars were parked near the site of the explosion, their headlights trained on what just moments earlier had been the rear wall while their sirens wailed in unison with the one on the roof. No one paid the least attention to them as Max lowered her to the ground. Lora stood up just as Max jumped down beside her. The brown sedan was parked nearby, a chain still dangling beneath it. Max caught her hand and sprinted toward it, dragging her with him. Clemente was ahead of them. Two men, prisoners from their clothing, darted past them to vanish in the darkness. Then Clemente was opening the sedan's door and flinging himself into the driver's seat. The engine turned over.

They reached the car. Max jerked open the rear door and thrust her into the backseat, then jumped in beside her, slamming the door shut. As soon as they were inside, Clemente gunned the car; the shriek of tires joined the infernal din of the shrieking sirens. As they sped down the hill away from the riotous confusion of the police station, Lora saw another police car screech to a halt beside the pile of mortar that had once been the rear wall. A heavyset man climbed slowly out, staring at the destruction as if he couldn't believe his eyes. With a shudder Lora recognized the captain. . . .

"I don't believe this! What have you done?" Lora turned to fix accusing eyes on Max as Clemente sent the car careening through the night. The rattle of the chain beneath them grated on her ears.

"Gotten you out of jail. Don't bother to say thank you.

Step on it, Clemente, we've been gone too long already. Tunafish'll be getting antsy.''

"Sorry I took so long, Max, but that idiot cop wanted to call Mexico City to confirm my identity. Good thing we cut the telephone wires. Everything went well after that—until the lady here decided to give me a problem." This last was accompanied by a reproachful glance at Lora, thrown over Clemente's narrow shoulder.

"I—" Lora started to defend herself, but was silenced by a warning shake of Max's head.

"You know women, *amigo,* always arguing," he said to Clemente with a shrug of his broad shoulders. "Not an ounce of proper gratitude."

Clemente nodded once in reply, his attention focused once more on the dark road as they left the lights of the town behind.

"You think I should be grateful to you?" Lora's voice rose incredulously. "I would never have been in jail in the first place if it hadn't been for you!"

"You wouldn't have been in jail if you'd listened to me," he retorted coolly, turning those eyes that gleamed like twin hunks of jet in the darkness on her. "I told you not to go to the police."

"Criminals always say that. Victims rarely listen. Of course I went to the police. You kidnapped me! Besides, you took all my money! What was I supposed to do for gas?" Her earlier grievance rose to the fore, and she gazed at him indignantly.

"I forgot about that," he admitted, not sounding particularly regretful. "But you still shouldn't have gone to the police. That was really stupid."

Lora stared up at him, totally at a loss for words. That was not to say that she couldn't think of anything she wanted to say to him. The problem was, she could think of too much.

And all of it was insulting. She bit back the words. Arguing would serve no purpose now. For better or worse, she had let him "rescue" her from the clutches of the police. There could be no going back. She didn't like to contemplate what the captain's reaction would be to her escape. Certainly she didn't want to experience it firsthand.

"How did you know where I was, anyway?" That question had been teasing at the corners of her mind.

He turned his head to look down at her again. The faint moonlight filtering through the tinted window formed a triangular wedge on his cheekbone. The rest of his face was deep in shadow; she could barely make out the villainous mustache and square, unshaven jaw—but she had no trouble at all seeing the glitter of the darker-than-the-night eyes.

"One of Ortega's hangers-on spotted the car in front of the police station, and after it stayed there for several hours reported the information back to Ortega, who is always very interested when one of his recent guests decides to visit the police. Ortega conveyed his interest to me. I assured him that your sudden chumminess with the authorities could have no connection with him, but I'm not sure that he believed me. I decided to check it out, as I was still in the area, though I couldn't believe that you were actually stupid enough to go to the Mexican police. But there couldn't be two orange Volkswagens with their front ends smashed in in this part of Chiapas. I had Clemente make some inquiries, and it wasn't hard to find out what happened. In a town the size of Comitán, everyone knows everyone else's business. I thought about leaving you to the wolves, but since I had to assume some responsibility for the predicament you were in, I decided to get you out. Although not without some misgivings. You are a real pain in the ass, you know."

"So are you," Lora said with feeling, and would have said more if Max hadn't leaned forward suddenly.

"It's up here on the left. Keep an eye peeled, it's easy to miss."

"Sí." Clemente too was leaning forward, scanning the seemingly impenetrable wall of jungle that rose on either side of the narrow road. "Ahh." He braked suddenly, throwing Lora forward. Before she had recovered her balance, he and Max were out of the car, dragging what seemed to be a narrow section of jungle to one side. Then they were back in the car and driving through the opening they had created. Clemente stopped again on the other side, and both men got out to drag the concealing foliage back into place. They got back in, and the car moved slowly forward without lights along what seemed to be a surprisingly good road. All around the car the jungle loomed, dark and menacing. In the distance came the scream of a small animal as a predator claimed it. Lora shivered, shrinking back into the velour upholstery of the backseat. She would have liked to scoot closer to Max, but she wasn't feeling too sure of anything at the moment, especially him.

"Where are we going?" The question had a quavery quality to it she hadn't intended.

Max turned his head again to look down at her. This time there was no beam of moonlight to illuminate his face. This far into the jungle, the foliage blocked out every moonbeam.

"There's a small airfield up ahead a ways. We have a plane waiting to take us out of the country."

"What on earth is an airfield doing in the middle of the jungle?"

He grinned. She could see the white gleam of his teeth even through the darkness.

"A well hidden airfield is very useful in some professions."

"Like what?"

"Oh, drug running—there's probably more dope grown in these mountains than corn, it's big business around here, and the growers need a way to get it out of the country; then there are the guys who smuggle guns into Nicaragua and El Salvador; and the other guys—or sometimes even the same ones—who smuggle refugees out; and it's useful for men like Ortega, who can't pass through a border in most of the free world without worrying about being arrested. He needs an airfield where he can fly in and out."

"What exactly does Ortega do, anyway?" The question, which had been nagging at her ever since she first stepped into the man's elaborate parlor, was almost a whisper. In the front seat, Clemente snorted.

Max looked at her for a moment. She thought he was going to refuse to answer. Then he shrugged and said, "He's a businessman, pure and simple. He'll turn his hand to anything that offers a big enough profit. Drugs, guns, phony money, refugees—you name it, he's got a finger in it. But he's smart about it; in all these years he's never been nailed with the goods. I've known him for quite a few years, and we're friends of a sort, but I wouldn't trust him across the street and back—not unless he was being well paid to be trustworthy."

Lora listened to this chilling recitation with growing horror. The worst part about it was that Max seemed so unconcerned about Ortega's crimes—was Max involved in drugs and guns and all of that, too? She didn't want to believe it, but the evidence was overwhelming. No wonder the police were so eager to arrest him. He would probably go to jail for the rest of his life if he was caught. And deservedly so, she told herself firmly, trying not to think of him pinned in a small cell until he was withered and old. A criminal deserved to pay for his crimes.

"Here we are."

They pulled out of the jungle into a cleared area the size of perhaps three football fields placed end to end. There, barely visible in the darkness, was a lumbering, propeller-driven aircraft painted in shades of camouflage green. Lora stared at it with some misgivings. They were going to fly in that? It looked like something left over from World War II! Clemente drove up beside it, and a door over the wing slid open. Obviously, their approach had been observed.

"You took your own sweet time, Maxwell!" A leonine head with overlong black hair thrust out of the door in accompaniment to the angry voice. Lora looked up at the heavyset stranger as Max, who had pulled her from the car, thrust her toward a set of steps that led to the wing. Clemente brought up the rear as the propellers began to turn, slowly at first and then with increasing speed.

"We were gone just as long as it took," Max replied coolly. "You—" He was interrupted by the sudden blaze of lights that seemed to spring up out of nowhere to bathe them all in a noonday glow.

"Alto! Federales!" The words, yelled over a loudspeaker, froze them all momentarily in their tracks.

"Christ! Get out of the way, Minelli!" Max recovered first, grabbing Lora around the waist and lunging up the steps and into the plane with her.

"Alto!" The command to halt boomed again as Clemente leaped through the door right behind them. A loud burst of gunfire exploded. Bullets raked the plane just as the man called Minelli banged the door shut. Max shoved her to the floor of the cabin as bullets whined and twanged above, hissed, "Stay down!" and sprinted, bent almost double, for the cockpit. Clemente, Minelli and the other man in the cabin dropped to the aisle between the seats, lying on their stom-

achs with their arms covering their heads. Lora, after one quick horrified glance, followed suit.

"Tunafish, let's get this baby out of here!" The roar was Max's. It was punctuated by more gunfire. A profusion of bullets thudded into the metal fuselage in a series of staccato ta-tats. Lora winced and covered her head as round after round of ammunition spat at the plane that started bumping over the ground, gaining speed, and finally, sluggishly, lifted into the air.

XI

—

"How in hell did the feds get onto us?" The enormous black man at the controls of the C-47 Gooney Bird relaxed his fierce grip on the wheel as the plane climbed safely into the night sky.

"Got me." Max shrugged, taking over control of the plane from the copilot's seat. "My guess is they weren't after us, particularly. They probably got tipped off to stake out the airfield, and we walked into it. Must have thought we were druggies. The feds have tightened up enforcement since that DEA agent bought it a while back."

"Yeah." The black man nodded. "Don't matter now, anyway. Did you get the woman?"

"Yeah."

"Any problems?"

"None worth mentioning. Except what you saw."

"Must be a hell of a woman for you to go to all that trouble."

Max lifted his eyes from the shifting clouds that all but obscured the moon and the mountains below to give the grinning man a quelling look. "Just drop it, okay?"

"Anything you say, boss." The grin widened, revealing strong white teeth that stood out vividly in the gleaming dark brown face. Max threw him an irritated look.

"Can it, Tunafish." Then he realized what he had said, and grinned himself. Tunafish's nickname was always good for a laugh or two, at least for everyone but Tunafish.

"Ha, ha." Tunafish did not much appreciate jokes about his name. In fact, he did not much care for the name itself, but it had stuck with him since boot camp days and, among his old friends anyway, he could not shake it. "I don't much like them greaseballs we sprung. Don't trust 'em."

Max looked over at him again, frowning. "They give you any trouble?"

"Nah. Only—they ain't what they're supposed to be. If they were locked up because they were carryin' a little grass, then I'm my grandma's pappy."

"Oh?"

Tunafish nodded slowly. "They're too slick, too careful what they say. Used to giving orders. And to packing a piece."

"How do you know that?"

"We got stopped by a cop on the way down here. Ran a stop sign, no big deal. When the guy came up to us, Minelli reached for his pistol. He didn't use it, but he reached. Automatic like."

Max digested this information in frowning silence. He should have figured—had figured, in fact, though he hadn't wanted to acknowledge it—that there was something fishy about the two men that he had been hired to break out of the prison at Mazatlán. The money had been too good, for one thing—a hundred and fifty thousand dollars, plus expenses; he was used to working for perhaps a quarter of that, but of course there'd been two of them and that particular prison was a tough nut to crack. To add to his inner disquiet, instead of a distraught wife or parent putting up the cash, there'd been a man in a business suit. Max had learned to distrust men in business suits on general principal. And there had been too damned much security at the prison, which had led to Lowenthal being killed and the rest of them having to separate. He had been the one playing the official from the Red Cross, and he had been the one whose face the guards could identify as part of the band orchestrating the escape. The thing had been a disaster from beginning to end; first, Clemente had timed the blast that was to serve as a distraction too early, and he and Minelli and the other man, DiAngelo, had still been in the company of three armed guards and the warden. He had had to take the warden hostage at gunpoint to get the three of them safely out of the prison, and even then it had been a near thing. He had sweated constantly for fear the guards would decide that the warden's life was expendable in the cause of stopping an escape from their maximum security institution. Second, outside the prison, Lowenthal, charged with providing cover fire should anything go wrong, had been shot. Max had not seen him fall, but Tunafish had. Tunafish said he had died instantly with a bullet through the brain, and they had had to leave him where he lay.

Outside the prison, Clemente and Tunafish had waited in one of the two cars that Max always insisted on—two in case one should not start. He had quickly dispatched Minelli and DiAngelo with them, and forcing the blubbering warden to drive him, had taken off in the opposite direction in the other car. There had been no pursuit then. But he did not fool himself that every police officer in the country would not be hard on his tail. He had told the warden to drive east, while Tunafish went south, hoping to throw pursuit off the other car's tail. In Puerto Juárez, he had freed the prayer-muttering warden and ditched the car, hoping the authorities would think that he had used that port town to leave the country. Instead, he had hopped a bus to Cancun, and seen himself featured on the evening news while he was eating a meager lunch with what was almost the last of his few pesos. (Not having been prepared for the fiasco that had occurred, he had not had much money in his wallet, and the warden had been equally broke. Under the circumstances, it would have been too risky to use credit cards with his name on them; no point in handing them his head on a silver platter.) He had hurried without giving the least appearance of hurrying to the tourists' market, bought himself a huge sombrero to hide beneath and a cheap Hawaiian print shirt in hopes of blending in with the tourists. Then he had walked back out to the street, wondering what he should do next—and seen a lone woman in an orange Volkswagen stopped at a traffic signal. It had seemed like fate. He had taken full advantage of this manna from heaven and jumped in beside her. Having Lora and her car for cover had worked well to get him—almost—out of the country safely, but it had disadvantages. Namely, the woman herself.

She turned him on. Why, he couldn't exactly say. Her smooth, almost blond hair, calm blue eyes, and delicate, regular features were in marked contrast to the luscious shape of her. She tried to disguise her voluptuousness by dressing like a septagenarian old maid, but unless a man was blind her curves were unmistakable. Those full, thrusting breasts and curving hips with the tiny waist between made him think of Dolly Parton. Add long, slim legs and a skin as soft and smooth as a baby's, and you had a dynamite combination. For him at least.

She liked his looks too, he knew. He'd had enough women to know when one had the hots for him. She'd cast too many sidelong glances at him when she'd thought his eyes were occupied elsewhere for him to have any doubts about that. He turned her on, but she wasn't easy, wasn't the kind of woman to indulge in a quick lay just for the fun of it. She was the kind who had to have a relationship—God, he hated that word!—the kind who, before the much-ballyhooed sexual revolution, would have held out for marriage; the kind bitter experience had taught him to run a mile from. Only it was hard to run from a woman you'd kidnapped, and before he knew it his sexual urges were getting the better of his good sense. So far, his good sense had won out—barely. That morning at Ortega's, when he had awakened to find her cuddled up against him—God, she had been hot, and he had been hot to take her, until it was forcibly borne in on him that she was just using him to get her jollies. Once she got it off, she had no more use for him than a pregnant cow had for a bull. And he hadn't liked it, not one little bit. As she'd told him—little bitch!—he could have gone ahead, but the sizzle had gone out of it. He wanted her hungry, damn it, hot and wild and sweet, burning up with wanting him. And if he couldn't have her that way, he'd decided, he didn't want her at all, which was probably for the best. The last thing he needed was to get mixed up with a lady schoolteacher from the cornfields of Kansas. So what was she doing in the cabin of his airplane?

"Shit!" The word emerged from his mouth unbidden.

Tunafish looked over at him, grinning. "Like I said, must be a hell of a woman."

Max glared at his friend and told him what he could do

with himself in three succinct words. Tunafish chuckled, unperturbed, lacing his huge hands behind his head and leaving the flying to Max.

"Max, I brought the lady up here. Those two are giving her looks I do not like." Clemente poked his head through the curtained doorway as he spoke. Then, without waiting for a response, he thrust Lora through the curtain and disappeared. She stood just inside the cockpit, her eyes shadowed as she looked uncertainly from Max to Tunafish.

"If I'm in the way . . .

"You're not." Max's reply was clipped.

Tunafish was grinning widely. "Ain't you goin' to introduce us, boss?"

"Lora, this grinning ape here is Theodore Francis Cassaroli, better known as Tunafish. I'll leave you to figure out why. Tunafish, meet Lora Harding."

"My pleasure." Tunafish beamed at her, a wicked glint in his eyes as they moved over her.

"Hello." Lora's polite smile was faintly wary. The man was a giant—he dwarfed even Max, which was no easy feat. He was dressed conventionally enough, in sneakers, blue jeans and a light blue windbreaker, but his massive frame was awe inspiring. She recognized him as one of the men who had emerged from the jungle, weapons drawn, to remove Max from the VW. He had frightened her nearly to death then, and she wasn't much less afraid of him now.

"You can take the jump seat back there. We won't be in the air long."

"Where are we going?" Lora sat down as she spoke. Tunafish was grinning at her, and she smiled back nervously before shifting her attention to the back of Max's unruly black head.

"Guatemala City. We've got about forty-five minutes of flight time left."

"Oh." There was a lot she wanted to ask him—such as who were the two oily looking men in the cabin who had been giving her the kind of looks that made her skin crawl—but she didn't feel comfortable with Tunafish's grinning brown eyes on her. The sheer enormity of the man—to say nothing of the memory of him pointing a pistol at her—made her uneasy.

"It's a—nice night for flying," Lora said after a few moments of uncomfortable silence broken only by Tunafish's cheerful humming. The sound appeared to annoy Max; from where she sat, she watched a muscle grow progressively tighter in his jaw as the off-key rendition of what she thought she recognized as "That Old Black Magic" reached a crescendo and then ended with a flourish.

"Sure is." The reply came from Tunafish. Max hadn't bothered to respond to her inanity, and she didn't much blame him.

"That big full moon up there, with them little slips of cloud floatin' across it and them tiny little stars just a winkin' and a blinkin' in the night sky, why, they make a man think of romance. Don't they, boss?"

Lora missed the glint in the sideways look Max cast at Tunafish, but she heard—and puzzled at—the faint suggestion of gritted teeth in his response.

"Everything makes you think of romance, buddy. We should've nicknamed you Salmon instead of Tunafish. You've got nothing but spawning on your mind."

"That's right." Tunafish tipped his head back in easy agreement. "Ain't nothin' more important than . . . Be-Jesus, Max, would you look at that!"

The sudden change from easygoing humor to alarm in

Tunafish's voice brought Lora's as well as Max's eyes swinging around to where Tunafish was pointing at a gauge with a long, thick-knuckled forefinger. "We must have caught a bullet in the tank."

"Sweet Mother Mary." Max expelled his breath in a long, slow whistle. "Here we are flying over the deadliest range of mountains on the continent of North America, and we're about to run out of gas!"

XII

Lora came around slowly, her eyes blinking groggily open once or twice before realization set in. The plane had crashed and—wonder of wonders!—she had survived. Strapped into a cabin seat, her head pillowed on her knees and a fervent prayer on her lips—funny how, in that time of crisis, the only one that came to mind was, "Now I lay me down to sleep"—she had winced as first one engine and then both had died, leaving them hurtling down toward the treacherous mountains in an ominous silence broken only by the tinny wail of automatic alarms and Clemente's muttered, "Hail Marys" as he sat with eyes closed tight in the seat right across the aisle. Behind her, Minelli had kept up a steady stream of profanity. How he could face death with words like that on his lips she didn't know. She had tuned them out, repeating her own childhood prayer over and over again until she heard Max shout, "This is it!" and braced herself, her mind blank with terror. She waited to discover what it felt like to die. . . .

There had been a terrible grinding noise as the vulnerable underbelly of the plane made tearing contact with the tree-tops. The plane lurched violently, rolling onto its side and losing both wings as it continued to crash through the jungle. Quick, terrified upward glances had shown her branches thrusting through the hole left by the shearing off of one of the wings, shedding swirls of tattered foliage as they had been torn off and left behind, then followed by more . . . Clemente—she thought it had been Clemente—screamed; there was a gurgling, followed by an ear-shattering, grinding noise as the plane had slammed into solid earth with a scream of crunching metal. Then something slammed into her head, silencing her own scream as the world went black. She had thought, in that last, horror-filled instant, that that was what it felt like to die. She had expected more pain. . . .

Only she hadn't died. She didn't even seem to be much hurt. Lora sat up cautiously, almost afraid to move in case she discovered some mortal wound she hadn't been aware of. But she seemed to be in one piece, limbs intact. . . . Her head hurt a little, but that was all.

Soft gray daylight filtered through the hole torn in the opposite side of the plane. She looked toward it and saw Clemente, still dressed in his dapper business suit, white shirt strangely dark as he sat with his head thrown back and eyes open and staring. . . . Lora felt nausea rise in her throat and averted her eyes, fumbling with her seat belt. It took her a few minutes to recall how the release catch worked and to actually open it. Her fingers shook as she took in the unearthly silence and tried to work out what it meant. Was she alone—Dear God, was she the only survivor? Clemente looked dead. The men behind her, strapped into seats on either side of the aisle, sagged limply forward in their seats. They looked dead, too. . . .

What about Max? The thought brought Lora staggering to her feet. She had to see . . . She lurched forward, at first thinking that her sideways gait was due to some injury she hadn't yet discovered and then realizing that the plane lay at a crazy angle, nose down and almost on its side. She brushed through the curtains, slowing her forward impetus by catching the side of the cabin door as her breath caught on a painful sob.

Max sat with his shoulders slumped forward, head resting against the control panel, hands hanging limply at his sides. He was not moving, and in that dim light did not seem to be breathing. Beside him, Tunafish was in a similar position, but Lora had eyes for no one but Max.

"Please, God!" she whispered as she let go her hold and lurched forward again, catching herself on the back of his seat which she saw had torn partially out of its moorings. She bent over him, her hand on his shoulder, his neck, his head as she checked for signs of injury. There was blood on his face. . . . She felt it, warm and sticky on her hand, and shuddered. The windshield was shattered. The left side of his face was uppermost, and it seemed to be intact. The blood was on the right, covering part of his right eye and cheekbone and then trickling onto the control panel and from there to the floor, where it formed a puddle. Dear God, was he dead? Her hands were shaking so that she could not trust herself to determine that he had no pulse. Perhaps she simply couldn't find it. Was she feeling in the right places? Beneath his ear—the inside of his wrist—she was afraid to move him to lay her hand against his heart. He showed no signs of life, but she couldn't believe that he could be dead. Dear God, what should she do?

"Max?" She called his name, whispered it really, right

into his ear. There was no response. She called him again, going crazy with fear. Then, to her overwhelming relief, he moved. It was just a tiny move, a slight shake of his head, but it showed he was alive. Lora sucked in a deep breath of air, steadying herself as she leaned over him again. Her hands didn't shake quite so much this time as she lightly grasped his shoulder.

"Max!"

He groaned. Lora gently shook his shoulder, urgently needing him to regain consciousness. She would not feel at ease until he looked at her, spoke—just because he was not dead did not mean he could not die. Perhaps he was gravely injured. . . . There was no medical help for maybe hundreds of miles. The plane had crashed in the middle of the rugged, montana jungle in one of the remotest areas of continental North America. But, of course, Max would have radioed for help before they crashed, so a rescue party was probably on its way at that very moment. They should be found soon. . . .

"God!" The barely audible murmur made her lean over him again, a profound relief filling her as his eyes flickered open. Injured or not, at least he was alive.

Those obsidian eyes fixed on her for a moment, and she wondered if he remembered who she was. Then he said, "Lora?"

"Yes." His hands moved to the control panel as he spoke, and he used them to try to push himself upright. It must have hurt, because he winced and faltered.

"Don't try to move," she told him, but he persevered.

"Are you all right?" His question was thick, and Lora wondered again if he was seriously injured. He was sitting upright now, and she could see that the whole right side of his face was smeared with blood. Most of it seemed to come from a jagged cut high on the right side of his forehead. At least his right eye seemed to be all right. It was regarding her rather groggily, but no more so than its fellow.

"Yes. I think so. What about you? Your head is bleeding badly—do you hurt anywhere else?"

"My head—" He lifted a hand to his head and, on coming into contact with the still oozing blood, withdrew it, looking down at his smeared hand. "I remember hitting it on the windscreen. It hurts like hell, but the rest of me seems to be okay. God, look at Tunafish!"

Max half rose out of his seat, but the still-fastened seat belt restrained him and he fell back. Lora's eyes went from him to Tunafish, for whom she had barely spared a thought until that moment.

"I'll see to him," she said, but before she could move in that direction, Tunafish stirred and sat up with a groan.

"Jesus, my leg!" He leaned his head back against the seat as his hand clutched his left leg. Lora saw that it had already swollen to perhaps three times its normal girth, and that, from halfway down the thigh, it jutted out at an odd angle. Stricken with concern and guilt, she moved to his side, looking down at the hulking figure slumped in the seat. Before she could say anything, Max was at her side, his face alarmingly pale and deep lines of what could have been pain bracketing that mustachioed mouth.

"You shouldn't move—"

"I'm okay." Max brushed her protest aside with an impatient shake of his head as he knelt to examine the swollen leg. Lora looked down at Max's bloodied face and knew that it was very far from being true, but she also saw that it would be useless to protest further. All his concern was centered on the sweating figure of his friend, who was looking at him with a twisted grimace as Max rendered his verdict.

"It's broken."

"Hell, I know that. Nothin' could hurt this bad if it weren't broke." Tunafish tried a grin, but it quickly turned into another grimace of pain. "If that's all that ails me, I'll live. At least the plane didn't blow up, not with no gas in it. What about the rest of them?"

Max looked at Lora, who shook her head.

"I'll check," he said, and turned toward the cabin. He looked back over his shoulder at Lora before he went. "You might look for the first aid kit while I'm gone. It should be under the jump seat. Maybe you can give Tunafish an aspirin or something for the pain.

"Thanks, buddy." Tunafish's mouth twisted. With a brief smile, Max disappeared through the curtain while Lora went to do his bidding. Sure enough, there was a small first aid kit where Max said it would be. The white box was marked with the universal symbol of the red cross. Lora opened it, rummaging around inside. Its supplies were pitifully meager: a roll of gauze, surgical tape, a small pair of scissors, a pair of tweezers, antiseptic, aspirin, and bandages of varying sizes. For serious injuries such as Tunafish's leg, there was nothing.

"Anything worth knowin' about?" Tunafish's voice sounded strained.

Her eyes darkening with compassion, Lora looked across at him. "What Max said. Aspirin."

"Shit!" Tunafish suddenly looked self-conscious. "Uh, sorry."

"Don't mind me." Lora carefully crossed the tilted cabin to kneel at his side. "I'd probably say the same thing myself. Or worse. You must be in dreadful pain."

"You're one nice lady, you know? No wonder the boss . . ."

Whatever he had been going to say was lost as Max appeared in the doorway. Lora and Tunafish both looked at him silently. His face was paler than before; his eyes were shadowed, and his mouth was grim.

"Well?" Tunafish asked the question for both of them.

"Clemente's dead." There was no emotion in his voice; the pain was all in his eyes. "The other two are all right. At least, as far as I can tell. DiAngelo's unconscious, but I think he's coming around."

"Lord Jesus! And Juanita just over havin' the baby. Clemente was so damned proud—a boy, after three girls."

"I know."

No one said anything for a long moment. Lora, looking at Max with concern, saw how dark and shadowed his eyes were.

Tunafish must have seen the same thing; his voice when he spoke was rough with sympathy. "Not your fault, boss."

Max looked across at him bleakly. "Isn't it? I talked him into coming. He wanted to quit after the last one—Juanita thought it was too dangerous. But I said just one more job. And with her pregnant, he needed the money, so he came."

"You're not God, man. What happened was none of your doing. The good Lord called him, and he went. Same thing with Lowenthal. Not your fault."

Max took a deep breath, and moved away from the door. "I know. It's just that Clemente was so damned proud of that boy."

"You'll see to it that he doesn't want—that none of them want. That's all you can do."

"Yes."

Both men were silent again. Max stood with his hand on the back of Tunafish's seat for a moment, staring out the shattered windshield at the tangle of branches pressing against it. Lora knew that he was seeing nothing of what was before him. She looked up at him from her crouched position, her heart aching for the pain obvious in the hard-bitten, masculine face. She had not realized that he was capable of such grief. . . . There was nothing she could say, so she said nothing. After a moment, Max seemed to come to himself. He looked down at her.

"Is there a bandage in that thing?" He indicated the first aid kit, which she still held in her hands.

Lora nodded. "There are some sterile pads, and a few Band-Aids."

"Stick a Band-Aid on my head, will you? Then we'll get you out of here, buddy."

Max swiped the sleeve of his windbreaker over his bloody forehead as he addressed this last to Tunafish, who was gritting his teeth against a renewed surge of pain. Lora stood up, looking at Max with knit brows.

"That cut needs to be cleaned first. It could get infected."

Max shook his head. "Not now. Just put a bandage on it so that the blood doesn't keep running in my eye."

"But, Max, it's a serious cut! It's probably going to need stitches! At least let me—"

"Don't argue with me, please, Lora. This isn't the time for it."

He was right, of course. Tunafish's injury had to take precedence over his cut. The question was, what did he think they could do for Tunafish? Wouldn't it be wiser to wait for someone to rescue them, so he could be transported to a hospital? She said as much, and Max looked at her impatiently.

"Lora, it may be days—or longer!—until anyone finds us! Any search party will have hundreds of miles of mountainous jungle to cover and we must be practically invisible from the air. We'll have to take care of ourselves for a while—so quit arguing and do as I say, please!"

Lora didn't say another word. Instead, she extracted a

sterile pad from the kit, adjuring him to crouch down and then hold the pad in place while she wrapped gauze around it to secure it. There was no way any kind of adhesive, such as Band-Aids or tape, would stick to his gore-smeared skin. It was only as she was tying a neat knot in the gauze to hold the pad in place that a horrible thought occurred to her.

"Max, you did radio for help, didn't you?" She asked the question in a very small voice. He looked at her impatiently.

"What do you take me for, a lunatic? Of course I sent a mayday."

"I only thought that, under the circumstances ... Well, you might not have wanted to let the police know where we are."

"Under the circumstances," his voice mocked her, "I'd a hell of a lot rather be found by the police than not found at all. Believe me."

Lora did, and it afforded her considerable relief. The thought of being stranded in one of the remotest jungles on the continent of North America was terrifying. But surely it wouldn't be long before a search party located them. It couldn't be long. . . .

As soon as the knot was tied and the dangling end of gauze cut, Max's attention was all on Tunafish, who was sweating profusely as he lay back in his seat with his eyes closed. Lora, looking up at her handiwork as Max frowned down at Tunafish, bit her lip as the white pad slowly began to stain with red.

"It's still bleeding, you know, and there could be glass in there."

"You can play ministering angel later. For now, go in the cabin and ask Minelli to come out here, would you? He's the big guy."

Lora did as he asked. Between them, Max and Minelli managed to get Tunafish out of the cockpit and into the cabin, not without considerable, heartfelt cursing on Tunafish's part. He kept apologizing to Lora for his language until at last Max told him not to be such an ass. Lora seconded the sentiments exactly, noun and all, and both Tunafish and Max stared at her. Tunafish grinned, relieved.

"That's one fine lady, boss," he said to Max as the two men wedged him against one rounded wall of the crazily leaning plane. They had moved him to the back, where the seats had been cleared out, to leave more room for cargo Lora presumed. The plane had landed so that the floor with its worn carpet formed part of one wall. The ceiling formed part of another, and it was against this that Tunafish sat.

"Ahhh!" Tunafish groaned as Minelli accidentally jostled his broken leg, and Lora looked down just in time to see Tunafish pass out in a dead faint at her feet.

"Just as well," Max said, looking at his friend's prone form. "I'll set the leg while he's out. Minelli, I'll need your help. Lora, see if there's anything you can do for DiAngelo, there."

Lora obediently made her way to DiAngelo, a tall, thin man with longish dark hair and a receding chin, who had not yet moved from his seat. He was still groggy, Lora supposed from a blow to the head, but other than a few scrapes and bruises he seemed to be unharmed. She was asking him in slow, distinct tones whether anything hurt, her attention focused on his pale face as she tried not to look at the blanket-shrouded figure of Clemente, still strapped in the seat, when Tunafish screamed with pain.

Looking around, she saw Max, grim-faced, pulling on his broken leg while Minelli held a struggling Tunafish still. . . . Shuddering, she hastily shifted her attention back to DiAngelo as Tunafish sobbed and groaned. When she looked at Tunafish again, she was relieved to see that he had fainted once more.

Max had broken two reasonably straight branches from the myriad that invaded the cabin on its opposite side, and was binding them on either side of Tunafish's broken leg with strips torn from his windbreaker. It made a crude splint, but under the circumstances it was the best anyone could do.

When Tunafish was resting as comfortably as could be expected, Max hefted Clemente's blanket-wrapped body and carried it out of the plane. When he returned some twenty minutes later, his eyes were somber. Lora didn't like to ask what he had done with the body. In this climate, it would not last long in its present state. When rescue arrived, Lora supposed that the remains would be recovered and returned to Clemente's family. She shuddered. She did not like to think of that vital young man lying dead out there in the jungle—or of his family. . . .

After that, Max could not seem to settle down. He paced, and finally stopped at the hole that had been left in one side of the cabin when one wing had sheared completely off. He stood for a while, staring out at the jungle, his arm resting on the jagged metal above his head.

Finally, he said over his shoulder, "I'm going to look around," and jumped.

Lora saw him disappear, and with a quick glance at the plane's remaining occupants decided to follow. She didn't want to remain essentially alone with Minelli—for that was what she would be, with Tunafish unconscious or asleep and DiAngelo not quite having regained his wits. She had not liked the way Minelli watched her while Max was gone before. . . .

Careful not to cut herself on the ripped metal, she jumped lightly to the ground and found Max, standing, staring, among the dense jungle growth not ten feet away.

"What—" she started to say, when he moved forward, his

eyes suddenly blazing, to lean inside a large hole torn in the plane's green-painted underbelly.

"What's wrong?" She followed him, nervously watching where she placed her sneakered feet. Beneath the thick carpet of vines and plants covering the jungle floor, anything could have lurked; snakes, or those dreadful tarantulas. . . .

"That son of a bitch!"

"What?" She reached his side and stared up at him uncomprehendingly as he continued to glare furiously into the hole. Since it was obviously the source of his anger, Lora leaned around him to look into the hole, too. What she saw made her eyes widen. The plane's cargo bay was packed with wooden crates. The impact of the crash had broken open perhaps a dozen of them, and from the broken slats spilled dozens of small, clear plastic bags filled with a snowy white powder.

XIII

"That son of a bitch Ortega was using us to run dope!"

Lora gaped at him, but Max barely saw her as his mind worked furiously. That reception at the airfield had been intended for them after all, it seemed. Or at least, for who the *Federales* thought they were: drug-runners! Max wanted to spit. No wonder Ortega had been so amenable to lending him a plane! He had thought it rather strange at the time—Ortega was a careful man, not one to get on the wrong side of the law for any reason but his own advantage—but his mind had been on other things and he had let the suspicion wash over him without really registering it. And why? Because of her, of course! Lora. He threw her a glance of such acute dislike that she actually took a step back from him, her eyes widening. Never before had anyone ever caught him this flat-footed! Hell, he was no saint, but he drew the line at running dope! He *hated* dope! And Ortega, the oily son of a bitch, knew it.

When the feds caught up with them—and they would, they'd been there at that hidden airport waiting for them—they'd probably tracked them on radar, and to top it off he'd sent that damned mayday, mainly for Lora's sake. Crashing in the wild, nearly impenetrable Sierra Madres was a nightmare; surviving the crash with no chance of rescue was a worse one, especially for a woman. But if he had known what was in the cargo bay he would never have radioed their position as they had been going down. By doing so, he had done his best to put himself and Tunafish, to say nothing of the two men he'd been paid to bring safely *out* of jail, in a Mexican prison for more years than he, for one, had to spare. He hadn't even done Lora a favor, as it turned out. The police were quite likely to decide that she was as guilty as they, and throw her in jail, too. . . . There was nothing to do but wait for the feds to show up. Alone, he could walk out of the jungle; under the circumstances, he would have even been willing to take a chance on walking out with the triple encumbrances of Lora, Minelli and DiAngelo. But there was Tunafish with a broken leg. And Tunafish weighed close to two hundred fifty pounds, all of it solid muscle. Max thought of the almost impassable terrain of the montana jungle and groaned. How could he carry Tunafish over nearly a hundred miles of uncharted, uninhabited jungle alone? The answer was, of course, that he couldn't.

"Goddamn it!" He swore, bitterly, and turned to see Lora regarding him as if he'd grown two heads. He scarcely glanced at her, because a few feet behind her stood Minelli, who had obviously heard most of the previous conversation. Wordlessly, Minelli brushed by Lora to look into the cargo bay himself. What he saw made him whistle.

"There must be ten million dollars worth of stuff in there!

Enough to get every junkie in New York high for a month.''
The words were said softly, as if to himself. ''Smack?''

Max shrugged, stepping closer to look through the hole
again. ''Probably.''

Minelli caught the sides of the hole and pulled himself up
and through. Max watched him a minute, then followed.
Lora, coming up to look through the hole after Max disappeared
inside it, watched as Minelli picked up a bag, tore a small
hole in it, touched the powder with a finger and put the finger
in his mouth.

''Smack,'' he said.

Putting down the bag, he picked up a loose board and pried
up the lid of an intact crate. More powder-filled bags appeared.
Max followed suit. By the time they had opened all the
crates, they had, by Minelli's muttered count, uncovered
perhaps a thousand bags of smack—in response to her question, Max told her that it was the street word for heroin—and
at least a hundred thousand dollars in U.S. currency.

The discovery of the cash, in a suitcase hidden in one of
the crates, seemed to add the final fillip to Minelli's excitement. His small eyes glittered and his thick lips quivered
with the sudden quickening of his breathing. Max's face, in
contrast, had grown increasingly grim. He was watching
Minelli, his eyes hard. Then Minelli looked up to find Max's
eyes on him. His expression changed, growing bland again
although nothing could erase the excited glitter in his eyes.
The two men eyed each other for a moment, then Minelli
abruptly got to his feet. Max rose more slowly, his eyes never
leaving Minelli's swaggering back as the man moved away
and then jumped down from the cargo bay. Lora stood back
as he landed beside her. Then Max was jumping down too,
and Minelli walked quickly away, shouldering through the
dense foliage and stepping up on a thick branch apparently

felled by the crash to grab the sides of the hole and hoist himself back inside the cabin. Max stared after him, frowning. Lora frowned at Max.

"That bastard's going to make trouble."

"Over the money?"

"And the dope. He wants it. Hell, it's white gold! That son of a bitch Ortega! I may have to kill him."

This last was said softly, more to himself than to her. Lora was horrified.

"Ortega?"

"Minelli." The answer was short, clipped. Looking up into Max's rigid face, fiercer looking than ever now with the white bandage wound around his forehead, Lora was irresistably reminded of the way he had looked when he had first kidnapped her. The face of a killer—she had thought so then, and she thought so now.

"You can't kill him!" She caught hold of Max's arm, staring up at him, appalled.

"Why not?" He sounded cold, deadly cold. Lora shivered, but hung grimly onto his arm. She would not let him do this thing—why, she didn't even consider.

"Because . . ." She stared up into eyes that were as black as a winter night. This was the part of him she feared. "Because he's a human being. You can't just go around killing people, for heaven's sake!"

"Can't I?" To her dismay, his eyes grew even more remote, seeming to focus on something that was beyond her line of vision. "Remind me to tell you about Mei Veng sometime."

Her brow knit. He shook his head. "A place in Vietnam. It doesn't matter. Come on, I want to check on Tunafish and see what Minelli is up to."

This last was muttered, but Lora heard it. Max's hand on

her arm propelled her forward. She walked ahead of him, making her way carefully over the downed trees. Sunlight filtered through the dense green treetops far above. The canopy of intertwining branches, leaves and vines was so thick that it was almost impossible to tell where the plane had torn through. Brilliantly colored birds flapped from treetop to treetop, their raucous calls joining with the whirr of swarming blue-bodied flies and the rustle of fallen leaves as things—Lora refused to speculate about what kind of things; she knew that she was better off not knowing, if the tarantulas were any guideline—moved through them. A fine mist rose from the jungle floor as moisture from yesterday's downpour evaporated in this new day's heat. A small brown monkey appeared, chattering, to survey the wrecked plane. Lora smiled at the sight of the creature balancing on a rock, and turned to call Max's attention to it.

What she saw as she turned made her blanch. He had extracted his gun from the waistband of his jeans and was checking the magazine. Apparently satisfied, he thrust it back into his jeans, pulling the hem of his t-shirt down to cover it. Then he looked up to catch Lora's eyes upon him. She expected an explanation, at least, but all he said was, "Come on," before taking her arm and helping her up into the plane.

As the hours passed, the atmosphere on the plane became so thick that it could have been pureed in a blender. Waiting, like war, was hell. Lora so strained to hear the sounds of approaching rescue that she gave herself a headache. Minelli paced restlessly, his eyes sliding away from Max, who spent most of his time staring at nothing with cold, expressionless eyes. DiAngelo slept; beyond checking to see that he was all right, there was little anyone could do for him. Lora spent most of her time with Tunafish, who was in dreadful pain though he tried to hide it. Sweat rolled freely down his face and his clothes were soaked with it, which wasn't surprising; the interior of the plane became like an oven as the day wore on. Bugs flew through the holes in the metal fuselage to feast on whoever happened to strike their fancy. Curses and slaps were practically the only sounds, and they were nearly continuous.

The humidity was dreadful. Lora almost welcomed the onset of the afternoon downpour—until she found that the loud click-click striking the metal was not caused by rain-drops alone. The force of the rain washed ticks down from the treetops, causing them to fall by the hundreds. Several dozen of them fell into the plane; Lora scrambled to her feet, shuddering as she first identified the repellant things. Max scooped as many as he could find onto a folded magazine and out into the jungle again, but Lora knew that he couldn't possibly have captured them all. The thought of ticks made her want to scream, but screaming would have been useless. So she set her teeth, and sat back down on the floor beside Tunafish. She didn't need Max's quiet warning of disease to make her keep a sharp eye peeled. The thought of ticks crawling on her was revolting enough by itself.

After the rain cleared, Max grew increasingly restless. He prowled up and down the plane, then finally stopped by the hole.

"I'm going to scout around for water and something to eat. Minelli, you can come with me."

It was an order, and from the look on Minelli's face he didn't like being given orders. For one frightening moment Lora thought the confrontation that she was rapidly beginning to regard as inevitable would occur there and then, but Minelli shrugged.

"Why not?" he said, and followed Max out the hole.

They were gone for perhaps an hour and a half. During that

time, Lora mopped Tunafish's sweating brow with what was left of Max's windbreaker, and chewed slowly on half a Hershey bar, all that was left of the four that Tunafish, a chocoholic according to Max, had stowed in his jacket pocket. Once that was gone, there would be no more food, unless there was something growing in the jungle that they could eat. Or perhaps the men could hunt. Max seemed perfectly at home with a gun. Surely he could shoot something to eat. Or maybe they would be rescued before it became necessary. Lora tried to cling to that thought, but as minutes turned into hours it was gradually losing its power to comfort.

At least water would be no problem, Lora thought as she murmured soothingly to Tunafish, who slept restlessly with his head pillowed in her lap. Puddles of it still shimmered against the cockpit wall, which was the lowest point of the plane. She was thirsty, and looking at the water made her thirstier still. When Tunafish woke, she would swallow a handful. . . . DiAngelo was sleeping, too. At least, Lora hoped he was sleeping. He hadn't moved for some time; perhaps he was comatose—or dead.

Minelli's head and shoulders appeared through the hole without warning. An instant later, he laid a squat black pistol on the floor. She hadn't realized he was armed. . . . Lora watched, wide-eyed, as he heaved himself inside and picked up the gun. What was he doing with it? Vivid images of mass murder flitted through her brain. It took an effort to dismiss them as ridiculous. She did not like him—something to do with the way he looked at her, she supposed. His eyes moved over her body from time to time with such intimacy that it gave her the willies. The last time, those loose lips had almost seemed to drool. . . . Lora shuddered. Face it, she just didn't like the man. And she didn't trust him.

This time, however, Minelli hardly spared her or the

sleeping men a glance as, gun in hand, he made his way down to the cockpit and disappeared behind the torn curtain. Lora heard him thumping around, heard a faint whine and static, but she was hardly paying attention. Like an alert terrier, her mind was quivering with alarm as soon as it registered that Minelli—armed with a pistol—had returned alone. Where was Max? He had said that he might have to kill Minelli—had Minelli reached the same conclusion about Max? And carried out his plan more quickly? The mere idea of it made Lora's heart beat faster. She couldn't sit here and worry, she decided, she had to find out for herself. Carefully, she lifted Tunafish's massive head from her lap and placed it on one of the flotation cushions she had removed from a seat. In the process Tunafish's spaniel eyes opened.

"What . . ." He frowned at her for a moment, then his eyes narrowed and his face whitened. One hand made an abortive movement toward his splinted leg.

"I'm sorry I woke you," she began, when it occurred to her that she needed an ally. Tunafish could not move about, but maybe he could tell her that she was being silly. . . .

"Where's the boss?"

Tunafish did not appear to have lost any of his mental faculties despite the pain, Lora concluded as she looked into eyes that seemed aware as well as awake. Which was a relief. If something had happened to Max, if he was injured or—she hated to even think the word—dead, Tunafish would be the only one she could turn to. Surprising how, under the circumstances, she had so quickly come to feel she could trust him; with her life, if necessary, certainly with Max's.

"I don't know. That's what I want to find out. He left with Minelli—and Minelli's back. Without Max. And with a gun."

Tunafish had heard from Max what the plane carried, and

his opinion of Ortega had been even less elegantly expressed than Max's. At this new piece of information, Tunafish frowned. "Probably nothin' to worry about," he said finally. "Minelli's got no reason to harm him—yet. And believe me, lady, the boss is one tough dude. He can take care of himself. I can't see Minelli gettin' the drop on him."

"That gun . . ."

Tunafish shrugged. "I gave it to him myself, when the trouble started back in Mazatlán. Could be carryin' it out because of the jungle. I would myself. No tellin' what a man might run into out there."

"I'm worried." Lora muttered, and would have stood up if Tunafish hadn't caught her hand.

"Wait."

"I just want to see. . . ."

Tunafish shook his head. His hand tightened on hers. "Boss wouldn't want you runnin' around in the jungle. Dangerous. Besides, ain't nothin' you could do for him. If he's dead, he's dead, and if he ain't, he'll be back."

This way of looking at it did not soothe Lora, and she opened her mouth to tell him so when Max himself appeared, levering himself through the hole. Like Minelli, he carried his pistol in his hand.

"Minelli back?" he demanded as he stood upright. At Lora's frightened nod and gesture toward the cockpit, his face tightened. He made his way quickly toward where the rumble of Minelli's voice could now be heard.

Lora's head swiveled toward the sound—who on earth could Minelli be talking to?—just as there was a deafening burst of gunfire from behind the curtain. Lora's mouth opened as Tunafish, eyes widening, jerked her down on the floor beside him. DiAngelo jumped in his sleep and Max jerked the curtain back to reveal Minelli emptying the magazine of his pistol into the radio set in the control panel.

There was an instant of electric silence. Then, as Minelli straightened and turned, balancing on the balls of his feet and hefting the gun, Max pointed his own weapon straight at the other man's belly and demanded, "Who did you call?"

Minelli shrugged. As he looked down at the pistol Max held, his eyes were wary. Lora could see the tension in his fingers as he gripped his own gun.

"You're going to tell me, one way or another. Better start talking."

Minelli seemed to hesitate, then said with an assumption of ease, "No harm telling you, I suppose. I called some friends to come and pick us up. Seeing as how your transportation service leaves something to be desired."

"You told them about the dope, I suppose." Max sounded almost bored. Lora might have believed he was—if it hadn't been for the tension evident in the hard muscles of his back through the white sweatstained t-shirt.

"Suppose all you want. I'm not saying anything else."

Max stared at him. Lora could almost feel the prickles rise on her own neck under the icy ferocity of that look.

"Oh, I think you'll—" Max began, lifting the pistol with a cold certainty that made Lora's nerves scream.

"Drop it, Maxwell!" The hoarse command came from the seat just in front of Lora and Tunafish. Both their faces registered shock as DiAngelo, whom they had totally forgotten, rose rather unsteadily to his feet. In his hand he held a pistol, which he had trained on Max. Max, after one arrested look over his shoulder, slowly lowered his gun and then, on DiAngelo's repeated command, dropped it.

"Kick it over here." Minelli resumed control, grinning widely from Max to his buddy. "Well, well, well, Maxwell, the shoe's on the other foot, now, isn't it? You should've been nice while you had the chance. Back up.'' Minelli's voice was brutal as he stepped forward, gun at the ready, forcing Max to move back to where Lora knelt and Tunafish lay.

Lora's heart thumped painfully in her chest as Max slowly obeyed. Minelli would kill all of them for what lay in that cargo bay, she had not the slightest doubt.

When Max stood beside where Lora and Tunafish were frozen in position, Minelli said to DiAngelo, ''Check those two for guns.''

Max sent a single, quick glance down at them. Lora could see a muscle jumping in his jaw. His hands hung loose at his sides, as if he was having to force them not to clench into fists. Then DiAngelo was beside her, his pale blue eyes cold as he reached down to grab her arm and haul her to her feet. Lora shivered and closed her eyes with revulsion as his hands ran over her, slowly and with obvious relish. She thought of herself worrying about him, and wished with more venom than she had known she was capable of that he had died in the crash. The feel of his hands on her made her want to vomit. . . . But finally it was over, and he was stepping away from her and bending over Tunafish while she shuddered.

''Now, boss!'' The yell was Tunafish's, and after that things happened with lightning swiftness.

DiAngelo cursed and fell to the floor, helped by a sudden sweep of Tunafish's splinted leg. Max dived at Minelli just as his attention was distracted for that split second by Tunafish's shout and DiAngelo's fall. The force of Max's body bore Minelli to the floor and sent the gun flying. While those two wrestled, Tunafish and DiAngelo were grappling for the gun that DiAngelo had dropped. Lora screamed, then screamed again in automatic reaction. None of the men paid her the least attention. But even as she screamed her eyes were on

Minelli's gun. It had skittered across the cabin to come to rest under the rear pair of seats. She darted for it, scrabbling under the seats to get it. When her hand closed for it— gingerly!—she turned back to survey the fray. DiAngelo had the other pistol in his hands now, and Tunafish was forcing him to keep it pointed toward the ceiling. Max and Minelli had death grips on one another's throats.

"I've got a gun," she called clearly. She might as well not have spoken as the men continued their fight. Hesitating, she looked down at the ugly black weapon in her hand. What did she do now? She wasn't about to fire the damned thing— she'd undoubtedly hit either everyone or no one. Then she saw DiAngelo lift his foot and kick down hard into Tunafish's broken leg. Tunafish screamed, DiAngelo snatched at the pistol—and Lora pointed the hated gun skyward and, with a muttered prayer, pulled the trigger.

A deafening blast of gunfire brought all four men's eyes darting around as the noise made her wince and screw up her eyes. As they saw the gun in her hand—it kept spitting out bullets, and Lora realized that she still had her finger on the trigger—all four men, friends and foes alike, hit the dirt. Bullets tore through the metal fuselage over her head, and one whistled alarmingly close to her ear. She had forgotten about the possibility of ricochets. . . .

"For God's sake, let up on the trigger, Lora!" As Max's voice called to her with almost comical dismay, Minelli was on his feet and running toward the hole. Max dived for his legs, but missed, cursing as he hit his shoulder on the metal frame of a seat.

Gun in hand, Lora watched Minelli disappear from sight. There was no way that she was going to purposely shoot anyone, even Minelli, despite Max's and Tunafish's frenzied shouts. Seconds later Max was at her side, relieving her of the weapon and turning it on DiAngelo, who quickly subsided. Then it was all over—for the moment. Lora felt her knees quiver, and looked surprised as they slowly buckled beneath her.

XIV

"You all right?" Max hunkered down beside her, keeping a wary eye on DiAngelo while at the same time managing to spare her a glance of concern. His hand just touched her arm—and there it was, the jolt of electricity. Lora shivered. With all that had happened, she had almost forgotten the physical chemistry that ignited between them at the slightest touch. Or hoped that, now that she was no longer precisely his captive, it was a thing of the past. Stockholm Syndrome should no longer apply. . . .

Max felt her shiver and looked down at her, frowning. Lora met his eyes with a dazed look in her own. All her life, she had dreamed of a man who could make her bones turn to mush just by touching her. It was, she supposed, the ultimate female fantasy. But not this man! Please, not this man!

"Lora!"

Something in her expression must have alarmed him, because his hand moved up to her face and he lightly touched her cheek with his fingers. And there it was again, that frisson of pure animal attraction. Lora stared up into those eyes that were blacker than the night, at the harshly carved features and tough masculine mouth, and despaired.

"Boss! Look out!"

Tunafish's warning shout made Max jerk to attention. The pistol snapped up as his eyes sought DiAngelo, who had taken advantage of that moment of inattention to bolt for the hole. It was already too late. DiAngelo was at the hole, and there was no way that Max could stop him—except shoot. He raised the gun, aiming.

"Max, no!" Lora cried, horrified, and Max hesitated for that crucial split second. Then it was too late.

DiAngelo was gone. Max stared at a panorama of jungle that was all that was visible in the space where DiAngelo had just stood, his expression as unreadable as stone. Then, slowly, he turned his eyes back to Lora as he lowered the gun. The look he gave her was unfathomable. The black eyes were as impenetrable as the jungle itself.

"Cripes, boss, you let him get away!"

Lora was vaguely aware of Tunafish shaking his head in disgust as she stared back at Max. He returned her look for a long moment, unspeaking, then got abruptly to his feet.

"Are you all right?" he asked almost formally, his eyes hooded as he looked down at her where she knelt at his feet.

Lora was taken aback at the cold remoteness of his expression. He was looking at her as if she were a stranger, and one that he didn't particularly want to get to know. She stared into those unreadable eyes, and slowly nodded.

"I'm fine. It was just—the excitement, I think." At her words, something flared briefly in his eyes. They burned down into hers for a second, and then he turned abruptly away.

"You shoulda shot him." Tunafish was still bemoaning DiAngelo's escape as Max dropped to his knees beside him. "He and that bastard Minelli will be up to God knows what out there. One thing's sure, they'll be comin' after us. And the dope, and the money."

"I know it." Max laid what looked like gentle hands on the broken leg. DiAngelo's kick had knocked loose the makeshift splint. "We'll have to mount guard over the plane. I don't want them getting their hands on that stuff. It's our ticket out of here. Now, shut up for a minute, will you? The boards from those crates will do a lot better job than branches for your leg. I'll be right back." He laid a hand on Tunafish's shoulder, stood up, crossed to the hole, and jumped through it, all without sparing Lora so much as a glance.

She stared after him, then looked at Tunafish. Tunafish shrugged his ignorance of Max's behavior. Lora was still frowning as she crawled across to Tunafish's side.

When Max returned, he asked Lora to watch for DiAngelo and Minelli. She stood at the hole looking out over the teeming jungle, secretly thankful not to have to help. She liked Tunafish and she hated to see him in pain. And he was in pain. She heard him groan, and swear, and groan again as Max did what had to be done. When it was over at last, and Tunafish lay sweating profusely, propped up against the curving wall, Lora turned to look at them again. To her surprise, Max pulled a silver flask out of his pocket and offered it to his friend. Tunafish accepted it gratefully, uncapping the lid and taking a long swallow. He then offered it in turn to Lora and Max, both of whom refused, before settling back with a happier expression.

"That sure hit the spot. Where'd you get it?"

"Clemente had it on him."

Tunafish didn't reply, but took another quick swallow from

the flask. There was a brief silence, then Tunafish said slowly, "Those guys Minelli radioed—mob?"

Max shrugged. "Probably. The arrangements were that a boat would be waiting for them off Puerto Barrios in the Gulf of Honduras. My guess is that he made contact with whoever is on that boat."

"Mob," said Tunafish gloomily. "They'll have an army up here after this stuff. From what you said, it must be worth coming after."

There was another brief silence. "I imagine Ortega will be along, too. He'll want his property back. And the feds. They must have known, or guessed, what we were carrying. Seems like they were after us, after all, back there at that airport."

Tunafish grimaced. "Think they'll find us?"

Max looked grim. "Eventually. It might take them a while. Ortega knew the route we were taking, and knowing him I would guess that this plane is equipped with a homing device. He wouldn't let that much dope out of his care without some sort of insurance that it would turn up where it was supposed to. I imagine Minelli told whoever he was talking to where we took off from and where we intended to land, and how much flying time we had before we crashed. So they should have a pretty fair idea of the general area we're in. And I sent that damned mayday, so the feds will be hot on our trail. Ortega and the feds have a head start—they were probably monitoring us on radar when we went down—but for the kind of haul we're talking about here, I imagine the mob will do a pretty good job of playing catch up. In fact, they're probably all three hot on each other's tails right now. So it's just a matter of who gets here first: Minelli's pals, Ortega, or the feds."

"Shee-it." Tunafish pursed his lips in a silent whistle,

while Lora listened to this litany of disaster in wide-eyed silence.

"Look on the bright side," Max offered with the flickering of a grin. "If we weren't loaded down with all this dope, no one would give a damn where we were. At least we can be sure that someone will be coming after us."

"Yeah, the lions, the tigers and the alligators. It's just a matter of who swallows us up first." Tunafish rolled his eyes. "Man, we got to get out of here."

Max shook his head. "We can't walk out of these mountains. No way."

Tunafish looked at him steadily. "*You* could—and take Lora here with you."

"I'm not leaving you, pal."

"Don't be an ass, boss. Think about the lady. Whoever shows up first, it ain't goin' to be pretty."

"Lora?" Max turned to look at her where she still stood by the gaping hole. Those black eyes met hers steadily. "You heard. You're involved here, too. What do you say?"

Lora looked from him to Tunafish. The idea of being in the center of a maelstrom of violence was frightening, but also slightly unreal. What was real was the sweat on Tunafish's brow and the pain in his liquid brown eyes.

"I vote we stick together."

Max's hard eyes softened almost imperceptibly as they met hers, and then he was turning back to Tunafish.

"You heard her. I agree. So we stay."

Tunafish snorted. "I never knew you had a suicidal streak, boss."

"Just goes to show you don't know everything about me. Besides, I don't mean to get killed—none of us will. I have a plan."

"Oh, Lord." Tunafish rolled his eyes again. "Here we go.

Lora, hit him over the head for me. Everytime he has a plan, I wind up gettin' hurt. It was his idea to borrow the plane from Ortega. And—''

''There's no use raking up old grievances, pal. Come to think of it, I can recall a few ideas of yours that were real disasters. But that's neither here nor there. Everybody who's coming after us is going to be looking for the plane, right? If we stay with it, we'll be sitting ducks. But while I was scouting around this morning I found a cave. A lot of them, actually; the whole mountain is honeycombed with them. I think we ought to hole up there and take the dope with us. It's our ticket home. We're going to hide it—and we don't tell where it is until we're safely out of here.''

Tunafish nodded slowly. ''Makes sense.''

''Lora?''

''It makes sense to me, too. Only—what about the drugs? It seems wrong to just let Ortega or the mob have them, although I suppose the *federales* are all right—they're the police, after all.'' She brightened. ''If the others get here first, couldn't we just pour the drugs out?''

Both men gave her long looks. ''Honey, I can see you ain't never had any real dealin's with real bad men. They'd grind you up for hamburger if you did that.'' Tunafish shook his head at her naivete.

''We can't do that anyway. The dope is our life insurance policy. Ortega, the mob, the feds—they'd all kill their grand-mothers to get their hands on this much dope. You've got to realize that they're not just going to waltz into the jungle, find the empty plane, shrug their shoulders, and waltz out again. They're going to look for that dope—and us. And Ortega's the only one we can do business with. If the feds show up first, or Minelli's pals, we'll have to stay out of sight until Ortega gets here. If the feds get their hands on us we'll go to prison for a long time—yes, you too, Lora. Do you think they will believe you had nothing to do with this? You've had some experience with the way they think, so don't kid yourself. As for the mob, I'd say our chances of coming out of this with a whole skin are slim to none once the mob gets its hands on the dope. So we wait for Ortega. We can trust Ortega—to a point.''

Tunafish looked skeptical. ''I wouldn't trust that little runt across the street and back.''

Max looked at him. ''You got any better ideas?''

''No,'' Tunafish had to admit.

''Then that's what we'll do. Anyway, Ortega has no reason to kill us—unless he thinks he's made an enemy of me by tricking me into running the stuff. Ortega doesn't like having enemies running around loose if he can help it. Well, I'll just have to convince him that I don't hold a grudge. It shouldn't be too difficult—he's convinced that one day having a more than nodding acquaintance with an ex-DEA agent will pay off. Besides, he'll be more interested in getting his merchandise back than in us.''

''You hope,'' Tunafish snorted.

''Shut up, will you?'' Max said fiercely with a significant look at Lora, who was looking ever more alarmed. ''Everything's going to work out fine. But I think it would be better if I'm the only one who knows exactly where the dope is. That way, there'll be less chance of anything going wrong.''

''Yeah, like somebody torturin' the whereabouts of the dope out of us before you can make your deal.''

''Damn it, Tunafish!'' Max glared at his friend.

Tunafish looked apologetic. ''Sorry. Uh—you know some place to hide it? That's a lot of dope to just make disappear.''

''I found the perfect place. That's what gave me the idea.''

Max grinned suddenly at Tunafish. "You got your leg broken on purpose, didn't you, you bastard, so you wouldn't have to help me haul those crates up a mountain?"

"It was totally premeditated," Tunafish returned solemnly. "Well, boss, there's no point in sittin' around. You may as well get started."

"Yeah." Max got to his feet. Crouching so long must have hurt his knee, because he flexed it briefly, his mouth contorting in a grimace. But he quickly banished any sign of discomfort when he saw Lora's eyes on him, and turned back to Tunafish. "You feel up to standing guard over the stuff here? All you have to do is sit in the shade with a pistol."

Tunafish looked insulted. "What do you think I am, some kind of pansy? I can do anything you can—except walk, and maybe some other things I ain't thought of yet."

Max grinned. "Just asking. Okay, you keep watch here and I'll move the cargo up into the cave. Lora, you'll stay with Tunafish."

"But I can help." While she might not be able to lift as much as he could, there was no reason why she couldn't carry lighter loads. If he did it all by himself, it would take him hours. . . .

"You stay with Tunafish." It was a brusque order. Lora's eyebrows lifted at the highhandedness of it. Her mouth opened to protest, but Tunafish forestalled her.

"I don't need no babysitter. And you need someone to ride shotgun for you."

Max looked from one to the other of them. They stared back at him with identical expressions of determination. His mouth moved wryly.

"Whatever you say, both of you. But Lora, it's a steep climb and I'm going to have my hands full. Don't expect me

to help you.'' His voice was much cooler when he addressed
her.

Lora lifted her chin at him. "Fine."

"Let's get on with it, then. Tunafish, put your arm around
my shoulders. Lora, get under his other arm."

XV

It was almost dark by the time Max finally got the contents of the cargo bay up the mountainside and into the cave he had found. The work was backbreaking, and Max had, of necessity, done it all himself. Lora's job had been to walk along beside him with a pistol in her hand, in case Minelli or DiAngelo should take it into their heads to jump them. As it happened, they had encountered nothing scarier than a foraging anteater, which made Lora jump but didn't count as threatening. Lora was so nervous she was not sure that it wouldn't have been a relief to have Minelli and DiAngelo stage an ambush, just to get it over with.

The cave was about half a mile up the mountain, situated so that it overlooked much of the jungle valley below, including the site of the crashed plane, although the thick quilt of treetops hid the plane itself from view. It took more than three dozen trips through the dense jungle undergrowth and over a steep, narrow path (made by goats according to

Max) up through the rocks before the job was finished. Lora was exhausted as she stood armed guard over the entrance to the cave while Max made one final trip back down to the plane to get Tunafish. All the dope was inside, but he had told her not to enter. He had a surprise for both her and Tunafish, he said. Lora didn't much trust his surprises. She didn't know what worried her more: the dark, echoing, hopefully empty cave at her back, or the possibility of Minelli and DiAngelo appearing. She would shoot them, if necessary, she told herself, fingering the trigger of the pistol and praying she wouldn't be put to the test. To be perfectly honest, she wasn't sure she could.

When at last Max came into sight with Tunafish slung over his shoulder, Lora heaved a sigh of relief. She walked forward quickly, meaning to help them.

"For God's sake, don't shoot us." Max sounded edgy, and Lora was affronted until she looked down at the gun. With Max in view, it had no longer seemed necessary to keep a deathgrip on it, so she had let it slump and its nose was, to her chagrin, pointed directly at the center of Tunafish's broad back, which happened to be covering Max's heart. Even she knew better than to point a gun of any description, much less one that she knew was loaded, at anyone. . . .

"Sorry," she said, and made no protest as Max reached out with his free hand and removed the pistol from her grasp, tucking it into the waistband of his jeans as he continued to help Tunafish toward the cave. Tunafish was sweating profusely, and if ever a black man could be said to be white under the dark pigmentation of his skin, Tunafish was that man. His complexion was a chalky gray. . . .

Lora could perceive no way she might help, so she trailed along behind, feeling useless. Worse, she felt like a burden. She was more helpless than Tunafish in this hostile environment, and without Tunafish's excuse of a broken leg. Max was already carrying Tunafish inside the mouth of the cave, and Lora followed glumly, scrambling over the loose shale. It took a few minutes for her eyes to adjust to the cool darkness, but when they did they widened.

All around her, flat sedimentary rocks rose in tiers to form a huge, round cavern. The ceiling must have risen to a height of thirty or more feet. Lora cast an uneasy glance up into the lofty darkness, at the stalactites like huge stone teeth dripping from the ceiling, and tried not to imagine what else could be up there. She was sure she didn't want to know. Max had built a fire close to the mouth of the cave, and had stuck leaf-wrapped sticks into clefts in the wall to serve as torches for illumination. The effect was eery, as if they had gone back thousands of years in time. On the walls, faded paintings of feathered warriors with flattened foreheads and ferocious dark eyes seemed to leap as the flames threw shadows over them. Lora stared at them, moving closer.

"Are they real?" she asked, scarcely daring to believe what she was seeing.

Max had gotten Tunafish settled, seated on a rocky shelf with his back propped against the wall, and was watching her. "Authentic Mayan cave drawings," he confirmed. "Probably over a thousand years old."

"That's unbelievable," Lora breathed, eyes wide as she pondered the ancient beings who had stood just where she was standing centuries before. She took another step forward, and something crunched beneath her feet. Looking down, she saw that the smooth stone floor was littered with broken bits of pottery. From the same Mayans, she presumed, crouching to touch some reverently. She glanced around to see what other ancient wonders waited for her discovery. There was nothing else. Literally nothing.

"What did you do with the drugs?" Her voice echoed her amazement. She had watched with her own eyes as he had carried crate after crate of bagged white powder inside.

Max shook his head. "We have an agreement, remember?"

Lora knew she was better off not knowing, so she didn't ask again. But she wondered madly.

"I'm going to go back and see what else I can rummage up—maybe there are some blankets or something in the plane's overhead compartments. I won't be long."

With that brief comment, and after wordlessly handing her back the pistol, Max disappeared back into the deepening gloom of the jungle. Lora looked after him with a frown. He was so distant with her—had been ever since she had made that instinctive protest against him shooting DiAngelo. Was he angry at her? She hated the idea of Max being angry with her. He was all she had, out here in this savage wilderness. She realized that she depended on him utterly, and didn't much like the realization. It wouldn't do to let herself come to need him. . . . Was this a part of Stockholm Syndrome, too? Lora wished she could remember more of what she had read on the subject, but at the time she had never expected to find herself in this situation. But something was happening between her and Max, had been happening ever since she had first laid eyes on him, in fact, and she had to know what it was. She was too sensible, too sane and levelheaded to get involved with a man like him—so why was she so worried about his safety as she watched him disappear into the night? Why did she care that he might be angry with her?

"You like him, don't you?" This was Tunafish, speaking in a more serious voice than she had yet heard him use. Lora turned to look at him, having to strain to see him in the deepening shadows.

"Who?" The question was purely defensive, and at Tunafish's

skeptical look she realized that she sounded like a coy teenager. She smiled wryly, and inclined her head. "Sometimes."

"He's a good man. One of the best."

"Have you known him long?" She shouldn't want to know about him, Lora thought. It was safer not to know too much. She didn't want this disconcerting physical attraction between them to go any further. It would be disastrous if she started to see him as a man she could learn to care for. . . . But she couldn't stop the question. She wanted to know all she could about the enigma that was John Robert Maxwell, whether it was prudent or not.

"Since we were kids. We grew up together in Houston. We kind of lost track of each other after I dropped out of school and Max went on, but we met up again in 'Nam. He was my C.O. over there for almost three years. When Bravo Company got him, he was a lieutenant right out of college, green as grass, and if I hadn't stood up for him there were a few times that some of the guys might have blown his ass off—uh, sorry. But he learned fast, and when he did, there wasn't a better officer over there. Most of us got out alive because of him."

Lora moved closer without even realizing that she had done so. "He—you both—fought in Vietnam? In the army?"

Tunafish nodded. "We ended up in Army Intelligence. Recon work, mostly. Behind the enemy lines, real hush-hush stuff. But relatively safe. At least, if we did our job right. We were not supposed to let the gooks know we were there while we found out what they were up to, and if they didn't know we were there they couldn't shoot us. Elementary, huh? Only it didn't always work."

"Were you wounded?" She was standing right beside him now, and as she spoke she unconsciously dropped to her knees at his side. The fact that she was nominally supposed to be on watch had completely faded from her mind. The gun dangled unnoticed from her hand, its barrel resting on the cold stone floor.

Tunafish grinned at her, the whites of his eyes and the gleam of his teeth very bright in the darkness. "Everybody who served in 'Nam was wounded, I think. Don't ask me where I got hit, 'cause I ain't tellin'. It's downright undignified. Max got it in the knee. Shrapnel. That's why he limps. He's lucky he didn't lose that leg."

Lora was silent for a moment. "Tunafish—have you heard of Mei Veng?"

The grin disappeared from Tunafish's face as abruptly as if someone had wiped it away. "What do you know about Mei Veng?" The question was harsh; his eyes on her were wary.

"Max mentioned it in connection with killing people."

"Yeah." Tunafish's face was very bleak. Lora waited, but he said nothing else, just stared off into the distance as though he was seeing something in the darkness that she could not.

"Tunafish?" Her voice seemed to surprise him, because he almost started as his eyes turned back to her. "Tell me about it. Please."

Tunafish looked at her for a moment, unspeaking. Then he shook his head.

"I'm real surprised Max even said the name. As far as I know, he's never told anyone about it. We've never talked about it between us. It's not the kind of thing you talk about."

"Tunafish, please. I want to know. I—need to know."

Tunafish stared at her for a long time. Then his eyes moved again to look out at the infinite darkness beyond the mouth of the cave.

"Mei Veng was a village in 'Nam. Little village, you know, with old men and women and little kids. We were checking it for reds, it was supposed to be sympathetic toward the Vietcong, when this little kid in a diaper walks up to some of our guys. Well, we were ready to shoot anyone who made a move, but who wants to shoot a little kid? Only the kid had a grenade stuffed in his diaper. It blew him to hell along with three of our guys. That's where Max caught the shrapnel. Then all hell broke loose.''

He stopped. His body was tense beside hers. Lora noticed that sweat had reappeared on his upper lip.

"Yes?'' she said weakly. Did she really want to know anymore?

"We killed them all,'' he said simply, staring out into the night. "Every living soul in that village. We killed them all.''

"Dear God,'' Lora breathed with instinctive horror. Her mind shied away from picturing the scene that he was obviously recalling so graphically, but she could not stop the images from forming. Blood and death—and children. . . .

"Dear God,'' she said again. She had wanted to know about Max, and she was well served that what she had learned was ugly, ugly. But then, war was ugly, it was hell they said. How could she, who had never been in one, make judgments? She didn't want to. She didn't even want to think about it. Her eyes refocused on Tunafish, who was sweating profusely as he stared unseeing out into the night. He looked like a man who was picturing unthinkable horrors . . . Her conscience smote her. She had forced him to recall this. Her arms went instinctively around his shoulders. He patted her arm.

"It's all right,'' he said.

Lora slowly withdrew her arms and they sat without speaking for a long while. Then she asked slowly, "Is he married, Tunafish?'' The question seemed to come out of nowhere, but as she said it she realized that the possibility had been troubling her for some time. And now she needed to know.

Tunafish's face recovered its customary good humor. "I ain't sure I should answer that. You better ask the boss."

"Please, Tunafish! Tell me. I—need to know."

"No, he ain't married. He was, a long time ago, but he got a divorce. He was kinda messed up for a while there after 'Nam, and I guess she couldn't take it. Anyway, somethin' went wrong, and she left."

"They didn't have any children?"

"No. No kids."

A ticklish feeling that Lora eventually identified as relief curled round and round in her stomach. She had been afraid, really afraid, to get an answer to her question. What would she have done if he had had a wife and half a dozen children tucked away back in the States? Nobly tried to forget this sexual attraction that pulled her to him despite the best efforts of her common sense? But she had tried that already, and it hadn't worked. Two dozen wives with six kids each probably wouldn't have made any difference to the way he affected her.

"So how did he—and you—get into this line of work?" Her tone was considerably lighter as she asked that, and Tunafish too seemed to relax, leaning back against the curving wall and reaching into his pocket for a pack of cigarettes and a lighter.

"From very different roads," Tunafish said, chuckling as he lit the cigarette. "After 'Nam, after he'd recovered a little, Max went to work for the government. Undercover DEA. There came a time when he needed an expert to help him with a bust, so he came lookin' for me. See, I went into the family business when I got out of 'Nam. My granddaddy was a burglar, my daddy was a burglar, and I was makin' a pretty decent livin' at it myself. But then Max—uh, persuaded—me that crime doesn't pay, and I went to work for him. Doin' the same thing, burglin', only it was legal. Then this fool kid we were watchin', hopin' he would lead us to the big boys, got busted in Mexico for smugglin' in a trunkful of pot. He was only seventeen, and if you ain't never seen a Mexican prison you don't want to. Max felt bad about that—we could have busted the kid ourselves a month before and our court system wouldn't have done much to a kid his age. Max felt kind of responsible, so we went in and got him out. And word kinda got around, and people started offerin' Max money—big money—to get their kids out of jail. And here we are.'' Tunafish looked around, looked down at his leg, and then looked at Lora before grimacing comically. "I shoulda stuck with burglin'. At least then I ate good.''

"Quit yer bitchin', Cascieroli.''

The voice was Max's, and Lora looked up with surprise as he walked into the cave and dumped a pile of gear on the floor. She had been so absorbed in what Tunafish was telling her that she hadn't heard him approach. "I've got some good news; Ortega did put a homing device on that plane. I found it in the right engine. So we should be found before too long. And I got something for us to eat. There's a banana grove out there.''

"Bananas!'' Tunafish said, groaning, while Max grinned.

"Unless you'd rather eat a monkey. I've heard they're pretty tasty.''

"You're joking.'' Lora was afraid he wasn't.

"I'm not. If we're here long, we may be eating monkeys. Tunafish here won't last long on a diet of bananas. Neither will I.'' To prove his point, Max reached down into the bundle at his feet and tossed a banana to Tunafish, who caught it, and another to Lora, who didn't.

"You'll just have to find something else. Than monkeys, I

mean. They're almost human," Lora said firmly as she scrambled after her banana. It was small and green, but it was surprisingly good, she thought as she finished it in a few quick bites. She hadn't realized how hungry she was. Tunafish, too, for all his groaning, finished his quickly. So did Max. Then they all ate another. When the fruit was gone, and a comfortably full feeling had replaced the hollowness in her belly, Lora went to help Max sort out the gear he had brought back with him.

By the flickering firelight Lora was able to see that he had brought three blankets, two pillows, an unopened bottle of whiskey, a carton of cigarettes, the first aid kit, and a flashlight all wrapped up in a fourth blanket. Max stood as Lora sorted through his booty, running his hands over the stubble on his chin and looking around.

"We need more fuel for the fire," he said, and before either Lora or Tunafish could say anything he turned and left the cave again, returning moments later with an armful of brush and a few branches, which he proceeded to pile to one side of the cave's mouth.

"Any more matches?" he asked, displaying a nearly empty pack which he removed from his jeans pocket. Tunafish wordlessly displayed his lighter.

"Good. Here's water." He displayed an empty whiskey bottle filled with clear liquid, which he set beside the pile of brush.

"Looks like we're in business," Tunafish drawled.

"Not quite," Max replied, while out in the jungle a jaguar screamed. Lora shivered, and moved a little closer to Tunafish, who was closest. The dangers they faced were only just now beginning to come home to her.

Max went out again to gather more branches to make beds. He was gone more than half an hour, by Lora's calculation, and she was imagining all kinds of horrible fates that might have befallen him when he returned, the blanket on his back filled with cut tree limbs and leaves.

"Check those for ticks," he said to Lora, indicating the leaves as he dropped the bundle on the ground and proceeded to extract several of the cut branches. Lora stared at the jumble of leaves, horrified. The thought of ticks in her bed made her shiver. While Tunafish steadily sipped at Clemente's bottle of whiskey—Max had warned him to ration it, because the quarter that was left in there and the other bottle Max had found on the plane was all the alcohol they had—Lora shudderingly checked the bedding for invaders and Max made three pallets of branches, leaves, and blankets. When that was done he joined Lora and Tunafish, who were sitting against the wall near the fire.

"I'm going to bed for a while. Lora, you wake me in a couple of hours. I'll take the first watch. Tunafish, you can have the second."

"What about me?" Lora asked, indignant that she had been left out. It had never occurred to her that someone would have to stand guard all night, but now, with Max's words, she wondered that it had not. If all three of them slept at once, what was to stop Minelli and DiAngelo from creeping into the cave and blasting them as they slept—or that ravening jaguar she had heard from turning them into a midnight snack?

"I told you, you're on for the next two hours. But if you see or hear anything, you wake me up. Don't start shooting. From what I've seen so far, you shoot worse than you drive, if that's possible."

"Oh, shut up." She glared at him.

Tunafish grinned wanly. His leg in its makeshift splint stuck out stiffly before him; his face was drawn and gray.

Even his eyes were tinged with gray. He was suffering, and his face showed it even if he refused to say so.

"Come on, pal, let me help you to bed. You need to get some sleep, if you can." This was addressed to Tunafish, who slanted a look up at him.

"Yeah, all right," he grunted. Then he looked at Lora. "Got any more of that aspirin?" In answer, she scrambled to her feet and went to fetch the bottle of tablets from the first aid kit. Tunafish grimaced as she shook two tablets out onto his palm. Before he could swallow them, Max tossed one of the plastic bags of dope in his lap.

"Smack is the best painkiller in the world," he said matter-of-factly. "Just use a little when you have to."

"Thanks, man." Tunafish looked from the bag to Max's shadowed face. "For now, I think I'll try the aspirin." He swallowed the two in his hand, then tucked the bag of dope between two rocks. They said nothing more about it as Max caught Tunafish under his armpits and half-supported, half-carried him to one of the beds he had made of branches and leaves. Wrapped up in a blanket, his injured leg carefully supported by a strategically placed pillow, Tunafish still looked miserably uncomfortable. He was in pain, Lora knew.

"Here." Max handed her his pistol. She took it gingerly, careful to keep it pointed toward the mouth of the cave. "Like I said, don't try to fire it unless it's an emergency. If you hear or see anything the least bit suspicious, yell and I'll be right beside you. Understand?"

"Yes, sir," Lora said, snapping him a mocking salute. He gave orders like he was born to it, which was fine, as long as he didn't think she was born to take them. In this particular situation, she was willing to do as he said to a certain extent, but she didn't want him getting the idea that he could bark orders at her like a drill sargeant.

He eyed her grimly, clearly not much liking her flippant response, but all he said was: "And don't forget to wake me in about two hours."

"I won't. Sir."

This earned her a scowl as he turned away to wrap himself in a blanket and lie down on the bed he had made. The three beds were close together, with not more than two feet of space separating one from the other. Max had chosen to sleep closest to the entrance, and his bed was not far from where she sat by the small fire. The bed in the center, complete with blanket and pillow, was empty, and Lora presumed it was for her. Tunafish lay on his back with eyes closed on the other side of the empty bed. Lora doubted that Tunafish was asleep, but from the soft snores that were already assaulting her ears, Max was. The man seemed to have a positive genius for falling asleep whenever and wherever he chose.

Lora stared at the long form that lay curled with its back to her. Shoulders hunched, rough black head pillowed on a bare forearm, the rest of him shrouded in a nondescript brown blanket, and snores rattling from his throat every fifteen seconds, he still appealed to her. She wanted nothing so much as to crawl over to that bedroll and curl up beside him. . . . Lora remembered how his hands had felt on her body, how his lips had felt on hers, and shivered. What would it be like to make love with him—really make love with him, with both of them naked and her free to touch him as she liked? The very thought made a frisson of heat quiver up from her loins. It would be heaven—but the heaven would, eventually, lead to hell. For her, not him. She knew herself well enough to know that an affair based on nothing more than sex, however passionate, however longed for, was not for her. She needed more than that. She needed to know that he cared for her as a person, not just a female body, and the only one around at that. He was attracted to her, she knew, but she feared that his attraction might have its roots in nothing more than proximity, his hormones responding instinctively to the only game in town.

Lora thought over what Tunafish had told her about Max. He was divorced, he had served in Vietnam and been profoundly affected by the experience, he had worked for the government as an undercover agent, and had gotten into his present line of work because he felt responsible for some boy. And he hated drugs, yet he had given Tunafish a bag of heroin to ease his pain. Taken all together, the facts added considerable shadings to the tough-guy image he projected. They pointed to a sensitive, caring man hiding beneath a macho shell. Lora pondered that at some length, comparing all that she had learned during her experience as his captive with that conclusion. And, she decided, it fit pretty well. He had frightened her, but he hadn't really hurt her when she had provoked him a dozen times. Most men would have floored her if she had punched them in the nose—to say nothing of wrecking the car, kicking him in his bad knee, and trying repeatedly to escape. The kind of man she had thought him to be would have raped her, she thought. Max hadn't even taken advantage of her obvious attraction to him to so much as make a pass. She was honest enough to admit that she had instigated that encounter in Ortega's bed. . . . Even after that, he had not taken what another man might have decided he had earned. In all honesty, she almost wished he had. If he had taken her, then, she could have told herself that it was against her will. And that was much safer than admitting how much she wanted him. . . .

Something had changed. Lora frowned, alert now. She didn't know what it was, but something had changed in the atmosphere around her. Had her subconscious sensed a sound that she hadn't consciously heard? Or . . . Her hand tightened on the gun, and she turned her head to call for Max. He still slept with his back to her, huddled into his blanket. As she looked at him, loathe to wake him for what might be no more than a foolish fancy, it struck her that he was no longer snoring. That was what had changed. The cave was now silent except for the harsh rasp of Tunafish's breathing. Looking over the bedrolls at Tunafish, Lora thought that he might now be asleep.

Max was moving his head, and then his arms and legs, in small jerky movements that made Lora wonder if he was dreaming. Then he rolled over on his back, his head, no longer pillowed on his arm, tossing on the blanket beneath it. She frowned, watching him. He was scowling in his sleep, and a muscle was working at the corner of his mouth. And then, as she watched, he sat bolt upright. His eyes opened to stare blankly at nothing. The muscles in his arms clenched beneath the short sleeves of his t-shirt.

"No!" he cried, his voice hoarse. "Oh, God, no!"

Lora jumped at his cry, staring at him. He was shaking . . . It was a nightmare, she realized as she abandoned her post and the gun to rush to his side.

"Max!" she said, taking hold of his shoulder and giving it a hard shake. "Max, wake up!" His face turned toward her as she knelt beside him, and for a moment she thought she had gotten through to him. But his open eyes were still blind. . . .

"Max!" she said again, and then his arms were coming around her, pulling her onto his lap, and he was hugging her to him as if she was the only warmth in a cold world. His hold was rough and painful, the strength of it threatening to crack her ribs, but she didn't care. Her heart ached for the pain that had caused him to reach for her. She wrapped her arms around his neck, holding him close, her hands coming up to stroke that rough black head. It burrowed into her shoulder. To her horror, she thought she heard the ragged indrawing of a sob.

"Max, darling," she whispered into his hair. "Max, it's all right. It's all right, darling. Shhh."

He continued to hold her so tightly she could hardly breathe, his arms imprisoning her like a straitjacket, the muscles of his thighs hard beneath her. Over his head she saw that Tunafish had awakened, and was watching them from beneath beetled brows. Lora held a finger to her lips when he would have spoken, and continued to stroke Max's hair. A tenderness like nothing she had ever known crept over her as she held him, this big, hard, rough-and-tough man, like a child in her arms. He needed her. . . .

"Shhh, now . . ." She was crooning to him when he suddenly stiffened. She felt the change in him with every nerve in her body. Abruptly, he sat up, half a head taller than her even though she sat on his lap, and stared right into her eyes. He was awake, she saw, and started to smile at him, all gentleness and concern. He glared at her, those obsidian eyes crystal hard beneath ferocious brows. Lora stared back at him in surprise.

"What the hell do you think you're doing?" he growled.

"You had a nightmare," she said, thinking that he still did not understand.

"So what the hell is it to you?" he demanded roughly, his arms coming to remove her suddenly limp ones from around his neck and almost fling them back at her. He moved, practically dumping her off his lap, and got to his feet. His eyes as they moved over her looked like they hated her.

"Max . . ." Hurt surprise was in her voice, and his face tightened.

"I'll stand watch now. Go to bed." And with that he scooped up the gun and strode from the cave, leaving Lora to stare after him with wounded eyes. Tunafish whistled softly, and Lora turned to look at him.

"What did I do?"

He shook his head. "You comforted him. There are times when a man just can't take comfort, especially from a woman. And especially from a woman he likes like Max likes you."

XVI

He was in trouble. Max sat on a stone near the edge of the small, spring-fed pool he had found, and skipped a much smaller rock across the gleaming blue surface of the water as he faced the fact. It was just after noon of the following day, and he had been out looking for food when he stopped to quench his thirst with a couple of handfuls of water. As he stared down into it, the damned fathomless quality of the pool had reminded him of Lora's eyes. He cursed softly, hating the poetic thought. He never had poetic thoughts. They were as foreign to his nature as curses were to hers. He couldn't understand what was happening to him. She wasn't beautiful; he hadn't even thought she was more than passably attractive when he had first climbed into her car. And most of the women who had, in one way or another, left their mark on his life were pretty, at least, and exciting. He liked his women exciting. Lora certainly couldn't be described as exciting, not by any stretch of the imagination. She had a great body, granted, a body that he would give quite a bit to have naked and writhing beneath him at that precise moment, but though physically it was the match of any he'd possessed, Lora herself did not match her body. She was about as exciting as homemade bread. And he was a man used to a steady diet of chili sauce.

Maybe that was her attraction for him. Maybe, as old age crept up on him—he was thirty-seven, after all, only three years from forty—he was ready for milk instead of whiskey. Maybe he needed a change of pace. A prim little schoolteacher from the cornfields of Kansas, to be exact. Max thought of the last lady who had figured prominently in his life, and had to grin; whatever else Conchita was, she was certainly no lady. She was hot and wild and always ready, a tempestuous Latina with masses of curling black hair and eyes as dark as his own. And a body—Max thought of that body with the appreciation of a connoisseur. Her body was womanly and ripe, just the way he liked his women to be. Though, he reflected, it wasn't any more voluptuous than Lora's. . . .

The comparison annoyed him. What the hell was he doing, sitting out here on a rock in the middle of nowhere mooning about a woman who clearly regarded him as a cross between Al Capone and Richard Speck? Oh, she was hot for him, he knew. It would be damned easy to take her to bed if he wanted to. Max grinned without much humor. If he wanted to! Who was he kidding? He was dying to take her to bed, hungry to take her to bed, physically aching to take her to bed—but it went against the grain to make passionate love to a woman who looked at him at least half the time as if he'd just crawled out from under the nearest rock.

That was partly his fault, he acknowledged, but the acknowledgment didn't make him feel any better. All right, so he had kidnapped her, and scared her a little in the process—what else could he have done under the circumstances? He was running for his life at the time, and it hadn't been a moment to be too particular about his methods. If he had it to do over again, he would have done everything precisely the same. . . .

Well, not everything. He would have made her. He'd had lots of chances, and he'd blown every one of them. When, for example, partly to teach her a lesson and partly to get her out of those damned wet clothes that she was afraid to take off in case she incited him to rape her, he'd stripped her naked and tied her to the bed. . . . Max thought of how she'd looked naked, her lush, creamy body stretched helplessly against the brightly patterned blanket, her eyes as they stared up at him frightened and at the same time fascinated. . . . No matter what she probably would have yelled afterward, it wouldn't have been rape. He could have had her wanting him in a matter of seconds, but something had held him back. What? A sense of decency, perhaps? Max quickly rejected that. If he'd ever had a sense of decency, it had vanished long ago.

So why hadn't he fucked the hell out of her that morning at Ortega's? That was the real question, the one that had been eating away at him ever since. She'd wanted it that morning, been as hot as Conchita at her horniest. He'd woken to find her rubbing her butt (crammed into those skintight blue jeans, another ridiculous precaution on her part against rape) against his crotch, savoring his hardness. Max thought about how soft her skin had felt beneath his hands, the way her breasts had overflowed in his palms, the stiffness of her nipples beneath his questing fingers, her soft moans of pleasure. He had given her much pleasure. . . . Max pictured her as she had been then, her back to him, her head thrown back as she writhed and moaned with excitement. . . . He could see her, smell her, feel her wetness. . . . The mere memory made him hard as a spike. Just like he had been then. But though he clearly had had every right after that, though he knew he could have had her moaning for more in a matter of minutes, he had allowed the loathing in her eyes after he had pleasured her and she had come to herself again to stop him from doing what he had, at that moment, wanted to do more than anything in the world. He was not used to women looking at him like he was a pile of fly-covered shit. . . .

She had been horny, and she had used him to get off on. That was the unvarnished truth of that incident. He had realized it the moment he had seen that look of revulsion on her face as she floated back down to earth and remembered exactly who and what he was. The knowledge had angered him so much that he had been stopped in his tracks. Like a fool . . . If he had it to do over again, he would drill her until she fainted from exhaustion, and to hell with how she looked at him. But that was the trouble with life: one never got to do anything over again. Do something once, and it was carved in stone.

He could still have her, he knew. Anytime. It would require no work at all on his part. She would fall like a stone if he so much as kissed her cheek. She wanted him every bit as badly as he wanted her, if not more. So what the hell was holding him back?

Max knew the answer to that even as he asked himself the question. He hadn't made a woman like her in years. A nice woman, a lady. Not since he'd last made love to Marybeth, his ex-wife. Sweet little Marybeth, whom he'd married just after he got out of 'Nam and who, in the course of a few months, had torn him up as badly as ever the Vietcong had. She'd wanted too much of him. He hadn't been able to give her a steady, solid husband with a nine-to-five job, a nice house in the suburbs, two point five kids. . . . She had wanted a rock to lean on, and at the time he had needed a rock himself. What she hadn't wanted was a husband who woke up in the middle of the night screaming with nightmares, who broke into tears at the drop of a hat, who limped and shied at every sudden noise and couldn't hold a job even as a grill cook at a McDonald's. . . . He had known he was a failure as a husband, known that Marybeth was unhappy, and he hadn't even much cared. Her very gentleness had goaded him to hurt her. And when he'd said the nastiest, most hurtful thing that had come to his mind and watched the tears drip down her cheeks, he hadn't even felt like the bastard he knew he was. He'd just felt angry with her for marrying him. She should have known what she wanted, should have known that he wouldn't fit the bill. She'd been over twenty-one, after all. But of course, women didn't have that much sense. Women—ladies, in particular—all seemed to want white knights and heroes, and he was fresh out of heroics—then and now. And that was the reason he was wary of Lora: like Popeye, he was what he was and that's all that he was. He wanted her like hell—but just for a little while, just until he got his fill of screwing her. While she—he knew her type. She would hate herself if she had sex without being in love, so she would sooner or later convince herself she was in love with him. Then she would want commitment, marriage and kids, and a house and a job for him . . . God, no! He wasn't falling into that trap. Not again.

There was another reason, too, although he didn't like to admit it even to himself: with Lora, he was vulnerable. And he hated being vulnerable. He hated needing anyone or anything. If life had taught him just one lesson, it was the value of self-sufficiency. And Lora was making him feel less self-sufficient than usual. Last night, when he had had the nightmare again—he hadn't had the damned thing in years, it must have been seeing all that dope that had brought it back—he had welcomed her arms around him like a baby welcomes its mother's. God, he had actually cried in her arms. . . . The thought made him sick to his stomach. When he had recovered sufficiently to realize what he was doing, he had been horrified—and even more horrified to discover how good it felt to be held by her, comforted by her. She brought out a side of himself that he thought life had stamped out of him, and it frightened him. He didn't need her, didn't want to need her, didn't want anything from her except a little sex. He certainly didn't want her motherly comfort or her pity—or, if she should talk herself into it, her love.

The very idea made Max jump off the rock and start to stride away from the pool. He had taken only a few steps when he became aware of a discordance in the atmosphere. There was a faint, almost imperceptible noise behind him. Max heard it, and his body stiffened in preparation. He was too canny a jungle fighter to show that he had heard—whatever it was would be on him in an instant. Instead, he trained his every nerve toward the faint rustle of the undergrowth and continued to walk, poised and ready.

The faint sounds behind him continued. A twig cracked, then another. This was no animal stalking its prey. The movements were too clumsy. Therefore it almost had to be Minelli or DiAngelo, or both. He had been expecting an ambush sooner or later. . . .

"Maxwell."

To his surprise, DiAngelo stepped out from behind a tree dead in his path. Funny, he hadn't been expecting that—they were more clever than he'd thought. DiAngelo held a pistol, and Max remembered that he had escaped with one. And that pistol was aimed straight at his own heart.

"What do you want, DiAngelo?" Max was alert but calm. Clearly audible footsteps told him that Minelli was walking up behind him, making no effort to conceal his presence now.

"Guess." DiAngelo smiled evilly, the grin splitting his thin face. Minelli reached around him to pull the pistol from his waistband.

Now was the time, Max knew. Now, while Minelli was close. With two of them, he would have to make it fast and good. For a split second, Max wondered if his body was up to it. The last time he had tried it, during his stint with the DEA, his knee had thrown his timing off. But then he'd only had one opponent, so timing hadn't been crucial. In this case, with two fit men and a pistol trained on him, he'd better get it right. Or die . . .

He caught Minelli's reaching arm, jerked him around in front of him, and chopped down hard on the man's neck with the side of his hand. Minelli crumpled without a sound. The pistol DiAngelo held blasted, but Max was already diving beneath the line of fire. The bullets whistled harmlessly over his flying back as his head sank with a satisfying thunk into DiAngelo's cadaverous belly. DiAngelo toppled backward with a bellow. While he was still recovering his senses, Max performed a particularly nasty maneuver on his balls. He had used that trick a time or two before, and it had never failed to incapacitate. It didn't fail this time, either.

Max rolled off DiAngelo, who was gasping for air and rolling about on the ground in agony. Glancing over his shoulder, he saw that Minelli was just beginning to come to. Max scooped up the pistol, stationed himself so that he could cover Minelli and DiAngelo impartially, and waited. He could not help a pardonable pride that, despite being out of practice and having the disadvantage of a bum knee, he had not forgotten his training.

"You bastard!" This was Minelli, who was rubbing the side of his neck and glowering at Max.

"Easy, boy." Max waved the pistol at him and Minelli subsided, sitting down heavily on the mulch-covered ground and rubbing his neck with a groan.

"Oh, God, I think you've crippled me." This moan came from DiAngelo, who was still lying on the ground clutching his balls, although he had quit squirming like a worm on a hook.

"Probably." If Max sounded indifferent, it was because he felt indifferent.

"What are you going to do to us?" This was Minelli again, looking up at him apprehensively. Max pursed his lips and lifted his eyebrows, but didn't say anything.

"You can't kill us!"

Minelli sounded alarmed, as well he should be, Max thought. Every instinct he possessed warned him to shoot both of them here and now, before they could cause anymore trouble. If he didn't, if he let them live, they would cause him no end of headaches. He was as sure of that as he was that the sun would come up in the morning. But there was a problem: he was, to a certain degree, responsible for Minelli's and DiAngelo's well-being. He had been paid, well paid, not only to break them out of jail, but also to deliver them in one piece to whoever was waiting at Puerto Cortés. Of course, the situation had changed drastically, but he still had his reputation to think about. To date, he had never failed to deliver the goods as promised and paid for.

He scowled, and his fingers tightened on the pistol. Minelli looked alarmed, and DiAngelo actually let go of his balls. Max looked at them in disgust. If he had had any sense, he thought, he would have left them to rot in prison. His instincts had warned him about this job. . . . Well, it was too late now.

"All right, I'll keep you two sleazeballs alive. But I warn you, one wrong move from either of you, and you're both history. I could always tell your pals that you died in the crash." That had just occurred to him, and it was tempting. He could waste them where they were, bury the bodies, and no one would be the wiser. Except Tunafish and Lora. Lora would wonder where Minelli and DiAngelo had gotten to sooner or later, and if he wanted her to keep her mouth shut he would have to tell her. . . . Then she really would look at him like the creature from the Black Lagoon. Goddamn it, he swore bitterly, and lifted the gun menacingly.

"Just give me a reason. Please," he growled.

The look on his face must have reflected his inward fury, because Minelli held up both hands, palms outward in surrender, while DiAngelo looked like he wanted to piss in his pants. Max stared at them in disgust. Christ, how did he get into these situations?

"Stand up, turn around, and put your hands behind your backs. Both of you."

They obeyed with an alacrity that would have been funny if he had been in a mood to laugh; he wasn't. Scowling, Max kept the pistol trained on their backs with one hand while he took off his belt with the other. Then he had DiAngelo tie Minelli's hands. Max checked Minelli's bonds, then tied DiAngelo, who he considered the lesser threat, to the other end of the long thong himself, using his teeth to tighten the knot. With the two men roped together, it would be impossible for one to try anything. A fact he viewed with some regret.

"All right, move. To your right." The two men, sullen-faced and silent, obeyed. Staying carefully behind them, the pistol at the ready although he didn't expect to need it, Max directed them back toward the cave. By the time they reached the foot of the cliff, both men were panting with exertion. Blood ran down their faces from dozens of scratches inflicted by branches that they had been unable to push out of their way with their hands tied. Flies and mosquitoes swarmed around the bloody scratches. Max directed them to climb the crumbling rock, totally unmoved by their obvious misery. They could count themselves lucky he had not killed them outright, as every vestige of his common sense was still shouting that he should. Talk about vipers in the bosom. . . . .

XVII

The presence of Minelli and DiAngelo in the cave further complicated an already tangled situation. With Tunafish unable to stand without assistance, there was only Max to find food, fetch water, assist with Tunafish's most private requirements, and keep guard over the two men. Lora did what she could, but those things were largely beyond her scope. She could not go into the jungle alone. Neither could she stand guard over Minelli and DiAngelo. If they managed to get free of their bonds, they would overpower her in a matter of moments, gun or no gun. Tunafish could guard them, but Tunafish was at times almost out of his mind with pain. He didn't complain, even managed to joke about it from time to time, but Max had known him too long. He could see the desperation in Tunafish's eyes. Max knew that he was inhaling smack when the pain was worst, but under the circumstances, who could blame him? Max was almost glad they had the damned dope. . . .

The jungle was beautiful with a wild, savage beauty that he admired despite the harrowing circumstances. Everyday, as he fished in the pool that still reminded him of Lora's eyes, much to his annoyance, or gathered fruit or branches for the fire or performed one of a hundred other tasks, he discovered new wonders. Like the flowers. Gorgeous tropical flowers that covered the jungle floor like a carpet in places. Orchids in lush shades of purple and orange and white grew everywhere, thrusting up from the ground like weeds. So did poppies. Amapola poppies, with their velvety scarlet and black petals and heady aroma that caused giant bees and flies to swarm around them like addicts. These poppies grew all over Mexico, in vast fields. They were a cash crop, raised and razor-harvested for their white gold: opium.

Seeing the poppies growing wild brought back memories, some bad and others worse. In his days with the DEA, Max had spent a goodly amount of time in the remotest areas of Mexico. The *mestizos* who populated the villages raised poppies like Americans raised corn. It was their livelihood. Most times it was done willingly; sometimes the peasants had to be coerced into the business. But if they valued their lives, they cooperated. The Mexican drug families were a vicious lot. They thought nothing of wiping out entire families, entire villages. When word of these atrocities got around, the next village was more amenable to doing as it was told. The authorities rarely interfered. They were well paid not to. But since the highly publicized murder of that DEA agent, the authorities had—reluctantly, and only after much whip cracking by the United States—begun to crack down. Not that it would do any good. The smart ones would just lay low until the heat was off and then resume operations again.

Since 'Nam, Max had never touched so much as a single joint. He had seen what drugs could do to seemingly civilized men, and he hated it. He hated drugs. . . . He hated what drugs did to people; made them crazy, violent zombies with only one goal in life: to get more of the substance that was killing them. He hated seeing kids who thought they could make a quick buck caught up in the dark world of the drug families. Many died. More became addicted. Some went to prison, in the States or in foreign countries like Mexico that had never heard of prisoners' rights. And some turned into animals as bad as the men they worked for. He thought of Ortega using him to run drugs, and his fingers twitched with longing to close around the man's pudgy throat. Ortega knew better than to pull such a thing on him—or if he didn't, he soon would. As soon as Max got himself and the rest of them out of this hellish paradise.

It was a hellish paradise. Max was not the only one to think so. Trapped in a cave with four men, two of whom were bound most of the time and had to be kept under constant guard, with inadequate food, clothes that were growing more repulsive by the hour, and the constant fear of snakes, insects, or other creatures who might decide to explore the cave, to say nothing of the nervous tension caused by waiting, waiting for whatever hostile rescue party would arrive first, Lora thought she might actually go crazy. It was like being snowbound for months, she thought, only worse. Because at least someone who was snowbound did not have to contend with flies and mosquitoes and huge fire ants that stung like hornets if you were unwary enough to put your hand down on them, daily downpours that left the world smelling of mildew, and the contrast of hot, steamy days with cold nights; to say nothing of the constant threat of danger from Minelli and DiAngelo, who were sullenly threatening as they sat bound hand and foot through the seemingly endless hours. And then there was Tunafish's suffering, which was painful to watch. The heroin helped when he took it, but he only did so when the pain was dreadful. As a schoolteacher, Lora thought that drugs were an abomination second only to the devil, but in this one instance she had to admit that without them Tunafish's situation would have been unbearable. If he had been in a hospital, they would have given him painkillers, but they could not get to a hospital and the heroin was the only painkiller available. Under the circumstances, Lora could not think it wrong for Tunafish to take it. Guiltily, she realized that she even found it interesting to watch. Tunafish sprinkled the powder on a large flat leaf, rolled another leaf into a cigarette-sized hollow tube, and used the tube to inhale the drug. Lora actually caught herself thinking, so that's how they do it! and immediately banished the subject from her mind.

Max was another problem. He kept his distance, speaking to her only when necessary and then in a cool, distant way that she hated to admit hurt. Even Tunafish had noticed, and commiserated with her with raised eyebrows and a grimace when Max wasn't looking. Lora didn't know for sure what ailed Max, but it was beginning to bug her as much as the enforced confinement. Surely he was not still angry at her because she had witnessed him having a nightmare. . . .

He was apparently uneasy about leaving her and Tunafish in the cave with Minelli and DiAngelo any more than he had to, but necessities such as food and water dictated that he leave the cave several times a day. During those periods, Tunafish would sit watching Minelli and DiAngelo, a gun propped in his lap. Though those two had never tried to cause any more trouble, Lora was always jumpy when Max was gone. Ten million dollars worth of drugs and a hundred thousand dollars in cash was enough to tempt many law-abiding men to murder. And Minelli and DiAngelo had never, she thought, been law-abiding, even in their cradles.

They made her uneasy for another reason, too, or at least, Minelli did. He watched her with an insolent attention that made her feel unclean. She always got the feeling that he was mentally undressing her, and as the days passed the feeling grew stronger. Even though she performed her daily ablutions—a sponge bath, with a cupful of tepid water and a rag made from the remains of Max's windbreaker—behind a bush just outside the cave and definitely out of sight of Minelli's avid eyes, she still felt uneasy about removing her clothes. As a result, she usually just pulled off her t-shirt and sponged herself as quickly as she could. Which, after three days, left her feeling grungier than she had ever felt in her life.

The two men were a problem at night, too. Max bound them more securely then, because even he had to sleep sometime. Their pallets—sans blankets or pillows—were on the opposite side of the large cavern from where she and Tunafish and Max slept, but that did not stop Lora from feeling particularly vulnerable when she lay down and closed her eyes. Tunafish now stood the early watch, while Max took the late one. They clearly didn't trust her enough with a gun to let her stand her share of watching, and Lora didn't much blame them. She didn't trust herself much that way, either. But with Minelli and DiAngelo across the cave, whether they were bound and supposedly sleeping or not, she found herself inching imperceptibly closer to Max. Until now her pallet was so close to his that there was scarcely a palm's width between them. If he had noticed her creeping encroachment, he had not said anything. But then, he didn't say much to her nowadays.

On the afternoon of the fourth day since the crash, Lora couldn't stand it any longer. She thought she would die if she didn't get out of the cave. The daily downpour had already passed, leaving that sickening sweet smell of rotting vegetation that she was beginning to think would suffocate her. Minelli and DiAngelo sat with their hands bound loosely in front of them, their backs resting against the curved wall of the cave as they seemed to doze. Tunafish was standing guard, but he looked as apathetic as the rest of them. His splinted leg must be hurting him badly, she thought, but as Max was out hunting for food he could not seek the relief of sleep or dope-induced insensitivity.

Adding to the misery, Lora had at least a dozen mosquito bites that were itching to distraction. Max had warned her not to scratch. She had tried it once, disregarding his curt caution, and found that scratching only made them swell up and itch four times as ferociously. After that, she had not argued about coating her exposed skin with the mud that he said was the only remedy for the itching and swelling, and the only way to guard against future bites. He had been right, of course, but she felt almost as miserable with smears of mud on her cheeks and neck and arms as she did with the mosquitoes chomping on her.

More than anything in life—except rescue and a decent meal—she longed for a bath. But that was clearly impossible. Although there was a spring somewhere nearby, according to Max, she didn't know where, and even if she did she didn't dare wander about the jungle on her own. Every night she heard the yowl of big cats and the screams of their prey, and every day ticks and snakes were washed onto the shelf of rock just outside the cave. Danger lurked everywhere out there, and she wasn't stupid enough to brave it alone. She was stuck. Stranded. Unable to go further than a few feet from the cave that was rapidly growing more confining to her than the prison cell Max had rescued her from.

There was no reason Max couldn't take her with him on some of his expeditions, Lora told herself, feeling a righteous anger begin to build. Just because he was nursing some ridiculous grievance against her was no reason to treat her like she had leprosy. When he came back and Tunafish had had a chance to rest, she meant to demand that he take her someplace where she could breathe, and perhaps bathe. If he refused—well, he wouldn't refuse. That was all there was to it.

To her surprise, he didn't. He looked at her rather narrowly when she told him with more than a hint of belligerence that she needed a bath, but after eyeing her up and down he didn't argue. Lora didn't much like that when she thought about it—it was insulting to have someone agree that one stank— but she wasn't going to quarrel with the results. He meant to go fishing for their supper, and he agreed to take her with him, provided she did as he told her, and didn't wander off.

The spring-fed stream that trickled down the side of the mountain near the cave widened as it cut through the jungle. Max led her along it via a path he had already cut through the thick vegetation until, without warning, the stream shot out into space with a shower of sparks, to tumble down a staircase of gray rocks before cascading into a small lagoon perhaps twelve feet below. As waterfalls went, this one was nothing spectacular, but Lora found it beautiful. When she and Max had worked their way down over the steplike rocks on one side of the waterfall to stand looking up at the falling torrent of water, Lora felt the first rush of exhilaration she had known since the plane crash. The scene was like something from *Green Mansions,* which she had her students read every year. Framed by lush, hanging greenery, with sunlight falling tangentially through the canopy of leaves to glisten on the sparkling drops that shot away from the main fall of rushing water, the view before her took her breath away. Garlands of scarlet hibiscus trailed from the trees with which they were intertwined to hang over the water. Exotic orchids of nearly every color imaginable grew in thick patches along the sides of the lagoon itself. Near the rocky banks, a profusion of water lilies flourished. Their waxy white blossoms and dark green leaves glistened with water droplets that sparkled in the sun. Birds fluttered in the trees overhead, while monkeys chattered as they swung from branch to branch. Nearer at hand, a snake slithered across a rock, but Lora was so caught up in the beauty of it all that the snake didn't seem frightening at all, but natural. Even the rustling of a particularly dense patch of greenery on the far side of the pool didn't disturb her rapt appreciation. This was the jungle of Edgar Rice Burrows and Anya Seton. This was the jungle of Tarzan and Sheena. This was the jungle as she had always thought it would be.

Now, except for the occasional squawk of a parrot or the sudden chatter of a monkey, the dull roar of the water itself was the only sound. When Max spoke, she jumped. She had been so lost in admiration that she had nearly forgotten why she was here.

"If you want to take a bath, make it quick. We want to be away from here before sundown. That's when the animals come to drink."

His sour voice didn't detract from the validity of the warning. Lora shuddered at the idea of still being here when lions and tigers and pythons and God only knew what else came to claim the pool, and turned to survey the glistening water. She saw a flash of scales beneath the surface, and had a sudden thought.

"Is it safe?" She must have sounded doubtful, because she

thought she saw a touch of humor in the black eyes that had been as remote as glaciers for the last few days.

"Yep," he answered, sounding as if he had copied his conversational style from a TV western. "Just stay near the edge and me, and you'll be fine. But watch out for the piranhas."

"What?" Her eyes were enormous as she silently begged him to admit he was kidding. His face, that expressionless stone face, did not change by so much as a twitch.

"Don't worry, they won't eat you. At least, as long as you don't go out in the center of the pool. Go on, do you want to take a bath or don't you? We don't have all day."

He had moved a little away from her as he spoke, settling himself down on a convenient rock and extracting the fishing line he had made from laboriously unraveling a thread from his windbreaker, which was made of nylon and therefore made the thread much stronger than it looked. At the other end was a hook which he had fashioned from a safety pin in the first aid kit. The result was crude but effective, as their dinners for the last two days attested.

Lora looked at him uncertainly. "You're joking, aren't you?"

"About what?"

"About the piranhas?"

"No."

"But I can't go into a pool that's swimming with piranhas!"

"Yes you can. They're not vicious. As long as you're not bleeding somewhere. You're not, are you?"

It took a moment for Lora to register this as the very intimate question it was. Her face burned.

"No!"

"Well, then." He seemed to consider the matter settled.

Lora glared at him, then looked nervously at the pool.

Surely Max would not send her into the water only to be devoured by woman-eating fish! No, he would not. Of course he would not. Whether he admitted it or not, he was just teasing her. . . .

Still, Lora hung back, staring at the water. Then, taking a deep breath, she walked to the edge of the pool and climbed carefully down the shallow rock bank. When she reached the edge of the water, she took one more uncertain look at Max, who was staring at the place where his fishing line disappeared beneath the water with a look of intense concentration. He would not let her go into a piranha infested pool—would he?

Clothes and all, she waded in. Since she only had the jeans and t-shirt and single set of underclothes she had been wearing when they crashed, and the clothes were as filthy as she was, she saw no reason to remove them before bathing. If she was clean while they remained filthy, she would never be able to put them back on. Better to get them soaking wet and let them dry on her. At least they would be clean—and she would not have to worry about him looking at her while she was naked.

"Max?" She was waist deep now, and the cool water felt marvelous, even through her clothes. She just had one problem: soap. She could not get clean if she had no soap.

"What?"

"What should I use for soap?"

"God, you are helpless, aren't you? Scoop up a handful of mud and use that."

Lora stared at him. He was looking down at her impatiently from his perch on the flat gray rock. The late afternoon sun was slanting down through the leaves, its rays just touching his hair. Even unwashed and uncombed, its rough black texture looked vibrantly healthy. So did the sun-bronzed tone of his skin, darkened dramatically since the crash. Even the four days' growth of whiskers on his face became him. Lora decided that he was a man who could turn disreputable into some kind of masculine chic.

She decided he wasn't kidding. He didn't look like he was kidding, and, anyway, he hadn't been much for jokes lately. So she scooped up a handful of mud, stared at it rather dubiously for a moment, and then began to work it into the skin of her arm. To her surprise, she did feel considerably cleaner once she had rinsed it off. Heartened, she scooped up another handful and rubbed her face and neck and hair with it. After all, she reasoned, everyone had heard of mud packs. . . .

"Heyee!" The cry came from Max, and it almost drowned Lora. She screamed, starting, and promptly lost her footing among the slippery pebbles and mud which made up the bottom of the pool, falling with an enormous splash. She floundered beneath the surface, kicking frantically for a foothold. Finally, she found one and shot up, choking. Water streamed down her face from her soaking hair. Her waterlogged jeans hung from her waist as though they were made of lead.

"What's wrong?" Lora dashed the hair and water from her face and opened her eyes to look nervously around the pool and then at Max.

He was scowling at her from the rock, those ferocious black brows meeting in a wide vee over his nose. He was standing instead of sitting, and beside him curled the thin string of his fishing line, with neither fish nor hook in sight.

"Damn it, you made me lose him!"

"Who?"

"The fish! The damned biggest catfish I've ever seen! On my line—until you yelled and made a splash a blue whale couldn't match!"

"I yelled? *You* yelled first, and you almost drowned me in the process! Don't you yell at me for yelling, you, you—"

"I'll yell at you anytime I damned well please." He was yelling, his fists balled on his hips and his mustache quivering with anger all out of proportion to the subject of the argument. Those black eyes shot fire at her.

Lora, too, was suddenly furious. She was sick and tired of putting up with his ill temper and she meant to let him know it.

"Well, then, I'll yell right back!" she said, yelling herself, glaring up at him with an expression to match his. "Who do you think you are, anyway? You've been sulking around for days—ever since you had that stupid nightmare! If I'd known it was going to make you mad, I would have let you cry all by yourself—baby!"

There was a moment's charged silence.

"Why you little—" He bit off a word, but his eyes said it for him. They spat anger at her like twin black machine guns. His hands were no longer balled on his narrow hips, but hung at his sides where the fingers flexed and unflexed as if they itched to close around her throat. Beneath the short-sleeved white t-shirt, the brown muscles of his arms tightened until they resembled rolling hills. He looked as if he was about to explode.

Lora knew that she had hit below the belt by referring to his nightmare, but she didn't care. It was about time Mr. Macho Stud was brought down a peg or two.

"Crybaby!" she said, taunting. The absurdity of the nursery school name did not even occur to her. She wanted to make him mad, and she knew with unerring accuracy that that was the way to do it.

She was right. She could practically see steam come out of his ears. His fists clenched at his sides, and she could see the muscles of his thighs bulge against the material of his jeans as his whole body tensed.

"Shut up, Lora." The command was a grim warning, uttered through clenched teeth.

Lora lifted her head and looked him squarely in the eyes. "Crybaby, cry, stick your finger in your eye," she sang softly, and with a bellow he was diving off the rock into the center of the pool, his big body splitting the water as cleanly as a knife. She barely had time to consider the depth of the pool before he was surfacing just a few feet from where she watched, wide-eyed.

He stood up, one large brown hand coming up to sluice water and lily pads from his face, and fixed her with eyes that glittered like jet. Lora instinctively took a step backward, only to lose her footing again on the slippery bottom and fall down. He was upon her in an instant, hauling her out of the water by her shoulders. As she surfaced, spitting and gasping, and shedding as much water as the waterfall, she caught a glimpse of his face and thought she would almost have rather stayed beneath the surface.

"Say it again. I dare you." His lips barely parted to reveal the glinting white teeth through which he spoke. Lora felt his hands hard on her upper arms, saw the murder that glittered in the black eyes, and for an instant was transported back to when they first met and she had thought he was going to kill her every other minute. He looked as frightening now as he had then . . . only now, she remembered, she wasn't afraid of him.

"Not so brave at such close quarters, are you, lady?" he sneered.

The sneer was a mistake. It reminded her of her grievances with him. She straightened her spine and glared at him through the trailing, dripping strands of her hair. "Crybaby!" she said again in a soft, goading tone.

He stared down at her as if he couldn't believe his ears. His hands tightened on her arms so that his fingers dug into her soft skin, and he gave her a warning shake.

"Shut up."

"Crybaby!"

"Shut up!"

"Crybaby!"

"Argghh!" It was a growl much like a tiger's, and like a tiger he looked ready to spring. One hand tightened ferociously on her arm while the other lifted, hovering open-palmed in the air. Looking up into his rage-infused face, Lora was certain that he meant to strike her. Every instinct for self-preservation that she possessed urged her to keep quiet, but something, some unnamed thing like a thorn in her flesh, was driving her on. . . .

"Crybaby!" she cried, glaring up at him defiantly, her eyes daring him to do his worst.

He growled again, deep in his throat, and she could see the hot blood throb in the artery in his neck. His black eyes glittered with it. But he did not slap her. Instead, the hand that had been poised above her face shot to the back of her head and grabbed a handful of soaking hair. Then he was jerking her toward him, eyes still glittering with murder as his face came down.

His mouth descended on hers like an avenging fury, assaulting and punishing as it forced her lips apart. Lora felt her lower lip split as he drove it back against her teeth, tasted her own blood in her mouth, felt the harsh rape of his invading tongue. Stunned, she hung in his arms like an sack of flour, too shocked to fight. His fist gripping her hair hurt. His arm that had slid around her shoulders to crush her to him hurt. The hard, unyielding body that bent hers backward hurt. Even his mouth hurt. But she didn't fight him, didn't even want to fight him. Dimly, with some still-functioning part of her brain, she realized that this was why she had goaded him. This was what she wanted. . . .

"Oh, Max," she groaned into his mouth, and then she was responding to that rapier tongue with a passion that even in his fury he couldn't mistake.

"Lora . . . " Her name was a tormented whisper as he kissed her harder, fiercer than before, as if he was starving for the taste of her mouth. She twisted in his arms, not trying to get away but to work her arms free. . . . She managed to push them up through his crushing hold and lock them around his neck. He groaned deep in his throat, and she groaned too in protest as his mouth suddenly left hers. He was looking down at her, his breathing heavy, a wild glitter in his eyes. Lora lifted one hand from the corded nape of his neck and lightly stroked the rough, wet edges of his hair.

"Kiss me, Max," she whispered, her mouth reaching for his even as she spoke. Plastered against him as she was, she felt him shudder. She heard the sudden, harsh indrawing of his breath as she touched his mouth with hers. Still, he held himself a little away from her; she could feel the beginning of resistance in his body and it galled her that she should have to be the one to encourage him. Where was her rapist now? she wondered hazily, remembering how she had feared him that time that seemed like eons ago but was actually little more than a week. She had known him just one day more than a week. . . .

"Please." And she was begging for him. She, Lora Susan Harding, a "nice girl" who had never, ever done anything like this in her whole life, was begging this man to kiss her. To do more than kiss her. . . .

"Oh, God," he groaned as if he was being condemned to eternal hell fire, and bent his mouth to hers again.

It was a kiss so devouring that Lora closed her eyes and surrendered her soul.

His hand came up to crush her breast, and at the heat and strength of it burning through the flimsy cloth of her wet t-shirt and bra, Lora trembled. Her knees quivered, and she felt them give beneath her weight. He was bending her back over his arm, both of them thigh-deep in gleaming green water, his mouth locked to hers and his hand on her breast sending shuddering jolts of electricity through her body. Her nipple was stiff beneath his cupping palm. When he found it with his fingers she gasped. Even through the cloth, his touch made her shiver and burn. . . . Only her arms around his neck held her upright as he abandoned his hold on her waist to cup her breasts with both hands. His mouth ate hers greedily as his hands pushed up beneath the wet cloth of shirt and bra to find her bare skin. . . .

Lora felt as if she were falling. She *was* falling. She was slipping down into the water, her knees no longer able to support her, her arms around his neck losing their grip. Tremors coursed through her like electric shocks and she could no longer bear it. . . .

His arms were around her again, lifting her, carrying her. She opened her eyes to find his face hard and taut, his eyes still glittering with that dangerous wildfire as they looked down into her face. She knew her own eyes must be heavy lidded with passion, drugged as Tunafish's were after he made use of the dope. Because that's how she felt—as if she were lost in a thick, unbearably sweet fog from which she might never escape. Little slurping noises sighed a protest as the water released Max's sneaker-clad feet. Then Max was scrambling up the bank with her cradled tight against his chest. She grasped his neck again, holding tightly as he slipped on the wet rocks, not even caring if he dropped her as long as they fell together. But he didn't, he made it safely across the rock shingles and then he was walking through the knee-high patches of flowers, bending and lying her down in a bed of orchids. Lavender and cream orchids, higher than Max's knees so that they closed around her as he put her down, enveloping her in perfume so exotic that it was intoxicating. She was intoxicated by the heady scent of the orchids and the surrealistic green beauty of the jungle canopy overhead, by the softly filtered sunlight and the muted cries of birds, by the meandering flight of purple and gold butterflies as they flitted from flower to flower, and the sibilant rustle of the flowers' slender green stems and leaves. . . .

And she was intoxicated by him. By Max. Her heart pounded as he dropped to his knees beside her, uncaring of the fragility of the exotic blooms he crushed beneath him, uncaring of everything except her and the passion that arced between them like great bolts of lightning crashing to earth and then roaring back to heaven. On his knees beside her, he stared down at her for a moment, his face with its ferocious mustache and eyebrows and harsh blade of a nose and square, unshaven jaw aggressive even in passion. She looked at the linebacker's shoulders straining against soaked white cotton, at the tufts of curling black chest hair just visible in the hollow of his throat, at the corded muscles in the sun-bronzed arms, and felt the quiver in her belly that had started with that first kiss expand and grow until she was quivering all over, visibly shaking from head to foot like a lovestruck teenage girl. Then she looked again at the strong brown arms that were supporting his weight as he stretched his length beside her and saw that he was trembling, too.

And in that instant she knew that he was as vulnerable as she.

"You're shaking." There was wonder and excitement in her whisper.

He smiled slightly, crookedly, as he leaned over her, his chest not quite touching hers as he supported himself with one hand braced on the ground near the shoulder farthest from him.

"I want you." His voice was a whisper too, husky and dark and unbearably sexy.

"I know."

"Well?"

Lora looked up at that hard face, at the bristly jaw and villainous mustache and glittering black eyes, and thought about what she was doing. She, who had never had so much as a parking ticket in her life, was on the verge of giving herself to a man who was involved with all kinds of nefarious characters, a man on the run from the law, a criminal. . . .

"What's taking you so long?" she murmured with a broken little laugh, and suddenly he grinned too, swiftly, and his face lightened into tenderness in that instant before he took her mouth again.

XVIII

His kiss was hard and hot and slow, with a lazy quality to it that had not been there before. There was passion, much passion, but it was as if he had put the brakes down hard on his libido for some reason Lora couldn't quite fathom. Not that she was up to fathoming much. Even with the brakes on, his kiss was enough to make her blood pound in her ears.

When he lifted his head at last, she had to grit her teeth to keep from hauling him back down to her. Her arms dropped from his neck to the ground beside her, and her hands clutched handfuls of lavender petals to keep from clutching at him. If he could control himself, she could, too. She was not an animal. . . .

Or so she kept telling herself as he pushed her t-shirt and bra up until her breasts were bared.

"You are so goddamn beautiful," he murmured as he stared down at the naked, pink-tipped breasts his hands had uncovered.

Following his eyes, Lora looked down at herself. The contrast between her own soft, milky white skin and the dark brown skin of his hand as it rested on her rib cage just under her right breast was unbelievably erotic. Her breasts, already full and swollen with passion though he had not yet so much as touched them, swelled even more, their brown-pink nipples tautening until they were almost painful. Never, never had she ever imagined that she could be so hungry for a man. The sight of his body in the wet white t-shirt that clung to his broad shoulders and sculptured chest and allowed tantalizing glimpses of the curling black hair beneath was so erotic that she had to fight an urge to rip the shirt from his back. The wet jeans encasing his narrow hips had an unmistakable bulge in the front that was so erotic that just the sight of it made her toes curl in her wet shoes. The sight of her own naked breasts was erotic. Even the soaking t-shirt and bra that he had pushed up out of his way and that now stretched in a twisted line from armpit to armpit struck her as erotic. The cold wetness of the jeans covering the place that she had never so much as been able to call by name did nothing to quench the heat that was raging between her legs. She wanted him to put his hand there . . . oh, how she wanted him to put his hand there!

He was still staring down at her breasts, his expression unreadable as he slowly lifted a hand to touch a nipple with a gentle forefinger. The sensation that shot through her at that slight touch was unbelievable. Lora had to grit her teeth to stifle a moan. When his finger moved to her other nipple, still just barely touching, she could not stifle it. The sound reverberated from her throat, soft and shocking in its animalism. But Lora was too far gone to be shocked at anything. She wanted him to touch her, wanted him to kiss her, wanted him to make love to her more than she had ever dreamed it was possible for her to want anything in her life. Her body arched up off its bed of orchids in silent demand; her hands clenched into fists at her sides as she fought to control the impulse to lock her arms around his neck and drag his head down to her throbbing breasts, to catch his hand and place it on the pulsating ache between her legs.

His hand was covering her breast now, testing it, weighing its softness against his hard palm. The feel of his calloused palm against her skin made her want to writhe. She wanted to feel it everywhere on her body—wanted to feel him everywhere on her body. She wanted him to love her until she begged him to stop. She remembered what he had done to her before, remembered how expertly he had given her ecstasy with only his fingers, and had to clench her thighs together hard. She wanted him to do it again. . . .

But he didn't. He caressed her breasts, his hand gentle, the other one propping up his head as he stared down at her, a funny kind of half smile quirking his mouth. How could he be so damned dispassionate when she was going out of her mind and a minute ago he had been too.

"What's taking you so long?" The question, which she had meant to be a joking echo of the one she had uttered earlier, did not sound as if she was joking at all. Her gritted teeth might have something to do with that, she thought. But she couldn't help it. Her self-control was stretched dangerously thin as it was. What *was* taking him so long? From the ragged sound of his breathing, he was just as turned on as she. . . .

"I told you before: I like my women hungry." This reference to their last abortive lovemaking session should have made her go crimson with embarrassment. It didn't. She looked up into those glittering black eyes, at that masculine, whiskered face, at that passionate mouth beneath its silky mustache, and abruptly all her inhibitions went into hiding.

"I *am* hungry," she whispered shakily. Something flared briefly in his eyes before being sternly brought under control.

"Prove it." The husky whisper was almost casual, except for the rasp of his breathing and the faint tremor of his fingers on her breast.

"How?" She was whispering too. Her voice shook. Her eyes locked with his, and she felt the heat between her legs flare hotter. His eyes glittered with passion. . . .

"For starters, you can take off your clothes." That deceptively casual voice would have fooled her if she hadn't been able to see into his eyes.

"All right." She sat up, willing to do whatever he said. Her hands found the edge of the twisted t-shirt.

"Uh-uh." He stopped her. She looked at him inquiringly.

"Stand up."

Lora stood up. Her knees were shaking so much that she wasn't sure they would hold her, and he didn't help any by looking at her as if he might jump on her bones at any moment. But somehow she managed to pull the t-shirt over her head, to find the hook in the twisted bra and unfasten it, letting the bra drop to the ground. She kicked off her shoes, then felt a little shy as she unsnapped and unzipped her jeans. As she pushed them down her legs and stepped out of them she felt even shyer. She could have taken off her panties, the same white panties that he had stripped off her in that never-to-be-forgotten night in the farmhouse loft, but some lingering instinct of modesty made her leave them on. Or maybe some newly burgeoning erotic instinct was urging her to spin out the striptease. . . .

"Those panties turn me on."

She looked at him, sitting cross-legged on the ground not

three feet away, his eyes burning as they inched over every millimeter of her skin. The huskiness of his voice sent her senses quaking. Her hands shook as she hooked her thumbs in the waistband of the panties.

"Leave them on. And come here." The words were almost a growl. His black eyes almost scorched her as she met them.

Lora swallowed, and took the single step toward him that was needed to put her within reach. Before she could drop down beside him, his arms came around her and he pulled her close, burying his face in the vee between her legs as his hands crushed the roundness of her bottom, his fingers finding and sensuously exploring the crevasse through the thin nylon. . . .

Lora caught her breath, her heart pounding so hard that she was aware of no other sound as he opened his mouth against the silky cloth covering the apex of her legs. She could feel the heat of it in burning contrast to the cool dampness of the material elsewhere. He opened his mouth more, pressing harder against her, and she could feel the soft slither of his tongue as he sought and found the secret point that quivered and throbbed in aching need. Her hands came up to clutch at the rough blackness of his hair, holding his head in place with two tight fists as his tongue caressed her. He hadn't even parted her legs. . . . Lora's eyes shut tight, and she moaned at the feel of his tongue and mouth gently but insistently urging her highter. . . . The very fact that her panties formed a thin barrier between his mouth and her flesh made what he was doing to her all the more exciting. Even in her wildest fantasies she had never imagined a man doing anything like this . . . or herself feeling anything like this. . . .

She couldn't stand it anymore. Another second and she would surely die. Her knees buckled, and she slithered down in his hold, collapsing in a heap in his lap. Her barely clad bottom planted on a jeans-clad leg; her naked breasts came into surprisingly arousing contact with a hard chest wall covered with a cold, damp t-shirt. The shock was just enough to bring her back from the edge. Her eyes opened to find him looking down into her face. That maddening half smile was still there, but she didn't care. She only cared about the black eyes that smoldered and smoked, and about the ache that radiated out from between her legs to make her body throb from head to toe. . . .

Eyes blind with passion, her arms came up to circle his shoulders and her mouth found his, her lips soft and shaking and seeking. Her tongue found its way between his lips and kissed him with an intensity that she would have thought, before, to be utterly foreign to her nature. His arms tightened around her body, holding her close as he returned her kiss with lips and teeth and tongue, and yet she sensed that he was not giving all of himself—yet.

"Damn you, what do you want?" she whispered, goaded, pulling her mouth away from his and almost glaring into those too-controlled black eyes. She wanted him in the same state as herself, on fire with passion, driven mad with passion.

"I told you, I want you hungry."

The words were soft, factual, but they drove Lora into a frenzy. She snarled at him, baring her teeth, her fists beating down on his shoulders until he caught her wrists in his hands and deftly twisted her until she was no longer sitting on his lap but lying flat on her back on the broken stalks of ruined flowers. With a deft movement he released her hands and stripped the panties from her, leaving her lying naked as he straightened and looked down at her, his eyes suddenly flaming. It took him just seconds to pull the t-shirt over his head, to slide out of the shoes and jeans and shorts, to lay the pistol that he always carried tucked into the waistband of his jeans on the ground nearby, but to Lora it felt like an eternity. It was all she could do to keep from moaning and writhing where she lay. She had to clench her thighs together to fight the impulse. . . .

Then he was coming down beside her. She gasped as he moved over her, and her eyes closed tight with passion. The crush of his lower body on her legs and belly and thighs was just what she craved. Her legs parted instantly to allow him access. She arched her back in anticipation, feeling the quaking between her legs intensify to a fevered pitch. Now he would take her. . . .

But still he didn't. She could feel him everywhere, his thighs hard and hot and rough with hair between her shaking legs, his abdomen hard and hot and rough too against her silky stomach and lower, against the slight protuberance of her femininity, and the enormous, red-hot male part of him she ached for prodding at her with unsatisfying restraint. He was teasing her. . . .

Her eyes flew open. They were a dark, brilliant blue as they flamed at him. Her hands which had been clutching his back turned into claws that dug into his shoulders. "Please, Max, now!"

He smiled then, a slow smile that sent the blood racing through her veins. Lora felt the throbbing inside her intensify until she was sure she would not be able to stand it another second as he slowly, oh, so slowly, lowered his head. His target was her left breast. Lora felt his hot mouth close on the straining nipple, felt him tug the crest of her breast into his mouth to rub it with the rough wet surface of his tongue, and cried out in a frenzy of need.

And in that instant he took her.

She climaxed at once as he squeezed inside, enormous and

hard and fiery hot and filling her to bursting. She cried out again, sailing away in a firestorm of brilliantly colored sparks, shaking, gasping for breath, clutching him to her urgently. When it was over, when she came floating back to earth, it was with some surprise that she realized that he was still enormous inside her. Of course, he was still hungry. She wasn't. Definitely wasn't. She was so tired, so replete, so completely spent that it was all she could do to breathe. . . .

Then he moved. A little quiver of something sprang to life again inside her. He moved again, pulling himself almost all the way out before slowly, slowly , squeezing his way back in again. Lora stiffened. Despite her exhaustion, he felt good. . . .

His hands braced on either side of her rib cage, he stiffened his arms until his weight was almost completely off her. Their only point of contact was where their bodies joined. Slowly, he moved in, then out, until she lifted her hips slightly with involuntary anticipation every time. Then he bent his head and took her breast in his mouth again.

She groaned.

Lora thought that it would be impossible to equal the desire he had roused in her with his first torturous possession. She was wrong. His slow movements and erotic mouth brought her back to a fever pitch of passion, and this time he came with her. When at last he had pushed her to the point of screaming frenzy, he was there too, and his hoarse shout joined with her cry as they fell over the edge together. It was a long, long time before he could summon up the energy to roll away.

"We've got to get back."

"What?" Lora sat up and stared at him. He was sitting up too, gloriously naked and gloriously masculine against the feminine background of swaying lavender orchids. She wanted to reach over and trace the outline of every ridged muscle and indention with her fingers. But something in his tone bothered her. She looked searchingly at him. He stood up, reaching for his clothes.

"Is something wrong, Max?" The question was quiet. She hadn't expected a declaration of undying love after what they had just shared, but she hadn't expected the cold shoulder either. Staring up at him as he stepped into his damp briefs and jeans and squeezed his feet into wet shoes, she felt an absurd hurt begin to seep into her heart.

"What do you mean, is something wrong? Nothing's wrong. What could be wrong?" He was pulling the soggy t-shirt over his head as he spoke. The action gave him the perfect excuse not to look at her, she thought, but it could not quite disguise the suppressed savagery of his tone. Watching him tuck the pistol into the waistband of his jeans, she began to get angry in turn.

"Silly me. Of course nothing's wrong. You always act like a lion with a thorn in its paw," she agreed coolly, standing up and beginning to dress herself. Ordinarily, she would have been shy with his eyes on her nakedness, even after what they had just shared, but temper was simmering in her veins and as it heated it obviated such concerns as modesty. Besides, she realized as she dragged on her own wet jeans with about as much grace as a fat woman getting into a girdle, he wasn't looking at her. At all.

"For God's sake, Lora, you're not one of those women who wants to have a rehash every time she has sex, are you? It was great, okay? But it's over, and we've got to get back now. We've been gone a long time."

The harsh impatience of his tone was as hurtful as his words. Lora looked down at the clammy bra that she was having trouble fastening, and deliberately took her time about getting each little hook secured before sliding it around and working it up to its proper place. If she said anything before she had a chance to calm down, she was afraid that he might realize just how much his casual attitude was hurting her. They had had great sex, huh? Was that all it was to him? She felt like a slab of prime rib. Nice, when one was hungry, but barely memorable when the hunger was gone. She pulled the water-darkened hot pink t-shirt over her head with a jerk that should have split the seams. Luckily, the garment held together, but Lora was so angry that she didn't much care either way. The cold wet clothes sent goosebumps popping up all over her skin, but she didn't care about that, either. Under the circumstances, she thought, sizzling, she probably needed something to cool her off. Before she told Mr. Macho here what he could do with himself and his great sex.

"Come on."

He barely waited for her to slip her feet into her shoes before striding back toward the lagoon. Lora followed him, glaring furiously at the broad back and tight derriere that looked infuriatingly sexy in the wet, clingy t-shirt and jeans. He walked with an easy lope that made her grit her teeth. Male sex appeal personified, that was him. And she had fallen like a ton of bricks for all that tanned skin and steely muscle, fantasizing about him as a lover, dreaming about him as a lover, yearning for him as a lover. Well, wasn't there a saying about being careful what you wished for because you just might get it? She had wanted him to make love to her so badly that it had been almost a physical ache inside her for some time now, and she had finally gotten what she wanted. And the sex itself had been great, just great as he had said. Lora ground her teeth, remembering the casual way he had dismissed something that had threatened to profoundly change her life. She had been on the verge of making a drastic error in judgment—but luckily he had brought her back to real life before she could commit the monumental folly of really thinking she was falling in love with him. She ought to be grateful to him, she told herself, not angry. He certainly hadn't strung her along. He had merely described the situation as he saw it—great sex, indeed!—and she couldn't be angry at him for being honest. It wasn't reasonable. It wasn't fair. To hell with being fair, she thought, and glared daggers at the broad-shouldered form that was climbing nimbly up the shelf of rocks at the side of the waterfall.

They made their way back to the cave with scarcely a word exchanged between them. If Max was aware that she was murderously angry at him, he gave no sign of it. He went on about the business of relieving Tunafish and supervising Minelli's and DiAngelo's exercise period as if nothing at all out of the ordinary had occurred. Lora got the job of preparing the supper of bananas and papayas—there was no fish, to Tunafish's loud disappointment and later razzing comments about Max's abilities as a fisherman. As she passed around the fruit that all of them were heartily sick of, she gave serious thought to poisoning Max's. And Tunafish's, too, if it would stop his needling guesses about what might have distracted Max's attention down at the pool. Although Max was as cool as that damned escaped fish, Lora felt that their mutual experience must have branded her visibly for life, like Hester Prynne with the scarlet letter. And the feeling maddened her. By the time the meager supper was finished, she had worked herself up into a state of silent fury. And it was no help to lie down on the miserably uncomfortable pallet, tossing and turning for hours as she tried with abysmal success not to relive any part of the day, including the "great sex" that she and Max had shared, and discover that, within minutes of being relieved by Tunafish and lying down on his own pallet beside hers, the object of her scorn was sound asleep. And snoring!

Lora lay awake in the dark for a long time, taking some comfort from mentally devising a hundred and one ways to silence a snorer—violently.

XIX

Something warm and dry was sliding over the skin of her arm, touching her softly, slithering. Lora frowned in her sleep, and inwardly muttered a few choice words to the man who, in her dream, was trailing a hard brown finger up and down her arm. He was smiling that unexpectedly charming smile, his black eyes radiating sex appeal as he tried to talk her into bed. . . . Well, she was having none of that. No way was she going to fall for an ungrateful, churlish, violent, insulting, probably mentally disturbed criminal, be he ever so sexy! She opened her mouth to tell him so—and to her outrage he chose that moment to pull her close and kiss her right on her open mouth. She shuddered as she felt the hot touch of his lips, and she had to fight an urge to melt like butter in his arms. Instead, infuriated, she struggled against his steely hold. . . .

She struggled so hard that she woke herself. Her eyes shot open to discover, to her relief, that it had been a dream after all. The sensation of him kissing her had seemed so real. Her body was still reacting hotly to the imagined contact. She could feel shivers running over her skin. . . .

Lora went very still as she realized that the shivers were not imaginary. There was something warm and soft and smooth moving over the arm that she had flung out of the pallet in her sleep. Almost afraid to look, she was equally afraid not to. Something was crawling over her arm. She moved her head slowly, cautiously, careful to make no abrupt gesture that might startle whatever it was until her outflung arm was within her vision. When at last she had her head tilted back, what she saw was the embodiment of her worst nightmare. The tiny hairs on the base of her neck stood up, and she had to fight a violent attack of the shivers. She had a feeling that if that arm moved much, even as much as it might when in the throes of a violent attack of the trembles, it might be one of the last movements she ever made.

A long, slender snake with alternating bands of coral and black and yellow undulated across the white skin of the underside of her wrist toward the palm of her hand. Lora knew very little about snakes, except that she loathed them. Just seeing pictures of snakes was enough to make her shudder. Watching the reptile crawl across her skin made her want to jump up and run screaming for the nearest exit. But every instinct for self-preservation she possessed warned her not to move. The snake could very well be poisonous. . . . Lora looked at the small sleek head with its darting tongue so close to the blue veins of her wrists and felt a sick shudder start in her stomach that she frantically suppressed. If it was poisonous, and it bit her there, she would surely die. . . .

"Don't move." The quiet warning came from above and behind her. Lora was afraid to look, but she would recognize Max's harsh tones in a dark hole in China. Ridiculously, the knowledge that he was there, that he was aware of her predicament, calmed her considerably. Although there was nothing he could do to help her, she realized. The snake rested almost wholly on her arm now. Only its tail still trailed the ground. Its head was in her palm as it slithered toward her fingers. Lora had to struggle not to clench her fist. She couldn't bear the idea that the snake was going to slide over her helpless fingers. . . .

"Relax, Lora." Max's voice was low and soothing. "He's not going to do anything if you stay still. He'll just crawl off your arm and go somewhere else. Just stay still and it will soon be over."

Lora shut her eyes, letting his words wash over her. She concentrated on that husky, brown velvet voice. She loved the sound of Max's voice, she realized, with its drawling Texas accent. That was one of the first things that had attracted her to him. That and his linebacker's shoulders . . . Lora thought of those shoulders, pictured them naked and gleaming bronze, concentrated on the width and breadth and strength of them as the snake slithered across her palm and over her fingers. She concentrated so hard that she wasn't even conscious of the sweat that was drenching her body. . . .

"Blammm!" The explosion of a pistol almost in her ear sent her screaming upright, her hands flying out from under the snake as she jumped to her feet. Max was there behind her, and she fell against him as she turned with blind panic. His arms enfolded her, holding her against him, one hand soothing as it slowly stroked her back. His other hand held the pistol. . . . Lora shuddered and gasped into the soft cotton of the t-shirt covering his broad chest, the terror that she had managed to hold at bay until now making her quake with tremors from head to toe.

"What the hell?" The yelped question was Tunafish's as

he jacknifed into a sitting position on his pallet, but Lora scarcely heard it.

"Coral snake," Max said briefly. "I took care of it, go back to sleep."

"She all right?"

"Yes. Go back to sleep. All of you." The tone made it an order that was also addressed to Minelli and DiAngelo, who had started up at the sound of the gunshot and now sat staring at Lora in Max's arms with identical smirking expressions.

"Anything you say, boss." Tunafish lay back down and ostentatiously shut his eyes. So did the other two, with snorts of disgust. Lora was scarcely aware that they were even present. She could not get the image of that brilliantly striped snake on her white skin out of her mind. She clung to Max as if she would never let him go.

"It's over now," he murmured into her hair, his head bent so that his mouth was pressed somewhere near her ear. "The snake's dead, and you're safe. It's over."

"It felt so—warm," she gasped, shivering. "I always imagined a snake would feel—cold."

"It must have been lying in the sun when something disturbed it. Put it out of your mind. It's over."

"Oh, my God, I'll have nightmares for the rest of my life. I hate snakes."

Against her hair she felt a movement of his face that made her think he was smiling.

"So do I. They give me the creeps."

That so surprised her that she pulled a little away from him to look up at him. He was smiling, she saw, a crooked, boyish smile that charmed her utterly. When he was like this, she found herself thinking, it was easy to imagine that he was someone she could love. . . . Her eyes widened with horror that she could even in her wildest imaginings couple that word with this man. Of course she couldn't love him—she didn't even like him. Or at least, not often. It was just a case of her perfectly normal female hormones responding as they were meant to to an inordinately sexy hunk of masculinity. . . .

She pulled away from him, her hands on the hard muscles of his bare arms setting him at a little distance. He looked down at her inquiringly, and she found that she had to look away from that too-aggressively masculine face. He disturbed her on every level.

The body of the snake, its head shot off, caught her eye, and effectively banished Max from her mind. She shuddered again, feeling her stomach heave. All at once she knew she was going to be sick. . . . She ran for the entrance to the cave and fell to her knees on the crumbly rock in front of it. There, with small shaggy bushes tickling her cheeks and green leafy treetops almost at eye-level, she vomited until there was nothing but clear liquid left inside her. When it was over, she sat weakly back, to find Max beside her. She didn't even care that he had seen her at her repulsive worst.

"Here," he said, passing her a bit of gauze bandage that he had hastily doused with water. "Wipe your face, you'll feel better."

"Thanks." She took it from him, shakily, and passed it over her face and neck. The cool wet cloth did make her feel better.

"Rinse your mouth out, then take a couple of sips," he ordered next, passing her the empty whiskey bottle which he had pressed into service as a canteen. Lora obediently took a swallow from the bottle, swished it around her mouth and spat. Then she took a couple of sips as he directed, and handed him back the bottle.

He let her sit there for a moment, soaking the warmth of the sun into her shock-chilled system, then he pulled her to her feet. She clung to his forearms, her eyes lifted to study his face. She didn't know it, but the newly risen sun caught the tangle of curls that framed her face, turning it a bright and shiny gold that glinted and glittered with life. All her unaccustomed outdoor activity of the day before had left her normally pale face flushed with rosy color from the sun. Her mouth was a deep rose, too, and her eyes were a dark, denim blue. The shocking pink t-shirt hugged her from shoulders to waist, and even though she was wearing a bra the contours of her soft, round breasts with their upthrusting nipples was unmistakable. And the tight jeans revealed no less of her curvaceous hips and long, long legs. . . .

Max's face tightened as he looked down at her. All the warm caring, all the tenderness and concern vanished, to be replaced by a craggy mask harder than the rocks they stood on. Those black eyes glittered down at her unreadably, and that hard mouth tightened into a straight line. Even the silky black mustache seemed to change: it was no longer charmingly masculine, but intimidatingly ferocious. Lora stared up into the ruthless face of the man who had first kidnapped her, and felt her eyes widen.

"Max?" His name was a soft, puzzled question. She didn't understand what had caused him to change so quickly. He'd been kind and gentle, and now . . .

She felt his forearms tighten under her hands. "Go back inside. I have some things to do. I'll be back later."

"Max . . ."

"Tunafish!" he roared over her head. "You're on!"

"Got ya, boss!" came the answering shout from inside the cave, and then Max turned his attention back to Lora.

"Go on," he said, stepping away from her so that her hands fell to her sides. Without even looking at her to see if she obeyed, he turned and started down the crumbly rock face of the cliff. Lora stared at the back of that black head, at the broad back and those long, jean-clad legs until they disappeared into the dense jungle below.

XX

"I want to talk to you."

It was late afternoon of the same day, and the daily downpour was raging outside. The rush of the water, which Lora sometimes found almost soothing, was threatening to drive her out of her mind. She was so sick of everything always being damp, and smelling of mildew! To say nothing of snakes and ticks and mosquitoes and—and men! Particularly one man. She glared at him challengingly as she cornered him at last, sitting at the mouth of the cave, pistol resting on his bent knees as he stared out into the pouring rain. He had taken good care to be out of the cave all morning, and she had a feeling he would have been gone now if conscience hadn't demanded that he take over the guard duties so that Tunafish could rest. Ever since he had come back into the cave—bearing fish, this time, which they had baked on a rock and eaten for lunch—he had been behaving as though she were a mere acquaintance whose name he had trouble remembering. She had taken it silently, because there didn't seem to be anything else she could do without making a fool of herself. But as he chatted with Tunafish, and even exchanged a few remarks with Minelli and DiAngelo while shepherding them outside to attend to nature's call, she felt her grievance grow until she thought she would choke on it. Damn it, she was not disposable! She could not be used once and then discarded like a—a paper plate! As Tunafish dozed and Minelli and DiAngelo stared sullenly off into space, Lora glared at Max's averted head and seethed. Suddenly, she made up her mind: as the advertisements said, she was mad as hell and she was not going to take it anymore! And so she walked determinedly to where Max stared out at the roaring rain and confronted him.

It seemed to take her words a moment to sink in. Then he turned his head slowly to look up at her. She stood, hands on hips, face belligerent as she glared down at him.

He sighed and lifted a finger to stroke his mustache. "Not now, Lora, okay?"

"Why not now?" Her tone was as belligerent as her expression.

He sighed again. "Would you believe I have a headache?"

"No."

"Well, I do."

"Want an aspirin?" Sarcasm stung through the seemingly solicitous request.

"That would be nice, yes."

"Too bad. Tunafish has taken them all."

Max sighed again, eyeing her.

"Just who the hell do you think you are?" The question burst forth from her throat of its own volition, fueled by the seething anger that had driven her to tell him off in the first place—and by the resigned way he was meeting her increasingly maddened eyes.

"This is about what happened yesterday, I take it?"

"You're darned right it is! I don't like being treated like a—like a—" she hesitated, searching for just the right word. To tell the truth, she didn't know exactly what he was treating her like. All she knew was that she didn't like it!

"Like a one-night stand?" he supplied helpfully.

Lora glared at him. "Yes!"

"I knew you wouldn't."

His calm response stopped her incipient tirade in its tracks. "What?"

He eyed her. The resigned look was back, but this time Lora was too confused to respond with the fury it deserved.

"Look, Lora, if we have to have this out, why don't you sit down? I'm sure Minelli and DiAngelo are having a ball trying to figure out why you're shouting at me."

Lora cast a furtive look over her shoulder. Like Tunafish, Minelli seemed to be dozing, but DiAngelo was watching them interestedly. She looked back at Max, who patted the floor beside him. She sat down with poor grace.

"If you want an apology for yesterday, you've got it. I apologize. Sincerely."

"I don't want an apology! I want to know what happened! Yesterday, when we were—were making love, you seemed—I thought . . ." Her voice trailed off as she found herself quite unable to put what she had thought into words, even in her own mind. "And then you changed," she added obscurely. "This morning, too."

Max looked at her for a moment, his expression unreadable, then turned to look back out at the slashing torrents of rain.

"Just what did you think while we were making love,

Lora?" The question was quiet, but the eyes that turned back to focus on hers were keen.

"I thought—I thought . . . " She floundered in a morass of half-formed sentences, and stopped.

"You thought that this might be the start of some kind of deathless love affair," he answered for her. That was exactly what she had thought, she realized with chagrin, but now that he had put it into words, it sounded hopelessly sophomoric. And from the way he said it, he thought so, too.

"Well?" he asked, probing.

"What if I did?" she answered, her chin lifting defiantly.

"That's what's wrong, Lora. It wasn't the start of a love affair. At least, not the way you think of a love affair. You're a forever kind of girl, Lora. You want an husband and kids and a home. You're not the type to just enjoy having sex with no strings attached, and that's all I have to offer. Good sex while we're stranded in this godforsaken jungle. That's it. After that, good-bye."

"And you think I couldn't handle that?"

"I know you couldn't. I've run up against girls like you before, Lora. You're like spiders, trying to wrap a man up in little silken threads until he's so bound to you that he can never escape in a million years. And once you've got him, you try to change him. I've been through all that, Lora, and I'm not going through it again."

"What about yesterday?"

"Yesterday was not all my fault. You had something to do with what happened, too, you know. You goaded me until I lost control of my temper, and when I lost my temper all my other controls went with it. But what happened was only sex, Lora. Good sex. Great sex. But only sex. Which you enjoyed as much as I did."

Lora stared up into that dark face, into the black eyes that were shadowed and guarded as they looked down at her. Her eyes touched on the square jaw almost black with whiskers, the hard, thin mouth, the silky mustache, the blade of a nose. They moved over the broad cheekbones, the thick black wings of his eyebrows, the forehead faintly lined with wrinkles as he frowned, the rough black hair that was growing longer so that it curled a little about his ears and neck. She looked at that face, at the muscular neck and broad shoulders and corded arms and the rest, and made a blinding discovery.

I've fallen in love with him, she thought, amazed. Something of her stunned expression must have gotten through to him, because he looked first puzzled, then faintly alarmed.

"You're not going to cry, are you?" There was a note of panic in his voice. Lora stared at him. "I'm sorry I was so blunt, but—"

"No, I'm not going to cry," she agreed absently. She continued to stare at him, unblinking. This was inconceivable—it couldn't have happened, but it had. Apparently, she was as much a sucker for great sex as he had feared. She couldn't let him know. That much was clear. Not now, not until she worked out what she was going to do. She had to have time to think—time to assimilate this catastrophic happening, this time bomb which had dropped out of nowhere into her heart.

"I think I'll go for a walk," she said, standing abruptly.

"You can't do that! Have you forgotten we're in the middle of the jungle? And it's raining." He stood up too, towering over her, staring down at her with concern.

He must have thought she had lost her mind, she thought, and after a moment's reflection agreed silently that she had. But not in the way he supposed.

"So it is," she agreed, staring out into the torrents. "Then I think I'll take a nap."

"Lora . . ." He caught her arm, frowning. "Are you okay?"

She looked up at him. Impossible to believe that she had fallen in love with this disreputable roughneck whom she had never even set eyes on two weeks ago, this macho male who made it clear that all he wanted from her was a little sex. Impossible. . . .

"I'm fine. Just tired all of a sudden."

"Oh." He pondered that, watching her out of those hooded eyes with concern.

Lora said nothing more, just turned away and crossed to her bunk. She didn't even lie down. Just sat there, staring off into space while he watched her with growing puzzlement. She needed to think. . . .

The rest of the day passed much as had every day since the plane crash: in preparing meals, sweeping out the cave with a broom made of leaves bound to a stick, shaking out the bedding and carefully examining it for unwelcome guests. Most of these tasks fell to Lora, whose semi-feminist soul would have been outraged at the men's casual assumption that she would assume all the "womanly" tasks except for one thing: since she and Max were the only two able-bodied persons available, and Max was called on to provide food, stand guard duty, watch over Minelli and DiAngelo, and help Tunafish with his personal care, that left only herself to do the other tasks that needed to be done. Her inate fairness made her realize that, in this case, the work she was allotted happened to be traditional woman's duties was just incidental. Here in the jungle, each did what life had best suited him for. Max was used to danger and guns and violence. She was not, but she could sweep the floor or cook a trout. So that's what she did.

Night fell with the suddenness of a breath snuffing out a candle, and once it did there was little to do except sleep. Except for whoever was standing guard—Tunafish spelled

Max throughout the night, but Max took on the bulk of the responsibility so that Tunafish could get enough sleep—the rest of the residents of the cave turned in nearly as soon as the sun went down. And rose with the sun as well.

Lora's abstracted silence ever since her conversation with Max did not go unnoticed. Max himself eyed her warily, as if she were an explosive device that might detonate at any moment. Tunafish noticed, too, and watched her with a thoughtfulness that Lora wasn't even aware of, so caught up in her own thoughts was she.

"You two have a fight?" Tunafish asked the question casually of Lora when she brought him his dinner of bananas and baked fish. He was sitting on a shelflike rock formation with his back leaning against the wall and his splinted leg propped on another rock. Looking down at him, Lora saw that, of all of them, he had fared the worst in this adventure. Besides the torture of his broken leg, which she knew still pained him a great deal despite Max's inexpert care of it, he had lost a lot of weight. His flesh seemed to hang about him in folds. His skin had lost both elasticity and tone, and beneath the dark pigment lurked an ominous charcoal gray. His eyes were dull, too, glazed over most of the time, the whites yellow and bloodshot, the irises without life. Of course, some of that could have resulted from his cautious use of the drug. . . . How much, Lora didn't know. Most of it, she hoped. She didn't like to consider the alternatives. The specter of gangrene rose in her mind, to be swiftly banished. Surely Max would know if Tunafish had developed something like that.

"No, we didn't have a fight." Because of her concern, she responded to that more gently than she might have. Ordinarily, she would have tartly told him to mind his own business. Tunafish saw too much, and this secret she had uncovered about the way she felt about Max was not for public con- sumption. She didn't want anyone to know; not Tunafish, and certainly not Max.

"Then how come you been walkin' around like you seen a ghost all day, and Max been watchin' you like you gettin' ready to grow another head?"

"It's your imagination, Tunafish. You've been shut up in this cave too long. Or else you've been sniffing that powder again."

Tunafish grinned crookedly. "No, I ain't. I ain't had any dope for days. I ain't comin' out of this a junkie, not if my leg falls off. I've seen too much of what that stuff can do."

Lora was suddenly curious. "Where, Tunafish?"

"Everywhere I've ever been, all my life. The worst was in 'Nam, though."

"Did Max ever take drugs? Is that why he is so against them?"

Tunafish cast a sneaking look toward where Max stood pointing his pistol at a sullen Minelli and DiAngelo, whose hands he had untied so that they could eat. They were on the far side of the cave, perhaps twenty feet away with a rock formation partially blocking the area between them and where Lora and Tunafish talked. Still, Tunafish lowered his voice to a near whisper.

"We all did—in 'Nam. Only way most of us made it out of there reasonably sane. Max didn't do nothin' real heavy—a little weed, some speed mainly. In our line of work, you had to stay on your toes. Doze off in some of the situations we been in, and that's the last nap you'll ever take." He drew his forefinger graphically across his throat, and Lora shuddered.

"Tunafish—did drugs have something to do with what happened at Mei Veng?" The question popped out of her mouth from nowhere, but even as she asked it Lora knew the

answer. It would explain so much—how Max came to participate in such an atrocity, his later aversion to drugs.

Tunafish nodded once, his eyes moving again to where
Max still stood with his back to them. "We was all wired out
of our minds at the time. Else we never would have done
it—not killed all them people, no matter what. But that stuff
makes you real paranoid and meaner than a black snake. Me,
I told myself that what we did ain't no worse than anything
else that happens in wartime, and I'm able to live with it.
Max is more sensitive. He has those nightmares."

"Yes." Lora followed his eyes to the subject of their
conversation. He was such a masculine man, tall and strong
and sure of himself, cocky almost. A male chauvinist to his
toenails, she suspected, as incapable of admitting to feeling
hurt and lonely and afraid as a pig was of flying. But he was
vulnerable too, enormously vulnerable. More than many
people who openly asked for it, he needed love. He needed
someone to hold him in her arms and convince him that what
he had done was not so bad, was not unforgivable, did not
put him beyond the pale of normal society. To convince him
that he was lovable. And loved. And she meant to be that
someone.

"Ain't you gonna eat?"

Lora's eyes snapped back around to Tunafish, who was
regarding her knowingly. She didn't even bother to scowl at
him, just looked down at the half-eaten plate of food that he
had managed to plod through while talking. Her own portion
of bananas and fish waited for her by the fire, but the
knowledge did not inspire her with enthusiasm. She was sick
of bananas and fish.

"I suppose so," she said without enthusiasm, and with a
quick smile at Tunafish moved off to eat her own dinner. Max,
she noticed, took care to stay away from the fire until she was

safely finished and in her pallet. But the fact didn't bother her. Now that she had, she thought, figured out what made Max tick, she had also figured out what to do about the problem of loving him: do it without telling him. She would sneak up on him, using the bait of sex to draw him close to her, hoping that by encouraging him to take her body she could find a way to take his heart. It was a dangerous scheme, one that could easily leave her bleeding to death if it failed. But it might work, she told herself. Anyway, it was the only chance she had.

Accordingly, she lay waiting for him when he finally came to his pallet. She judged the time to be around ten P.M., because that was when Tunafish usually took over to allow Max his scant four hours of sleep. She had been amazed to see how well he seemed to function on such a small amount of sleep; like the nightmares, another legacy of Vietnam, she guessed.

Her pallet was so close to his that she could almost feel the heat of his body as he wrapped himself in the blanket and settled down to sleep. She wanted to reach out and touch him, wanted to stroke that rough black hair and hold him in her arms as he fell asleep. But she knew that he was not ready for tenderness yet. What he thought he wanted from her was sex, and only sex. Lora was gambling on the hope that he was fooling himself. Her instincts told her that what he really wanted was love. But he was afraid of it, afraid of her, so he disguised his very human need as mere sexual desire, safe in the assumption that she would not permit him to simply use her for such a purpose. Or, at least, he thought he was safe. She meant to shatter that smug assumption into a thousand smithereens.

Cautiously, she lifted her head and looked around. At the entrance to the cave, on the other side of the small, flickering fire that served as much to frighten away whatever animals might be prowling in the dark jungle as to provide warmth, sat Tunafish, his broken leg thrust out stiffly before him, his arm around the bent knee of his good leg. A pistol lay on the ground beside him. One hand touched it absently as he stared out at the inky black night. Across the large cavern, Minelli and DiAngelo were rolled into their pallets, huddled under a single blanket. At night, for safety's sake, they were bound hand and foot. Lora always worried that some night they just might manage to get free and sneak up on Tunafish while she and Max slept—she never worried about anyone sneaking up on Max—but tonight was not the time to start thinking about that. She had other things on her mind.

Except for the small, orange glow of light cast by the fire at the mouth of the cave, the rest of the huge cavern was dark. Shadows leaped and danced up the walls, highlighting the Mayan drawings so that they almost seemed to come alive. A neat little fence of stalagmites provided a small measure of privacy between where Lora and Max lay on their pallets and where DiAngelo and Minelli slept, but there was only the darkness to shield them from Tunafish's eyes should he happen to look their way. Outside in the night came the sudden scream of a large cat. Lora shivered, and instinctively drew closer to Max.

She was huddled almost up against his back now, lying on the very edge of her pallet. She stared at the back of that rough black head, at the broad shoulders wrapped in the gray blanket, and for a moment her nerve almost failed her. She had never before tried to seduce a man. . . . But this wasn't any man, it was Max, proud, stubborn, unreachable Max, with his still bleeding war wounds and his fiercely hidden vulnerability. Max, whom she loved. Taking a deep breath, Lora scooted over until she had closed the small distance between them, until she was lying on his pallet with him, curled against his back, luxuriating in the warmth and hardness of his body. She waited for him to move, to speak, to make some acknowledgment of her nearness. What she got was a snore.

He was asleep! If that wasn't just like him. Lora felt mildly affronted, until she realized that of course he hadn't known that she had designs on his body and therefore could not have been expected to stay awake in readiness. Now that she thought about it, he had really made her job easier. Because he might just possibly have rejected her overtures at the outset, had he been awake. Now he wouldn't have a chance. . . .

She snuggled closer, her arm sliding around his body, hugging him to her. No response, except another snore. Her hand sought for and found the opening in the blanket, sliding inside the overlapped ends to seek his body. He was dressed in the t-shirt and jeans. Lora's hand encountered the smooth, soft cotton of the t-shirt, slid over it and down to the stiffer material of the jeans, where it hesitated, hovering around the waistband. She had never down anything like this before, and every ladylike tenet of her upbringing was screaming with shock. But after only a moment's hesitation, she plowed determinedly onward. Faint heart never won fair maiden—or, in this case, fair gent.

The snap of his jeans gave with an audible snap. For a second Lora froze, holding her breath, but nothing happened except another snore. Funny, to her the sound had been as loud as a gunshot. . . . Her fingers found the tab to his zipper and worked it downward, not without some tugging. But finally she had it open. He was all hers, to do with what she would. What should she do with him? Lora nearly panicked, realizing that she had never touched a man as intimately as she was about to touch Max. Making love with Brian had never included anything like this. But she couldn't stop now—not if she wanted Max. And she did want him, body and soul.

Her fingers moved, touched soft cotton covering a warm bulge. There, that was not so bad. Nothing frightening at all, just Max. She touched him again, more firmly, her fingers sliding up over the protuberance that swelled as she stroked it. She enjoyed the knowledge that she could do this to him. . . . Emboldened, her fingers slid back down over the front of his underpants, tantalized by the hardness and heat of him. The thin layer of cloth was no barrier at all. . . . Her hand slid up to the elastic waistband, briefly stroked the hair-roughened belly, then crept inside, sliding across the muscled, ridged abdomen to the object of her assault. It had grown even in the scant seconds since she had last made contact, she thought. . . .

Her fingers curled around the heated shaft, squeezing gently. It was burning hot against her skin, hard as a steel rod yet covered in skin that was silky to the touch. She squeezed again, then moved her hand up, then down. . . . He throbbed beneath her touch. Lora felt an answering throb deep in her own body. To her surprise, what she was doing was exciting her as well. Her breathing quickened, and she pressed herself closer against his sleeping back, enjoying the crush of the hard wall of muscles against her breasts. She pressed her hips against the hardness of his behind, and enjoyed that sensation, too. But most of all, she enjoyed the feel of him pulsing and burning in her hand. . . . Intoxicated by the sensation that she was free to do as she liked now that she no longer had to worry about modesty and being a lady and whether he would respect her in the morning—all the trappings of civilization that had been drummed into her head since her birth—she slid her hand lower, reaching for and finding the soft round protuberances, at the end of the shaft. She cuddled them gently for a moment, then reached up to grasp him again. . . .

"What the hell do you think you're doing?" His hand shot out to fasten over hers, trapping it against him so that it couldn't move. He turned so that he could fix her with disbelieving eyes. He was on his back and she lay on her side beside him, one arm curled beneath her head, the other flattened against throbbing, burning male flesh by his hand.

"I made a decision tonight." She smiled at him, sensuously moving her fingers beneath his imprisoning hand so that they kneaded him.

His face changed, and he shifted suddenly, so that she was no longer touching him. His hand closed more tightly over hers, pulling it away from him and holding it captive outside the intimacy of his shorts.

"What kind of decision?" His facial muscles were contracted as if he was in pain; his voice was hoarse from trying to emerge from between lips that barely moved. Lora saw the black glittering flame in his eyes and smiled a small, catlike smile.

"I decided to take you up on your offer of great sex." So large was her satisfaction at the sudden blaze of fire in his eyes that she practically purred the words.

He looked at her warily, his hand contracting over hers so that it practically crushed her slim fingers. She made not a single sound of protest. The unthinking strength of his grip went hand in hand with the rapid rise and fall of his chest as wariness battled with desire.

"It wasn't an offer. It was an explanation."

She liked the way he gritted the words at her. Her smile widened just a bit, and the hand that he was not holding moved out from under her head to run a soft, teasing finger across his full lower lip. He jerked his head back, but his eyes flamed even more in response.

Delicately, she lifted her eyebrows at him. "The way I remember it, you made me an offer. Good sex while we're stranded in this godforsaken jungle, and after that, good-bye, was the way I believe you phrased it."

"And you'd agree to that? I don't believe it! You're stringing me along."

Lora smiled at him, and her wayward hand came back to trail that provocative finger along the side of his neck and around the base until it twirled in the silky black whorls of hair at the hollow of his throat.

"I'm not, you know. I decided that you were right: I do need a husband and children and a home—some day. But not now. Now what I need is—you." Her voice dropped to a husky breath on the last word, and her eyes, soft with promise, locked with his.

He took a deep breath, his eyes moving from her eyes to her mouth and back up again in an unconscious gesture that spoke volumes.

"Why shouldn't we get some pleasure out of this awful mess? I've been miserable enough to die most of the time— except for yesterday afternoon. You made me feel good, Max. And I decided I like feeling good."

He was staring at her as if he couldn't believe his ears. Lora hardly believed that she was saying these things herself. The words, the sultry tone of her voice, seemed to come from some part of her that she had never been aware of before. The woman part, not the lady.

"Are you going to renege on your offer?" She asked the question softly, her lips parting invitingly.

He stared at her as if he was Adam seeing the serpent in Eden. Which, in effect, he was. When he didn't answer, she leaned over and kissed him, rubbing her lips sensuously across his hard mouth. The mustache tickled... His lips stayed closed beneath hers, so Lora traced the line where they joined with her tongue. Then his mouth parted on a harsh indrawing of breath. Lora leaned closer, as if to deepen the kiss, then, on a sudden instinct, drew back.

"Christ." He was staring up at her, his hard face clenched, his eyes glittering with passion. His body was rigid, his hold painful on her hand. "Any more of that and I'll take you right here in plain view of Tunafish and anyone else who cares to look."

"Does that mean that you'll keep your part of the bargain?"

He scowled a little. "If you'll keep yours. No strings, Lora. Do you hear me?"

"I promise. But you have to live up to your end of the deal, too."

"What's that?"

"Great sex, Max. You promised me great sex."

"Damn!" He jackknifed upright, grimacing, his arms coming up to hug his bent knees. Lora sat up too, and looked at him with concern.

"What's wrong?"

He eyed her grimly. "You should know. We've got to get out of here or I'm going to embarrass myself. Here, put your shoes on."

He retrieved her sneakers from the foot of her bed, shook them impatiently to check for intruders, and thrust them at her.

"Put them on. Now," he said impatiently in response to her surprised look. Puzzled but obedient, Lora took the shoes from him and began to slide them onto her feet.

Max reached down to snap and zip his jeans, wincing as he made some minor adjustments to accommodate the source of his discomfort, jammed his feet into his running shoes without even bothering to tie the laces, scooped the pistol out from under his pillow and stuck it into his waistband, then stood up, dragging her with him. Then he bent to grab the blanket from his pallet and fling it over his shoulder. Tunafish turned to look in their direction, his attention attracted by the movement. Max walked toward him, stiff-legged, pulling Lora by the hand after him.

"What's happenin', boss?" Tunafish's question was lazy as he took in the two of them, Max stalking past, his shoelaces flapping, with Lora's hand held in a crushing grip while Lora, pink-faced, hurried to keep up.

"We're going to get some air."

"Out there? At night?" Tunafish sounded amazed, but Lora saw the grin lurking under his carefully straight face. Max must have seen it too, because he scowled at his friend and continued on, pausing only to catch up the flashlight that rested on a rocky shelf near the entrance.

XXI

"Where are we going?" Lora was breathless as Max dragged her down the crumbling face of the cliff after him. She slipped and slid and nearly fell on her bottom more than once, but still he kept moving relentlessly forward. She would have hung back when they reached the edge of the jungle, but he didn't even pause and she was dragged into the inky black forest before she could protest. Still, she tried.

"Max, have you lost your mind? It's dangerous out here at night. There could be jaguars—snakes—anything! Can't we wait until morning?"

"The way I feel, I'll be lucky if I can wait ten minutes. If you didn't want it, Lora, you shouldn't have started it. You asked for it, and by God, you're going to get it!"

"I didn't know it would involve being dragged through the jungle at night! Where are we going?"

He turned to flash a single glinting look at her. "I don't consider sex a spectator sport. Don't worry, I know what I'm doing. I've been out here before at night, remember, and I haven't seen a thing more threatening than a bat.''

"A bat!" Lora moaned and shuddered, but was still dragged relentlessly on. Her eyes had adjusted to the darkness by now, and she was relieved—she thought—to find that it was not as inpenetrable as she had supposed. Dense black shadows lay everywhere, and with the absence of light each twisted vine and gnarled trunk took on a sinister aspect. The insect chorus was silent, and so were the birds. Lora found the absence of the incessant chattering and shrieking spine chilling. Even the faint rustlings in the undergrowth seemed more menacing in the dark. Lora could imagine a jaguar crawling through the undergrowth on his belly, gold eyes alight as he stalked them, his prey. . . .

"Please, Max . . ." She moaned in real fear, only to find herself jerked ruthlessly on.

"If you don't like it, you'll have to be more careful next time you take me up on an offer."

"I will." It was said fervently. "At least I'll be careful to do it in daylight. Max, this is insane."

"I feel insane."

There was no answer she could make to this, so she shut up and concentrated on not tripping over anything—she shuddered to be more specific—that might cross her path. If anything she was walking on was not dead leaves and fallen branches, she preferred not to know about it.

The shifting darkness disguised his destination until it loomed out of the night as a large, solidly shaped shadow in a landscape of shifting ones. The plane. She should have guessed.

"What if something's in it?" She hung back as he moved in the direction of the jagged hole.

"Don't worry, I doubt if anything much is. Our smell will

still be all over the place here, and wild animals don't like our smell. But if it makes you feel any better, I intend to check it out. That's why I brought the flashlight."

Lora had vaguely wondered why he hadn't turned the flashlight on during their trek through the jungle, but had come to the conclusion that he felt it would attract attention. Without light, they were just one of many creatures out roaming in the night.

He switched the flashlight on, aiming the beam down at his feet, then turned to look at her.

"You want to wait here while I check?"

Lora shuddered, and grabbed at the hand that had at last released hers. "Not on your life!"

"Stay close, then."

Lora reflected that if she had ever heard an unnecessary piece of advice, that was it, but then she didn't have time to think anymore because he was disappearing through the opening and she had to scramble to keep up with him.

The interior of the plane smelled musty, even mustier than the cave. Max swung the flashlight around the interior slowly, then moved down the aisle, shining the light carefully to the left and right. When he got to the curtain separating the cabin from the cockpit and moved it, there was a sudden burst of sound. Lora screamed as something took wing, then screamed again as a trio of small white creatures passed within inches of her head as they flapped toward the opening. The whole episode took less than a couple of seconds, but Lora was left shaking and staring wide-eyed at the gaping hole that led to the jungle at night.

"Just some bats. Nothing to be afraid of. The ones around here are harmless. All they eat are insects." Max was back, his arm sliding around her waist as he led her toward the rear of the plane where the seats had been removed. He stopped in the tail section, in an area with perhaps as much floor space as a double bed and maybe a few inches more than his own height in head room. Shining the light all around, he gestured for Lora to follow the beam with her eyes.

"See? We're all alone." He shook out the blanket as he spoke, while Lora watched with nervous eyes. Somehow she seemed to have gotten out of the spirit of the thing. She was perfectly willing to let his seduction wait until morning.

There was a faint click as he turned off the flashlight. Without its bright yellow beam, the inside of the plane was even darker than the jungle. . . . She was shivering as his arms came around her, and not with passion. Her cursedly vivid imagination was alive with creepy crawlies. . . .

He pulled her against him, and she was faintly comforted by the hard warmth of his body. He was reassuringly solid. . . . She snuggled against him, and felt one arm move as he reached up to slide a hand beneath her chin and tilt her face toward his. The darkness was like a veil shrouding his features, but she could clearly see the restless glitter of his black eyes.

"Not afraid anymore, are you? We're perfectly safe. Trust me."

His voice was the merest murmur as he bent down to brush her mouth with his. It could hardly be called a kiss, so brief was the contact. He straightened to look down at her, his hand dropping to gently stroke over the skin of her throat. Lora kept her face tilted to his, her throat arching under the soft caress. He bent his head again to take her mouth in a kiss that was slightly harder, slightly more stinging, but was still over in slightly more time than it might take her to blink. Lora frowned, and felt herself yearning upwards. If he was going to kiss her, he might as well do it right. . . .

He bent his head a third time, his arm hard around her

waist holding her against him as his other hand slid down the front of her t-shirt to find her breast. His palm, firm and warm, cupped the soft roundness, and Lora felt a sudden clenching in her loins. Her nipple sprang to sudden attention beneath his hand. He did not caress her, just held her with that penetrating warmth while she swelled into his hand, and somehow it was the most arousing thing he could have done.

"Max," she breathed, her arms coming up of their own volition to find the back of his head and pull it the rest of the way down to her lips. She felt the soft abrasion of his mustache, felt him smile a little bit against her mouth, and then he was kissing her as she longed to be kissed, hard and deep, his tongue in her mouth demanding her body's most primitive responses. She still shivered in his arms, but fear was the farthest thing from her mind. She shivered because her body was on fire for him and he seemed in no hurry to put out the flames. . . .

His hand was beneath the t-shirt now, leaving a trail of fire over her ribs as it slid around to find and unfasten the hook of her bra. One-handed . . . Lora would have marveled at his expertise if she had been capable of marveling at anything other than her body's responses. He was tugging the t-shirt up, and Lora was impatient as she had to let go of his mouth for the brief time it took to pull the shirt and bra over her head. Then her hands were on his shirt, pulling it off, and their naked chests were crushing together as her hands fumbled at the zipper of his jeans and his operated hers with more surety.

"Amateur," he goaded softly into her mouth as he began to push her jeans down her hips while she still fumbled with his zipper.

"My hands are shaking," she whispered in response, tugging at the recalcitrant zipper to no avail.

"So are mine," he said into her mouth, and she trembled more at the knowledge. Then he was releasing her mouth to slide both her jeans and her panties down her legs. He had to pull off her shoes before she could step out of the garments, leaving them lying in a heap where she had been. She felt his breath warm on her thighs and then her belly as he straightened, and remembering what he had done to her before she felt the clutching spiral of urgent desire spring to life between her legs. Wantonly, she pressed herself against him, going mad as her nakedness came up against the stiff material of his jeans. She wanted him naked, too. . . .

Her hand tore at the zipper now, and this time it gave. He stood unmoving as she bent to slide the jeans and shorts down his muscled legs, to remove his untied shoes. Then he was naked, gloriously naked, and as she straightened she pressed herself to him, somehow finding that her mouth was trailing up his thighs, open and moist as it caressed the hair-roughened muscles that clenched and trembled beneath her kisses. . . . He jutted out at a ninety-degree angle from the path she was taking, and she didn't even have time to consider what she was doing before some instinct that she hadn't even known she possessed told her to take him in her mouth. She did, and he groaned deep and loud, the sound agonized in the hush of the night. His hands clenched on her hair as she allowed her instincts to take over, loving him as he had loved her before, pleasuring him as he had pleasured her. Until at last he could stand it no longer.

"Stop," he ordered on a strangled groan. Caught up in what she was doing, Lora paid no attention. He groaned again, then pulled her away from him by her hair and held her there on her knees in front of him when she would have come back to him.

"Max!"

"Easy, babe, easy. Christ, I don't believe what you do to me." He was dropping to his knees beside her, his hands on her arms easing her down. Lora was barely conscious of the roughness of the blanket beneath her bare backside as he pinned her with his body, his thighs wedging between hers, spreading them wide. She needed no encouragement. She was ready for him, aching, hungry. . . .

"I love your tits." He muttered those words against the soft globes as his mouth rooted for and then found a nipple. He drew it gently into his mouth, rolling his tongue around the bud, biting it softly.

She could feel the scratch of his mustache and unshaven chin rasping against her soft skin. Lora cried out, her hands coming up to clutch his shoulders, her nails digging deep into his skin. His mouth moved to the other nipple, suckling, rasping, and Lora felt quivers of fire shoot up from her loins. She whimpered, writhing beneath him, her legs coming up of their own volition to wrap around his hips. He was hard and heavy and hot on her, crushing her down into the hard floor, and she loved it. The burning heat of him jabbed at the softness of her inner thigh, and she shifted restlessly, craving his possession. With every fiber of her being she wanted him. . . .

"And I love your ass." His hands slid all the way around her body to separately cup the twin halves of her behind, squeezing and kneading and stroking the dark crevice between.

Lora whimpered, stunned that she could be so aroused by such a caress, and then his mouth was on her breasts again and his hands on her bottom were lifting her against him, grinding her hips into his. She wrapped herself more tightly around him, clutching him to her with arms and legs, trembling, writhing, needing. . . .

"Please, Max, do it now!" she moaned as his mouth came

up to claim hers, unable to bear the throbbing tension that was rapidly turning into physical pain inside her another instant. In answer, his mouth possessed her, fierce and demanding and wildly sweet. And his body possessed her at the same time.

Lora groaned. The feeling was like nothing she had ever experienced. She quivered and quaked and cried out as he made love to her with passionate intensity, his body an instrument of both torture and ecstasy as he went first soft and slow, then hard and fast, then soft and slow again, keeping her always on the brink. Finally, she was mindless with passion, writhing as she cried his name. She needed him to give her peace. . . .

"How do you want it, Lora? Hard or easy?" It was a soft, insidious question, murmured as he traced the inside of her ear with his tongue.

She shivered and shuddered, her hands digging deep into his buttocks as he kept his movements teasingly slow. His hair-roughened skin was a penance against her aching breasts. His hard-muscled body kept her pinned to the floor, helpless to do anything to bring this agony to an end. She could only beg him to be merciful. . . .

"Harder. Love me harder," she groaned, driven far beyond inhibitions by the torment he was inflicting on her body.

She heard the quick indrawing of his breath, felt a reflexive clenching of his arms around her, and then he was slamming into her with the fierce rapidity of a jackhammer and she was loving it. She clung to him, gasping, matching her movements to his with frenzied abandon. He cried out her name at the end, stiffening, his arms clenching around her so that she could scarcely breathe. But she wasn't concerned with breathing. She was dying, and it was glorious. She was soaring above the clouds, and he was with her. . . .

It could have been seconds or it could have been hours before she drifted back down to earth. Lora rather suspected that it had been somewhere in between, because the interior of the plane was still inky dark, the blanket was still scratchy beneath her backside, and the man she loved still lay sprawled across her, breathing hard. She turned her head and found that his face was so close that their noses brushed. Smiling faintly, she brushed a kiss across his mouth. His eyes opened. Her eyes must have adjusted to the dark, because at such close range she could see every separate eyelash—he had surprisingly thick eyelashes—and every tiny line that fanned out around his eyes. She could see the glisten of moisture on his forehead and the dampness of the edges of the rough black hair. She could see the bump in the bridge of his nose and the chiseled line of his mouth beneath the villainous mustache. She could see the shadowed outline of his unshaven chin.

"Did I live up to my end of the promise?" There was a teasing inflection in his voice, and she could see a faint gleam of white teeth as his lips parted in a fleeting grin.

"Mmmmm."

"Oh, no. You'll have to do better than that. You weren't shy earlier." He leaned over to kiss her, drawing her lower lip into his mouth to nibble at it before releasing it. Lora stretched, loving the feel of his warm, sweat-damp body on her, and would have purred if she knew how.

"You want your pound of flesh, do you? All right, it was very nice." She kept her words deliberately prim.

"Very nice? Is that all you can say? Come on, Lora, you can do better than that."

She smiled a little, and her hand came up to trace the harsh outlines of his face. He turned his head so that his mouth nuzzled her palm.

"I really don't have a lot to compare it with, you know. Maybe you could demonstrate again?"

He stared at her for a moment, then chuckled. "You've got to be kidding."

She shook her head. "No-o."

"I feel like Dr. Frankenstein with his monster."

"And what did Dr. Frankenstein do with his monster?" It was silly, seductive teasing, and Lora reveled in it. She had never felt so warmly content, so at ease with a man. . . .

"I have no idea." He shifted, rolling onto his back and pulling her with him so that she was lying on top of him now, her legs between his and her arms around his neck while her fingers threaded through the thick softness of his hair. "But I know what I'm going to do with mine."

"What's that?"

"Guess." His mouth was nuzzling her neck, moving lower. Against her thighs she could feel the part of him that she thought was out for the count hardening again.

"Max, I was teasing!"

"I'm not."

And he proceeded to demonstrate his seriousness very expertly until they were both exhausted. Bright fingers of dawn were trailing down through the trees before they finally made it back to the cave.

XXII

Lora had only been asleep for a couple of hours when something—a faint, distant roar—startled her awake. Not that the sound was particularly loud. It was just the incongruity of it—man-made, mechanical droning out in the middle of the jungle. She started upright, frowning and blinking, to find Max snatching up the first aid kit and sprinting outside while Tunafish craned to see what was happening from his perch on the rocks just inside the cave's mouth.

"What is it?" she asked, scrambling up.

"Airplane overhead," Tunafish answered tersely, barely sparing her a glance as she joined him to look out at Max, who was tilting the silver metal surface of the underside of the first aid box so that it caught the sun. The roar was louder now, and Lora strained to see through the branches hanging out over the clifftop. She caught just a glimpse of a small white plane as it swooped overhead.

"We're here!" she cried, waving frantically. The certain

knowledge that the plane's occupants could neither see nor hear her made her stop. Max was still signaling with the first aid kit, but already the droning of the plane was fading. It was moving away.

"He didn't see us." Lora felt disappointment knot sickly in her stomach. She had not realized how badly she wanted to be safely back in civilization until that plane appeared.

"Maybe. Maybe not. He couldn't land even if he did. The only kind of aircraft that might be able to put down up here is a helicopter. Even if the pilot of that plane saw us, he would have to radio for reinforcements. He couldn't do anything himself."

"Oh." Max's calm pronouncement made her feel a little better.

"Who was it? Could you tell?" The urgency of Tunafish's question reminded Lora that even if the pilot had seen them, it didn't necessarily mean that they were any better off. If that plane had been sent by the mob, or the feds, they could be in serious trouble.

"No way to tell. The plane was unmarked, but that doesn't mean anything. The feds wouldn't be using marked planes for an operation like this." Max answered Tunafish as he moved back inside the cave.

Lora moved, too, sinking down on the rock beside Tunafish disconsolately. She had been so caught up in the magic of what was happening between her and Max that she had temporarily forgotten the danger they faced. But now she remembered, and the memory shook her—the danger seemed suddenly close at hand. When rescue did arrive—if it could even be termed rescue under the circumstances—the idyll she shared with Max would be shattered. If Minelli's friends were the victors in this race for the drugs, she and Max and Tunafish faced death. Their prospects with the feds were only slightly better. From her previous experience with the Mexican system of law enforcement, she imagined that they would all, herself included, face years of imprisonment. Only if Ortega arrived first would they be saved—maybe. Lora didn't like to admit the tiny niggle of doubt, but it would not be banished. Like Tunafish, she didn't have much faith in Ortega's trustworthiness. Across the cave, Minelli and DiAngelo were sitting upright, their eyes gleaming with interest as they listened silently to this exchange. Looking at them, Lora shuddered inwardly. If their friends should come out on top, she knew that she—to say nothing of Max and Tunafish—could expect no mercy.

"Hey." Seeing her wan face, Max caught her chin in his hand and tilted it so that her eyes met his. "Stop worrying. That plane might not even have been looking for us—or it might have been some of Ortega's men. But worrying's not going to change who it was. So you might as well put it out of your mind. Whatever happens, we'll deal with it when it happens. And we'll come out okay. Trust me."

Beside her, Tunafish snorted. Max shot him a killing glare. But as Lora turned his words over in her mind, she realized that he was right: worrying would not change a thing. She ought to concentrate on making the most out of whatever amount of time she and Max had left, and put the uncertain future out of her mind. She smiled at Max, and he smiled back, looking relieved as he released her chin. Whatever happened, she was resolved to take what came one day at a time.

Max promised Lora great sex, and he delivered. For the next two days, anytime he was not busy they went off alone together. They returned to the waterfall, and made love in the pool itself. They returned to the plane, and agreed that the second occasion there was even better than the first. They made love lying on flat, sun-warmed rocks, standing up with Max's back to a tree and Lora astride, sitting on an overturned tree trunk. They made love until Lora was worn out and Max had dark circles under his eyes from lack of sleep. They made love until they both were satisfied—temporarily. And then they made love again.

For Lora, it was a time of wonder. Although she had found Brian's lovemaking mildly pleasant, she had always thought that sex was somewhat overrated. Once, when she had overheard some of her girl students talking about being horny, and wailing that they would die if they didn't "do it" soon, she had been slightly shocked—nothing those teenagers could do could shock her much, after four years of teaching—but also curious. Did other females really feel that way? She didn't think that she had ever experienced a state that could be described as "horny"—detestable word!—and had certainly never thought that she might die if she didn't have sex. It was supposed to be a basic human need, like hunger and shelter, but she had never experienced her sexuality that way. In fact, she had never really thought of herself as having a sexuality. She made love with Brian because that is what engaged couples did nowadays, and she enjoyed it when it happened. It was all very civilized, very dignified, very controlled. She had found Brian's touch pleasant, and had therefore assumed that all was well in that area of their relationship. Smiling a little, Lora told herself that she hadn't known what she had been missing.

Making love with Max was a soul shattering experience that only improved with repetition. Lora had never dreamed her body could feel the way he made hers feel. She had only to look at him to feel her body quicken. And it wasn't because he was exceptionally handsome, because he wasn't.

Even as besotted as she was, she hadn't changed her opinion about that! Granted, he had a gorgeous body, but so did the Incredible Hulk and he had never done a thing for her temperature. No, it was something about Max himself. Lora didn't know what it was, couldn't find a single, isolated quality that made her react to him like a match to friction, but her response to him was nothing short of devastating. He thrilled her in ways she hadn't known existed, and she palpitated just thinking about them. And him.

Sexy. That was the word her students would have used to describe him, and it fit him to a tee. Everything about him quickened her senses, from his shaggy black hair to his size eleven running shoes. She had only to look into those narrowed black eyes, gleaming with wicked knowledge now whenever they met hers, to feel her heart start to beat faster. Her pulses fluttered over the configuration of battle-scarred nose, lean, bronzed cheeks, and square, unshaven chin. She even liked that ferocious mustache! She loved the way it trickled and rasped when that hard mouth trailed over her soft skin. And it went without saying how she felt about the rest of him. Broad shoulders, wide, hairy chest, narrow hips and long legs were definitely her cup of tea. Funny, she had always thought that thin, bespectacled, intellectual types like Brian attracted her. Lora had to smile at her own naivete. Who would have guessed that she, Lora Harding, would buckle at the knees over a hunk of male beef?

There was more to it than sex, of course. Much more. She loved him. And that surprised her even more than the way he could make her body feel. He was not her type, and that was the truth, but it didn't seem to make any difference. He had lived a hard life and it showed; he was right at home with the violence that was so much a part of his existence; he handled guns with a familiarity that should have given her pause. He had killed, she knew, and while what had happened in Vietnam might be excusable because he had been fighting a war, she had a suspicion that he had killed again in his work with the DEA. And she knew him well enough to know that he would kill again, if necessary. If Minelli or DiAngelo were to become a threat to their security, she had no doubts at all that he would take what steps he deemed prudent to eliminate that threat. And them along with it.

How could she love a man like that? Lora had asked herself that question many times. He was alien to anything she had ever known, to any expectations she had had of the kind of man with whom she would want to spend the rest of her life. But she loved him. There was no rhyme or reason to it. She loved him, and that was that.

He could be gentle. He was gentle with her. He was a man with a conscience, a sensitive, thinking man, as the nightmares he still suffered about what had happened at Mei Veng showed. He was a loyal friend; he could have left Tunafish to fend for himself and walked out of the jungle. Lora had no doubt at all that he would have made it through safely. Max was a survivor, if ever she had known one. And he was a man of honor. He had had her in a position where she was totally in his power in the early days after he had kidnapped her, and he had behaved, if not like a total gentleman, then at least better than many men would have done. He had neither raped her nor sexually molested her nor beaten her. And she had certainly given him cause to knock her senseless, at least. Lora remembered punching him in the nose, and her eyes danced and moved to seek out the object of her amusement, who was leaning a shoulder against the curved rock at the mouth of the cave, back turned, gun resting negligently against a muscular thigh as he studied the landscape below.

He wasn't aware of her eyes on him, but Lora smiled very tenderly at him nonetheless. Clad in filthy running shoes, tattered, faded jeans that were threatening to split in a dozen places, and a once-white t-shirt that was permanently stained with an infinite variety of substances, with more than a week's growth of black beard bristling from his cheeks and chin and a deadly looking pistol dangling negligently from his hand, he was definitely not the stuff of her adolescent dreams of romance. And still she loved him madly.

"Hey, babe, if you're spreading hot stuff around, why don't you spread a little this way? I know how to treat a broad right." Minelli's voice interrupted her reverie, and she looked down at him with distaste. He was filthy, too, his oily face obscured with whiskers, his clothes creased and stained. But he awakened only the liveliest repulsion inside her.

"I bet you do." Her words were dry as she handed him his lunch of one banana and one orange. He took the fruit from her, his stubby fingers brushing hers until she pulled them away pointedly, his eyes moving over her avidly, resting with a suggestive leer on her breasts. Lora had to suppress a shudder. She wouldn't give him the satisfaction of knowing he bothered her. She turned a shoulder on him to hand DiAngelo his fruit, glad that the smaller man was too sullenly miserable to be offensive any longer.

"You ought to give it some thought, babe. Big man up there won't be in charge forever. When my friends get here, everything's going to change, and you better start thinking about getting on the right side."

"I am on the right side." Lora moved away as she said it. She knew she ought to ignore Minelli, but he gave her the creeps. Having him in the cave was like having a fat white slug in a garden. She crossed to sit down next to Tunafish, who was munching his banana with a gloomy expression.

Tunafish took another bite out of his fruit, then looked sideways to watch her peel her own.

"You oughta tell Max if that slime-bag bothers you."

"You heard him, huh?"

"Enough to know that he needs his mouth punched. Ordinarily, I'd be glad to oblige, but . . . " He gestured at his splinted leg. "But Max'll take care of him for you."

Lora bit off a small portion of her banana and made a wry face. "That's what I'm afraid of."

Tunafish looked at her reflectively. "Afraid the boss might make it permanent, is that it? Well, you could be right. I ain't never seen him protectin' his woman before, but I once saw him break a man's neck over an airplane. And a woman is a lot more important than an airplane."

"I'm not his 'woman,' Tunafish." Her tone was repressive, and she concentrated on taking a series of small nibbles out of the side of her banana. She had always hated that term, and besides, it wasn't true. And even if it was, she hated everyone knowing. Anyone knowing. She wasn't comfortable enough with it herself yet. Anyway, true or not, she refused to be known as Max Maxwell's "woman"!

"Yeah. That's why the two of you are always sneakin' off someplace, and why Max ain't had more than two hours' sleep in two days, and why he was whistlin' under his breath this morning. I didn't even know the boss could whistle."

"He was whistling?" Despite herself, she had to follow up on this. The idea intrigued her. If Max was whistling, it must mean he was happy, and if he was happy in their current predicament then she had to be the reason. And she liked knowing that she made him happy. It was a step in the right direction.

"Mmm-hmmm. Sounded real cheerful. Ain't like Max."

Lora thought about that, then smiled suddenly at Tunafish. "Thanks," she said softly.

"What for?"

"For being such a nice man. For being my friend."

Tunafish looked suddenly embarrassed. His eyes dropped to his banana and he took a large bite.

"'S okay," he said around the mouthful. "Any friend of the boss's, you know."

"Yeah, I know," she said, mimicking his mumble. "Me, too." And with another warm smile at him she stood up and went to join Max at the mouth of the cave.

"You and Tunafish looked mighty cozy."

"Jealous?" The saucy question made him frown.

"Nope."

"Good. Then I won't have to worry about damaging your friendship when I tell you that I think Tunafish is a fantastic person."

"I think so, too. So does his wife, and three little kiddies." Max was grinning as he produced this information like a conjurer pulling a rabbit out of his hat.

"Tunafish is married and has children? You're kidding!" Lora was amazed. "He's never said a word!"

"Well, if he's not telling you about the wife and kiddies, then what does he spend so much time talking to you about?"

Lora smiled naughtily. "Wouldn't you like to know?"

Max shook his head. "I don't think so. My ears burn whenever you two get together. If I didn't know better, I'd think he was filling you in on my misspent past."

"Would it bother you if he was?"

"Nope. He doesn't know the best parts." He grinned down at her, looking piratical with those white teeth slashing out of the bristly black beard.

"You're scaring me," Lora replied, and Max's eyes narrowed wickedly.

"I'd rather be doing something else to you."

"Oh?" Lora cast a gleaming look up at him. "Like what?"

"I could show you, but Tunafish might be shocked."

"In that case, maybe you'd better not."

"I could show you in private."

"Sounds interesting."

"It will be. I guarantee it." And he bent his head to whisper in her ear, telling her exactly what he had in mind.

Lora tingled and blushed, and cast nervous glances at the three men behind them. Of course they could have no idea what Max was saying ... ! But as she listened to his outrageous suggestions, and felt her body quicken she felt almost as exposed as if they were carrying out his indecent ideas in full view of everyone.

"Stop it, Max," she breathed when he got so explicit that she trembled.

"Am I embarrassing you?" He looked down at her pink face and chuckled intimately. "I like embarrassing you."

"I always suspected you had a sadistic streak."

"I do. Didn't I get to that part yet? I want to bare your delicious little bottom and spank it until you—"

"Max!"

"You'd like it. I promise."

"Max! I'm not kidding! Stop it."

He grinned, unrepentant. "Spoilsport."

"Hey, boss!" The call came from Tunafish. Both Max and Lora turned to look at him inquiringly, Lora wondering self-consciously if, at a distance of perhaps fifteen feet, Tunafish could tell that her face was red.

"I'm on. You're off. Go root us up something decent to

eat. Like meat. I see another banana, I swear I'm gonna start swingin' from trees." Tunafish picked up his gun and got awkwardly up on one foot. Max moved to help him over to the mouth of the cave, and between the two of them they eased him into a position where he could watch both the valley below and the two men behind them, who watched the operation with sullen expressions.

"You all set?"

"Yeah. Get out of here. Catch me a fish. Or better yet, catch me a steak. As God is my witness, I'd kill for a juicy T-bone."

Tunafish rolled his eyes comically, and Lora laughed. The fire in her face had faded, and she felt comfortable again— until Max grabbed her hand and Tunafish grinned.

"Don't forget that steak!" Tunafish called after them good humoredly as Max pulled Lora after him down the slope.

"I won't—fillet of banana," Max called back. As Max pulled her into the shelter of the trees, Lora heard Tunafish groan.

"Where are we going?" Lora demanded, half laughing as Max dragged her through the jungle. A bright orange marmoset chattered down at them as it swung from branch to branch high overhead. Lora could just catch glimpses of it through the interlaced greenery. Moist looking green lizards flicked their tongues at her from the trunks of trees, but she barely noticed them either. She had become accustomed to such denizens of the jungle.

"You'll see," he answered, sounding mysterious, but Lora already knew. They had traveled the path to the plane quite a few times since the first night he had brought her there. He lifted her through the hole with his hands on her waist, then swung up beside her to catch her in a ferocious kiss. Lora returned the embrace with abandon, loving the delicate war of lips and tongues, loving the crush of his body against hers, loving the taste of him. . . .

"I thought we might try out some of my ideas," he said with a teasing leer, thrusting a hand down the back of her jeans to caress her bare bottom as he spoke. Lora jumped, laughed, and submitted. He had her to the point where he could do anything he liked with her, anything at all.

"You're gorgeous," he whispered moments later as he bent his head to press a kiss to the already aching tip of her breast. Lora felt the moistness of his mouth through the layers of her t-shirt and bra and squeezed her thighs together. Right this moment she was ready to take off her clothes and lie down with him. . . .

"You're too slow," she protested with teasing breathlessness as he transferred his attention to her other breast, still without removing a single item of her clothing.

"I thought women like a man with slow hands," he answered, biting down on her nipple in punishment.

"Not this woman," she answered, her hands making two fists in his hair to tug his head upward. "Not right now." She slid her hands under his t-shirt, stroking the satiny, hair-roughened muscles of his chest, tugging the garment upwards. He grinned and bent to catch her mouth with his, when suddenly he stopped in mid-motion and lifted his head.

"Listen—do you hear that?" he demanded, his hands catching hers and stopping them from pulling his t-shirt over his head.

"What?" Lora's eyes were on the expanse of bronzed chest she had bared, and her response was absent. He glared down at her, removing her hands from his skin and pulling down his shirt.

"Helicopters."

"Helicopters!" Now Lora was listening, too. And there it was, a faint droning, barely audible through the cacophonous jungle sounds. "Is that what that is?"

"I think so. Come on, we've got to get back to the cave."

Lora made no protest as he jumped down from the plane. She joined him, her sneakered feet sinking soundlessly into the thick cushion of mulch as she landed.

"Does this mean this is it?" Hope and alarm coursed in equal measure through her veins. The idea of rescue was dazzling. Civilization—she had almost forgotten about it! How wonderful it would be to eat a good meal—to take a bath—to sleep in a bed. With Max. She was very specific about that. But what did rescue mean to her and Max? She wasn't ready—wasn't nearly ready to put their relationship to the test. She needed more time. . . . Anyway, the coming of others need not mean rescue at all. It could mean violence, and death. . . . Her mouth went dry as she once again considered the possibilities.

"Maybe. Maybe not. Depends on who this is. It could be Minelli's friends, it could be the feds, it could be Ortega. Or it could be someone else. Or it could be someone who's not even looking for us. We'll just have to wait and see." He was making his way through the undergrowth as he spoke over his shoulder. Lora's hand was in his, but she practically had to run to keep up with him. She tripped over an exposed root and nearly fell. He slowed down, but not much.

"Max, do you really think your idea is going to work?" The prospect of having to bluff an army of violence-prone men that she had banished so firmly from her mind was suddenly, terrifyingly at hand. Unless the new arrivals—if there were really new arrivals and the sound of the helicopters had not been just a figment of Max's imagination, and if the new arrivals were after the drugs—agreed to Max's deal, they all had very uncertain futures. In fact, it was quite possible that they had no future. The prospect made Lora feel suddenly icy cold.

XXIII

"Hit the dirt!"

"Wha—" Lora was only half able to articulate the question before Max was thrusting her down into the softness of the jungle floor with his hand on the back of her neck. He crouched beside her, his hand still on her neck, keeping carefully behind a broad-leaved plant that bore some resemblance to a short tobacco stalk. She was just about to question him again, indignantly, when she heard it too: the faint squelch of footsteps in the loam.

"Who—"

"Shh!" He silenced her with a gesture, his face very grim.

Lora took one look at that expression and cowered silently behind the sheltering foliage. She had never seen him look quite so ferocious. His hand was moving to the waistband of his jeans, stealthily extracting the pistol that he was never without. Lora watched him heft it and silently release the safety. The pistol was leveled at whoever or whatever was

302

approaching through the undergrowth as the footsteps grew closer.

Lora peered cautiously through the screen of sun-dappled leaves, her heart in her throat. What she saw was not as frightening as what she had been imagining: there were perhaps half a dozen men, clad in a miscellaneous assortment of gear that ranged from hiking boots and army pants to jeans and sneakers, advancing toward them through the jungle. One held a small box about the size of a transistor radio in his hand. The box emitted a continuous series of beeps that seemed to increase in volume with every step he took. What on earth . . . ?

Lora cast an uncertain glance at Max.

"Transmittor. They're zeroing in on the homing device," Max whispered out of the side of his mouth, the words hardly louder than a breath of air across Lora's ear.

Then he frowned at her fiercely, his eyes plainly ordering her not to move, not to make a sound. Lora was willing to follow his instructions, although the tantalizing vision of imminent rescue was still dancing in her brain. But until they found out who these men were, she knew it was wiser not to reveal themselves.

They were moving in a straight line with perhaps twelve feet between them, their eyes darting nervously back and forth over the stunted plants and twisted vines and gnarled tree trunks that made up the rain forest. Every small sound of monkeys chattering or birds calling made one or the other jump and swing his rifle around. They were all armed with rifles, which they held at the ready as if expecting to open fire at any moment. At what? Lora wondered.

"Quiet now. Don't move." Max's words in her ear almost made her jump herself. The men were about ten feet away now, moving toward them in a line that would bring one passing within about four feet of them. The leafy bush would hide them—maybe. Lora looked down at her own bright pint t-shirt with something like horror. She must stand out against this background of emerald green like a parrot in a dovecote, and Max in his white shirt was not much better. Surely they would be seen. . . .

Max motioned at her, silently directing her to curl herself into as small a package as possible. Lora huddled, head bent to her knees, arms clutching her shins, scarcely daring to breathe as the men approached. Beside her, Max crouched, motionless, pistol unwavering at the man who was now less than six feet away. . . .

He was a white man with a swarthy complexion and oily black hair. Like Max, he had a mustache, a neatly trimmed, almost military looking affair that gave his full lips a cruel look. He was young, maybe twenty-five or- six at the most, and clad in army fatigues and hiking boots. His feet made crackling noises as he planted them one after the other in the soft carpet of rotting twigs and leaves. . . . He was almost directly opposite them now, his eyes swinging back and forth alertly, his hands keeping the rifle moving from side to side.

What was he stalking? Lora wondered again as she shut her eyes with the foggy notion that if she couldn't see him, he couldn't see her. . . .

"Ouch! Goddamn it!" The shout and curse came from a man farther to the left. Lora's eyes popped open automatically to find that all the other men's attention was momentarily centered upon the curser.

"What the hell's the matter with you, Jack?" This disgusted demand came from the man to their immediate left, the third man in line. The man on their immediate right, the one Lora had been studying as he approached closest to them, was shaking his head in disgust. Apparently, Jack's yell had startled the entire company, and they were only just now recovering from it.

"Damn branch. Walked right into it. For a minute there, I thought it was a snake." Jack's sheepish response was barely audible to Lora as he and the others moved on past without breaking their careful formation.

"Keep it quiet!" came the stern warning from the man who was apparently in charge, and the footsteps moved off as the men melted into the jungle in the direction of the plane.

"Who do you think they are?" Lora judged that it was safe to whisper once the men were out of sight. Max was crouched beside her, his shoulder brushing her arm. When he turned his head to look at her, Lora saw that his eyes were bright with an emotion she couldn't identify.

"Minelli's pals. They aren't Mexicans, that's for sure, so that pretty much rules out the *Federales* or Ortega's crew." He smiled, but the smile was as unpleasant as the hard, hot glitter of his eyes. "They think we're all there in the plane waiting for them like sitting ducks, with the dope and the cash ripe for the picking."

"What's going to happen when they find out they're wrong?" Lora's eyes were enormous as she tried to deny her own guess. After trekking all this way, she knew those men weren't going to just give up and go home.

"They'll start looking for us," Max said grimly, catching Lora's hand and rising into a half-crouching position. "Which is why we better get the hell out of here while the getting is good. Come on."

He moved stealthily off through the tangle of vines and plants, keeping low to the ground, pulling Lora after him. She tried to move in that half-crouch too, and discovered that it was murder on the back. Murder—that was a word that she wished hadn't come to mind. It seemed like a good possibility for her and Max's and Tunafish's ultimate fate at the hands of Minelli and DiAngelo and their friends. Lora thought about what Minelli and said in the cave earlier and shivered. Her fate at their hands would probably include more than murder. Minelli was the type to enjoy rape. . . .

"Shit! Get down!" Max tugged her urgently down into the loam, and Lora dropped like a Raid-zapped fly. Her heart pounded in her ears as she looked fearfully over at Max. He was lying full-length beside her, his hand pressing her deeper into the earth. Here there was no convenient broad-leaved bush to shelter them. Here there was only the sparse cover of leafless vines and tree trunks. . . .

Uniformed men on burros. Maybe a dozen of them, obviously Mexicans as they sat solemn-faced atop the long-eared animals. Lora would have laughed at the ludicrous picture made by men and beasts—the burros looked nearly as funny wearing saddles and bridles as the soldiers did riding such small, comical looking beasts—if the situation hadn't been so deadly serious. Because, unless she was very much mistaken, these were the *Federales*, the Mexican Judicial Police.

Lora scarcely breathed as the burros picked their way over vines and branches and around fallen tree trunks. The soldiers rode in stolid silence, never even glancing their way. Like Minelli's friends, they were being guided toward the plane by a beeping transmittor. Lora's eyes widened as she imagined the inevitable confrontation.

"What will they do when they run into the others?"

"God knows. I don't want to."

Max was on the move again, dragging Lora with him. They had traveled the equivalent of perhaps two city blocks when, from the direction of the plane, they heard the cry, "*Alto, Federales!*" and then, seconds later, the blast of weapons. Shouts and curses in English and Spanish punctuated the ear-shattering cacophony of exchanged gunfire. Max stopped, listening, then turned to Lora with a grimace.

"Wait here. Don't move so much as a nostril," he ordered, and without a backward glance, began to make his way back the way they had come.

Lora stared dumbfounded at that retreating back, looked wildly around the unfriendly jungle in which she had just been left alone, thought simultaneously of snakes and jaguars and stray bullets and capture, and took off after Max in a crouching run.

"I thought I told you to stay put!" he hissed angrily when she caught up with him.

"No way!" Lora answered with succinct though necessarily quiet force.

Max didn't argue, just shrugged and looked disgusted as he moved off through the jungle. Lora trailed him, imitating his movements, being as silent and inconspicuous as possible. The sound of gunfire had stopped. She didn't know if that should be reassuring or not. Did that mean that both groups had killed each other—or banded together and were even now moving back their way?

Max dropped to his belly, and Lora followed suit. They were lying behind a little thicket of inch-thick saplings—not a particularly good cover if it had not been for the leaves that had drifted to rest in a pile about two-feet high around the front of the grove. Peering over the leaves, following the direction of Max's eyes, Lora saw that the burros were tied to a rope strung between two vines. The soldiers were nowhere in sight.

"For God's sake, will you just stay here? I'll only be gone a couple of minutes."

Max's hiss in her ear made her jump. She turned her head to glare at him reproachfully, only to find her face on a level with his feet. He was already belly-crawling around their sheltering grove to slither through the undergrowth toward the plane.

Lora stared after him and debated. Should she follow? She argued with herself as she saw his long body moving snake-like over vines and piles of leaves and fallen branches. As soon as those white rubber soles disappeared into the trees, the issue was no longer in question. She was off through the trees like a shot, belly-crawling in a way that would have astonished her gym teacher, totally ignoring the assault to her bare arms and semi-protected knees.

Max was lying on his belly under a flat-leaved bush, and only looked briefly disgusted when Lora crawled up beside him. His attention was focusing on what was happening just beyond the sheltering leaves, and as Lora peered through the overhanging foliage, she saw why.

The *Federales* were lying on their bellies in a circle, their rifles uniformly pointed toward the ruined plane that lay half on its side, nose down and tail in the air in the circle's center. Through the ripped fuselage, Lora could see glimpses of movement inside the plane. She looked over at Max, surprised to find a grin splitting his face.

"The feds have Minelli's pals holed up inside the plane. Probably think they're us." His grin broadened, and he began to creep back away from his vantage point. "That should keep them both occupied for a while."

His hand on her leg tugged her back, too, and Lora followed him with many a painful grimace as he belly-crawled until he judged it safe to stand up. She stood up then, too, and would have examined her scratched and bruised forearms if he hadn't immediately grabbed her hand and dragged her after him as he jogged in the direction of the cave. She followed, willy-nilly, stumbling and wincing and trying not to gibber with fear at the sporadic outbursts of exchanged gunfire. When they reached the base of the cliff, Max sent her scrambling ahead of him over the crumbling shale while he followed just behind her.

Lora was breathless by the time she reached the ledge of rock just outside the cave. Her arms hurt, her knees hurt, and she thought she might be winded for life. She was really out of shape. . . . The darkness of the cave coming right on the heels of the brilliant light that bathed the cliff where it rose above the trees blinded her. Lora blinked as she entered. Then she gave a little choked-off scream as she was grabbed from behind.

"Don't make a single funny move, or I'll blow the broad's head off."

The voice was Minelli's, and it was clear that the words were addressed to the dark shadow that was Max, slowly walking into the cave in her wake. As Lora's eyes adjusted to the gloom, she saw that the arm that was hard around her throat, choking her, also belonged to Minelli. Her eyes rolled to one side to catch a glimpse of his sweat-beaded face. His eyes were fixed on Max, who had come to a poised halt, and his loose-lipped mouth curved in a triumphant grin. Lora felt something cold against her temple, and realized with a shock that he was holding a gun to her head.

"What makes you think I give a damn? You shoot her and I shoot you—takes no skin off my back." Max's tone was as casually indifferent as his words.

Lora's eyes goggled at him over Minelli's restraining arm. He was pointing his own gun straight at Minelli, his expression as untroubled as if he were contemplating the potential destruction of a fly. The gun at her temple pressed a little closer, and she felt sweat break out all over her.

"Come off it, Maxwell, you're not going to let me turn this little lady here to hamburger. Now drop the gun."

"You drop it." Max's voice never wavered. Neither did his hand holding the gun.

Lora stared at him with horror, felt the nose of the gun nuzzle at her forehead, and shut her eyes. If she was about to get her brains blown out, she wasn't going to look.

There was a moment of silence in which neither man backed down an inch. Lora felt herself wilting against Minelli's large frame. The classic Mexican stand-off—with herself in the middle! Dear God, she prayed, let neither of them decide to call the other's bluff!

"I'm going to count to three, Maxwell . . ." Minelli's voice trailed off ominously.

Lora's eyes flew open, to fix with helpless pleading on Max. He looked as cool as a Popsicle. She wanted to plead with him to throw down his gun, but her voice no longer seemed to work.

"One . . ."

"Better think about it carefully, Minelli. I can't miss at this range."

"Two . . ."

"You'll be hamburger right along with her. I'm aiming right between your eyes."

Lora shut her eyes again, squinching them up against the expected bang. Oh, God, she was going to die, she was going to die, and all because the pigheaded fool she was stupid enough to love thought he could play chicken with her life. . . .

"Drop the gun, Maxwell."

Lora opened her eyes to find that DiAngelo had come noiselessly into the cave behind Max, and now stood with a pistol pressed to his spine. Max dropped the gun, and Lora sagged with relief. Thank God for DiAngelo. . . . There was a clatter as Max's pistol bounced over the floor. Max grunted as DiAngelo jammed his gun harder into Max's spine.

"Over there. With your friend." Minelli released his chokehold on her throat as DiAngelo shoved Max in the direction of the stalagmite fence. Lora saw that Tunafish sat on the other side, trussed like a Thanksgiving turkey and gagged with his own shirt. His face and bare torso glistened with sweat, and Lora could only imagine the roughing up the two thugs must have given him.

"Tie him up." Minelli's arm slid around her waist as he spoke, holding her so that her back was pressed against his stomach. "Then he can tell us what he did with the dope before Fat Frank and the boys get here. Fat Frank doesn't like to be kept waiting." This last was said with a malicious smile at Max, who looked back at him expressionlessly.

"What makes you think your buddies are here, Minelli?" Max spoke with cool dispassion as DiAngelo moved behind him.

Minelli grinned. "Blackie here let out a yell when he saw choppers overhead. Got so excited he forgot about us. So we made our move."

"Sorry to burst your bubble, Minelli, but those choppers belong to the feds. We saw them out in the jungle."

DiAngelo looked over Max's shoulder at Minelli. "Tony?" His voice was uneasy.

"Another bluff, Maxwell?" Minelli sneered, giving DiAngelo a hard look. "Get on with it."

Max shrugged. His eyes never left Minelli as DiAngelo carefully laid his gun down on a rock behind him and reached to pull Max's hands behind his back, one at a time and with considerable force to judge from Max's wince.

Minelli was staring undecidedly at Max. "You tell me,

baby," he said suddenly to Lora, his arm tightening around her middle as he pulled her tighter against him. The strength of his grip threatened to crack her ribs. Lora silently sucked in air before she answered, praying that she would say the right thing. She had no illusions about the desperation of their position. . . .

"Answer me, baby." He tightened his arm violently. "Are the cops out there?"

Lora gasped. "Yes, they're out there!"

"How do you know they're feds?" His voice was hard, suspicious. The arm around her middle was causing her physical pain.

"They wore uniforms. They were Mexican. They looked like police."

DiAngelo spoke up, sounding frightened. "What we going to do, Tony? The feds . . ."

Minelli considered a moment. "So the feds are out there. So what? We hole up here and we wait. Fat Frank and the boys will be along soon. Hell, they're probably right on the feds' tails. We just got to wait."

Lora watched in despair as DiAngelo began to wrap the very bindings that Max had used on him around Max's wrists. Soon she would be at Minelli and DiAngelo's mercy— she had no doubts at all about Minelli's intentions as far as she was concerned. And he would just as certainly kill Max and Tunafish. Tunafish was totally out of commission, and Max was just as helpless with a gun trained on him and his hands being tied. Once the restraints were secured, they would have no chance. That left only her to do something, anything. . . . But what? If she could somehow manage to distract Minelli, Max might be able to overpower DiAngelo and get his hands on a gun. . . .

Lora took a deep breath—or as deep as she could with Minelli's arm crushing her ribs.

"At least we got entertainment," Minelli was saying, his tone jovial. "The broad here's been giving you a real good time, Maxwell. She can start spreading it around a little while we wait. But we don't mean to deprive you altogether—you can watch."

Lora shuddered inwardly at this confirmation of the fate that awaited her at Minelli's hands. As if to emphasize his words, the hand that had been gripping her waist slid up to grasp her breast. He squeezed hard, his meaty fingers pinching her nipple. She cried out at the pain of it, then literally saw red. Without even having to think about it, she was kicking back to catch him in the kneecap. He groaned as the force of the blow caught him unawares and reached instinctively for his injured leg. The gun lowered and his hold on Lora loosened enough to allow her to whirl and jam the heel of her palm hard against the underside of his nose. The move that had served her so well all that time ago with Max worked equally well with Minelli. He howled, staggering backward, the gun forgotten as he clapped his hand to his bleeding nose. Lora tore free of his grasping hands and shoved him with all her might. He staggered, tripped over Tunafish's pallet, and fell. Behind her, Lora heard a shot and the sounds of a struggle. . . .

"I'm going to kill you, you bitch!" Minelli screamed, his hand coming away from his nose as he jerked the gun up to point it at Lora.

She screamed, dropping to the floor and covering her head as a shot exploded in her ears. Her scream echoed and re-echoed through the chamber, but she didn't seem to feel any pain. Minelli must have missed. . . .

She opened her eyes a fraction, lowering her arms so that

she could see what was going on. To her heartfelt relief, Max stood nearby, a gun held purposefully in his hands. Minelli was rolling around on the floor, groaning, his left hand clutching his mangled right arm, which was pouring blood. DiAngelo was high-tailing it out through the mouth of the cave. Max snapped a shot off after him, but to no avail: they could hear the sounds as he slipped and slid down the shale.

"You are one awesome lady, did you know that?" Max said, shaking his head in admiration at Lora, who was getting unsteadily to her feet. "I never did ask you: where did you learn that stuff? It's scary."

"I took a rape prevention course."

Max grinned widely, and Lora returned his grin, sparing scarcely a glance for Minelli as she moved to untie Tunafish, whose eyes were bulging over the gag. As far as she was concerned, Minelli deserved to bleed to death. . . .

"I don't believe it!" Tunafish burst out as soon as she eased the gag from his mouth. His head swiveled around so that he was staring at Lora. "You took that slime-bag out! All by yourself! Boss, do you believe it?"

Max grinned again. "Oh, yeah. She pulled that on me once. Hurt like hell, too. I've been real nice to her ever since."

Tunafish chuckled. "I noticed." Lora jerked on the rags binding his hands, and he winced, grimacing as she pulled them free. "Sorry about lettin' myself get ambushed like that. We heard the helicopters and then, bam! They were on me. Must have gotten themselves untied some time ago, and been waitin' their chance."

Max shook his head. "Don't worry about it. You okay?" Tunafish nodded. "Lora, tie something around Minelli's arm, will you? I'd kind of like him to come out of this alive—I was paid to deliver him."

"You're doing a hell of a poor job," Minelli snarled from the floor. Max snapped the gun around at him.

"I can do a worse one," he said tightly.

Minelli subsided.

Lora wrapped Tunafish's shirt around Minelli's arm and tied it with rags from Max's windbreaker, not caring that Minelli groaned and winced with pain. He was bleeding profusely from a large hole in his upper arm as well as from his nose, but not, she thought with some regret, enough to die from. When she was finished, Max hog-tied him with the leather thong and left him sitting.

"We've got a problem," Max said when he rejoined her and Tunafish. "Everybody out there must have heard those gunshots, so it's going to be just a matter of time until they find the cave. But only the feds and the mob are here so far, though I imagine Ortega is right behind them. He's probably hanging back, watching to see what happens before making his move. But what we're going to have to do in the meantime is get out of here and hide in the jungle. Those guys out there will be searching this mountain with a fine-tooth comb."

"What about Tunafish?" Lora could barely get the words out around the dryness that suddenly afflicted her tongue and throat. Her worst nightmares were coming true. Not only was Max's plan not going to work, Ortega hadn't even shown up! What if he never did?

"I carried Tunafish up here, I can carry him back down again. Thank God he's been on a banana and fish diet! Maybe he's shed a few pounds."

Neither Tunafish nor Lora bothered to respond to this bit of forced humor. Instead, Tunafish pointed at Minelli.

"What about him?"

"Leave him for his friends—or the feds." Max turned to

look at Lora. "Grab as much of our gear as you can carry, and let's get the hell out of here." Lora scrambled to obey as Max moved toward Tunafish. "Come on, buddy."

"You, *gringos!* This is the *Federales!* Throw down your weapons and come out!"

The shout made them jump. They looked at each other in nervous silence. It was too late to hide. . . . The moment of truth was at hand.

The three of them moved as one toward the mouth of the cave, Lora and Max on either side of Tunafish, helping him. Despite the fact that he was wounded and securely tied, Max kept an eye on Minelli, who was still rolling around and moaning and did not look to be in good enough shape to cause anyone any trouble at all. Lora dismissed him from her mind as, standing flush against the inside of the cave, the three of them peered out. What she saw below brought butterflies to her stomach

"You have three minutes to throw down your weapons and come out!"

The soldiers she and Max had seen earlier waited at the foot of the cliff, their impressive arsenal of weapons trained on the mouth of the cave. DiAngelo stood under guard at the rear of the formation; so did the six other men that Max had identified as Minelli's friends.

"What do we do?" The terse question was Tunafish's.

Lora looked at him, and then at Max. Then they all three looked back out at the waiting *Federales*.

"We hold them off for as long as we can and pray that Ortega gets here," Max said firmly.

Lora looked down at the waiting army and swallowed. Unbidden, the last scene from the movie *Butch Cassidy and the Sundance Kid* popped into her mind, when the two men, weary and wounded, were left facing the entire

Bolivian Army. She sincerely hoped that none of the three of them were about to suffer Butch Cassidy's fate. From the number of guns below, the police had come prepared for a massacre.

XXIV

The three of them were still staring gloomily down at the *Federales* when a squad of dirt bikes came roaring out of the jungle. Helmeted drivers revved the cycles toward the astonished feds, who had turned to gape at the emergence of the first shiny red motorcycle and still hadn't recovered the presence of mind to fire on them. About half the cycles had a second man riding shotgun, or machine gun in this case, and these gunners opened fire with whooping abandon as the cycles zoomed and leaped and skidded to form a moving circle around the feds, who were at last beginning to fumble with their weapons.

The scene reminded Lora of a modernistic version of settlers and Indians, with the feds taking the role of the embattled pioneers. She stared goggle-eyed down at the circus below. Max and Tunafish watched with no less astonishment. The feds had dropped to their bellies and knees behind every conceivable cover, but the rocks and squat bushes that dotted the base of the cliff were scant pretection from the darting enthusiasm of the bikers.

In the confusion, DiAngelo and the rest of the mob group managed to break away from the preoccupied policemen and flee in great leaps to the jungle. A few of the cyclists fired desultory bursts after these unarmed escapees, but, judging from the way they dived into the undergrowth, they managed to keep from being seriously hit. The cyclists obviously considered the policemen their main opponents, and they continued to roar around them in a circle, firing and laughing gleefully as the bullets tore into bushes and ricocheted twangingly off rocks. The feds gamely returned fire, but few of the cyclists fell. The cyclists had gradually tightened their orbit until they formed a circle around the hapless feds when the most mind-boggling thing of all happened: out of the jungle, big as Ike and trampling down small trees and undergrowth in its path, rolled something that looked like a cross between a bulldozer and a World War II vintage tank!

It stopped just short of the jungle, its long gun pointing in the direction of the hard-pressed feds. The hatch opened, and from the hatch emerged a rotund figure in a white silk business suit topped incongruously with a combat helmet.

"Ortega!"Max stared, then collapsed against the wall, chuckles turning into full-throated laughter as he took another good look at the antics going on below.

Ortega—for it was he who had half emerged from the hatch—had a bullhorn to his lips and was shouting something in Spanish at the stunned *Federales*.

"Surrender or die," Max translated for Lora's benefit. The shooting had stopped with the appearance of the tank (presumably the feds were as taken aback by its arrival as the three of them were) and there was a tense moment as Lora waited with baited breath for it to resume. These *Federales* were the Mexican equivalent of the FBI, after all. They would not just tamely surrender to a man of Ortega's stamp. They would lob a grenade or something, and go on to carry the day. . . .

A white handkerchief attached to the muzzle of a rifle rose from behind a rock and was waved slowly back and forth. As Lora watched, the cyclists whooped and zoomed enthusiastically while the feds got to their feet, threw down their weapons, and were taken prisoner by the dismounting riders. Meanwhile, Ortega and the tank rolled to the foot of the cliff. Ortega looked up at the cave, and raised the bullhorn to his lips again.

"Don't anybody move!'' You're all under arrest! This is the DEA!''

A rush of green uniformed soldiers emerged from the jungle without warning, and wild pandemonium ensued below. Ortega's men, thinking the battle was over, were caught unprepared. Most of them had dropped their cycles, and there was a mad scramble for rifles and bikes. They got off a few wild shots, but it was clear from the beginning that this new adversary had the advantage of discipline, weaponry, and surprise. Ortega's men were quickly rounded up. Ortega fared better. He popped back inside the tank, the hatch slammed shut, and the tank rolled back into the jungle, seemingly impervious to the shots fired at it, while a small contingent of the newly arrived soldiers ran after it.

"That you up there, Maxwell?"

"Good God, it's Barney,'' Max said to no one in particular, staring down at the crisply uniformed man who stood at the base of the cliff with his hands cupped around his mouth.

"Who's Barney?'' Lora demanded, while Max leaned out of the cave, grinning widely.

"Yeah, Barney, I'm up here. What the hell are you doing here?"

The man below snorted. "We're backing up the Mexican feds now. Mutual cooperation, if you can believe it. Can I come up?"

"Come ahead." Max waved him up and drew back inside.

"Who's Barney?" Lora asked again, while Tunafish looked glum.

"He was my boss at the DEA. Colonel Bernard Brackinridge. Great guy, Barney," Max replied, looking more cheerful than Lora had ever seen him. He was grinning, his hands stuck in his pockets as he watched the man called Barney ascend the cliff.

"Yeah, a real great guy." Tunafish agreed sourly.

Max said to Lora, "Barney and Tunafish never hit it off. Barney has a prejudice against former burglars."

"He'd like to fry my ass," Tunafish said gloomily, and then Barney was walking into the cave.

He was a tall, spare man with short sandy hair and military precision. He shook hands briefly with Max, acknowledged Lora with a smile, and nodded to Tunafish. When he saw Minelli, still bound and bleeding in the center of the cavern, he lifted his eyebrows.

"He's part of that mob group your boys are rounding up now," Max explained, and Barney frowned.

"What I want to know is, how the hell did the mob get mixed up in this?" He looked at Max, then shook his head. "Never mind, I don't want to know after all. I assume it's a long story."

Max grinned. "It is."

Barney nodded. "With you, it usually is. We had a fix on your position two days ago, you know. But we wanted to wait until we could haul in some warm bodies along with the dope." He chuckled. "Boy, did we ever get our wish! The *Federales* spotted a group searching the jungle this morning. They tailed them, thinking they were the Mexican druggies looking for their own downed plane. They thought they'd catch them red-handed with the goods. But damned if they weren't following the wrong bunch! The druggies were behind them the whole time! Lucky I held my men back. This mutual cooperation thing is crap, let me tell you. Talk about your screwups... Well, that's beside the point at the moment." He looked at Max again, his eyes growing suddenly keen. 'You do have the drugs?"

Max nodded. "Yeah, I do."

"If you'll just tell me where they are, I'll have some guards posted until we can get them lifted out of here. This is a hell of a big drug bust, you know." Barney sounded tough, cool and efficient as he took charge.

Max grinned slowly at him. "Not quite so fast, Barney. I want some insurance first."

"What kind of insurance?"

"Immunity from prosecution, for one thing. You know I didn't have anything to do with running the drugs—at least, not on purpose—but I want your word that none of us will be prosecuted for that, or anything else we may have done."

"Like kidnapping, Max?" Barney's voice was dry. His eyes sought Lora, who smiled feebly at him.

"Among other things." Max was still grinning, but Lora felt about two inches tall as Barney turned to her.

"You're the victim, I presume?"

"Yes."

"Do you want to press charges?"

"No."

"Mmmm." He looked her over, unsmiling, then turned back to look at Max. "I don't think you have a problem there."

"Actually, that wasn't quite the charge I was concerned with."

Barney grimaced. "You want me to try to persuade the Mexican authorities to forget murders, jail breakings, bombings, kidnappings—two besides the lady here—car theft and God knows what else? Oh, yes, I know what you've been up to. We've been keeping tabs on you."

"At least you didn't leave anything out," Max responded dryly.

"I can't speak for the Mexicans, Max."

"Then you'll just have to search the jungle for the drugs. They could be anywhere."

Max smiled sweetly at Barney while Tunafish muttered something about God and mercy under his breath.

"Tell me where the drugs are, and I'll do what I can to see that they go easy on you."

Max shook his head. "Not good enough, Barney. Come on, you're talking to me, remember? I know you can give me immunity. I've seen you do it before, in other cases."

"Yeah, but then we weren't supposed to be assisting the Mexicans. They want to hang you out to dry, Max, and the situation between our two countries isn't too good right now."

"There's about ten million dollars' worth of smack here, Barney. And some cash. A hundred thousand dollars of drug money. May be traceable."

Barney stared at him, looking undecided. Lora clasped her hands in front of her and prayed. Tunafish shut his eyes. Finally Barney nodded curtly.

"I'm probably going to get my ass kicked over this, but you've got it. Immunity from prosecution for any and all past crimes, in return for the drugs."

"You're a good guy, Barney." Max was grinning, and even Tunafish opened his eyes and looked brighter. Lora sighed with relief. Everything was working out perfectly. None of them would go to jail. . . .

"So where are the drugs?" Barney demanded.

"One more thing." Max's grin was wider than ever.

Barney groaned and said, "What?"

"I want a finder's fee. After all, I'm not working for the agency now."

"A finder's fee!" Words seemed to fail Barney. "How much?"

"One percent. A hundred thousand dollars. Pretty reasonable, considering the value of the shipment."

"Out of the question!"

"Face it, we did the agency a service. Think what this bust will look like in the papers! We deserve to be paid for our time and trouble."

"You are a pushy son of a bitch, Maxwell," Barney said bitterly. "All right, you have your finder's fee!"

"Thanks, Barney." Max clapped him on the shoulder while Tunafish and Lora looked at each other in disbelief.

"Now, where are the drugs?" Barney asked impatiently.

Max said nothing, merely crossed the room with a half smile curling his lips.

Lora, Tunafish, and Barney stared after him with identical expressions of confusion. Max walked right up to the wall with the mysterious cave drawings, put his hand on a rock just beneath the first warrior's spear, and pushed. With a creak and a groan, the whole wall moved.

"Well, I'll be damned!" Tunafish muttered in amazement, while Barney walked slowly forward to stare into the small room revealed by the sliding wall.

Lora followed him, slack-jawed. Who ever would have guessed. . . .

"You mean it was here the whole time?" Lora stared into

the small chamber, which was filled to the roof with the crates of white powder, while Max and Barney walked right inside. "What is it?"

Max looked back at her, an engaging twinkle in his eyes. "A Mayan burial chamber, I presume. At least, I think that's roughly the equivalent of a sarcophagus."

He gestured to one side of the chamber, where Lora saw a skeleton wrapped in tattered bits of cloth lying on the delapidated remains of a wooden bier. The room itself was painted with highly stylized figures, still intact pieces of pottery lay about on the floor, and it looked like it belonged in one of the tombs of Egypt.

"I suppose we'll have the archeological people bitching because you destroyed priceless antiquities," Barney grumbled, scarcely glancing at the sarcophagus as he counted the crates. "Where's the cash?"

Max pointed to where the brown leather suitcase leaned against a crate.

"You say there's a hundred thousand dollars here?" Barney picked up the suitcase, hefting it in his hand.

Max nodded. "That's right."

"Then here's your finder's fee. Keep it under you hat." Barney thrust the suitcase at him. Max accepted it with a slight bow.

"Now we've got to get you out of here. I think I'll have a better chance of persuading the Mexicans not to prosecute if you're nowhere to be found."

"Thanks, Barney." Max sounded suddenly sincere.

Barney shook his head. "Yeah, well, you were one of the best agents I've ever had. If you ever want your job back . . ."

"I'll think about it," Max said, and then Barney was leaving the burial chamber and crossing to the cave's mouth.

He yelled down for someone called Burrows. Minutes later, an out-of-breath young man appeared, saluting smartly.

"Burrows, I want you to escort these three to my helicopter. Have Dennis take them anywhere they want to go."

"Yes, sir."

"And Burrows—it might be best if it looked as if you were placing them under arrest."

"Yes, sir." Burrows's expression remained carefully wooden, but he shot a furtive glance at Lora.

He was no doubt madly curious, but she doubted that his curiosity would ever be satisfied. She certainly wouldn't be the one to tell him what was going on.

"What about him, sir?" Burrows pointed at Minelli, who was lying lifelessly on the floor.

"Is he dead?" Barney asked the question without much interest. Burrows went to check, bending to feel for a pulse and then straightening.

"No, sir."

"Then he is under arrest. Really under arrest."

"Yes, sir. If you'll excuse me, sir, I'll get some of the men up here."

"You do that, Burrows."

Burrows went to the mouth of the cave and yelled down. In moments six more men appeared.

"Michaels, Gibbons, and Patterson, you're to escort these three individuals at gunpoint to the colonel's helicopter. I'll be coming with you. Todd and Zigler, you're to mount guard over this cave. No one save the colonel or myself is to enter without permission. Raymond, this gentleman is under arrest. He is to receive emergency medical treatment and then be kept under guard. Is that clear?"

"Yes, sir!" answered a chorus of voices, and the men deployed as he had directed. Two of the soldiers were required to carry Tunafish down the cliff in a makeshift litter, while Burrows and an even younger man marched alongside Lora and Max, who parted from Barney with a handshake and a *hasta la vista*, escorting them at gunpoint from the cave and down the mountainside.

The *Federales*, having had their freedom restored, were getting their revenge by roping Ortega's men together and standing guard over the downed cycles. As Lora, Max, Tunafish and their escort passed by them, they saw that the mafia boys, including DiAngelo, had been recaptured and were being roped in with the others. Only Ortega and his tank were unaccounted for.

"Uh, sir..." One of the young soldiers spoke up hesitantly, beckoning to Burrows. After a whispered consultation, Burrows nodded and turned to Max courteously.

"It has been suggested that it would be much quicker to transport you to the helicopter on the captured motorbikes. My men can drive them, if you feel comfortable riding behind? Colonel Brackenridge seemed to think that speed was of the essence in getting you out of here."

"It will be a pleasure," Max answered with a quick grin at Lora. She was not so sure. She had never ridden a motorcycle before, but then she had never done a tenth of the things she had tackled since meeting Max. Riding a motorcycle was tame in comparison to most of them.

"I'm game," she said, lying only a little, and when Tunafish nodded it was unanimous.

Three cycles were brought up, and there was a short wait while Tunafish's leg was strapped to the side of the vehicle so that it would be jostled as little as possible. The boy driving him mounted gingerly, having to sit in an awkward position to accommodate Tunafish's leg. Max was laughing, and Lora was feeling mildly amused herself by the time the bike roared off to the tune of Tunafish's laments. After that, she climbed onto the back of the cycle piloted by Burrows with only the smallest hesitation. The young lieutenant probably drove very well, but to Lora it seemed as if he tore off like the hounds of hell were on his heels. She could have sworn she heard fiendish laughter as Burrows gunned the machine over bumps the size of hills and steered between trees that were close enough to scrape Lora's elbows. Looking to the left, where Max rode behind another boy almost alongside her, she saw that the laughter was not a figment of her imagination. Max was laughing uproariously at her. Lora turned a cold shoulder on him, clinging to Burrows's waist like a monkey in a hurricane, and vowed to get her revenge one day.

She made it to the top of the mountain in one piece, much to her surprise. There, on a flat-surfaced rock the size of a baseball diamond, sat three helicopters. Two were enormous, looking as if they belonged in a sophisticated military operation, while the other was small and white with sleek purple markings, obviously Barney's personal craft.

Lora climbed off the cycle and locked her knees to keep them from buckling, smiling slightly insincere thanks at Burrows, who had climbed off as well and stuck his head inside the helicopter for a word with the pilot. Then with a salute Burrows remounted the cycle, and he and the other young men were off the way they had come, sans passengers.

"I'll get you for laughing at me, you devil," Lora said feelingly to Max.

Tunafish, being laboriously helped inside the helicopter through a door that did not want to accommodate both his size and his unbendable leg, grunted in agreement. Max grinned.

"I can't wait," he murmured for her ears alone. His eyes were dancing, and the brilliant sunlight that was not shaded at all on this barren mountaintop brought out red highlights in his black hair.

Lora stared at the craggy features with resignation. He was grinning, obviously unrepentant, but looked so handsome she found it hard to hold on to her grudge. Her eyes fell on the battered brown suitcase he held in one hand, and she thought of another grievance she had with him.

"You can't keep that money."

"Why not? Don't worry, I'll see to it that you get a fair share."

"I don't want to share! It's drug money!"

"What do you suggest I do with it, then? Throw it away?"

"Give it back."

"To whom? If I give it back to Ortega, who is, I suppose, it's rightful owner, he may very well decide to have me shot on the spot. I doubt if I'm his favorite person right now. And after I'm dead he'll just go on to use the money to finance another drug deal. You wouldn't want the money to go for that, would you? And there's no point in giving it back to Barney. It would just end up mouldering away in a government vault somewhere."

Lora glared at him. He had her there. . . . She was unable to say precisely what should be done with the money, but she did know that Max had no right to it. But then, who did?

"Salve your prickly conscience, Lora. We earned it, and anyway, I mean to see that it's spent in a good cause. Clemente's and Lowenthal's family will get some of it, to begin with."

"What about Clemente?" Lora asked, suddenly remembering the body that they had left behind in the jungle.

"Barney said he'll bring the body out and see that it's returned to Clemente's family. I told him where to find it."

"And Ortega? Do you think they'll catch him?"

"Probably. He might even be arrested. But I seriously doubt if he'll ever go to jail. Ortega has friends in high places."

Lora looked up into those sparkling black eyes, twinkling piratically above the crooked blade of a nose and villainous mustache, and suddenly, impulsively, reached up to plant a quick kiss on his mouth.

His hand came up to catch her arm, and he looked down at her for a moment, his expression a mixture of surprise and something else she couldn't decipher.

"Lora . . ." But whatever he was going to say was lost as the rotor of the helicopter started to revolve, making further conversation impossible.

The pilot leaned out the door to yell, "You folks coming?" and then they were climbing inside.

They settled into the rear seats as Tunafish had taken the seat next to the pilot to give his leg more room. Then the whirlybird was lifting into the air.

As the helicopter gained height, the panorama beneath them was dazzling. Lora looked down with awe at the magnificence of thousands of hills that seemed to ripple into eternity in every imaginable shade of green. Misty clouds of steam from the daily downpour veiled the lowland areas. Stark rock cliffs, a few crowned with snow, stretched for the sky. The deep blue of lagoons and lakes and streams appeared unexpectedly from time to time in gleaming contrast to the vistas of rolling greenery. Lora wondered which one was theirs. . . . Seen from the air, the montana jungle looked like a verdant paradise. Glancing at Max, Lora decided that, despite everything, maybe that's just what it had been.

"Mr. Maxwell, where should I take you? Colonel Brackenridge has put me totally at your disposal."

They had been in the air about fifteen minutes. Lora had been so caught up in the beauty of the scenery—and a curious sense of loss that she could not quite explain—that she had not said a word so far during the flight. The pilot's question caught her attention. She looked up, her eyes going to Max.

"Tunafish needs a hospital, a good hospital, so I suppose you'd better take us to Guatemala City."

"I ain't goin' to no hospital, man. You know I hate hospitals."

"Well, I sure as hell am not taking you home to Ann like that. She'll skin me."

Tunafish looked uneasy. "Me, too. I done told her we was takin' a fishin' trip."

"And I'm not going to wetnurse you, so it doesn't look to me like you have much choice. It's either a hospital or Ann."

"Some friend you are," Tunafish grumbled, glaring at Max. Max looked at Lora with a grin. "Ann's his wife. Barely five feet tall and meaner than hell. She keeps Tunafish and those kids in line, believe me."

Tunafish grinned, too, looking in no way offended by this description of his wife. "I'm gonna tell Annie it's your fault I broke my leg."

Max shuddered exaggeratedly. "You probably would." Then he turned to look at Lora, his eyes suddenly unsmiling. "Lora, we can put you on a plane when we get to Guatemala City. You can be in Kansas by breakfast time, if you like."

Lora returned his look. She would rather say this in private, but there was no privacy to be had. Casting pride to the winds, she said softly, "I want to stay with you, please, Max."

Tunafish cleared his throat and looked away. The pilot suddenly became very busy studying his instruments.

"We'll talk about it later," Max said repressively, but his eyes were suddenly warm on hers.

Lora smiled at him, feeling ridiculously happy all at once. He had not rejected her. That must mean that he was not yet quite ready to say good-bye, as he had threatened, now that their jungle idyll was at an end.

XXV

By the time they landed at the airport in Guatemala City, got Tunafish into a taxi, waded through the red tape that was required before he could be admitted to a hospital, and found a taxi to take them to a hotel, it was nearly midnight, which in a Latin country like Guatemala is the top of the evening. The streets were teeming with traffic and pedestrians, the restaurants and lounges overflowing. After finally leaving Tunafish sleeping under a heavy dose of a sedative in preparation for surgery the following morning to rebreak and reset his poor thigh, Lora was exhausted, and Max looked as tired as she felt. The idea of spending the night in a hotel with Max was exciting, Lora thought, or at least it would have been if they both hadn't been so tired. Too tired? She glanced speculatively at the dark-shadowed face of the man she loved. That remained to be seen.

The taxidriver dropped them at the Hacienda Guatemala City, a small but elegant hostelry in the center of the city.

Walking through the ornate brass doors, Lora took one look at the casually chic clothing of the other guests and felt about two inches tall. She slunk across the marble floor of the lobby and hid behind a potted palm, feeling horribly self-conscious about her tangled, grimy hair, sunburned face and torn and dirty clothes as Max walked up to the desk and requested a room with aplomb. He did not seem a whit disgruntled by his own disreputable clothes or scruffy beard, Lora noted with some asperity. Her eyes popped as he extracted an American Express card from his pocket and handed it over. How on earth had he ever gotten that?

"It's not stolen, is it? The credit card, I mean," she whispered anxiously as they were shown to their room by a smiling bellhop, who had shruggingly accepted Max's firm refusal of an offer to carry their only luggage, the brown leather suitcase.

"Of course not," Max answered with a quirky smile. "I wish you'd rid yourself of this notion that I'm some sort of criminal. I'm not, you know. At least, not that sort," he amended with a grin as the bellhop opened the door and bowed them into the room. "I got it quite legitimately, just like everyone else."

"You can get an American Express card?" That idea was more mind-boggling than the other. "What on earth did you put for occupation? Jailbreaker?"

"I said I was self-employed, which is true," Max said soothingly, passing the expectant bellhop a bill—undoubtedly from her small store of money, which had survived unscathed in his pocket through all their hardships—and closing the door behind him. "I don't know about you, but I'd just as soon forget about all this stuff for a while. What do you say to dinner—room service? You can take a bath while I order.''

"A bath." Lora breathed the words, enraptured at the idea. She was so dazzled by the combined prospects of food and cleanliness that every other thought was instantly crowded from her mind.

"Through there," Max said, pointing at an open door. "Steak sound all right to you? That's what I want."

"It sounds heavenly." Lora sighed, thinking of a big, juicy sirloin. "With all the trimmings. Salad, and potato, and bread and butter. . . . ''

"You'll get sick," he warned, grinning. "If Montezuma's revenge doesn't get you, eating too much on an empty stomach will."

"I don't care, it's worth it. Go on, order all that. And a shrimp cocktail, if they have one. And dessert."

"You'll get fat." His grin was wider than ever as he picked up the phone.

"I'll worry about it later. Order." Lora stuck her tongue out at him, then disappeared through the bathroom door. Inside the bathroom, she stood for a moment marveling at everything: the white porcelain tub with its glass shower doors, the luxury of a flush toilet, the sink with a lighted mirror above. The floor was cool, black and white tile, and Lora kicked off her mangled sneakers and enjoyed the sensation of it against her bare feet as she closed the door. Sighing blissfully at the luxury, she let the water run into the tub while she washed her face with soap and the delightfully thick washcloth the hotel provided. They also provided toothpaste, but she didn't have a toothbrush. Not that a small inconvenience like that mattered. Humming happily, she squeezed toothpaste onto the washcloth and rubbed her teeth with that. The strong minty taste left in her mouth afterwards made her stomach rumble. She was starving. . . . Lora thought longingly about the steak she would soon be eating as she stripped off her clothes, made quick but appreciative use of the toilet, and climbed into the steaming tub. Her mouth watered as she pictured the thick slab of meat, brown and sizzling. . . . Her stomach rumbled, loudly, and Lora picked up the soap and washcloth and set to work with a will. As much as she would enjoy a long soak in the tub, her starving insides insisted she hurry.

Her hair was filthy, and she was contemplating washing it with the bar of soap in lieu of shampoo when a quick rap at the door was followed by Max's entrance.

"I didn't say you could come in," she protested, pressing the white washcloth to her breasts and feeling ridiculously shy as he looked her over with grinning appraisal from just inside the door.

"You're not getting modest on me again, are you?" His voice was teasing, but his eyes warmed as they took in her curving body, the taut, pink-tipped breasts gleaming with water and traces of soap, the tiny waist and the curve of her hips that was just visible through the veil of water. Her legs were bent at the knee, hiding quite a bit, but his eyes gleamed over as much of her as he could see.

"I brought you something," he added, holding up a brown paper bag tantalizingly as his eyes moved back up to meet hers. Lora had to smile at the lurking smile she found there. "Toothpaste, a toothbrush, a comb, shampoo, and some female junk that the hotel threw in for good measure. I called down to the desk and explained that the airline had lost most of our luggage."

"And they believed you?" Lora thought of the picture they must have presented in the lobby. No reputable airline would let passengers board looking like that!

"Why not? I'm a paying customer. They'll believe anything, as long as you pay for it."

"You're very cynical."

"You're very naive. And very, very pretty. How would you like your back scrubbed?"

"I wouldn't!"

"Well, I would. Move over, I'm getting in."

"Max, no!" The idea of Max joining her in her bathtub was almost as shocking as it was intriguing. She had never taken a bath with anyone, with the exception of her sister when they were small. Though she had made love with him on more occasions than she could count, and though he had seen, and more than seen, every millimeter of her skin, she still felt shy about him joining her in the bath. But he was taking off his clothes, and as she watched she felt a delicious flutter of nervous excitement. . . .

God, he was gorgeous naked. He had the most beautiful body of any man she had ever seen—not that she had seen that many naked men, of course. But his was just as she had always imagined a man's body should be, broad of shoulder and wide of chest, narrow of waist and hips and long of limb, to say nothing of brown and hairy and muscular and too sexy for words. Her eyes moved over him with kindling warmth as he stepped into the tub with her. From the wicked half smile on his face, as well as the other unmistakable physical evidence, he was as aware of the possibilities of this encounter as she was. She sat up straighter, bending her knees closer to her body to accommodate him as he sat down at the opposite end of the tub with a great sloshing overflow of water.

"Pass the soap," he said, and Lora obediently handed over the soap, watching with interest as he lazily soaped his chest.

The sight of white bubbles smeared across bronzed skin and whorls of black hair was captivating. Lora smiled at him as he lifted one hard-muscled arm to scrub beneath it. She could envision doing this every day of her life, until she was a little old lady of ninety-two. There was something about the intimacy of sharing a bath that made her want him to belong to her—permanently, forever, all hers—with an intensity that was almost physical. Her heart trembled and her lips quivered with the need to say, I love you, but she firmly clamped the lid on her foolish organs. Sex with no strings, she had promised him. Of course, she hadn't meant a word of it, but her deepest feminine instincts warned her that now was definitely not the time to confess to that. She had to wait a little longer—wait until he needed her a little more. Wait until he loved her a little. All of which was an awfully tall order. . . .

"You're looking at me like a cat at a mouse. You planning to pounce?"

This was so close to the truth that Lora was momentarily taken aback. But she made a quick recovery, realizing that he could have no notion that she had just been plotting his ultimate surrender. From the teasing glint in his eyes, he had interpreted her fixed attention as a sign that she wanted him. Which she did.

"I was giving it serious consideration." She stretched out a hand to stroke his hard-muscled calf, enjoying the feel of the wet, warm, hair-roughened skin beneath her palm. "But I think I'll have to wait until after supper. I'm starving."

"You mean you'd rather eat than make love? Tsk, tsk, Lora, you wound me." Max grinned, sinking down a little in the tub and then straightening abruptly as his back came into contact with the hot and cold fixtures. "This is uncomfortable as hell. Think there's room for me at that end?"

"No," Lora said, but he was already standing, grabbing her arms and pulling her up beside him.

"You can sit on my lap."

He was holding her by the upper arms so that she would not slip, and their bodies just brushed each other. The slight contact was electric. His eyes changed, the teasing glint darkening, turning into something both primitive and powerful. Lora knew her expression must have changed, too. She stepped closer or he pulled her closer, she wasn't sure which, but suddenly she was against him, with his arms tight around her waist and her arms sliding up to encircle his neck. His chest was slick with soap, and the contrast between that and the abrasion of his body hair was tantalizing. She rubbed her body against him instinctively, feeling her nipples harden and the now-familiar quickening between her legs. He felt so good—so hard and tough and male. Funny to think that she was such a sucker for old-fashioned masculinity. . . . Lora half smiled at the humor in it as his mouth came down on hers. Then she quit smiling, quit doing anything at all except kissing him back, her tongue and lips and teeth telling him what her heart was afraid to. She loved him. . . . She kissed him like a woman in love, and only hoped that he was too blind to notice.

Finally, he lifted his head, staring down at her with an expression she couldn't define. She smiled up at him dreamily, hardly aware of the soap that covered them both or the bathwater rapidly cooling around their calves, her fingers trailing over the broad expanse of his shoulders, sliding down to play with the soapy curls of hair on his chest. With a quicksilver forefinger she touched his flat nipple, then skittered away to the other one, barely sliding over the rough surface. His nipples reacted just as hers did. With a catlike smile at him, she leaned forward to press her lips provocatively to that first responsive nipple, drawing it into her mouth and nibbling at it as he did her own. It tasted of soap. . . .

"To hell with taking a bath. I want you." His voice was hoarse, his eyes burning as he drew in a rasping breath. Then he was pushing her away from him, his hands hard on her waist, steadying her. Lora yearned toward him with a little mewling moan, her arms reaching to encircle his neck once more. Her body cried out for the touch of his.

"Come here, baby." He stepped out of the tub, then lifted her out after him, careful not to slip on the cool tiled floor as he carried her into the bedroom. Lora was scarcely aware that they were moving. All her senses were focused on the hot fusion of their mouths, and the reaction it was setting off in her body. All he had to do was touch her and she caught fire. It was wonderful, unbelievable, a private fantasy given breathtaking life; a dream from which she never wanted to wake. . . .

He was dropping her on the roughly woven bedspread, falling with her, crushing her with his weight. Lora was conscious of the prickly cloth beneath her back, the electrically cooled air drying the moisture from her skin with its chilly breath, the heat and weight of his body on top of her. Then she was twisting and turning in his arms, her own arms capturing his head and pulling it down. She wanted him. She wanted him. She wanted him. She had no time to waste on preliminaries, and apparently neither did he. She twisted and squirmed in his arms until the maximum amount of her skin was pressed to his, entwining his legs with hers and urging him down to her. She felt the touch of him against her, fiery hot and urgent as it sought its home, and surged upwards. The sudden impact of their joining sent shudders of pleasure through her. Lora clung, gasping with need, as he claimed her with a frenzy to match her own. He took and took and gave and gave and she shuddered and shivered and matched his every stroke. . . .

There was a sudden brisk knock at the door. Lora scarcely heard it, but Max hesitated and she was aware of that. The knock came again, louder, more imperative.

"La cena, señor!"

"What a hell of a time for room service!" Max muttered a few other words that would, under normal conditions, have singed Lora's ears. But under the circumstances she was totally in accord with the sentiments he expressed.

"Leave it outside the door! Christ, he probably doesn't speak English." Max repeated the command in Spanish.

"Sí, señor!" There was a slight rattle of crockery, and then the faint sound of retreating footsteps.

Max looked down at Lora. "Now, where were we?" His lips were curled in a half smile.

She moved beneath him suggestively, employing her own version of the slithering technique that had been driving her out of her mind.

"Somewhere about there, I think," she said politely as her hands slid over his buttocks and pulled him deep inside her. The smile deepened, warmed just before he bent his head to catch her lips.

"I thought it was more like here," he murmured against her mouth, withdrawing himself until he was just barely inside her.

"Ummmm, wherever." Lora's fingers clenched on his buttocks, her nails sinking deep into his flesh, and he came into her again with a laugh and a groan.

"Animal," he accused against her mouth, and then he was kissing her and loving her and there was no more talking at all.

Later, much later, after a quick shared shower in which

Lora finally got to wash her hair, Max wheeled the dinner cart inside and they sat down to eat clad in nothing but thick towels. As Lora lifted the cover from her meal of steak and potato, she closed her eyes in rapt appreciation of the savory smell. Then she opened them again to see Max sniffing with equal enjoyment across the table. She smiled at the picture he presented with his black hair damp and tousled and his torso bare. He looked good enough to eat. . . . Her eyes slid over his naked chest with much the same rapt appreciation she had felt for her steak. If ever anyone had told her that she would be dining with a man dressed only in a towel slung low on his hips, his hairy flesh prominently on view across a very small table, she would have been disgusted. Only beer guzzling, belly scratching morons came to the table without a shirt, and Lora had always thought that if she were unlucky enough to encounter one, she would know how to deal with him. But Max was dazzling half-naked. Besides, with her hair in a beige towel and her shoulders and the tops of her breasts bare above a large brown one, she wasn't in any better shape than Max. And from the warm smile he was giving her, he didn't mind at all. Lora smiled back at him as she picked up her knife and fork. It was cozy eating dinner this way, she decided. She felt as if they had been married for years.

The steak was cold, of course, and so was the potato, and the salad was correspondingly warm, but that didn't detract a whit from the first decent meal either of them had had in two weeks. They wolfed their food with gusto, gobbling up every last bite of bread and butter and salad dressing. The wine served with the meal was a very good burgundy, and after the food was gone they sat talking about nothing, laughing as they polished off the bottle. Lora told him little snippets from her childhood, about Janice and her mother and father and her house and her job. He listened in attentive silence, leaning back in his chair as he swirled and sipped at the wine, as she described her ambivalent feelings about her mother and the guilty relief she had felt at her death. Lora thought she must have been a little tipsy form the wine, because she told him feelings that she had never expected to confide to another soul. By the time she had finished, the wine was gone and they were lying naked in the double bed, the room dark around them and his arm warm and comforting around her shoulders. Lora lay back, replete with food and drink and this sharing of her deepest secrets with the man she loved, and waited for him to do his part by confiding the details of his life. But he didn't.

"Tell me about you," she prompted finally in a drowsy murmur.

His arm tightened around her shoulders, and he turned her so that she was lying half on his chest, her head pillowed on the resilient muscle beneath his collarbone and her hand spread out across his chest.

"Nothing to tell," he answered, his fingers lightly stroking her upper arm. Like Lora, he sounded half asleep.

"Of course there's something to tell," she replied in exasperation. "Do you realize that I don't even know how old you are?"

"Thirty-seven. There, does that make you feel any better?"

"No." There was so much she wanted to know, but she was so tired . . . too tired to play the role of inquisitor. Obviously, he had no intention of talking about his past unless she pried every single fact out of him. And she wasn't sure if he would even tell her everything then. If it hadn't been for Tunafish, she wouldn't have known anything at all about him except his name, the fact that he kidnapped women and was wanted by the Mexican police, and now his age. It was as if he was determined to hold her at arms length on every plane but the physical. She realized what he was telling her without words, but what he didn't know was that she was equally determined to sneak under his guard, to make him need her as she had come to need him: as fundamentally as food to eat, water to drink, air to breathe. But tonight was not a good time to start prying his secrets from him, she decided. She was just too tired. There was always tomorrow. Thank God for tomorrow, she thought with a sleepy smile.

"I was born on October twenty-seventh. I believe that makes me a Scorpio. Satisfied now?"

"No." But she had to smile again at the ridiculousness of it, and he must have felt the movement of her mouth against him because he smiled too.

"Neither am I."

"What?" She was so sleepy that the question was the merest breath of sound.

"Satisfied."

"What?" It took her a few seconds to make sense of this. It might have taken her longer, but his mouth was on her breast and he was turning her onto her back and coming with her. The exquisite suckling sensation made her curl her toes, even half asleep as she was. Then his hand moved down between her legs, seeking and caressing. . . .

"You're not sleepy, are you?" The question was murmured as he switched his attentions form one aching nipple to the other. Lora quivered, and her legs parted instinctively to encourage his wandering hand to explore further.

"N—no." It wasn't true, of course, she was so sleepy she could scarcely keep her eyes open, but what he meant was, was she too sleepy to make love with him again and she was never too sleepy for that, never, never, never, never. . . .

"Sure?" His fingers found the part of her that most cried out for his possession, and slid inside. Lora moaned.

"Yes."

"Good." He moved on top of her, replacing his fingers with himself as his mouth continued to nibble at first one and then the other quivering breast.

Lora moaned again, writhing beneath him despite the waves of exhaustion that his caresses were just barely holding at bay. She could barely keep her eyes open, but she wanted him, wanted him. . . .

She arched and moaned and clung, and their union was all the sweeter because of the lethargy that threatened to claim her. When at last the exquisite explosion of feeling made her cry out, clasping him tightly to her, he was right behind her, crying out himself, gasping her name. They fell back to earth together, clinging, and were still joined as they were both engulfed by waves of sleep.

It was later, much later, when Lora awoke. She wasn't sure what woke her as she lay blinking into the darkness. There was only a sense that something was not quite right. Something . . . Max moved beside her, turning violently from his stomach to his back, muttering. Lora turned on her side facing him, frowning. He was not usually a restless sleeper—but then, she didn't have much experience sleeping with him. Maybe he was a restless sleeper, and she just didn't know it. . . .

His head twisted from side to side, and the restless muttering increased. Lora sat up, staring down at him, wondering if she should wake him. Wondering if it was the nightmare again. . . .

"Oh, God, what have I done, what have I done? Those people—those people!" He sobbed, clutching at his head, his fingers tearing at his hair.

Lora bent over him, catching the rigid forearms and shaking them gently, trying to awaken him.

"Max! Max, wake up! Max!"

"Oh, God, oh, God, oh, God . . ."

"Max!"

She caught him by the shoulders, shaking him roughly because his pain frightened her. He was hurting, and she couldn't bear to see him suffer like that. When he still continued to moan and writhe, she shook him as hard as she could, calling out his name. He sat up then with a great cry, his arms flinging wide. The right one struck her and sent her sprawling backwards.

"Max!" She regained her balance and crawled toward him, half frightened of him in this state. But her love was stronger by far than her fear. She caught the arm that was bent at the elbow now as his hands covered his face, shaking it, calling his name, praying her voice would penetrate through the clouds of nightmare. . . .

"Max!"

Her hands were still on his arm and slowly, so slowly at first she thought she might be imagining it, she felt the tension seep out of it. The agonized sound of his breathing slowed, steadied. Finally, his arms dropped to his sides, and his head turned. His eyes were wide and fathomless in the darkness as they focused on her.

"Lora."

"Oh, Max, are you all right?" She crawled close to him, and would have taken him in her arms, but he held her off, his hands on her shoulders.

"Did I hurt you? Scare you?" His voice was rough, but beneath the roughness was indescribable weariness.

"No, Max, no, darling. You didn't hurt me or scare me. You just had a nightmare, and I woke you."

"You mean I just turned into a raving maniac in my sleep." His voice was bitter. "My ex-wife used to run screaming into the bathroom and lock the door when it happened. I didn't blame her. Who knows, I might have hurt her one day. I might have hurt you."

"You didn't hurt me, and your ex-wife sounds like an idiot," Lora said hotly, the pain in his voice making her long for a few seconds alone with the woman who had hurt him so. She had a totally uncharacteristic longing to rake her nails down the lady's selfish face.

"She was a very nice girl. Believe me. Kind of like you that way. I seem to have this fatal attraction to nice girls. . . ."

"There's nothing fatal about it. Here, darling, why don't we lie down? You're cold." She had managed to put her arms around him, and she could feel him shivering. She wasn't sure if it was cold or the aftermath of his nightmare, but she thought that either way he would be better off under the covers. In her arms. . . .

Max let her push hi down onto his pillow and cover him with the disordered blankets.They she lay down as close beside him as she could get, her head on his chest, her arms around him. After the briefest of hesitations, his arms came around her, enfolding her tightly. He was still shivering. . . .

"Max, can you tell me about it? About what happened at Mei Veng? That's what your nightmare is about, isn't it?"

He laughed, the sound a bitter breath on the artificially cool air. "Tunafish told you about it, didn't he? About Mei Veng. I'm surprised you don't think I'm a monster."

"I don't think you're anything of the sort. You're a man, that's all. A man who was caught up in a hellish situation and may have made a mistake. A man who has enough of a conscience to have tortured himself about it ever since. In my book, that doesn't make you a monster. Far from it."

"Oh, Lora, you're the best thing that's ever happened to me, do you know that? I had forgotten that girls as kind and decent as you exist."

"Tell me about the nightmare, Max. Please."

She felt him quiver, and then he sighed. The sigh sounded very, very tired, as if he had been carrying his burden for a long time. Then he began to speak, his words halting and barely audible at times, his voice hoarse with emotion.

XXVI

"My father was a minister, you know. The Reverend John Thomas Maxwell. He was a good man, I suppose, but stern and strict with my older brother and me. When I was a little kid and knelt beside my bed at night to say my prayers, his was the face that would appear in my mind. I thought God must be like that—thin and bony-faced with a wide forehead and cold, blue eyes. And so good. He was always so good—a virtuous man. I always knew that I could never measure up to what God expected of me—and I could never measure up to what my father expected of me. They were pretty much the same to me then, I guess.

"He was a very patriotic man, and when Paul—that was my brother—graduated from high school he raised no objections to him joining the army instead of going to college. My father said there was plenty of time for college after Paul had served his country. I remember my mother cried when Paul left for boot camp. But she never tried to stop him. My mother never gainsaid my father in any way.

"After boot camp, Paul was immediately shipped off to 'Nam. I was a senior in high school myself, but unlike Paul—and my father—I was against the war. Actually, I knew very little about it, and my feelings weren't based on any kind of politics. Looking back now, I can see that proclaiming myself anti-war was a way of rebelling against my father. And it worked very well. I drove him crazy in those few months before I went off to college.

"Texas A & M had a very vocal anti-war group, and I joined them as soon as I walked on campus. I let my hair grow and carried anti-war signs and protested and had a fine old time driving my father around the bend. He got so he would scarcely talk to me, by the end of my sophomore year. All he could talk about was Paul. Paul had been decorated for bravery, Paul had been wounded and been awarded a purple heart, Paul was promoted to sergeant, Paul was coming home. Only Paul never made it home."

Max stopped talking, and Lora felt him take a deep, shuddering breath. She lay quietly, not moving, hoping to comfort him just by being a warm, sympathetic presence. And after a moment he started talking again.

"Paul was killed in October 1968. After that, everything changed. My father seemed to shrink. He became very quiet, no longer ranting endlessly about religion and patriotism and all those things. You know, I almost missed his shouting all the time. It was like he died with Paul. Or I did. My father never seemed to see me after that.

"My mother died a year later, almost to the day. October 17, 1969. I was twenty-one ten days later. The following May, I graduated from A & M with an engineering degree.

The next day, I joined the army. Three months after that, I was shipped off to 'Nam.

"Vietnam was a nightmare from start to finish. They say war is hell—they've never seen combat in 'Nam. From what I've heard of hell—and believe me, I heard a lot about it, growing up—it doesn't even come close. We were recon, I was the lieutenant and I didn't know shit about what I was supposed to be doing. Some of my men died because I didn't know what I was doing. I learned on the job, a hard way to learn when men's lives are at stake. But I learned. . . . We were always scared. Scared to death. So scared we couldn't sleep even when we had the chance. We'd seen too many corpses who'd had their throats slit while they slept. All we wanted to do was stay alive and get the hell out of that damned country.

"Mei Veng was a tiny little village near the border of Laos. We'd had reports that they'd been harboring gooks. We went to check it out. God, I'll never forget that day as long as I live. It was a beautiful day in a beautiful country. If it hadn't been for all the killing that was constantly going on, 'Nam could have been a model for the Garden of Eden. It was gorgeous, the sun was shining, the sky was blue and the air was sweet—and out of one of those little huts came this baby in a diaper."

His voice cracked, and Lora longed to shush him. His pain made her ache. But he needed to talk, needed to share this nightmare that he had held inside him so long. Her arms tightened around him as she listened and wished she was not.

"They had planted a grenade in his diaper. He got right up to us—none of us was going to shoot a baby who could barely toddle—and the damned thing went off. The baby was blown to hell. Two of my men—Hardy and MacLaren, good guys both—were blown to hell with him. I was hit in the knee—funny, there was all this blood and I hardly even felt it, I've cut myself shaving and felt more pain. Another guy— Philip Winslow, he had just turned nineteen the day before— had his leg blown off. He lay there screaming that his leg hurt—and it lay off by itself about six feet away. He was clutching that damned stump and it was gushing blood and he was screaming. We were all screaming. Then a woman came running toward us out of the same hut the baby had come from. I don't know, maybe she was the kid's mother or maybe she was a Vietcong sympathizer—or both. I don't know. Harvey, one of the men, shot her. Tunafish was trying to help Winslow, and the rest of us were moving in on that hut. Another woman was in there, crying and trying to hide. Somebody shot her. Then—you know, I don't remember this very clearly—we were herding all these people out of the huts, old men and teenage boys and women and children and they were screaming and crying and calling out to us in their damn language and then one of the boys—he must have been about twelve—pulled a gun. We shot him. We shot them all. Every last one.

"You know what I hear in my nightmare? The sound of babies crying. I hear babies crying and I see all those people lying dead in the sunlight and I smell blood."

His voice was shaking, and Lora could feel the tremors that racked his body. She didn't know what to say to ease his pain, so she said nothing. She just held him tightly, closing her mind to the horror that he had described so graphically. Whatever had happened to him in Vietnam, whatever he had done or was done to him was a part of him now. It could never be changed or, she thought, forgotten. But he could learn to live with it. She would help him. Her love would help him.

"My dad died two months after I was sent home from

'Nam. I was in a VA hospital all that time, and I had only seen him once. I—never told him I loved him. And he never said he loved me. I did it all for him—and we were strangers. That hurts most of all.''

This tortured confession was whispered. Lora reached up to stroke his cheek, not surprised at the dampness she encountered there. He was crying—Max, super-cool, super-confident, super-macho Max. Her heart ached for him.

"I'm so sorry, darling." It wasn't much, but it was all she could think of to say. She longed to comfort him, but there were no words to ease the pain he was suffering. He had to bear it, come to terms with it, live with it. "I'm so sorry."

She didn't even feel the tears running down her own cheeks. She only knew that she hurt, ached as if she had been kicked in the stomach, that her throat throbbed with suppressed tears. She moved, inching upwards so that she could lay her cheek against the warmth of his. Their tears joined and ran together down onto the pillow.

That was the way they fell asleep. When she woke up, she was alone.

XXVII

"What happened to you?" Janice met her at the airport in Wichita, her blue eyes that were so like Lora's widening as she took in her sister's tanned face, sun-streaked hair and slimmer figure. "From what you said on the telephone, I expected you to be practically on your death bed. You look wonderful!"

"I don't feel wonderful," Lora assured her. Janice's carefully maintained blond hair was perfect as usual, and her slightly plump body was set off to advantage by the pale yellow cotton blouse and skirt she wore. Janice looked a lot like Lora, only better. Or so Lora—and Janice—had always thought. Now, for the first time in her life, the older sister found herself envying the younger's looks.

"Tell me everything," Janice insisted, only to be interrupted by two squealing voices.

"Aunt Lora! Aunt Lora!" Heather and Becky threw themselves on their aunt, their thin little bodies hugging her tightly. Lora hugged both girls in turn. She was really very fond of them—and they served as a very effective barrier between her and her sister.

"Later," Janice said resignedly, giving Lora a speaking look.

Lora smiled in reply, and hugged the girls again, saved for the moment. But she knew Janice well enough to know the reprieve was only temporary. When Janice wanted to know something, she pestered you until you told her. It never failed. No one Lora knew could hold out against her. Not Bob, Janice's husband, not the girls, not Lora herself.

"Lora!" It was a masculine voice, and Lora looked up from hugging the little girls to see Brian advancing toward her. Funny, with all that had happened she had almost forgotten that she was engaged to Brian. Tall and thin and bespectacled, his fair hair receding slightly from a high forehead, and immaculately dressed in a sport coat and tie even in the summertime, he hadn't changed a bit. Lora looked him up and down, frantically trying to revive some of the emotion she had surely felt for him at one time. But there was nothing there. He might as well have been a stranger. But she would work on it, she told herself. She was not going to let an unfortunate interlude with a man who had made it very clear that he didn't want her tear apart the fabric of her life.

"Brian." She rose to greet him, and the little girls hung around her legs.

Brain leaned close, catching her hands, and brushed his lips over hers. His mouth felt cool and dry. . . . And did absolutely nothing for her nervous system. Well, she would work on that, too.

"It's good to see you, Lora," he said quietly. "When

Janice called to say you were safe it took a tremendous load off my mind. We've all been extremely worried about you ever since the fellow from the State Department called to tell us there was a possibility you'd been kidnapped in Mexico.''

"Is that how you found out?" Lora was momentarily intrigued. How had the state department gotten into the act? Well, it didn't matter. What did matter was that she was home, among the people who loved her. Which was more than she could say for some ungrateful scoundrels whom she wasn't missing at all.

"Of course, I was worried when you didn't come back from that uncivilized country when you were supposed to, but I never really suspected anything like kidnapping. . . . But I told you all that on the phone.''

Yes, Janice had said all that and more, much more, when Lora had phoned her sister from the hotel the day before, after she finally accepted that Max had left without her. She had waited for hours for him to return, and then, when lunchtime finally came and went, she thought of checking with the desk clerk to see if he had at least left a message. Maybe something urgent had come up—maybe Tunafish had had a relapse. . . . There was no message, or at least not of the kind she wanted. Max had paid the bill and left his credit card with the desk clerk for her, along with instructions to use it to buy herself a ticket home and whatever else she needed. There was nothing else, no good-bye, nothing. Lora remembered the desolation she had felt, and hardened her heart. She would not hanker after a man who had proved so conclusively he did not want her. She would not!

"I warned her about vacationing in Mexico. I don't consider it safe. As this has certainly proved.''

Brian was speaking to Janice as if Lora were not present.

He did that a lot. Janice was smiling at him. She did that a lot. He was a great favorite of hers, although Lora suspected that Janice would be inclined to smile at anyone who was willing to marry her little sister—with the possible exception of a kidnapper with criminal connections. Not that the question would ever arise, of course. Max didn't want her. She would probably never see him again, much less get the chance to introduce him to Janice. And she was not going to break her heart over it. She was not!

"Listen, we can talk at home. For now, we'd better get going. We're blocking the way and Lora must be tired to death. Let's get her home."

Lora smiled at her sister, feeling genuinely thankful to her for one of the few times in her life. She was tired to death, and all she wanted was to go home. She didn't want to think about Max. . . .

The loudspeaker blared, people rushed by them, the girls demanded and got cotton candy, and Janice and Brian both talked at once, describing their reactions to Lora's disappearance. Lora barely heard any of it. She was getting accustomed to the noise, the hustle and bustle that had been so markedly absent from her life for a period that seemed much longer than two weeks. Only two weeks . . .

They walked out onto the tarmac. The sun shone brightly down on the blacktop parking lot. Janice's bright red Ford Escort was parked nearby. The same Escort that had taken Lora to the airport two weeks before. It seemed like a lifetime.

"You're very quiet." Brian's voice penetrated the fog that seemed to envelop her.

"I'm tired," Lora said truthfully as Janice started the car and pulled out into the traffic whizzing away from the airport.

But it was more than just tiredness that afflicted her, and she knew it, though she refused to admit it even to herself.

"Aunt Lora, were you really kidnapped?" Becky asked, wide-eyed, from the front seat.

"Let Aunt Lora alone," Janice ordered firmly. "She'll tell us all about it later. She's tired now."

And to Lora's great relief, they did leave her alone. For the time being.

Over the next few days, she told judiciously edited versions of her story to just about everyone she knew. Janice got the most accurate and detailed account; keeping secrets from Janice was practically impossible. Brian's version left out much about Max, but enough slipped through to make him actively jealous. Finally, on the first Friday night she was home—they always went to dinner and a movie on Friday nights, and Lora was not surprised to learn that nothing had changed in Brian's fondness for precise scheduling—Brian asked her outright if she had slept with Max. Lora hesitated a moment, then with a feeling of throwing her cap over the windmill admitted she had.

"Oh, my Lord! Lora, you can tell me—did he—use force?" Brian sounded both scandalized and faintly intrigued.

Lora looked at him, sitting on the pink, flowered couch that had sat in her parents' living room for as long as she could remember, his face flushed as he waited for details. Something about his expression made her think of a Peeping Tom. Lora thought without volition of Max, pictured him as clearly as if he was standing before her at that moment. It struck her suddenly that his attitude was healthier by far than Brian's. Max enjoyed sex unashamedly. She could not imagine him drooling as he pressed for details that she suspected would titillate Brian while he affected great shock at her behavior. Brian was a hypocrite, she realized with a sigh, and also

realized something that she had secretly known since she ha[...]
first seen him again in the airport. She was kidding herself b[...]
trying to act as if nothing had changed. Everything had
changed. And she had changed most of all.

"No, he didn't force me, Brian. I made love with him
because I wanted to." Brian looked shocked, as she had
expected, and opened his mouth to say something else. Lora
forestalled him with an upraised hand—the hand that should
have worn his ring. Damn it, she had wanted a ring! That was
just one small symbol of all that was wrong between them.
Brian was sensible and levelheaded and careful. Lora had
thought she was all those things, too—but she wasn't. There
was a secret Lora inside that wanted romance and adventure
and diamond rings and great sex. And with Brian, she
wouldn't have any of it.

"I think we can both see that this isn't going to work,
Brian," she added, standing up and moving a few steps away
to look back at him. "We're just not right for each other."

"We were perfect for each other until you went to Mexico!
You're breaking our engagement over some criminal you've
had a dirty affair with!" He jumped to his feet, sounding
outraged, and his narrow face grew alarmingly red. "Lora,
this isn't like you. You're still in shock from your ordeal."

"Yes, it is like me." Lora threw up her head and met his
pale blue eyes squarely. He was glaring, and once she might
have backed down. But not any more. The Lora Harding that
she had discovered in Mexico could stand up for herself
against men a lot more intimidating than Brian Curry! "The
real me. If you think about it, Brian, you'll realize you don't
want to marry me. Not now. I'm not the same person that I
was."

"You're certainly not the girl I've been engaged to for four years," he agreed with a huff. "She would never have willingly slept with a—with a criminal!"

"No, she wouldn't, would she?" Lora agreed cordially, moving pointedly toward the door. "So you see, you've had a lucky escape. Good-bye, Brian."

Brian moved to stand beside her, looking down at her with an angry frown. "Don't think you can call me and make this up," he warned.

"I won't call you," Lora promised. Brian stood glaring down at her for a moment longer, then turned on his heel and strode out of the house, banging the screened door behind him.

"I can't believe it!" Janice almost wailed when Lora told her.

They were sitting at the kitchen table in their parents' old home—Lora had trouble thinking of it as her house, now—and the girls were playing in the backyard. Janice had made the coffee, and both women had been sipping it when Lora made her announcement. Now Janice was choking on hers.

"How could you have broken up with that nice man? He's perfect for you."

"He's not, Janice."

"He *is!* You're so much alike! Lora, he wouldn't care that you can't dance and you do your taxes two months early and you go to bed at ten o'clock every night! He does that kind of thing himself! It's a match made in heaven! How could you have done it?"

Lora just shrugged and sipped her coffee. Janice stood up agitatedly.

"It's that man, isn't it? That Max. Lora, you told me yourself you're never going to see him again! Honey, it was an affair! We all have them! But we don't let them mess up our whole lives!''

Lora was suddenly intrigued. ''Janice, have you ever...''

Janice looked down at her impatiently. ''Of course I have. Lora, grow up, for goodness sake! You're twenty-seven years old! Everybody has affairs these days, they're lots of fun, but they don't mean anything. Do you think I'd throw Bob over for a man I just wanted to sleep with? I'd never be so stupid!''

''Does Bob know?'' Lora was fascinated by these intimate revelations. She had thought her sister had the perfect marriage, just as Janice always had the perfect everything. It was enlightening to know that she did not. Maybe in this area, too, she had been looking at life through a distorted lens.

''Of course not. Although he does the same thing. He thinks I don't know, but I do. You can't keep secrets long in a town like Augusta. But we're not talking about me, we're talking about you. Lora, I am your sister and I love you, but you were always as dumb as a bunny about some things. Especially men. Call Brian and tell him you're sorry, that you don't know what got into you, that you want to make up. He'll do it, I know he will. He loves you.''

''But I don't love him, Janice.'' Lora took another small sip of her coffee while her sister paced agitatedly.

''What's love got to do with it?'' Janice demanded, rounding on her sister. ''Marry Brian, Lora. Love—the way you mean love—isn't real. It doesn't last. But the kind of life you can have with Brian—that's forever.''

Lora looked up, her eyes wide as she studied her sister. She had never realized how much was lacking in Janice's life. She had thought her sister was perfectly happy—all because she had never opened her eyes and seen what was right before her nose. She started to reply, but before she could say anything, the doorbell rang.

"Must be the girls," Janice said irritably, glancing out the kitchen window and presumably not seeing her daughters. "I told them to stay in the backyard, so it stands to reason they're out front ringing the doorbell. Stay put, I'll see what they want."

Janice vanished into the hall leading to the front door, and moments later returned, carrying a brown paper wrapped parcel.

"It was a man from UPS," she said with some awe, holding the package out to Lora. "It's for you. Who would be sending you a package?"

"I have no idea."

"Well, open it!" Janice handed the parcel to her and hovered over her impatiently as Lora complied.

Inside the brown paper wrapping was a sturdy cardboard box. Lora lifted the lid from the box—and sat staring blankly at its contents. It was filled to the brim with stacks and stacks of hundred dollar bills!

"My God," Janice breathed, reaching out a hand to touch the cash as if to make sure it was real. "There must be thousands here! Lora, this can't be for you! The parcel service must have made a mistake."

"They must have," Lora agreed as soon as she regained her voice, picking up the paper that the box had been wrapped in to doublecheck the address. Before she could locate the address, a small, rectangular piece of white paper fluttered out from the torn wrappings she held in her hand. Lora bent to pick it up, her heart suddenly pounding. It was a business card. On the front, in bright blue lettering with a drawing of a keeling yacht attached by a fishing line to an enormous, rampaging swordfish for illustration, were the words: "Tunafish's Fishing Fleet. Boats and crews available for rental by the day or week; we know where they are—you catch 'em!" along with an address in Puerto Santos, Guatemala. On the back, scrawled in bold black ink, was written: "Your share of the finder's fee. Max."

Lora sat staring at his sloping signature while her blood drummed in her ears and a sizzling anger began to build inside her. How dare he send her this dirty money? How dare he! Was his conscience bothering him for deserting her the way he had, without a word, after all they had shared? It should bother him—but he was not going to buy it off with cash!

"What does it say?" Janice practically danced around the chair as Lora, her face slowly turning crimson with suppressed rage, stared at the note. Unable to stand the suspense any longer, Janice finally grabbed the card from her sister and read both sides of it. When she finished, she handed it back, her eyes wide.

"How much is there?" She sounded awed. Lora shook her head, glaring at the business card.

"I don't know and I don't care. I don't want his dirty money!"

"But Lora—you have as much right to it as he does! More, after all he put you through! I must say, there must be more to him than I'd thought for him to send you this! It's almost like an apology!"

"He can take his apology and—stick it where the sun don't shine!" Lora spat, borrowing one of her students' favorite expressions as she jumped up from the chair and started bundling the parcel back together.

"Lora!" Janice was almost wailing. "What are you doing?" You don't mean to send all that money back to that—that criminal!"

"You're right, " Lora said with savage satisfaction. "I'm not going to send it back to him. I'm going to take it back to him! And throw it in his face!"

And despite all Janice's arguments and horrified protestations, the next morning Lora boarded a plane bound for Guatemala City carrying a flight bag holding a few clothes—and another one crammed with money.

XXVIII

From Guatemala City she caught a commuter plane to Puerto Barrios, which was as close to Puerto Santos, a small fishing village on the eastern coast, as she could get by air. En route, it had occurred to her that the address on the card was for Tunafish's Fishing Fleet, which presumably belonged to Tunafish and where she might find him but not Max. But it was the only address she had, and she was certain that, if Max was not there, Tunafish knew where to find him. And she was not going home until she had thrown Max's conscience money in his face and told him what she thought of him. Lora dwelled on the names she would call him with pleasurable anticipation; she would start with coward and end up with selfish beast!

By the time the plane landed in Puerto Barrios, it was midafternoon. Her stomach still shaky from the turbulent ride, Lora tottered out of the airport on unsteady legs, bright red flight bag clutched in hand, to rent a car for the short drive to Puerto Santos. Lora had vowed that she would never again drive anything but an automatic, but there were no automatics available. In fact, there was only one car: a dilapidated, rusted Volvo with a stick shift. Lora accepted it with resignation forged by experience. Besides, she had less than twenty miles to go. How many times could she have to shift in twenty miles?

An hour and a half later, as the car stuttered into the tiny town of Puerto Santos, Lora had the answer: too many. She shifted savagely down into first with much groaning from the engine to make it up the steep grade leading to the harbor. The Volvo shuddered and whined, but it slowly climbed the hill. At the top, it gave a gasp, and died. Lora was left to coast down toward the sparkling blue waters of the Bahia de Amatique, where she had been informed she might find Tunafish's Fishing Fleet.

The harbor was filled with a colorful assortment of boats of various sizes and degrees of repair. Lora stopped the car, set the brake despite a strong temptation to let the blasted vehicle roll straight into the bay, and climbed out, sniffing appreciatively at the fresh, salty tang of the air. Finding Tunafish's Fishing Fleet among this lively collection of people and boats might take awhile.

As it happened, it took just about five minutes. Lora only had to show the business card to a cheerful, white-garbed bait vendor to be pointed toward a small wooden building with a blue flag flaunting the same illustration that had been used on the card waving over it. ''Tunafish's Fishing Fleet. We find 'em, you catch 'em'' proclaimed the sign out front. Lora walked beneath it, squinting a little as she passed from the brilliant sunlight outside to the shadowy interior of the building. Any minute now she expected to see Tunafish. . . .

"May I help you?" The voice was definitely not Tunafish's. Lora's eyes adjusted finally to find herself being studied by a slender, pretty black woman clad in a loose cotton blouse and flowing skirt. Despite the two-inch heels of the espadrilles on her feet, she must have been just over five feet tall. Lora stared at her, guessing at once who this had to be.

"You're Annie, aren't you?" Lora asked with a smile, holding out her hand.

The woman looked briefly surprised, then with another swift, appraising look at Lora she smiled, too, a warm, generous smile with a lot of humor to it, and shook Lora's hand.

"That's right, I am," she agreed. "And you must be Lora. I had a feeling I'd be meeting you one of these days."

Now it was Lora's turn to look surprised. "You did? I'm surprised you've even heard my name."

Annie looked amused. "Oh, I've heard more than your name. Theodore is always talking about Lora this, Lora that. He says Max is stuck on you real bad. Max isn't talking, but he has been one soreheaded son of a bitch ever since he got back."

It took Lora a minute to remember that Tunafish's given name was Theodore, and to assimilate the fact that Max had apparently been in a rotten mood since parting from her. Which knowledge pleased her mightily. He deserved every rotten feeling his conscience visited upon him!

"Is Tunafish here?" Lora asked, wanting to get on with the real reason for her journey while her temper was still smoldering.

"Yeah. He's up at the house, tied to the bed by a traction pulley the doctor rigged up so he could come home. Tunafish hates being in the hospital, but he hates being home in bed almost as much. But you didn't come all this way to see Tunafish, did you?'' She smiled broadly again, her large brown eyes twinkling at Lora. ''You came to see Max.''

Lora felt a brief flare of embarrassment, which quickly died under Annie's warm smile. ''Yes, I did,'' she admitted with a smile of her own.

''And about time, too,'' Annie said with satisfaction. ''Max lives right up the hill. . . .'' She took Lora to the door and pointed toward where a row of narrow adobe town houses painted in bright pastel shades rose from the cliff overlooking the bay. ''In the pink one. And he's home, now, too.''

''Thank you.'' Lora turned to smile at Annie with real gratitude. From what she had seen of the smaller woman, she could readily believe that Tunafish and his children were ruled with an iron hand. Despite her small size, she had the feeling that Annie would be dauntless in the face of any adversity or opposition. She also had the feeling that Annie would make a good friend.

''My pleasure,'' Annie said, shooing Lora on her way. Then she added with a wide grin, ''Give him hell, honey,'' before vanishing back inside the shop.

With a single thought for the car—which would probably never run again, with her luck—Lora decided to walk. It didn't look so very far. . . . But by the time she arrived, panting and breathless, at the foot of the dauntingly steep flight of steps leading up to the door of the pink house, she felt as if she had taken a journey of a thousand miles. The road was steep and uneven, the sun hot. Her feet in their flat sandals ached. Her aqua pedal pushers and striped t-shirt were damp with sweat and clung uncomfortably to her skin. Her hair was disheveled and, she feared, starting to curl, perspiration beaded her face and her arm ached from lugging the damned bag. And her temper, which had cooled slightly from its first hot flaring when she had received the money, was flaring hotter than ever. She glared up at the white painted door, stiffened her spine, and marched up the steps like a general going into battle.

"*Si?*" Whatever she had been expecting, the sultry brunette who opened the door in response to her brisk pounding was not it. Lora gaped at the woman—a voluptuous creature barely dressed in a red halter top and tiny white shorts—while the woman in turn eyed her up and down with barely veiled insolence.

"I—want to speak with Max." Lora put up her chin and refused to be put off by this unexpected occurrence. Perhaps she had the wrong house, or maybe this Latin Mae West was Max's housekeeper. It was within the realm of possibility.

"Max, he is busy."

At least the woman spoke English, Lora registered just as the door started to close very decisively in her face. Lora stared with disbelief at the closing door and felt her smoldering anger flame to blazing life. She had not come all this way to be told by some half-naked sexpot that Max was too busy to see her! She was up the remaining step with a bound, and shoving her way through the door. The brunette fell back under her onslaught, and stood glaring at her, fists planted on round hips. Lora glared back.

"I want to speak with Max," she reiterated with a distinct edge to her voice.

The woman replied in shrill Spanish accompanied by unfriendly shooing gestures with her hands. Lora stood her ground, thinking that she might just have to take matters into her own hands and invade the house further to search for Max herself, when he spoke.

"What the hell—Conchita, *que pasa*?" He was standing at

the top of the stairs that hugged the whitewashed wall to the left of the door, looking down over the wrought iron railing, an irritable frown on his face. His voice died away as his eyes lighted on Lora.

She stared up at him, meeting those black eyes, thinking that he had never looked worse or, conversely, better. At least to her. His face was unshaven, his hair stood up untidily around his head, his cut-off jeans were so faded that they barely seemed to have any color at all, his baggy white shirt hung outside his shorts and had the breast pocket half torn off, and his feet were bare. His expression changed as he recognized her; the scowl vanished to be replaced by an inscrutable scrutiny as he slowly descended the stairs. When he reached the bottom, Conchita threw herself at him, her arms going around his neck, her brightly painted mouth babbling away in Spanish just inches from his. Under Lora's affronted eyes, she finished the diatribe by planting a passionate kiss on Max's mouth. He caught her arms, pulling them down from around his neck and holding her a little away from him.

"Hello, Lora." This was said over Conchita's dark head. Conchita wailed at him in Spanish. Max ignored her, looking at Lora with unreadable black eyes.

"Hello, Max." Despite her best efforts, she could not keep a savage inflection from coloring her response. "You have lipstick on your mouth."

"Do I?" His response was absent. With a brief word to Conchita, who visibly sulked, he released her to swipe at his mouth with the back of his hand. The scarlet stain that had acted on Lora like a red flag on a bull disappeared. "To what do I owe this honor?"

Lora's eyes sparked. "Oh, I just happened to be in the

neighborhood," she replied, as sarcastically as he had once said the same thing to her.

"I presume you got my—message?" His voice was politely inquiring.

Lora nodded curtly. "Yes, I did. And now I've got one for you. Here!" She heaved the bag at him, right at his stomach, hoping that it would hurt when it landed.

But he was too quick for her. He caught the bag in both hands, hefting it with a slight grin as he realized from its weight what it contained. She glared at hm, disappointed not to be leaving him doubled over in pain, and turned on her heel. All the things she had been going to say to him were impossible under the circumstances. He had a woman with him. . . . Lora felt as if her heart was being squeezed in a vice. She also felt coldly furious. He had a woman here!

"Lora, wait!" He came after her as she marched, head high, down the steps, catching her a few steps from the bottom.

"Let go of me!" She tried to jerk her arm out of his grasp, but he wasn't letting go. Tired of jerking, she glared at him.

"Surely you didn't come all this way just to throw the money in my face! Don't you want to tell me what a bastard I am?"

"Yes!"

He grinned, a warm and carefree grin that she rewarded with an even fiercer glare. He had no right to look so damned sexy—not when he had just wiped another woman's lipstick from his mouth!

"Why don't you, then? The way you look, you'll burst if you have to go all the way back to Kansas with all that temper inside you."

"I have nothing to say to you," she said frigidly, her snapping eyes belying her arctic tone. "Nothing at all, you

low-down, sleazy, lying, cheating, cowardly son of a bitch!''
Her voice deteriorated into an infuriated hiss as she spat out
that last.

He laughed. "Come in and chew me out in comfort, why
don't you? The house is air conditioned—and there isn't
another bus out of here until tomorrow morning.''

"I drove.''

"Oh, my God.''

His rueful shake of the head did it. Her temper exploded.
She had had enough of his cowardly retreat from relation-
ships, his animadversions on her driving, his women. . . .
Before she even realized she meant to do it, her hand was
arcing through the air to connect with satisfying force against
his cheek. The sound of the slap resounded sharply through
the cheerful droning of voices and vehicles as residents of the
area went about their business on this sunny afternoon.

Max clapped a hand to his rapidly reddening cheek, staring
down at her, his own eyes suddenly alight. Then he reached
for her, grabbing her by the upper arms and hauling her hard
against his body as his head swooped to capture her mouth.

He kissed her soundly, there on the steps of his house with
white seagulls and brown terns wheeling and calling in the
bright blue sky and interested neighbors watching from nearby windows and the street. In the doorway above, Conchita
watched with a gathering scowl. As Max released Lora,
looking down at her with a bewitching smile while Lora
stared back at him, bemused, Conchita stormed down the
steps, spitting a torrent of Spanish. She shouldered between
the two of them, confronting Max with wild gesticulations
and angry words while Lora staggered backwards, on the
verge of losing her balance on the narrow step.

Before Max could react, Conchita hauled off and slapped
him too, on the very same cheek. Then she flounced on down

the stairs and up the street to the tune of laughter and clapping by the gleefully watching neighbors.

"And that goes double for me!" Lora said when she had recovered from the shock of it. Max looked at her out of those glinting black eyes, grabbed her arm, and hauled her up the steps after him. The watching neighbors cheered.

"Why did you come?" he asked quietly as he closed the door on their interested audience.

Lora looked at him stonily in the shadowy quiet of the hallway. That slap had only relieved her feelings—it hadn't eliminated them.

"It should be obvious, but if you like I'll spell it out! I don't want that dirty money. I came to return it."

"There's twenty thousand dollars there, Lora. One-fifth, the same amount that went to Clemente's and Lowenthal's families and Tunafish and me. That's a lot of money to turn down for a scruple."

"At least I have scruples!"

"Meaning that I don't? But I do—at least where you're concerned. I could have fed you this big line about being in love with you to get you into bed, but I didn't. I played it straight."

"Am I supposed to give a big cheer or what?"

"You're supposed to return the favor. Tell the truth, Lora. Why did you really come?"

"I told you, to return the money."

"Liar." He said the word softly.

Lora stared into those glinting black eyes and felt hot color begin to creep up her neck.

"I did. . . ."

"I've missed you, Lora. I think you've missed me, too."

She stared at him. He looked very tall and very dark as he towered over her in the narrow hallway. Overhead, a large hanging fern caught the light from a window at the top of the stairs. The hanging greenery reminded her of the jungle. . . .

"I can see you've been very lonely." The sarcasm was a defense against desperate need. More than anything on earth she wanted to throw herself into his arms and beg him to hold her, make love to her, love her. . . . But she couldn't. She couldn't just meekly surrender to whatever restrictions he chose to put on their relationship. She couldn't stay with him, loving him, knowing that it would last only for as long as he wanted her body, knowing that he might leave her at any time—or turn to another woman, as he had clearly already done. . . .

"If you're talking about Conchita, and I can see you are, it's been over between us for a long time. Since before you and I met. She just came by today to see if she could restoke old coals—and I had already told her nothing doing before you arrived. That's why she slapped me."

Lora stared up at him. He smiled back at her, a little coaxing smile that ordinarily would have charmed the heart right out of her. But not today. Today there was too much at stake. Lora saw suddenly, clearly, that he was right: she hadn't come to return the money at all. She had come to reclaim Max, but this time on her own terms if she could.

"Anyway," he said, the smile fading, "what about your math teacher?"

"I broke our engagement."

"Ahhh." The smile reappeard again, broadened. "Why, Lora?"

"Because I realized I didn't love him." The admission was as quiet as it was honest. The time had come to lay her cards on the table. It was a gamble, but she couldn't go through life wondering and worrying and hoping that someday she might hit on the right gambit to make Max return her love. Max had to know how she felt, and if the knowledge scared him into running again, then it was better to find out now than later, when her emotional commitment would be even greater.

Taking a deep breath, she twined her hands in front of her and looked up to meet those glittering black eyes. "I love you, Max."

His eyes flickered. That was absolutely the only response he made while Lora stared up at him with hope and fear mixed in equal parts in her eyes. This was the man who couldn't stand commitment, who couldn't let anyone too close, who vanished when he thought he might be growing too vulnerable. And it looked very much as if he was getting ready to run again. Lora braced herself to hear words that would crush her soul.

"So you love me." The words were very quiet, drawn out, as if he was looking them over for flaws. "I'm no great catch, Lora. I haven't held a steady job in years, I have friends you wouldn't let in the front door, I have a bum knee and those damned nightmares. You'd probably be better off with your math teacher."

"I don't want the math teacher. I want you." She reached out to touch him, her fingers trailing down the length of the strong arms to catch and hold his hands. He made a sound then, half laugh, half groan, and pulled her close, his arms coming around her to hold her in a crushing embrace.

"I want you, too," he said, his voice muffled by her hair. "So damned much. Why do you think I sent the money? I knew it would bring you running. If it hadn't, I would have had to swallow my pride and come after you."

"Would you really have come for me?" She pulled a little away from him to look up into his face. Her own face was ablaze with happiness. He wanted her—and not just for a little sex. He might not love her, but at least he cared a little, and that was enough. To start with, anyway.

"Oh, yes. Two days after I left you I knew I'd made the biggest mistake of my life. The rest of the time I spent figuring out how to get you back without groveling."

"Max, darling, I'd love to watch you grovel," she whispered, reaching up to plant a kiss on his hard mouth. He returned her kiss with a hot leisureliness that made her bare toes curl up on the soles of her sandals. Her arms wrapped around his neck, and then he was picking her up and carrying her up the stairs. . . .

"So you'd like to watch me grovel, hmmm?" It was later, much later, and they were cozily ensconced in his big bed while gentle night breezes blew in through the screened window to cool their overheated bodies.

'Mmmmm." She was tired, blissfully tired. Turning in his arms, she snuggled closer. He was warm and damp and his hairs tickled her nose and she loved him. . . .

"You could make me, you know."

'Mmmmm."

"Damn it, woman, here I am trying to tell you I love you and you're going to sleep on me!" The gruff voice roused her before the words had a chance to sink in.

Lora sat bolt upright, staring down at him. "What did you say?"

He crossed his arms behind his head and looked up at her, his big body very dark and muscular against the white sheets. "You heard me."

"Say it again."

He grunted, reaching for her, pulling her down to lie sprawled on top of him. "Maybe I will—in twenty years or so."

"Twenty years?" Her heart stopped. She lifted her head to

stare at him. Was he saying what she thought, hoped, prayed he was? Those black eyes met hers with an intensity that rocked her heart.

"Maybe fifty," he muttered defiantly, and kissed her.

Two days later, she was wearing the diamond ring she had always wanted, with a gold wedding band to match.